Change of Heart
'Charlotte Bingham's devotees will recognise her supreme skill as a storyteller . . . A heartwarming romance which is full of emotion'
Independent on Sunday

'A fairy tale, which is all the more delightful as it is not something one expects from a modern novel . . . It's heady stuff'
Daily Mail

The Season
'Her imagination is thoroughly original'
Daily Mail

Summertime
'Destined to become one of the season's bestsellers, this is great summer escapism'
Choice

Distant Music
'As comforting and nourishing as a hot milky drink on a stormy night. Her legions of fans will not be disappointed'
Daily Express

The Chestnut Tree
'As compelling as ever'
Woman and Home

The Wind off the Sea
'Heartwarming and full of period charm'
Daily Express

Daughters of Eden
'Compelling'
Woman and Home

The House of Flowers
'A rip-roaring combination of high romance and breathless excitement'
Mail on Sunday

The Magic Hour
'An engaging, romantic and nostalgic read'
Wendy Holden, *Daily Mail*

Novels with Terence Brady:

VICTORIA
VICTORIA AND COMPANY
ROSE'S STORY
YES HONESTLY

Television Drama Series with Terence Brady:

TAKE THREE GIRLS
UPSTAIRS DOWNSTAIRS
THOMAS AND SARAH
NANNY
FOREVER GREEN

Television Comedy Series with Terence Brady:

NO HONESTLY
YES HONESTLY
PIG IN THE MIDDLE
OH MADELINE! (USA)
FATHER MATTHEW'S DAUGHTER

Television Plays with Terence Brady:

MAKING THE PLAY
SUCH A SMALL WORLD
ONE OF THE FAMILY

Films with Terence Brady:

LOVE WITH A PERFECT STRANGER
MAGIC MOMENTS

Stage Plays with Terence Brady:

I WISH I WISH
THE SHELL SEEKERS
(adaptation from the novel by Rosamunde Pilcher)

IN DISTANT FIELDS

Charlotte Bingham

BANTAM BOOKS

LONDON · TORONTO · SYDNEY · AUCKLAND · JOHANNESBURG

IN DISTANT FIELDS
A BANTAM BOOK : 9780553817782

Originally published in Great Britain by Bantam Press,
a division of Transworld Publishers

PRINTING HISTORY
Bantam Press edition published 2006
Bantam edition published 2007

3 5 7 9 10 8 6 4 2

Set in 11/13pt Palatino by Kestrel Data, Exeter, Devon.

Bantam Books are published by Transworld Publishers,
61–63 Uxbridge Road, London W5 5SA,
a division of The Random House Group Ltd.

Addresses for Random House Group Ltd companies outside the UK
can be found at: www.randomhouse.co.uk
The Random House Group Ltd Reg. No. 954009.

Printed and bound in Great Britain by
Cox & Wyman Ltd, Reading, Berkshire.

The Random House Group Limited makes every effort to ensure
that the papers used in its books are made from trees that have been
legally sourced from well-managed and credibly certified forests.
Our paper procurement policy can be found at:
www.randomhouse.co.uk/paper.htm.

This book is dedicated to those heroes and heroines of the Great War (1914–1918) who lie in distant fields, and to those who loved them, and were left behind.

IN DISTANT FIELDS

Prologue

They had spent long hours building the sand-castle and its surrounds, and it was truly magnificent. It had an outer wall with four towers, complete with make-believe narrow windows. It had a central portcullis, and a moat, which surrounded a keep, which in turn proudly flew its flag – a long stick to which the inevitable piece of seaweed had been neatly attached.

It seemed, as sandcastles always do, to be impregnable. Once it was complete, and they had duly admired it, ice creams were produced, brought down to the beach on wooden trays. After which the ladies went paddling, while the men – their boaters protecting their fair skin from the sun – stared out to sea, passing binoculars backwards and forwards between them, as they studied the horizon, watching the shipping that passed to and fro between the outer limits of their vision.

And so the pretty scene continued, until the sun which had shone on them all afternoon, started to sink, and the tide, creeping surreptitiously and almost soundlessly, started to make its way up the beach.

Perhaps they had all been enjoying themselves too much; perhaps they had been distracted by the ice creams, or the dreamy preoccupation with the ships and boats. Certainly the arrival of the insistent tide, the onrush of the sea water, seemed to surprise them. Indeed, it seemed almost to be upon them before they were quite able to find their shoes and snatch up their buckets and spades. Excited laughter followed, and before very long everyone on the beach had fled up to the house, leaving the castle to stand alone and face the oncoming rush of water.

With the increasing tide first the outer towers succumbed, only for the house, its moat now filled to overflowing, to swiftly follow, taking with it the gaily fluttering flag. Meanwhile the joyful workforce – the fair-skinned young men, the pretty girls and their siblings who had put so much time and energy into the castle – were nowhere to be seen; so that as the lights in the house into which the happy party had disappeared, shone out on to the beach, it could be seen that the magnificent castle, built on sand, had disappeared without anyone even noticing.

Chapter One

The Invitation

Partita draped a fine wool shawl around her shoulders and, seating herself nearer the log fire the housemaid had set for her, she took up her old schoolroom pen and licked the nib to free it, before carefully wiping it on her handkerchief and dipping it in the ink pot in front of her. Writing a letter was not something to which she could look forward, but write this letter she just must. She began with the date. It should have been in Roman numerals, but she was very uncertain of her Vs and Xs so she merely wrote the day, the month and 1913.

'I've been invited to Bauders Castle for Christmas!' Kitty stared at Partita's letter.

'May I see?' Her mother held out her hand for the letter.

Kitty hesitated before giving it to her. 'Imagine. Bauders Castle. Of course I can't go,' she finished quickly.

Violet shook her head. 'But you must go. It is what you should be doing.'

'I couldn't leave you alone at Christmas-time, really I couldn't.'

'I insist on it, Kitty. You must go, whatever happens.'

'No, Mamma, I could not, truly.'

Kitty turned away, went to the window of their narrow first-floor drawing room and stared out at the traffic below – new motor cars, and horses and carriages – everything mixed up, moving in and out of each other.

On the other side of the room, Violet stared ahead of her, all of a sudden hearing only music and laughter from what now seemed long, long ago.

'Of *course* you must go, Kitty darling,' she replied finally. 'I would not hear otherwise. No, no – no, my bewilderment is not at your having been invited, but at Lady Partita's atrocious handwriting, and as for her spelling . . . !'

Violet went to the window and gave the letter back to her daughter with an amused expression. 'She cannot be learning very much at Miss Woffington's Academy, if that is how she writes, dearest.'

Kitty reread Partita's misspelled missive.

'Do com, pleese,' the letter read. 'We shood all luv it, really we shood. I am shore I will dye of boardom if you do not. Pleese deer Kitty promiss you will com! Your loving friend – Partita.'

'At least she can spell her family name now,

16

Mamma,' Kitty murmured. 'When she first arrived at Miss Woffington's she kept writing to her father as "the Duke of Ed-*on*", instead of "Ed-*en*"! Woofie could hardly believe it.'

'What could her governess have been thinking?'

'Not her governess, her gover*nesses*, Mamma,' Kitty corrected her. 'Apparently Partita has had a succession of governesses, all of whom left after a very, very short time. That is why she ended up going to Miss Woffington's. I told you, her father does not even know she is going to a proper school. He thinks she's just having private tuition in London, and it seems no one has dared to tell him because none of the girls in the family has ever been away to school before.'

'No, no, of course not . . .' Violet murmured, her thoughts once again elsewhere.

'But as it has turned out, Partita told me, the Duchess much prefers London to the Shires, loving to keep up with the fashions. Her Thursday afternoon "At Homes" are always such a riot of people and personalities, it is really better for the Duchess if Partita does not have a governess. But have no fear, Mamma, I shall not leave you to Papa at Christmas, really I won't.'

'Oh, I think you must, Kitty, really I do. In fact, I insist that you do,' Violet replied firmly, ignoring the implied slight to her husband. 'Such invitations are not offered lightly. Besides, it will be quite an adventure for you.'

'They say the Duchess is extraordinarily

beautiful, that her figure has been so much admired and painted. Partita says she is still known as one of the most beautiful women in England, even at her age.'

'Oh, she has always been beautiful, Kitty, I assure you. I remember, when she first came to England from America, seeing her at Lady Carrington's ball, and she is every bit as beautiful as they say. She and Consuelo Vanderbilt were the beautiful catches of that year, heiresses from America being all the rage in those days. Poor souls, they little knew of just what awaited them in their ducal husbands' large draughty castles.' Violet sighed. 'American women have done so much for our interiors, of that there is no doubt, but just how much work would be required to make these old castles at all congenial does not bear thinking about. And I mean, Kitty, places like Bauders Castle are *impossible*, they are so medieval. Little wonder the Duchess prefers Knowle House in London, for however fine a seat Bauders Castle may be, the drains alone would give cause for worry. I believe they even have a nightwatchman still. Besides, the Duchess being a great beauty, she numbers so many, many clever, famous men among her friends, country life would not be congenial to her in the same way her London salon would be. But still, we must find a way to send you for Christmas to the castle, Kitty, really we must. I know we can.'

Violet's face was alight with enthusiasm, and for a second Kitty too looked enthused, before giving a sigh and leaning back against the wall, her gaze once more returning to the scene outside the window, which seemed suddenly to be full of people going somewhere exciting.

'There is no possibility that I can go, Mamma, when you think about it,' she said wistfully, tucking in a long strand of dark hair that had escaped from the black bow at the nape of her neck. 'Apart from anything else, I have no suitable clothes to wear, and no pennies to buy anything new.'

'If there is any way we can possibly afford for you to go to Bauders Castle, then afford it we most certainly shall.'

Kitty looked doubtfully at her mother, well aware that they were so financially straitened it was difficult for her to pay Bridie or the maid of all work. Their sad circumstances were due entirely to her father's profligacy, not to mention his reckless gambling. As she contemplated this, she found herself wondering yet again at the fact that her mother and father had remained married.

'We must see if Aunt Agatha sends us her usual gift. Let us hope she does, and in time too.'

'Could we not ask Papa for once?'

'What can you be thinking, Kitty?' Her mother smiled and Kitty sighed.

'But surely he might want me to go to stay at Bauders? Partita told me her father and my father are known to each other.'

Violet, too, sighed. 'Yes, Kitty, but not I fear for

19

the right reasons. Besides, even if your father had the money, you know he would not spare it, fond as he is of you. Your father, alas, has only one use for money and that is to gamble with it – which is why we never have any.'

Kitty might be only just seventeen, but the constant vagaries of their life over the past years were apparent to her. Even now she could never hear a knock on the door without thinking it might be the bailiffs. How her mother had managed to clothe and educate her, let alone find the money to send her to Miss Woffington's Academy, she hardly knew. Certainly her father seemed to contribute little to their welfare, and nothing at all to their happiness. His presence in the house always seemed to signal an immediate downturn in their fortunes.

The moment he came home from some house party to which only he had been invited, Violet became pale and tense; and as far as Kitty herself was concerned, just the sound of his voice was enough to send her scurrying to her bedroom.

Once in her room, Kitty felt safe because she knew her father would always be either too lazy, or too drunk, to walk up so many stairs to the third floor. Fortunately, because the lure of the gaming tables took him away to play in the houses of the newly rich for long periods, he was rarely at home for more than a few days at a time, which meant that Violet and Kitty were left to pursue their own little economies, work out how best to bring their dresses up to date, and manage their lives as thriftily as was possible.

'The problem – as always – is going to be keeping secret from your father anything Aunt Agatha may care to send you,' Violet murmured. 'Let us pray that if Aunt Agatha does choose to remember us, it is at a time when we have the house to ourselves, Kitty.'

But the fates deemed otherwise, for on the morning that Violet found the much-longed-for envelope, postmarked Suffolk, among the letters on the salver in the hall, Evelyn Rolfe threw open the front door.

Violet was no actress but she did her best to try not to look as anxious as she felt, as she quickly hid the letters behind her back, while staring at her dishevelled husband with frozen fascination.

'Good morning, Evelyn. Have you had breakfast? Because if you have not I will call down to Bridie—'

'I had breakfast at the club, before coming on,' Evelyn interrupted curtly. 'Where's the post, Violet? There's an IOU due.'

'The post?' Violet hesitated. 'Let me see – I think Bridie might have taken it through to the dining room, thinking you were expected for breakfast. Would you like me to fetch it for you?'

'I need the post immediately it arrives,' Evelyn replied, walking slowly past her into the drawing room, leaving a trail of alcoholic fumes behind him as he did so.

Once he had disappeared from view, Violet began to sort feverishly through the Christmas letters.

'You were wrong, of course,' Evelyn remarked, returning almost at once. 'Bridie has not left—' He stopped. 'Which is hardly surprising since I see what post there is, Violet, is in your hands.' As Violet stared at him, he went on in lightly sarcastic tones, 'There is a mirror right behind you, Violet. I can see the letters.'

'I was just sorting through them,' Violet stammered. 'I didn't want you being upset by seeing so many bills, Evelyn.'

But Evelyn was intent on ignoring her.

'Give them to me.' He rifled impatiently through the letters. 'Is this all there is, Violet?'

'As far as I know, Evelyn, yes . . .'

'Well, in that case you don't know very much, Violet, for there is a letter on the floor over there.' He stared past her as if he had seen a mouse scuttling by.

'I don't think so, Evelyn,' Violet said, turning as if to look, in the wild hope that she could nudge Aunt Agatha's letter out of sight.

'Hand it to me, Violet,' he said, in a tired voice.

Violet frowned, pretending to be surprised by her discovery. 'It's nothing. Just something trivial for me, I think, Evelyn, notification of a doctor's appointment.'

'Give it to me.'

'But it's addressed to me, Evelyn. So it really cannot be the IOU you were expecting.'

But he had snatched it from her hand and was now examining the postmark.

'Suffolk, I see,' he muttered. 'From your ghastly aunt, I dare say.'

'No, no, probably it is just the recipe for damson cheese that she promised me.'

'Well, we'll soon see, won't we, Violet?' Evelyn returned. 'As I remember it, your aunt can be quite munificent at times, can she not?'

Evelyn eyed Violet while he slowly unstuck the back of the letter, trying to remember, perhaps for the thousandth time, why he had married Violet Almondsbury. There must have been some good reason – but for the love of him every time he came home and saw her he could never remember what the devil it was that had made him think that marriage to her would turn out to be a good bet. It was not as if she had been a famous beauty, or an heiress. Indeed, it was difficult to see what the attraction of a slender, pale-faced girl who stood to inherit nothing could possibly have been to a scion of the ancient family of Rolfe.

He tore at the envelope, then threw it to the floor.

'I'm going on to Biddlethorpe Hall, Violet,' he told her slowly. 'I'm in for a change of luck – I am sure of it.'

Violet remained silent as always when faced with Evelyn's predictions as to his change of luck, but also because he had opened her letter and found her Christmas present from Aunt Agatha.

'Ah ha,' he said, without humour. 'It would appear my luck is turning already, even as I speak. Ah ha.' He looked up at Violet and the smug triumph in his face was worse to her than the fact that he was actually holding the means for Kitty's escape to a better world. '*Voilà*. Manna from heaven, so to speak. Shan't have to wait for the IOU now, Violet.' He waved the cheque at her. 'Generous old bird, Aunt Agatha,' he added, without a trace of a smile.

'I think that is for me, Evelyn,' Violet said quietly. 'If you wouldn't mind.'

Her husband stared at her outstretched hand and laughed. 'What is yours, my dear, is mine,' he said. 'Remember your marriage vows?' He folded the cheque carefully and put it in his top pocket. 'I shall deposit it in my account later. In the meantime, be good enough to tell that idiot maid that I require some coffee.'

'Evelyn,' Violet pleaded. 'Evelyn. Please, please don't take that money. It is meant for Kitty. You know what an interest Aunt Agatha takes in her – and that money is to help towards paying the fees at Miss Woffington's. Please don't take what is not meant for you, just this once.'

Evelyn, who had been walking away in the direction of the dining room, stopped and swung back round. As soon as she saw the look in his eyes Violet retreated from him.

'I've done me money, Violet – do you understand me? Now tell that girl who pretends to be a maid to bring me my coffee – and then go up and sort out some fresh linen for me. I shall be leaving as soon as I am changed.'

Violet watched him go through to the dining room and then she turned and put out a hand for the newel post of the narrow Regency staircase. Baccarat, that rakehell gambling game that destroyed so many, had Evelyn in its embrace, and it was a fiercer tie than any woman could ever be. She hurried through the green baize door to order Bridie to bring the coffee through.

As she slowly climbed the stairs to her bedroom she thought she could once again hear her father's voice warning her not to marry Evelyn Rolfe.

'They're a bad lot, the Rolfes, Vi. They've bad blood, and nothing to be done about it. They might be an old family, they might be aristocratic, but they're rotten on any level – gamblers and wastrels, all of them . . .'

But of course Violet had known better. She had been swept off her feet by the dashing, handsome Evelyn, and no one could talk her out of him. She had paid the penalty for her obstinacy, and doubtless would spend the rest of her life doing so.

'Mamma?' Kitty's voice called from what seemed a great distance, but was actually only from the hall.

Violet hurried back down.

'Ssh, Kitty. Your father is home.' Violet nodded towards the dining room, where breakfast and the *Morning Post* were always laid ready for Evelyn, no matter what.

'Oh . . .'

'You might well say "oh", Kitty,' Violet replied in a low voice. 'And he has Aunt Agatha's letter.'

Kitty stared at Violet, who looked suddenly quite faint.

'Then I shall go and ask him for the letter back.' Kitty looked momentarily indignant. 'That letter is addressed to you and me, or at any rate to you, not to him.'

But her mother drew her into her small study, and half closed the door behind them.

'Don't go near your father, Kitty. Please. He is not – well, he is not himself. He will be leaving soon for Biddlethorpe Hall, so it is of no matter if we leave him to his own devices.'

Kitty stared at her mother, who had begun to remove her diamond engagement ring.

'What are you doing, Mamma?'

'Take this to the shop on the corner, Kitty. He will give you a good price.'

'But, Mamma—'

'*Quickly.* There simply is no time for argument. I will go in to him, as you go out.'

'You can't pawn this, Mamma. This is your engagement ring. Papa will most certainly notice.'

'You can leave your father to me, Kitty,' Violet insisted, steering her daughter out of the study. 'I can handle your father – or at least I can try. Now do as I say. Go on with you, Kitty – go on.'

Kitty put the ring in her skirt pocket and

started to hurry across the hall, only to find herself confronting her father.

'Good morning, Papa,' she said, curtsying, all filial submission, at the same time plucking at her coat, which she quickly pulled on while maintaining her dutiful expression.

'Where the hell is the coffee?'

'Bridie is just making it, Papa. Oh, look,' Kitty quickly pointed out of the window. 'Look, Papa, there's the Earl of Caulfield's Rolls-Royce. How smart it looks, wouldn't you say?'

Her father turned quickly and without a word went back into the dining room, shutting the door behind him, and Kitty slipped quickly out of the front door. What a boon for her to know that her father still owed the Earl of Caulfield a great deal of money.

She shot out of the front door and started to walk at breakneck speed towards the pawnbroker's shop, always and ever known discreetly in their house as the 'shop on the corner'. Pawnbrokers always gave a better price than jewellers. She would always loathe going there, but this morning she cared less, for if Mr Trinder would give her enough money to go to stay at Bauders Castle, she would be only too grateful.

'*Good* morning, Miss Rolfe. How nice to see you again.'

Mr Trinder was tall, with an ample figure that Kitty always thought must be a direct result of all the money he had made from everyone else's misfortunes.

'Good morning, Mr Trinder.'

Kitty seated herself on the gold chair by the counter, placing her mother's diamond ring on the cushion in front of them both. As soon as he saw it Trinder took out his enlarging glass and studied it, before wordlessly disappearing into the back of his premises.

Kitty waited. She knew the ring was worth a great deal of money. It had the blue glow that valuable old diamonds always had. Mr Trinder returned shortly, looking poker-faced, if slightly pinker.

'Just remember I am not a bank,' he said with a sigh, stroking his double chin slowly and pretending once more to smile. 'Everyone hereabouts thinks I am but I simply trade on interest. I hardly make a thing on the gewgaws people bring to me. I hardly make a farthing, let alone a penny, let alone a shilling.'

He laughed rather too loudly at the thought of making a shilling, shaking his head slowly while all the time carefully watching Kitty.

'Hmmm,' he said as he replaced the ring on the cushion. 'This is a delightful piece. Quite delightful. It will be an honour to have this in my case.'

He smiled again, and Kitty wished for perhaps the twentieth time that he would not. Mr Trinder's smile was not a pretty sight.

'I am quite sure it will be an honour,' Kitty told him primly. 'It is a beautiful diamond.'

'Yes, yes,' he said. 'As I am saying, this is a

delightful piece, most delightful. And I dare say you are expecting a sizeable loan on this, are you not? I most certainly would be, on such a delightful piece of jewellery, most certainly. So today I might have to be even more generous than is my custom. Particularly since it is soon to be Christmas, and the time when we should be thinking of others – and doing our best to put our good feet forward. Do you not think so? Most certainly I do, most certainly. So shall we perhaps say this? Would that be satisfactory, young miss?'

Having written a sum on a pad on the counter, Trinder turned it round so that Kitty could see. Fortunately Kitty had been brought up by her mother to cope with the Mr Trinders of this world, tradesmen who presented their accounts twice, and all manner of other tricks.

'That will not be enough, Mr Trinder, and you and I both know it.' Kitty did her best to look stern and unyielding.

'You are, of course, right, Miss Rolfe. Perhaps we may settle on my second figure? I do hope we may.'

Kitty stared at the second hastily written figure, and then at Mr Trinder.

'Very well, Mr Trinder, plus, I think, a little more, don't you?'

Some minutes later Kitty left Mr Trinder's premises, an envelope full of more money than she would have ever hoped to possess stuffed in her coat pocket.

Afraid of going home and bumping into her father before he left for Biddlethorpe Hall, she headed for the park, for the sight of the ducks and the swans, the other people, their dogs and their children, all the time grasping the envelope in her pocket so tightly that it might almost have been a helping hand held out to her, which in so many ways she knew it was.

By the time she allowed herself to return home, her father had left for Biddlethorpe Hall, and her mother had hastily written to accept Lady Partita's invitation to catch the Thursday afternoon train to Bauders Castle.

'Have you ever seen so much money, Kitty? Have you ever, ever seen so much money?'

Kitty shook her head.

'And now all we have to do is spend it!'

Half an hour later the two women, dressed for the winter weather, umbrellas over their arms, expressions as bright as the sky above them was grey, left for the shops, where they spent the rest of the day, not to mention the following morning too, buying everything that Kitty would need for her visit.

At last Thursday dawned, and the little household was up at dawn, packing and preparing for the journey ahead.

'I have told Bridie to attend to your every need,' Violet informed Kitty. 'But don't be surprised if she appears a little over-excited. She says she has never seen a castle, let alone visited one.'

'I keep feeling so guilty, Mamma. How will you manage on your own here, without Bridie?' Kitty paused. 'I keep wondering what you will do if Papa comes home.'

Violet shook her head. 'Stop wondering, Kitty. It is not your place to worry about me. Even should I need Bridie, which I will make sure that I don't, I have told you, you cannot possibly visit a place such as Bauders without a maid. It would not be understood.'

'Yes, but, Mamma, what will Bridie do when we *are* there?'

Violet paused in her folding of one of Kitty's new blouses.

'She will do as the other maids do for their young mistresses, Kitty. She will help dress you, and generally tend to your needs.'

'But then how will you cope, without anyone but young Mary coming in to clean?'

'I will cope, dearest, really I will.' Violet smiled suddenly at Kitty. 'Now don't forget to remind Bridie to hand the keys for your luggage to the butler on your arrival – that is *de rigueur*. She will not want to look like a hayseed to the other servants, for they will make quite open fun of her if she does, believe me.'

Kitty smiled. 'We will both try to be a credit to you, I promise.'

Mother and daughter stared into each other's eyes for a second, each knowing as she did that this invitation to Bauders could well change Kitty's life, and for so much the better.

'Take heart, Kitty, really. You will be everything that I could wish. I know that.'

Later Violet watched Kitty, followed by Bridie, climbing into the waiting hackney carriage in her new travelling outfit. She looked a picture in her feathered hat and fur muffler, her new blue coat as elegant as anything either of them could wish. Bridie, of course, was dressed in her customary black since she always seemed to be in perpetual mourning. Her mind and spirit appeared to reside permanently in or around the churchyard.

'Pray to the Lord our God to keep us safe on this journey,' the maid muttered as the cab took them across the park to the railway station. 'And may He keep us and preserve us from the attentions of strangers and free from all pestilences on our journey – because you would do well to remember, Miss Kitty,' she said more loudly as she focused on her mistress, 'that one soul's careless sneeze may be another's early demise. Wasn't my poor Uncle Fergus just such a victim, God rest his soul indeed, for didn't he take a train journey to Cork for a Nationalist meeting on the one day, and wasn't he dying in hospital on the next, and wasn't it all due to travelling in a train and being proximous to the afflictions of others? May God preserve us on this journey, Miss Kitty, for He will surely need to.'

They had barely settled themselves and their luggage into the railway carriage when Bridie took out her rosary beads and started to murmur her prayers and to toll the beads.

Kitty felt embarrassed, until after a short time she came to realise that as soon as the other passengers clapped eyes on Bridie tolling her beads they climbed back out of the carriage as quickly as they had climbed in. It seemed that Bridie's devotions meant that not only did her prayers put her in good stead with the Almighty, but they afforded the two travellers the most splendid privacy all the way to their station in Northamptonshire.

It was disappointing, but waiting at the station for Kitty's arrival was not as amusing as Partita had hoped it might be. Normally when visiting guests arrived at the Halt, they would be met by one or two of the servants, and transported back to the castle in one of the Duke's many ponytraps or another small horse-drawn carriage, but on this occasion Partita had insisted on going to the station to meet Kitty herself. She had been too excited to stay at home and wait. Now, however, she had cause to regret her eagerness, because besides half freezing to death in the back of Jossy's trap, she was discovering what everyone else knew, namely that there was very little to do at stations.

Of course, a small part of her had hoped that if she managed to get herself to the station on her own, without her maid, the ever-possessive Tinker, there might be some sort of adventure to be had. Perhaps a chance encounter with some dashing young cavalry officer in the waiting

33

room, or even a minor accident in a siding that would require the services of the estate fire engine, instead of which there was only the platform populated by a particularly idle-looking station-master who, despite the bitter nature of the wind, was leaning on one of the posts reading a stout almanac of some kind.

Partita sighed and finally took refuge in the Ladies Only waiting room, which was currently occupied by a harassed-looking woman and her three small sons, who immediately stopped trying to annoy each other to stare at the young woman beautifully dressed in velvet and furs, now standing in front of the waiting-room fire warming her gloved hands. A moment later one of the boys, prompted by a whisper and a nudge from his mother, offered Partita a seat, for which she thanked him, but demurred. Finally, having read every poster and notice hanging on the walls at least twice, she decided once more to brave the elements rather than endure the increasingly toxic fug of the overheated room.

Happily, and only five minutes late, the London train finally steamed in to the Halt and Kitty, closely followed by Bridie, disembarked.

An aged porter appeared from nowhere to fetch their luggage from the guard's van while Partita hurried down the platform to greet her friend, noting the thin whey-faced girl she assumed to be her maid walking behind Kitty, carefully carrying, as was the custom, a small black leather jewellery case.

'I cannot tell you how happy I am that you could come, Kitty,' Partita smiled, absurdly relieved that Kitty had finally arrived. 'I so hoped you could. Really I did.'

'Mamma was not going to let me stay at home once I received your invitation, Partita,' Kitty replied, as they exchanged light kisses on the cheek. 'It was so dear of you to ask me.'

'I cannot think of anyone I would rather see at this moment, Kitty,' Partita said, smiling. 'Christmas will be so wonderful now.'

She took Kitty's arm to steer her towards the exit and the patch of grass where Jossy was already standing holding open a little door in the side of the pony carriage.

'I hope you don't mind the wind in your hair, Kitty,' Partita said, having climbed the steps into the trap after Kitty. 'Papa refuses to enter the age of the motor car, alas. He declares he will always be a horse-drawn man until his dying day.'

'Not a bit,' Kitty smiled, settling herself in under a warm wool travelling rug. 'I can think of nothing more exciting than arriving at Bauders in a ponytrap.'

'I would have driven myself, but Jossy here would not countenance it, would you, Jossy?'

'Not after you turned my best rig over in the summer, young lady,' Jossy returned over his shoulder as he picked up the reins. 'You was lucky to get away with that, and only a few scratches to show for it, I can tell 'ee.'

'It wasn't my fault a wheel came off, and you know it, Jossy.'

'If 'ee goes round t'corners on one instead of two, that'll be thy fault,' Jossy returned. 'If I were 'ee, young lady,' he continued, now addressing Kitty, 'I would think more 'an twice about letting young Lady Tita 'ere pick up the ribbons.'

Jossy handed Bridie up on to the seat beside him, and then with a gentle slap of the ribbons on the pony's flanks they were away, heading down the lanes towards the great estate. Kitty sat back smiling, but glad of her fur muffler.

'I actually thought you might not be able to come, Kitty,' Partita said, pulling the travelling rug right up under her small chin. 'That your papa might not like you to come.'

Partita already knew all about Kitty's father, and was quite openly envious. It seemed to her to be really rather thrilling to have a father who was such a notorious gambler and womaniser, compared to which her own father seemed dull and conservative to a degree. He might be a duke and come from a distinguished line, but Kitty's father was notorious, which was so much more exciting.

Despite the fact that it was a bitterly cold winter's day so there would be little to admire in most people's gardens, as Jossy's little equipage turned into Bauders' parkland, Kitty marvelled at how much there was to admire in the Duke's domain. Against the winter sky white deer seemed to be constantly moving in and out of centuries-old oak trees, lakes and follies seemed to have been flung, almost carelessly, over acres and acres of carefully landscaped ground, and birds of every description flew between reddened shrubs and white-barked birches, while all the while, miles up the drive, the house remained barely discernible, tantalisingly distant.

As they drew nearer, the castle at last began to be defined as a long three-floored palace with ornamental battlements and vast windows at which Kitty imagined people might be standing gazing out across the park, watching the deer and the wildlife, perhaps feeling as awestruck as she was herself at being, however temporarily, a part of this great holding built so long ago. As they drew nearer to the house, Kitty was able to observe the arches of the forecourt, under one of which Trotty eventually clattered into a cobbled area, where the trap at last drew to a halt.

'Nanny's door.' Partita nodded towards a side door before taking off her gloves, putting two fingers into her mouth, and emitting a piercing whistle.

'You've no business whistling that way, Lady Tita,' Jossy grumbled, frowning at her. 'You bin told about that time and again, and you know who'll be carryin' the can for that if her ladynobs gets to hear you.'

'And rightly so too, Jossy,' Partita teased him. 'Since it was you who taught me.'

'Maybe it was, Lady Tita,' Jossy nodded,

37

having helped them all out of the trap. 'But you're a young lady now, not a child no more, and her ladynobs, Nanny Knowle, will be putting me in the corner if she ever catches you at that again,' he added with a nod towards Nanny's door.

'Nanny has retired to Seaford, Jossy, and you know it.'

Partita's eyes narrowed with a mischievous gleam, but since no boy was forthcoming in answer to her first whistle, she was about to repeat the offence, only for Jossy to quickly beat her to it with an infinitely louder and altogether more impressive whistle.

Perhaps because the boys being summoned knew how to differentiate between one whistle and another, or perhaps because like the dogs of the house they knew an old timer's whistle as well as their mother's bark, less than half a minute elapsed before two pages emerged at the double, coming to a halt by the pile of luggage, which they set about sorting out between them.

'If that'll be all, Lady Tita, I'll be off for me tea,' Jossy said, touching his cap. 'The lads'll take your things into servants' quarters, miss,' he added, addressing Bridie, who for once in her life seemed speechless. 'You'll have a boy assigned you to show you what's what and where's where, because make no mistake, folks has a habit of gettin' lost here, and not always on their first visit neither.'

He nodded while at the same time giving

Bridie an appreciative look, which, to Kitty's surprise, was returned with a smile brighter than Bridie had ever shown anyone in London.

Partita went ahead of Kitty up the shallow stone steps and into the house, suddenly increasing her pace as did the two pages following with Kitty's luggage.

At first Kitty could not understand what the hurry was. Then she felt the bitter cold eating into her as they scurried through a labyrinth of dimly lit corridors even colder than the freezing weather they had left behind outside, their breath coming in little wispy trails on the air.

'When the weather gets like this we don't only wear coats between rooms,' Partita sighed. 'We sometimes even wear them in bed!'

Finally they reached a large studded door at which Partita stood back, waiting for the page boys to push it open, which they very promptly did in the accepted manner of page boys everywhere – backside first.

'This, Kitty, is my room,' Partita announced proudly. 'And I did it all myself.'

Kitty went in and looked round. She had no difficulty in believing that Partita had designed the large purple-painted walls, the Bakst-style drapes looped around her ancient bed, the shell-encrusted mirrors and sparkling boxes encrusted with stage jewels. Nor would it have taken a genius to realise that Lady Partita Knowle's passionate love was the theatre.

Kitty gazed upwards to the great lantern that

hung in the centre of the room, the only light source for the immensely high ceiling, and as she surveyed the extraordinary room she felt oddly disconcerted. Partita's boudoir was such a dramatic contrast to her own modest room in South Kensington, decorated as it was in light floral wallpaper, with hangings around the bed of a pale primrose, and small brass-fitted electric lights, but here in this vast and astonishing room there was no sign of the twentieth century, no hint of modernism, no electricity or even gas, just a host of dark tallow candles casting a medieval glow on the room.

'Your room is through here,' Partita announced, leading the way through another large studded door to an adjoining room. 'You will have to keep your coat on until your bath is drawn,' she added factually. 'In weather like this you should keep your coat on at all times, but we can leave the adjoining doors open and talk all night – which I know we will.' She gave Kitty's arm a quick affectionate squeeze. 'Now we must go down to the library where everyone will be having tea. I shall instruct Wavell to tell Dixon to send your maid up to unpack for you. It really is so unendurably *lovely* that you are here, Kitty Rolfe!'

Kitty smiled in return, in spite of a sudden feeling of melancholy as she remembered the sacrifice her mother had made for her.

'To tell you the truth,' Partita was saying, 'I thought I would *never* make a friend at Miss

Woffington's, although I simply had to do or Mamma would not be allowed to be in London giving her At Homes and enjoying the kind of intelligent conversation which is not always available at Bauders, so when I suggested asking you, she thought it would be such a good notion, because my older sisters have each other for company while I have no one, because I am so much younger, and Mamma says that is *so* sad. Allegra has come out, and might soon become engaged to James Millings, once he has inherited, but Cecilia has no one, and has not been presented at court.'

She stopped to tilt her pretty head to one side as she examined Kitty's travelling clothes. 'I shall be changing for tea in the library, by the way,' she added diplomatically. 'So when you are ready, give a scratch on my door.'

Kitty smiled and, taking the hint, went immediately to change. By now, due to the miracles that Kitty would soon come to accept happen out of sight in grand establishments, Bridie had appeared in Kitty's room and was busy unpacking her cases, out of which Kitty took an appropriate change of clothes.

'I've never done this before, so I haven't,' Bridie muttered as she tried to help her lay out the right clothes. 'Would yous be wanting some kind of a belt to go with this, Miss Kitty, dotie?'

'No, no – thank you, Bridie, I will wear a sash. You'll soon get used to all this,' she added in a kindly tone.

'That's all very well, Miss Kitty, but sure, yous no idea how stiff it is down there. Surely to heaven, Miss Kitty, when I tells yous,' Bridie sighed, applying a clothes brush to the back of Kitty's immaculate new afternoon dress, a tightly tailored lace-trimmed blouse with gathered sleeves and a most becomingly cut dark skirt, 'when I tells yous I have a page of my very own, down there, the Lord save us. And what would my poor old mother – God help her indeed, if she were alive today – what would she be thinking of her little Bridie with her own page? She'd lather me with kisses, so she would.'

As Kitty started to feel Bridie's increasingly determined mood through the administration of the clothes brush she moved tactfully out of range of her heavy handed attentions, going instead to tap on Partita's bedroom door in the approved manner.

From the look in Partita's eyes it was immediately obvious that Kitty's new outfit had met with her approval, much to Kitty's relief, since she knew that the next few hours would be sure to determine her future at Bauders, that whether she liked it or not, the Knowles and *their* guests would be weighing up everything about Partita's guest. Partita herself was wearing a cream silk blouse with guipure lace at the neck and wrists, and a skirt of dark green velvet with a back pleat, which Kitty was able to appreciate as she followed Partita and they began the descent to the hall below, Partita chatting happily.

'Papa always says that this staircase is wide enough for eight people to pass down together; but then Mamma says that really only comes into play if you have a whole army staying. All those, by the by,' she went on, waving an artless hand up at the rows and rows of portraits hanging on the walls above them as far as the eye could see, 'they're all our ancestors. Most of them were a pretty dull lot, but one or two did do some rather tremendous deeds. Mamma says the rule is never to talk about one's ancestors unless to be funny, and even then not for long. Come on!' she urged all at once. 'You have to hurry through the Great Hall or you will be found frozen to death unable to utter a word, ready only for the next world!'

Taking her pace from her friend, Kitty began to run through the marble-floored hall set about with huge tapestries depicting medieval scenes, for despite the vast log fire burning brightly in the decorative fireplace, the temperature could not have been far above freezing point. Kitty found herself envying the attendant footmen in their heavy uniforms as she trotted after the figure of Partita, which was fast disappearing through two large doors being held open by those same footmen.

Once through the doors Kitty found herself in an immense room with mahogany ladders reaching far up to the ceiling, propped against innumerable shelves housing what she imagined must be thousands of beautifully bound books.

The room was illuminated by a vast selection of yet more candles, set not only into sticks and candelabra on the furniture, but also in the enormous chandelier that hung high above from the domed ceiling, leaving Kitty to wonder how long it took the servants to lower, light and replenish them at what must be all too regular intervals. Set everywhere were vast bowls of fresh flowers, perhaps supplied from hothouses on the estate, while yet another enormous log fire warmed those gathered for tea, most of whom seemed to be only too eager to stand within range of its heat.

Despite its being only tea-time, the women were beautifully dressed, their fashionable gowns being worn with discreet jewellery, their hair only recently dressed by their maids. Kitty watched them, momentarily fascinated, as they appeared to be listening to each other with interest, while all the time keeping constantly on the move within the area surrounding the fire, some choosing to sit to talk, others forming small groups to laugh quietly together, or to exchange quick asides. Perhaps because when they moved they took only small steps, and spoke in low and carefully modulated tones, their demeanour seemed almost geisha-like, certainly feminine and subtle, and quite obviously determinedly set on fascinating the men present, who, in their dark suits, provided an effective and sombre backdrop to the bright silks.

Of course Kitty knew none of the guests, the

only person familiar to her being the Duchess. Partita walked her across to her two older sisters.

'Allegra, Cecilia,' she announced proudly, 'may I introduce Miss Katherine Rolfe?'

'How do you do?' both the older girls murmured vaguely, while their eyes examined Kitty keenly.

The two older girls were both dark-haired and grey-eyed, in contrast to Partita's blonde hair and blue eyes. They were both also very pretty, but unlike Partita, they were not beautiful. Kitty realised that this, perhaps more than anything, was why Partita might be her mother's favourite. Out of all three girls she looked the most like the Duchess, who was now seated behind a magnificent silver tea service that included a gently steaming teapot and a fine samovar. She had obviously put herself in charge of pouring the tea, a custom that had become fashionable some time ago, but which, as Kitty now learned from Partita, still managed to shock the Duke.

'Papa is so medieval,' she moaned quietly. 'He takes absolutely no account of *progress* – which Mamma, being an American, accounts as absurd. She says we must progress or we will simply die out, and that is most certainly what my elder brother, Almeric, thinks. For instance, as Almeric says, we really have no need for a nightwatchman, but Papa told Almeric that he would be absolutely confounded without a nightwatchman. If he wakes in the night he must know the time. When Al succeeds Papa he will do away with poor old Birdie, the nightwatchman, which I do also find a *bit* sad, because, between you and me, I also enjoy hearing him calling out the hours through the night. But Almeric says it belongs to the age of jousting, which I find a little exaggerative, although I sometimes wish they did still joust. For I would certainly enjoy seeing a knight dying for my favour.'

At that moment, however, Kitty felt comforted to see the Duchess doing something as ordinary as pouring hot water from the samovar into her large ornate silver teapot, because it made Kitty feel at home in the grand house, although the guests had not the same sort of refreshment as she and her mother in South Kensington, where a thin slice of bread and butter was the order of the day. Here, Queen Alexandra sandwiches and small French gateaux were being presented to everyone by the footmen.

Kitty was put even more at ease when, having been presented to the Duchess, she found herself being lightly kissed on the cheek by her hostess, who then proceeded to walk her round the assembled company.

'Julia?' the Duchess enquired of one of her friends. 'May I present Miss Rolfe. Miss Rolfe – Mrs Wynyard Errol.'

Kitty curtsied, carrying her curtsy off so delightfully that both the Duchess and Mrs Wynyard Errol beamed approval.

'Delightful,' Mrs Wynyard Errol said, turning to the Duchess and lowering her voice. 'She is just as delightful as you said, Circe. One always fears the worst when it comes to gels one's children might meet at a school.'

The Duchess smiled and the two friends' eyes met in a vaguely conspiratorial manner. They both knew that really the Duchess could not have cared if Miss Katherine Rolfe looked and behaved like an organ grinder's monkey, since it was thanks entirely to Partita's refusal to study at Bauders with governesses that her mother was now able to live in London during the term time, enjoying the kind of intellectual and artistic company in which she revelled.

'I do most sincerely hope that is not for me,' Mrs Wynyard Errol murmured, noticing the butler approaching her with a telegram on a tray. 'Although I fear it might well be,' she added.

'For whom is that telegram, Wavell?' the Duchess asked.

'It is for *Mr* Wynyard Errol, Your Grace,' the butler replied. 'Newly arrived.'

'Like us.' Mrs Wynyard Errol sighed, glancing at her husband, who was now opening the proffered telegram.

'Why is it that telegrams so very rarely contain good news?' the Duchess wondered out aloud to no one at all.

The ladies formed an anxious little circle around Ralph Wynyard Errol, a tall, good-looking man, a theatrical manager, as Kitty soon learned, with a particularly mellifluous voice that, according to gossip, he used to great effect on the ladies, most especially those of the chorus.

'Oh dear,' he sighed, folding the cable up and addressing his wife. 'It seems my dear mamma has had a relapse. This is from her doctor. He advises I return at once.'

'How sad for you,' the Duchess offered. 'And how sad for your poor mother too.'

'I have to go, of course, Circe,' Ralph replied. 'You know how it is.'

'Indeed. Such a shame, with the festivities about to get under way. Wavell? Please be good enough to inform Mr Wynyard Errol's valet that Mr Wynyard Errol is leaving for London.'

'Yes, Your Grace.'

'And, Wavell? Be sure to tell Cook to prepare a picnic for his journey – something warming to counter this inclement weather.'

'Yes, Your Grace.'

As Ralph Wynyard Errol took leave of his hostess and his wife, Kitty marvelled at his behaviour, his impeccable style and manners. Mr Wynyard Errol made no fuss nor showed any undue emotion, nor indeed the disappointment he must surely be feeling at being forced to return to London and miss much of the festivity at Bauders.

'When Valentine arrives will you tell him that Grandma is not at all the thing, lovie?'

'Of course, Ralph dearest,' Julia replied. 'We shall all miss you quite dreadfully. It is all too dreadfully disappointing, and at this time of year too, it really is all so dreadful.'

Ralph took one of his wife's hands and squeezed it gently, and so, so lovingly, before turning on his heel and going. As she watched him, Kitty found herself wishing her own father showed as much consideration for her mother as Mr Wynyard Errol was showing to Mrs Wynyard Errol.

'Upon my word, how dreadfully, terribly sad, Ralph Wynyard Errol having to go back to London to spend Christmas with his ailing mother. And *so* unusual.'

Kitty looked round in surprise to find Partita pulling a comic face at her.

'Is it *not* unusual?'

'I would say not. Not in the least unusual. Rayff, dear Rayff, keeps a little poodle in Putney, doncha know,' Partita murmured, straight-faced. 'And as for the way Wavell deals with it, I do wonder how he gets through the little pantomime every Christmas,' Partita continued, lowering her voice still more, while not losing the look of mischief in her eyes. 'Each year the same – the old lady's doctor advises Mr Wynyard Errol's most *immediate* return – upon which news everyone becomes positively *suffused* with concern, and her son departs at once to return to his poor mamma's bedside.' Partita paused. 'Her doctor must be a medical genius, the way he has been keeping her alive over these last few years – and *always* with the same good effect, because once the New Year is upon us, *et voilà*, old Mrs Wynyard Errol is once more as right as rain.'

Kitty would have loved to hear more, but perhaps suspecting that her youngest daughter might be spreading scandal, the Duchess now looked across to where the two girls were standing and, with that particular look that all mothers know how to give, silently beckoned her youngest daughter over.

'Here is Valentine newly arrived even as his father has to take his leave, Partita. Be so good as to introduce him to Miss Rolfe, if you will.'

'You must be so worried about your grandmamma,' Partita said to Valentine after they had been introduced to each other.

'We *are* very worried about Grandmamma,' Valentine stated bravely. 'She is getting really quite old and her health is very delicate.'

'She seems more than anything to be allergic to Christmas, would you not say?' Partita continued mischievously. 'She has a habit of falling ill at Christmas.'

'Papa believes it is something chronic,' Valentine stated, not looking at Partita.

'Let us hope she gets better in time for the New Year.'

'So worrying always when an elderly relative becomes ill . . .'

Kitty was rescued from any more conversational essays by the arrival of Partita's brother, still in his hunting clothes.

'Forgive me, everyone,' Almeric said, making a dramatic, mud-spattered entrance. 'Forgive me,

Mamma, but we have had such a day and I am thirsting for a cup of your delicious tea, and some cake.'

Almeric Knowle padded in bootless feet across to the fireplace where he collected a cup of freshly poured tea from his mother.

'We shall forgive Almeric for his *déshabillé*, shall we not?' Circe wondered, watching with affection as her son tucked into his tea while warming himself in front of the welcoming fire.

'Everyone forgives Almeric,' Partita sighed. 'He is the son and heir.'

'Not quite true, dearest, not quite true,' Circe said, smiling.

At home Kitty would have helped pass round sandwiches, if there were any, but at Bauders she could only stand, one of a group, while footmen in their country tweed livery, their carefully padded stockings making their often sadly thin legs look flatteringly muscular, circled with plates of delicacies. Everyone talked and laughed as they were meant to do. The truth was, she felt as if she was taking part in a play but, as yet, did not quite know her lines, and yet wanted nothing more nor less than to learn them, before the curtain fell.

'There seems to be something on that mind of yours, Miss Kitty,' Bridie remarked through chattering teeth as Kitty sat by her bedside fire, trying not only to warm herself, but also to come to a decision as to what exactly to wear for the evening. 'You have the look of a broody hen, so you have.'

'It's nothing, Bridie,' she told her maid, who was now standing to one side of the fireplace, offering her thickly mittened hands to the warmth of the flames. 'I'm just a little fatigued after the journey.'

It had all seemed so simple when she and her mother were shopping; they had thought that two or three outfits for the daytime, and the same number of gowns for the evenings would prove quite sufficient, and in more modest households they would have done, but not at Bauders. Yet it wasn't the amount of dresses and outfits Kitty now guessed she might need that concerned her, but their quality. The clothes she and her mother had purchased were shop bought, while every gown and ensemble Kitty had seen so far were all couture, which was why she was now frightened that she might look unfashionably cheap.

Partita opened the intervening door between their rooms.

'Scratch – scratch?' she said from the doorway. 'I don't know what you're planning for this evening, but Mamma sent her maid along with this. She thought it might fit you.'

Partita was holding up a simple silk dress inset at intervals with Brussels lace. The gown was not only exquisite it was quite obviously couture and bang up to the minute, being in the Grecian style, slim and close-fitting.

'Your mother is very kind—' Kitty began, only to be overridden by Bridie, who was obviously going to have none of it.

'Miss Katherine has dresses of her own, so she does,' Bridie told Partita. 'She has no need to be borrowing of a gown from anyone at all, God love you all the same. Tell Her Grace thank you, but Miss Katherine will be addressed in one of her own gowns, so she will.'

'It's not that at all,' Kitty stated, feeling and looking mortified at Bridie's outburst.

She could have spared herself the embarrassment, because it seemed Partita had long ago summed up the maid for what she was – a fashion devotee. She sidled up to Bridie.

'Now, Bridie, I know you have the best taste in the world because my maid, Tinker, too has the best taste in the world, and so I know when you look closer at this you will appreciate the work that has gone into it. There was, after all, nothing like Mr Worth's gowns, and this was made by his pupil, Monsieur Soren, whom, as you know, some people feel could be even more inspired than his master. Do see.'

Bridie paused. She had a friend who worked in one of the back rooms of the great couture houses. She knew of the work that went into the new gowns, of the outworkers crowded in a stifling room, who ruined their eyes stitching and sewing to make such dresses as Partita was holding up in front of her.

'Sure wouldn't I know it was couture, just to

look at it? Just one look and you could tell,' Bridie conceded. 'This is a gown designed by Monsieur Soren, did you say? Well now, he is, as you say, gifted all right.'

Partita smiled. 'Take a closer look, Bridie. See the way he has had the pearls set so delicately in the lace insets?'

'There's a lot of women's work gone into that, Lady Partita, a great deal of work. Sure I know that just from glancing at it.'

'I'll leave you to talk it over with Miss Kitty.'

Partita slipped from the room, and when she returned it was to find not only Kitty looking ravishing in the dress, but to overhear Bridie's version of recent events.

'And there was I, frightened to death you was going to refuse to wear it,' Bridie sighed, walking round and round Kitty in order to make sure everything was perfect. 'Sure you could hardly be too proud not to wear such a lovely gown as this, Miss Kitty.'

'I love this high belt with the pearls strung across it.'

'And couldn't it just have been made for yous?' Bridie was adding, with one final tug at the hem, which was so strong it nearly unbalanced the wearer. 'Which is why Her Grace must have gone especially to find it for you, for must not she have known in an instant that this dress could have been made for yous and yous alone?'

'It is beautiful,' Kitty agreed, looking at herself

54

in the looking-glass and feeling once again that she had stepped into a world that had little reality but was somehow lit by its own magic.

The mood was further enhanced when she once again followed Partita down the great wooden staircase to the marble hall. By now, due either to the mighty fires, or the ever increasing population of the castle, the temperatures everywhere seemed happily to have risen. The marble Great Hall glowed even more at night, the colours of the stone warmed by the candlelight and the flames of the log fire. Partita had marked Kitty's card as to the progression of events. It seemed everyone was to congregate for drinks in the Chinese Room, followed by a formal dinner for forty guests.

'This is really dull,' she sighed, stopping to check her hair in an ancient silver-framed mirror hanging on a nearby wall. 'Allegra and Cecilia commandeered Tinker – so now I keep wondering whether or not my mother's maid has made a drover's pudding of it.'

Kitty, who had put up her own hair into a perfectly formed chignon held at the side with a dark tortoiseshell buckle, stood behind her.

'It looks perfect, Partita, really quite perfect.'

To reach the Chinese Room they had to pass down a long ornate Gothic corridor, hung about with rows of ancient leather fire buckets, along which, and quite out of keeping with the decoration of the Great Hall, were arraigned an endless array of magnificent stags' heads, all staring across the corridor into each other's dark soulful eyes. The guests then mounted another set of stairs lined with footmen in white wigs, the gold facings of their dark blue coats gleaming in the candlelight. By the time they reached the top of the stairs, two of the tallest footmen, clothed in faded green velvet laced with gold, flung the double doors open on to the Chinese Room, so named because it was inevitably hung about with eighteenth-century wallpaper and hangings in the Chinese manner.

Across the room the young bloods waited, fresh from their day's hunting, fired up by their sport, the champagne, and now the notion of the festivities to come. Groups of older relations and friends, such as are always invited everywhere at Christmas-time, had stationed themselves together, gossiping and chatting, their jewellery reflecting the light of the hundreds of candles above them, the women's priceless diamonds giving out a pale dullish blue.

The arrival of the girls did not occasion any particular stir among the older guests, but a great deal of interest among the young bloods.

'Ah ha. That must be Partita's new friend with her, ain't it, Almeric?' Teddy Heaslip asked.

'It certainly is, Teddy,' Almeric replied, without turning to look at him since he too was busy surveying the room.

'Quite delightful, wouldn't you say, Hughie?' Teddy continued.

'Positive delight to the eye,' Hughie Milborne

agreed, turning his large, dark, and oddly sad countenance momentarily to the red-haired Teddy. 'In fact, positively so.'

'Still,' Teddy sighed, taking another glass of the champagne offered to him from a silver tray held out by a footman, 'can't mind her. Duchess's instructions are for me to take Partita in to dinner, so off I go before some other fellow gets clever and jumps the queue.'

Teddy wandered off towards Partita, watched in some amusement by his friends, who all knew that Teddy, along with most young men of her acquaintance, had fallen hopelessly in love with Partita when she was hardly more than fourteen years old.

'Who is it precisely that's alongside Partita, Almeric, old fellow?' Hughie asked. 'Take it she does have a name?'

'As a matter of fact she's Evelyn Rolfe's daughter.' Almeric raised an eyebrow. 'You know who I mean?'

'Yes, I know who you mean,' Hughie replied. 'We all know Sir Evelyn.'

Indeed almost everyone who was anyone knew of Sir Evelyn Rolfe, brilliant horseman, incurable gambler and notorious rake.

'How he is still actually in circulation, not fled the country, is something that is beyond everyone,' Hughie continued, turning to Almeric.

'Quite, particularly since the chap's game is baccarat, which my father always describes as a game played by bores.'

There was a small silence as they all contemplated Kitty's father's indelibly black reputation.

'Poor child.' Peregrine Catesby spoke for the first time, and as he did they all turned slowly to look at him.

Peregrine Catesby was the eldest of the group of friends by some six years. He was not so much handsome as actually beautiful, and already as famous for his brilliant scholarship as Kitty's father was for his vices.

'Poor, poor beautiful child,' he murmured again, staring across at Kitty, who had produced a little fan and was waving it about her face against a sudden flush of high colour caused by the candles. 'Introduce me, Almeric. There's a good fellow.'

'Of course.'

'Miss Rolfe,' Almeric said after the two men had crossed the room, 'allow me to introduce you to Mr Catesby.'

Kitty nearly found herself staring a little too long into Perry Catesby's famously handsome face.

'Mr Catesby.'

'Miss Rolfe.'

Peregrine turned to indicate Almeric. 'Lord Almeric here has just told me that I am to have the pleasure of escorting you in to dinner.'

Almeric managed a smile, despite the fact that he himself would have liked that privilege, but in common with everyone else at Bauders Castle, including the Duke and Duchess, he could refuse Perry Catesby nothing. Quite apart from anything else, everyone knew that if it had not been for Peregrine Catesby's inspired coaching, Almeric would never have got a place at Oxford.

'I shall just confirm this with Mamma,' Almeric went on, a look of envious resignation on his face.

Left on her own with Peregrine, Kitty found herself about to become tongue-tied. Perhaps Peregrine sensed this, because with that ease that is second nature to the kind-hearted, he proceeded to make pleasant conversation, looking round the room in which they were standing as a museum guide might.

'This and the Marble Hall at Bettingsby are perhaps two of my favourite rooms in England,' he said. 'It is more tasteful than the Brighton Pavilion, which I always think verges on the vulgar, while this is light and graceful. Do you have an interest in domestic architecture and design, Miss Rolfe? Or do you find such matters too trivial?'

'By no means. I am fascinated by architecture and domestic design.'

'I truly believe, like that great philosopher Thomas Aquinas, that design is a moral issue.'

'I dare say it must be,' Kitty agreed. 'After all, where and how we live must influence how we think. It must be difficult to be dirt poor, I should have thought, and put your trust in God.'

Peregrine stared at her without speaking for a

few seconds. This was not the kind of reply he had expected, nor the kind of conversation to which he could normally look forward when escorting a young lady into dinner. Perhaps because he refrained from saying anything that could be construed as being patronising, in no time at all they found they were both discussing the merits of various exhibitions that had taken place lately at South Kensington, before taking their places in the line of guests forming a queue behind the Duke and Duchess, who were now beginning to proceed into dinner.

The happily chattering crocodile of guests followed their hosts through a long picture gallery, on into the great gilded dining room with its elegant coffered ceiling, beneath which they sat down to dine at a magnificent long table set about with tall, flower-bedecked silver epergnes, vast gold ivy-decorated candlesticks and gold knives, forks and platters, while a ten-piece orchestra, seated on a podium at the far end of the room, played a selection of Strauss waltzes for their entertainment.

Once the first course had been finished and the plates removed, Partita turned her attentions to Valentine who, like Teddy Heaslip, she liked to think was liable to become impassioned by her, although thankfully not in the habit of delivering books of handwritten poems to her. But as she chatted and flirted, she observed Peregrine turning his attention once again to Kitty, whom, she noted, had been escorted by him into dinner.

Peregrine can't like Kitty. He can't!

By the time the ladies had withdrawn from table, leaving the men to pass the port, Partita realised that no matter how *she* might feel, Peregrine might feel very differently.

Chapter Two

Christmas at the Castle

Once the candlestick by her bed had been blown out and a great carpet of darkness seemed to have been thrown over her bedroom, Kitty lay feeling only relief at having somehow got through the evening without making a fool of herself.

Her most trying time had come after dinner, when the ladies had retired to the great red and gold withdrawing room. There, as cherubs and gods and goddesses frolicked on the painted ceiling above them, the crimson hangings moved in the night breeze, and the ladies tried to pretend they were not freezing, Kitty knew that the Duchess's many female friends and relations would set about scrutinising, not just herself, but all the young girls present. A too-loud laugh, an ugly gesture, a doubtful comment, too forward a manner would be duly noted and put in their little black books. So now as she lay in bed listening to the nightwatchman tolling the bell and calling out the hour, while far away in the vast park the unmistakable cry of a vixen rang out, she remembered with gratitude that the Duchess had kissed her goodnight. For a girl like Kitty, a young woman with no means and, perhaps worse, a notorious father, the Duchess kissing her publicly as if she was a relative meant a great deal.

'You must be congratulated, Kitty. You have won all hearts tonight, and, believe me, that is not easy,' the Duchess had whispered as she kissed her young guest.

But now it was Christmas morning when everyone of the same faith as the Duke – family, servants, tenants and friends – was expected to attend Matins in the private church on the estate. The Duke and Duchess customarily entered from a side door to seat themselves to the right of the altar directly under the pulpit, much to the Reverend Mr Bletchworth's discomfort, while their friends, with their children, occupied the front rows and the other guests sat behind them, and so on, right to the back pews, which were filled with the farm labourers and their families, everyone dressed in their Christmas best.

Kitty was placed in the family pew, between Partita and Allegra. Partita had, of course, made sure to wear a particularly fetching hat made up of feathers dyed to match her coat and gloves, while Kitty was demurely attired in a long fur-trimmed coat, a small fur-trimmed bonnet, and a matching muff, all once the property of her mother, but now altered to fit her. On entering the church and taking their seats, Kitty as much as Partita and her sisters attracted the attention of the men in the congregation, which was hardly surprising since many of them were attending church for the first time that year, and so feeling badly in need of entertainment.

The vicar climbed into the pulpit, full of the inevitable clerical feelings of gratitude that, for once, his church was full to brimming. He placed his notes in front of him at precisely the same time that the Duke placed his half-hunter pocket watch on the pew in front of himself.

'May I begin by welcoming everyone?' the vicar began.

'He can begin whichever way he chooses,' the Duke remarked. 'Just hope it's none of that Old Testament nonsense again.'

The Duke hoped in vain, and was soon giving every appearance of being fast asleep, while Kitty did her dutiful best to follow the sermon, which unfortunately very soon went right over her head, being all too full of biblical references and scholarly asides, and having nothing to do with the life that she saw around her. She started to allow her thoughts to wander. What must it be like to be a Knowle and part of such a grand historic family with tombs of marble and statues of ancestors littering your own church? What must it be like to worship all your life at Bauders, and never know what it was to have to scrimp and save?

At last the service was over and the Duke and Duchess, followed by family and friends, proceeded out of the church.

Kitty stood aside to the back as the family immediately lined up to greet the farmers and their families, the tenants and their children, not to mention all the servants.

'There'll be no one wanting for a goose or a hen on t'table while His Grace is alive,' she heard Jossy say with some satisfaction to his son Ben, as he waited in line to shake the gloved hands of the ducal pair. 'His Grace always makes sure we're all provided for at Christmas,' he affirmed proudly to no one in particular.

'You say that every year, Father,' Ben reminded him.

'So I do, Ben, so I do, and so I always shall. Just as well to remind ourselves that we are more fortunate than t'rest of t'world, and that is t'truth. You'd never have got into that regiment of yours without—'

'Yes, Father, I know. Without His Grace we'd all have t'bottom out of our trousers,' Ben agreed, mimicking his father's accent while at the same time turning to his older brother, Tully, and winking.

'I'll have enough o' that cheek of yours, Ben Tuttle.'

'Happy Christmas, Jossy.'

As the old head lad passed her, Kitty held out her hand to him.

'Thank you, miss,' Jossy replied, whipping off

his cap. 'Allow me to present my sons, Ben and Tully, if I might. Tully, Ben – this is Miss Rolfe, a friend of Lady Tita's.' He paused. 'She's from London.'

Tully and Ben were as tall and open-faced as their father, and they now turned identical bright blue eyes on Kitty as they too whipped off their caps and extended large hands, which Kitty shook. Ben smiled cheekily at Kitty while Tully's eyes soon slid from Kitty's face to Bridie who, having waited outside the church during the service, was now stamping her feet to keep them warm.

'Come away with 'ee, lads,' Jossy said, turning to them both and frowning. 'Stay in line. We're next off.'

The boys replaced their caps, but as they did so Tully made sure to keep his eyes on Bridie, whose dimpled face had caught his eye. There was no doubt that things, courting in particular, might have been a great deal easier had his mother lived, but she, poor woman, had died giving birth to Ben, so the boys had been brought up by their father and grandfather. The two men had been kind and attentive, but there was no real female influence in the house. All the years of their growing they had wanted for female company and the softening influence that mothers and sisters could bring to a household, which was possibly the reason that Tully was still glancing back at Kitty's maid as he stepped forward to shake the Duke and Duchess by the hand, only to be nudged to immediate attention by his father.

'Happy Christmas to you, Jossy,' the Duchess said. 'And to you,' she turned to Tully. 'Oh, and Ben. The army let you out for Christmas, did they, Ben?'

Ben stared into the Duchess's still beautiful face, which he had loved since he was a small boy.

'Yes, Your Grace, and a fine time I will make of these days, you can be sure.'

'Of course you will, Ben, of course you will. Happy Christmas to you, Ben.'

'Thank you, Your Grace.'

'And a Happy Christmas to you all.'

'That's for surviving the sermon, Jossy,' the Duke muttered as he pressed a gold coin into Jossy's hand. 'Valour in the face of insuperable odds.'

It was the same joke every year, but Jossy never minded.

'I thought it was a lovely service,' the Duchess said to the next in line. 'The singing was better than ever.'

'Sooner they ban sermons the better,' the Duke informed his cellar man a minute or two later as he shook his hand. 'All be able to get to table a dashed sight quicker, eh, Trump?' He turned back to his butler. 'I say, Wavell, if this cold spell continues, I dare swear we might be skating on the lake tomorrow.'

'I took the liberty of testing the ice only

yesterday, Your Grace,' Wavell murmured as he passed yet more sovereigns to the Duke to hand out. 'And I would say that you are going to be proved right.'

'Nothing like a skating party, Wavell, mark my words, nothing quite like it.'

Soon after the church party, family and servants made their way back to the house, some choosing to walk in order to sharpen their appetites and others availing themselves of the carriages and traps laid on by Jossy. The cavalcade of beautifully turned-out horses, smartly painted carriages and finely dressed pedestrians made a colourful sight against the landscape of the great parkland.

'It's almost like a scene from long ago,' Kitty murmured to Partita, looking back at the line upon line of tenants and farmers climbing into their own horse-drawn vehicles, the ribbons on the women's old-fashioned bonnets and their cloaks moving in the slight breeze.

'Don't you believe it!' Partita laughed. 'Long ago they were all so drunk at Christmas-time the vicar would never have let them in the church. That was what the arch of the lich-gate was for – for them to shelter under.' She turned back and pointed towards the old building. 'They were all in the habit of getting so drunk that that was as far as they were allowed, even to get married!'

Christmas luncheon at Bauders was a brilliant occasion, the orchestra playing throughout the feast, and tea being served in the Great Hall for everyone from the estate, all of whom were waited on by the family.

Every now and then, at odd moments throughout the day, Kitty found her mind straying to her mother. At best, Violet might be asked to luncheon by her artistic cousins who lived in bohemian isolation on the edge of Holland Park. There would be peacock feathers in large vases, and a permanent smell of oil paint, and a roast capon and small home-made presents, but no gold, no orchestra, no liveried servants, and certainly no real gold animals tumbling from the crackers.

In the evening the ladies changed into their best gowns and the men into white tie and tails. There was a running buffet for those who were still hungry, then a riot of games from clumps to blind man's buff, all of which were played with high energy and with much delight. Finally, as Birdie called the midnight hour, everyone made their happy but utterly exhausted way to their beds.

'Gracious, you are asleep already, aren't you?' an apparently shocked Partita exclaimed, making her slippered and candlelit way to Kitty's bedside.

'I'm awake now, Partita,' Kitty replied, sitting up quickly.

'I really should go back to my own bed,' Partita murmured, nevertheless climbing in beside Kitty. 'Brrrr,' she went on with chattering teeth. 'This is the coldest I can remember. The lake really must be freezing, so I dare say we shall have a skating party tomorrow.'

'I love skating.'

'Good, then you will stay until the ice melts, won't you?'

'I would stay for ever if I could. But I must think of Mamma – and Bridie. She cannot spare Bridie for ever.'

'You can send Bridie home,' Partita said with just a hint of impatience. 'We can share a maid. As for your mother, do you want me to ask Mamma if your mamma may be invited?'

'No. Thank you.'

There was a small silence.

'Is your mamma like mine, does she not like the country so much as she should?' Partita finally asked.

'No, she doesn't,' Kitty agreed. 'No, she is – well, very much a town person. She likes the exhibitions and the museums, and taking tea at Fontenoys.'

Another small silence followed as they both stared into the darkness.

'If we were to send Bridie back to London . . .' Partita began again.

'Perhaps it would not be so bad for me to stay on?' Kitty conceded.

'Of course you will. Now for some gossip.'

But it seemed gossip was in short supply, because it was only a matter of minutes later that both girls were fast asleep.

Long before the housemaids could be heard
clanking up the stairs with their water buckets,
the Duke had decided the ground was too hard
to risk his horses, so those gentlemen in the
house party who had prepared to go hunting
now took their guns to join the large shoot that
was preparing to leave. Once they were gone,
the Duke and Duchess turned their minds to
organising a skating party for the afternoon.
Everything was to be made ready: braziers and
flares to be lit around the perimeter, plenty of hot
food and drink at hand, while pages were sent
out on ponies to issue invitations to the neighbourhood.

'Can't remember when the lake was last frozen
so solid,' said the Duke. 'I really cannot. Must ask
Wavell – oh, there you are.'

'The last time the lake was sufficiently frozen
to permit skating was the January of 1908, Your
Grace,' Wavell offered. 'The fifteenth, if my
memory serves me.'

'You should be on the halls, Wavell,' the Duke
replied. 'As some sort of memory man. You're
infallible, really you are.'

'You are aware that tonight is the servants'
ball, of course, Your Grace.'

'That I had remembered, thank you, Wavell.
Haven't yet entirely lost the old memory marbles.'

'It is just that everyone will need time to prepare, Your Grace.'

'Well aware of that as well, thank you, Wavell.

Usual arrangements, of course. Long as there's plenty of grub for the lake party you won't hear me grumbling, I do assure you.'

'Thank you, Your Grace.'

Wavell went away satisfied that, as always on the evening of Boxing Day, the ball that the Duke and Duchess hosted would take place.

'It's just like an ordinary ball, except that we dance with the servants – or rather, they dance with us,' Partita explained as they took a late and lazy breakfast in Partita's room in front of a roaring fire and to a background noise of distant gunfire as the shoot got under way. 'Papa always opens the proceedings with Mrs Coggle, the head housekeeper, followed by Mamma and Wavell, who is a very neat dancer.' Partita stood up and went to the window. 'We could go skating now, if you would like. We could be the first. Come on.'

Well muffled up against the bitter wind, the two young women hurried happily out into the parkland.

'Awful thing is, they get stuck in the ice.' Partita nodded towards some bewildered-looking ducks and swans, as the girls sat on a frozen bench to put on their skates. 'Papa won't have it. Sends Jossy out on a ladder to pull the wretched birds out. Ice cracked one year and Papa thought he'd lost his head lad. That would not have done, I can tell you.'

'Who's that skating over there?' Kitty wondered, pointing to the figure of a young man who had appeared from the boat-house on the other side of the lake and, hands held firmly behind him, was now skating expertly in ever-increasing circles.

'That . . .' Partita replied, looking up and shielding her eyes against the winter sun. 'Oh, that. That is young Mr Harry Wavell – and would it not just be?'

They watched him in silence for a minute.

'He's a very good skater.'

'Oh, Harry is good at most things.'

'Will he follow Wavell into service?'

'Harry? Good gracious, no!' Partita laughed. 'Wavell would not want him to become a butler. Besides, Harry would be hopeless. No, Harry wants to be a poet, among many other things.'

'Writing poetry?' Kitty enquired. 'Do you mean poetry as in Lord Byron, and Mr Wordsworth and daffodils waving in the wind?'

'I'm afraid so. It makes Wavell despair, apparently.' Partita smiled and, having finished lacing up her skating boots, she stood up. 'Ready?'

At Violet's insistence, Kitty had learned all the accomplishments required of a young lady, from playing the piano to skating, a skill she had acquired at the fashionable Niagra skating rink in London.

'Heavens!' Partita called, as she whizzed past her friend. 'You are really more than a skater, you are an ice dancer!'

Partita was certainly no match for Kitty, whose natural grace made her a delight to watch. Partita

73

slowed down to idle along on the ice just so that she could watch her friend executing a perfect spin.

'Oh, bravo!' Partita called out in genuine appreciation.

Partita began to try to skate a little more quickly, longing to join Kitty, not just because she loved her, but because she knew that skating with Kitty would enhance her own performance. As the two young women skated alongside they were passed by Harry, hands clasped behind his back, long legs pushing him to ever greater speed.

'That's Harry cutting it too fine as always,' Partita sighed, as they were passed within inches for the third time. 'Good morning, Harry!'

Harry wheeled round sharply, sped back to them and, braking hard, pulled up amid a cloud of ice.

'Forgive me, Lady Partita,' he said, taking off his cap but, to Partita's amusement, not looking at her, but at Kitty. 'I didn't mean to be rude. I was just trying out something new and my manners went a little blind. Good morning, miss?' he added, still looking at Kitty.

'This is a friend of mine from London, Harry. Miss Rolfe. Kitty, this is Harry Wavell. How was France, Harry? I haven't really seen you since your return. Harry went to France to *write*.' Partita turned to Kitty, eyebrows raised.

'France was excellent good, thank you, Lady Partita,' Harry replied, skating along slowly beside them. 'I was fortunate to find a professor after my own heart.'

'And he is a poet too, by all accounts. Whatever next!' Partita skated on, turning round and then skating backwards in front of Harry and Kitty.

'Oh, look!' she cried happily, pointing to something only she could now see. 'There seems to be a drama!'

The other two turned on their skates and looked where Partita was pointing, to see a number of beaters running alongside a pony and trap that was being driven as fast as it was possible in the frozen conditions, all of them quite obviously making their way back to the house.

'I wonder if there's been an accident?'

'With a bit of luck, don't you mean, Lady Partita?' Harry muttered as he and Kitty skated after her, causing Kitty to turn and look at him in surprise. 'Oh, there's nothing Lady Partita likes more than a fire, or an accident.'

'Gracious . . .'

'Oh, yes, when it comes to a fight, Lady Partita is the one you want on your side.'

Partita tore off her skates and was soon running as fast as she could, skirts held up, across the frosty lawns. She caught up with the pony and trap and the party of beaters just as the party reached the circling yard outside Nanny's door, joined only minutes later by Kitty and Harry.

'One of the beaters has been shot!' Partita exclaimed, turning back to the other two, thrilled.

'It's always happening nowadays, with so many foreigners coming over for the shoot!'

'Is he hurt badly?' Kitty wondered as she watched the casualty being lifted out of the back of the trap and placed on a stretcher by his fellow beaters, surrounded now by a handful of housemaids bearing jugs of hot water and bandages, all in the charge of the Duchess, dressed in a huge and magnificent fur.

'He's hardly hurt at all,' Partita continued, hurrying round the other side of the pony and trap to get a closer look. 'He's apparently just got it in the beam end!'

'Sorry about this, Your Grace,' the stricken beater groaned from his stretcher as they prepared to carry him in. ''Tis only a bit of buckshot.'

'I trust you were not wounded by anyone in the house party?' the Duchess said, taking his wrist and feeling his pulse. 'That would be too much to bear, Huggett, really it would.'

'I'm afeard it was not a foreigner this time, Your Grace,' another beater informed her. 'Someone in Lord Bultash's party – Mr Balfour was it?'

'That would make perfect sense,' the Duchess replied, letting go of the wounded man's wrist. 'Mr Balfour can be the most wayward shot. Now come along with you all,' she exhorted the stretcher party. 'We have to get the shot out of this poor man's rump.'

'Should someone go fetch the doctor, Your Grace?' one of the bearers enquired.

'No, absolutely no need for Dr Jones,' the

Duchess replied. 'Besides, I doubt that he'll be quite himself, seeing the time of year. No, no, this is something that can easily be dealt with here.'

'Poor man,' Harry muttered to Kitty as the invalid was decanted into the house. 'I dare say he'd much prefer to hang on to the buckshot than endure what he's about to endure.'

'I don't quite understand.'

'Her Grace likes to keep her hand in practising minor surgery,' Harry replied. 'She has a small place prepared that she keeps for operating on the ground floor here. Do you feel like spectating?'

'There was really quite a lot of blood,' Partita ran back to tell them, with some satisfaction. 'Much more than you might imagine, given the spread of a shotgun cartridge. Now if you'll excuse me, I must go and help Mamma.'

'The Duchess isn't really going to perform surgery on that poor man?' Kitty wondered as Partita disappeared once more inside the house. 'I mean, surely not?'

'Don't worry – she has a supply of chloroform. Not that she'll spare it for such minor surgery, I shouldn't have thought,' Harry returned with a straight face. 'Probably get the poor lad to bite on an old chair leg.'

'You're teasing me, Mr Wavell.'

'I wish I were, Miss Rolfe.'

'But he'll be in agony!'

'One of my grandfathers was in the Crimea,

Father told me. He had his leg amputated without anything at all. No whisky, nothing, not even a chair leg.'

'How purely dreadful.'

Harry and Kitty glanced at each other momentarily.

In the distance the sound of guns came towards them, carried on a winter wind. Kitty pushed aside the image of dead birds falling silently from a sky that had now lost its bravely determined sun, and seconds later she excused herself and hurried into the house, leaving Harry standing by himself, staring over the familiar parkland, which now, for some reason he could not say, suddenly appeared to him to be vaguely different from before.

Kitty scratched on Partita's door.

'Come in, come in, do,' Partita called. 'I am so glad you are here, I am in seventeen different minds as to how I look.'

'You look stunning, Tita,' Kitty assured her, before noting Partita's day dress that was still lying where she had discarded it on a chaise longue. She turned away and then turned back as she saw there were bloodstains all down the skirt. She was so squeamish, the very thought of what must be the beater's blood spilling all over Partita was enough to make her feel quite faint.

'You really will enjoy the servants' ball,' Partita continued before noticing Kitty's expression. 'Are you all right?' She peered at Kitty. 'Gracious, you look white to the lips. Don't tell me, it's my dress! Don't mind it, really, it is only blood,' she reassured her, taking Kitty's hand. 'Fellow didn't die or anything. He just had the shot taken out of his beam. Mamma did a first-rate job, as usual. She really would have made a number-one surgeon – but there you are – instead she mends and patches here whenever she can. So don't worry – if you break an ankle dancing tonight, Mamma will have you back on your feet again as soon as you can say Viennese waltz!'

With one final look at her reflection, Partita swept out of her room, pulling Kitty after her.

Kitty found that Partita was right. There was no ceremony, no protocol and no precedence at the servants' ball, other than the usual pattern of general polite behaviour that was always observed at Bauders.

The Duchess, in deference to the importance of the occasion, took care to sport her tiara, always known affectionately among her children as 'the family fender', so everyone else followed suit and dressed in their best and finest gowns and jewellery, knowing that the servants would wish it. The family, after all, were the main attraction and they had to dress up; if they did not dress up, the servants would fear to, and half the fun of the evening would have been extinguished.

Everyone that worked at Bauders had looked forward to the ball for months. It was, after all, the one night of the year when they could all be expected to be at their best, the women's dresses being either borrowed finery, or home-made gowns sewn by doting grandmothers, while the men wore their liveries, as appropriate.

'Mamma always looks forward to this ball more than any other, because she really is *bohemian*,' Partita remarked as she and Kitty stood at the side, fanning themselves and taking in the scene.

Kitty was amazed, not only by the amount of people there – so vast was the castle there were people she had never set eyes on soon crowding the room – but also by the atmosphere, which was more lively than anything she had known.

The opening dance was an old-fashioned waltz, which the Duke led off with his head housekeeper, the stately Mrs Coggle. They were followed almost immediately on to the floor by the Duchess and Mr Wavell.

'Wavell dances really quite well, wouldn't you say?' Partita asked Kitty, viewing the butler, head on one side. 'He's so light on his feet Mamma says he should have been a dancing master, not a butler – oh Lordy, here comes Harry.'

'Don't you like Harry Wavell?' Kitty murmured, surprised, as she saw the young man walking towards them.

'Harry's all right,' Partita replied, a little sur-prised by the question since she had never considered whether she liked or disliked Harry before. 'No, Harry's – just, well – Harry, and I do believe he's going to ask you to dance.'

Partita laughed lightly as she was at once

confronted by Taylor, one of the footmen, always known in the servants' hall as Big Footman.

'Dance with me, Lady Tita?'

'Oh, very well, Taylor,' Partita said, a little glint now lighting up her blue eyes. 'Just as long as you don't try steering me into the conservatory as you did last year.'

'I could ask you to forget about that, Lady Tita!'

Taking Partita onto the floor, he danced her off into the ever-increasing throng, executing an energetic step that owed nothing to any known dance but which Partita was nevertheless seen to cope with in really quite a skilful manner.

'More like a large dancing bunny rabbit, wouldn't you say, Miss Rolfe?' Harry asked her as he watched them. 'I do believe that the only time poor Tom Taylor can keep is the one told by a clock.'

'I suppose you must know all the household,' Kitty remarked as Harry led her onto the floor.

'Yes I do, Miss Rolfe, and a right lot they are too,' Harry stated affectionately. 'How is your waltz?'

'I don't think I'll let you down. At least I hope not.'

Harry danced so well that Kitty was disappointed when she was confronted by a determined footman.

'Keep the last dance for me?' Harry called, before leaving Kitty to the slow, methodical, but not entirely unrhythmic two-step as performed by the utterly silent six-foot-tall footman.

'Miss Rolfe?'

The next request came somewhat surprisingly from Almeric.

'Lord Almeric. Are you not meant to be dancing with one of the maids perhaps?'

'Find me one and I might consider it,' he replied gravely. 'But at the moment every maid has been taken.'

Kitty looked round the ballroom. It was true. The only people sitting this dance out were the older guests and the older members of the household. She walked back onto the dance floor, and started to waltz once more.

'You dance divinely, Miss Rolfe.'

Kitty smiled, but as they spun past the onlookers to the side of the floor she could not help catching Harry's eye. He raised his champagne glass to her in acknowledgement as they passed him for the second time, but when they finally stepped off the floor, perhaps realising that Kitty had already captured the attention of the next Duke of Eden, he had vanished from the room.

Chapter Three

Dance Cards

The New Year was to be seen in, as always, by a ball given by Cecil and Lady Maude Milborne. Everyone at Bauders liked Lady Maude, who was a woman of infinite charm and sweetness. Unfortunately they disliked her husband in equal measure.

'Sometimes it would seem that one's friends cannot marry people equally pleasing, and why poor Lady Maude married Cecil Milborne we will never know, I don't suppose,' Circe confided to her maid, as she did every year when the subject of the Milborne ball was raised.

Browne, who was busy sorting through Her Grace's gowns, looked vague, as she always did when the Duchess confided in her. Only Circe knew that the vaguer Browne looked, the more truly interested she was.

Circe was not alone in wondering why Maude had married Cecil Milborne, who was neither titled, handsome, rich nor amusing. Maude also wondered – not all day, but certainly every day. In her heart of hearts she blamed her father, who had been frightened that she would become a spinster.

'You'll end up a spiky-faced woman with a moustache, never seen out of her gardening shoes,' was how he liked to put it.

Her father's anxiety over her marital status would have been touching had not Maude known that it was less concern for her happiness than fear that she would die without giving birth, and would, Maude being his only daughter, therefore prove to be the last in the line for, most unusually, the Earl's title could be passed through the female line. So marry Maude had, the first man who asked her, and it happened to be Cecil.

Cecil, who changed his name to accommodate her family pride, brought nothing except himself to their marriage, a union that became increasingly uncomfortable as his sense of inadequacy increased, but as with so many people who are unpopular, Cecil was quite sure that it was all the fault of the rest of the world, while Maude was equally sure that having made her bed, she would jolly well have to lie in it.

'Maude?'

Cecil was standing in front of her.

'Yes, Cecil?'

'I want a word with you, please. I have a bone to pick.'

How Maude hated that phrase of his, 'a bone

to pick'. So ghastly, as if they were both dogs in a courtyard.

'Some new complaint, have you, Cecil?'

Cecil always managed to look both cruel and petulant at the same time, which Maude thought quite a feat.

'The flower arrangements in the dining room are vulgar, Maude.'

'They are modish, Cecil.'

'I have had them removed. The servants have thrown them out.'

Maude rose from her chair and as she did so she cursed the fact that she knew she had lost colour. She hated to show Cecil that she had any feelings at all, at least as far as he was concerned.

'The servants are to do no such thing, Cecil.'

Every year it was the same – some new disruption, some new complaint, and always stored up for the day of the ball, something that he had probably planned for days.

He caught at her arm. 'Where are you going, Maude?'

'I am going to have the flowers replaced, Cecil. There are no more to be had anywhere on New Year's Eve, and you know it. The hot-houses are quite bare.'

'Too late, Maude. I had them burned, earlier.'

Maude stared at him, and fell to silence. The phrase 'murder in her heart' would be too mild for what she was feeling. She shook off Cecil's grip, and left the room.

*   *   *

Snow was making the countryside surrounding Bauders look enchanting. Darkness had long fallen when everyone inside was to be found preparing themselves for yet another ball.

'Myself, I find I have not the energy I used to have,' the Duke confided to Wavell. '*Autres temps, autres moeurs*, if you know what I mean, Wavell.'

'Yes, Your Grace,' Wavell nodded. He had no idea what His Grace was on about with his French, but cared less, since they were both enjoying what His Grace always alluded to as 'a jolly good snifter' in the snug near the servants' hall – a particularly good Highland snifter it was too.

However, if His Grace was feeling weary at the idea of facing another ball, the young were still very much on their toes, and showing no signs of flagging. Partita particularly seemed to be imbued with an endless amount of energy, dancing in and out of the rooms, Tinker following with an increasingly hopeless expression.

'You are a jumping bean, that is what you are, Lady Tita,' Tinker grumbled. 'Gunpowder is it, that you swallowed at luncheon today?'

'I love New Year's Eve,' Partita confided to no one at all, staring at herself in the dressing mirror. 'It is almost shuddersome, don't you think? Wondering what is going to happen to one next year? Wondering if by next year

86

one will be married with five children? Or still wandering the world in search of a beau?'

Kitty stared at her fleetingly. She herself felt really quite tired, and would not mind at all if she spent the rest of the evening on a wobbly gilt chair, watching everyone else enjoying themselves.

Yet once Kitty and Bridie had begun her *toilette*, accompanied by still more nonstop nonsensical chatter from Partita, Kitty seemed to forget all about her fatigue, especially since Bridie's method of brushing her hair was strongly reminiscent of the method she must use when beating Violet's rugs on the washing line in the back garden.

'Lady Maude is quite interesting, actually,' Partita said, lifting her arms up and not bothering to pause while Tinker, deftly balancing the dress between two sticks, lowered yet another ball gown over her newly coiffed hair. 'Interesting and fun, but her husband is horrid.'

'Now, now, Lady Tita,' Tinker clucked. 'If you don't take care, there'll be soap instead of paste on that toothbrush of yours tonight.'

'She and the *awful* Cecil live in what was her father's house. Lady Maude's family are Keepers of the Keys, do you see – of our keys, of the keys to Bauders. That has been their position for goodness knows how long,' Partita sighed, emerging from her now fully lowered gown. 'When a monarch visits, there's this elaborate ceremony with the Keys. It drives Papa to distraction because whenever King George and Queen Mary visit, he has to wait for boring old *Cecil*, who has now taken on the role of Keeper of the Keys for himself, to be done with all his bowing and scraping and special speech-making. It really is enough to drive the King, and Papa, to distraction.'

'Tut tut,' Tinker clucked again, frowning at Bridie. 'All this criticism of His Grace's friends, Lady Tita. It ain't fitting. It really ain't fitting.'

'Oh, never mind fitting, Tinker,' Partita replied, regarding herself in the dressing glass. 'I am quite sure that anything I say is as nothing compared with what you have to say in the servants' hall.'

'At least *we* waits till your backs are turned, Lady Tita,' Tinker said, giving her mistress's sumptuous gown one last adjustment.

'You would blush if you knew what I said about you, Tinker,' Partita said, pulling a face at Kitty. 'It would turn that curly hair of yours quite, quite straight. The fact is, Kitty – Cecil Milborne is to be avoided. Mamma says poor Hugh's asthma is entirely accountable to his father's beastliness.'

'Folk gets asthma from damp, Lady Tita—'

'Sure you should try the place where I was raised,' Bridie offered. 'There was so much damp Mam never had to draw water for washing, she just ran the flannel across the walls . . .' She left the sentence unfinished, shaking her head.

'Horrid for you . . .'

Partita made commiserating noises, while not really listening. She turned to Tinker.

'You've been an angel as always, Tinks, you know that, don't you?'

Tinker looked up momentarily from her tidying-up. 'I do know that, Lady Tita, and you have been a little devil as always.'

Partita blew her a kiss. 'You are my own dear Tinker, and you know it,' she said, smiling with satisfaction.

'Thank you, Bridie,' Kitty called back in her turn from the door, despite the fact that her head was still aching from the maid's attentions to her hair, but that was not something she could now do much about.

The carriages circled in front of Milborne House, the flares lighting up the grand parade of horses and harnesses, of coachmen and grooms, of doors painted with ancient coats of arms. The old, eighteenth-century stone house, with its long windows and flights of shallow stone steps leading up to central doors, seemed to be smiling down at the scene below. This, after all, was what the country house was for – entertaining friends, greeting neighbours and cementing friendships based on mutual interests.

Tonight the great rooms of the house were decorated with swags of holly, and thousands of candles, with great branches of ivy interlaced with gold and silver ornaments, so that not even Cecil could find fault with its proud displays.

The moment Kitty entered the Milbornes'

ballroom, Peregrine Catesby went straight to her side.

'Seeing how beautiful you look tonight, Miss Rolfe, I think I should quickly write my name in your card – before it is filled with the names of every eligible bachelor present.'

The moment Peregrine left her side to fetch refreshment, Almeric appeared from nowhere, leaning over her shoulder to read her dance card.

'Perry is being greedy, Miss Rolfe,' he said, scribbling his own name over that of Perry's. 'That will never do.'

Before Kitty could demur he took her hand and led her onto the dance floor.

'Of all the nerve,' Peregrine murmured, watching Kitty being danced away from him. 'You shall regret that, Lord Almeric. That is the last time I help you translate Euripides.'

He had replaced the two glasses he had fetched on a passing footman's tray, before he noticed Partita sitting on a gilt chair nearby.

'What, Lady Tita a wallflower? This will never do,' he said, and immediately led her onto the floor.

'I'm fast becoming bored of waltzes,' Partita sighed as they began to dance. 'Next time ask me for a two-step, will you, Perry? Or a bunny hug, anything rather than the dull old waltz.'

'Have you begun reading from the list I sent to you in London?' Peregrine enquired as he spun her expertly around the crowded floor.

'I read the list, Perry,' Partita stated in a bored voice.

'And have you become enthused by it?'

'Too many Latin poets, Perry, truly far too many.'

'Good poets. Don't be impatient. You'll get to love them, if you allow yourself.'

'Oh, very well,' Partita agreed, mock bravely. 'For you I shall endeavour to understand and appreciate them.'

'Allow your friend Miss Rolfe to help you. She was telling me how much she enjoyed Virgil's *Aeneid*—'

'Kitty enjoys everything that is good for her,' Partita interrupted. 'Sometimes I swear she is too good to be true, just as her father is said to be too bad to be true.'

'I don't think Miss Rolfe's virtue can be the result of her father's vices. Or her father the fault of her virtues.'

'That is a little too clever for me, Perry. All I know is that I feel sorry for Kitty.'

'Nonsense, Tita, one only feels sorry for someone one doesn't really like. I see there are some very long faces over there, Tita. Very long indeed. Do you think they know something we do not?'

Partita glanced in the direction her partner was looking.

'Papa has a bee in his hat about this Balkans business,' Partita moaned. 'The Balkans really are not my subject. I don't even know where they begin or where they end, and I'm not awfully sure that I care.'

'Still afraid of being taken for a blue stocking, are we, Partita?'

'No, not at all, just afraid of being found to be a bore. This is meant to be New Year's Eve, for goodness' sake!'

'It most certainly is,' Peregrine agreed. 'And we shall all put away our cares and dance this last night of the old year away, without a thought of tomorrow.'

After which Peregrine reversed expertly, whirling Partita well away from the party of older guests, who were still all standing together.

'I cannot for the life of me see why you gentlemen imagine we could get involved in some trivial border dispute in some place few of us have ever even heard of,' their host was saying.

'Hardly trivial, and hardly a border dispute, Milborne,' the Duke replied.

'Greedy bunch, the Habsburgs. They'd have annexed all of Europe, had they had the chance.'

'To my mind, the French are to blame,' someone else put in. 'They should have been curbed ages ago. The current situation is a direct result of years of their wretched promotion of liberalism, not to mention nationalism. They're going to reap the reward now, you mark my words.'

'Myself, I say it's a storm in a teacup,' the tall and distinguished Lord Rawley opined, and since he had spent most of his life in the diplomatic service, everyone noted his stance. 'Although these problems are certainly vexing the Kaiser and Franz Ferdinand, they are not Germany's problem, they are Austria-Hungary's – and if Vienna does initiate a war they will contain it to the Balkans, because that is where it belongs. Nowhere else. In the Balkans.'

'Romania has little affection for Austria-Hungary,' the Duke argued. 'It's all to do with the Magyars, apparently. They're a real thorn in Franz Ferdinand's side, so they tell me. There you are. Kettle's on the hob, or certainly Kitchener is, and we must see it doesn't boil over.'

'I think we have little real need for concern, Duke,' Rawley concluded. 'The smoke from any trouble brewing is not coming in our direction.'

'Precisely,' Cecil agreed, determined as always to have the last word. 'Besides, the Kaiser is hardly going to pick a fight with his cousin now, is he?'

'Do not be too sure,' the Duke sighed. 'Do not be too sure,' he finished, quietly to himself.

As it happened the Duke was not having a particularly good evening. He disliked Cecil Milborne, who had insinuated his way into the Duchess's inner circle for no better reason than that the Duchess had become very fond of Maude, the women sharing many confidences since their children were young and boisterous. Their husbands, however, shared no such confidences, and no matter how intimate his wife was with the Duchess, Cecil still found himself kept at arm's length by the social diplomacy of the Duchess, who managed always to include Maude whenever the social occasion was suitable, while whenever possible *not* including Cecil – except, of course, when they had to attend the Milbornes' annual New Year's Eve ball.

But social niceties were not the Duke's present preoccupation. He was worried about many things concerning his estates. The servant problem always vexed such enormous households as they lost more and more tenants to the nearby towns and their ever-growing industries. Then there was the land problem, a predicament regularly made worse by ever-increasing taxes brought in by the Liberals, taxes that were making it harder and harder to farm profitably but productively, which affected how many horses he was going to be able to keep. Hawkesworth, his estate manager, did not appreciate the Duke's preoccupation with the comfort and well-being of the horses. He was constantly trying to point out to His Grace that the main stables were full to overflowing, and many of the smaller outhouses sheltered long-outgrown children's ponies from whom the Duke could never part.

'Must keep them for when the grandchildren come along. Can't have them riding about on bicycles, Hawkesworth,' he would murmur every time the dreaded accounting day dawned.

'Can't keep every horse or pony we've bred either, Your Grace.'

'The stables need fodder, the stables need bedding; we grow both and employment is the result,' the Duke insisted.

Yet now, as another year drew to a close, he found he was being pressurised by Hawkesworth to pull in his belt.

'Hawkesworth'll soon be telling me I have to do without my tea and biscuits,' he would grumble as he did evening stables with Jossy and the lads. 'How the devil can you expect to keep an estate running without animals? Stands to reason, animals eat, food is grown, and eaten, by humans and animals, end of the year sees barns full, animals and humans happy. What else is there to be done? Which other way is there to go?'

'Search me, Your Grace – fact is, you can search me from head to toe but you'll not find an answer.'

'No, nor would you if you did the same to me, Jossy.'

'Without t'stable what would we 'ave? No cobbler, no saddler, no grooms, no employment, and we all know what towns do to folk. No, stables is the foundation of all that is good in our society, and we know that. Always will be, and always has been. Take the stables out of life and what do you have? Metal! And fumes! Metal and fumes!'

'And where do they get us when night falls?'

the Duke would return, patting Barrymore Boy, his favourite hunter, and pulling his generous ears. 'Nowhere at all, nowhere at all.'

But the Duke sensed he was fighting a losing battle. He was too shrewd a man to ignore what he saw as the wretched and ignoble march of progress, and while he privately subscribed to the school of philosophy that welcomed changes as long as they helped to keep everything the same, he knew that sooner or later, whether he liked it or not, his horses, as on so many estates, would start to be replaced by machines, and Hawkesworth's eyes would linger yet more over the cost of hay and straw and oats, and what not.

But there was still the New Year's ball to be got through, and he had not asked his hostess's sister for the pleasure of a dance, which was remiss of him. He walked across the ballroom to where she was seated, and as he did so he passed the young, all of whom were leaving to fetch refreshment for their partners, or seek out new ones. To the older man they all looked younger and bonnier than they had ever done, and comfortingly innocent.

He bowed to the lady of his choice. 'Lady Frances, might I have the pleasure?'

Lady Frances Tillingham smiled. 'Why, John, we haven't danced since my coming out, have we?'

'Come, come, Frances, that can't be true.'

'No, it can't be true, but it might be!'

They both laughed, and stepped onto the

dance floor, passing Partita and Peregrine as they did so.

'There is such talk of invasion . . .' Peregrine was saying.

'Invasion talk is so dull.' Partita's tone was deliberately flippant because she had just seen Allegra disappearing into the conservatory with James Millings. Cecilia too was nowhere to be seen, which was also quite suspicious-making since it seemed Mamma was too busy dancing and enjoying herself to notice.

'It will not be dull if you get up in the morning and find a boatload of Serbs at the castle gates, I do assure you, Tita. They are said to be arriving in their hundreds off the Norfolk and Cornish coasts, so the newspapers tell us.'

'Are they very fierce? Will they be armed to the teeth with sabres and cutlasses, do the newspapers tell us? Is the *Morning Post* warning us to keep our eyes and ears out at every point?'

'I have not the least idea, but I fear that they might be. What will you do when they arrive?'

'Man the ramparts with buckets of boiling oil, and pour it over their foreign heads,' Partita stated with evident relish. 'It's all the fault of the Liberals, of course. If they had not made such a mess of things, Papa says, we would at least have some oil to boil. Now because of them the whole world – America, Germany, everyone – is doing better than England.'

'Your father is right, little Tita, it is the fault of the Liberals,' Peregrine agreed as the dance ended. 'Now I must go and rescue my poor sister, who I see has been stationed behind the dowagers for more dances than I care to think about.'

'I do wish you would not still call me little Tita.'

As Partita looked up at him Peregrine saw that her large blue eyes were filling with tears.

He leaned forward, horrified. 'I did not mean to hurt your feelings. I was only teasing.' He leaned further forward, touching her lightly on the arm to comfort her, appalled at what he suddenly realised was his lack of sensitivity.

Partita's expression changed to one of mischievous triumph. 'Ha, ha, you see how good I am at acting? Now I must go and find *my* sisters. I have not seen them for some time.'

She walked off into the crowd.

'I dare say if you were not a Knowle I would think of a way to punish you,' Peregrine called after her, before looking across the room to where his sister was standing, idly fanning herself.

Poor Livia, she was standing behind the rows of older ladies, all of whom were watching the dancing, waiting for some impudent young man to be found waltzing some innocent girl into the conservatory, always a cause of consternation if it was not immediately followed by a proposal of marriage.

'Valentine,' Peregrine murmured to Valentine Wynyard Errol, who disliked dancing only a little less than he disliked his feckless father, Ralph. 'Valentine? Would you be so gallant, old chap, as to take my sister onto the dance floor and give her a whirl? She is standing behind Mary, Lady Bultash.'

Valentine looked across at Livia. In common with all their friends, he would do anything for Perry, even dance with his sister.

'Very well. Which one is she?'

'I told you, she is standing behind Lady Bultash, and beside Elizabeth Milborne. She is in the blue dress.'

As he stared at his sister, Peregrine felt resigned. They were not rich, to say the least, but even so, he always thought that Livia should be given a few new dresses, not always be sent off in some second-hand piece that one of the maids had washed and starched for her. Mind you, this particular evening, the Empire line still being so much in vogue, Livia did not look as out of fashion in her old blue dress as she might.

'The one in the blue dress, you say?' Valentine turned back to Peregrine. 'But she is very pretty,' he said, staring.

Valentine manoeuvred behind the row of old trouts seated on gold chairs, and touched Livia Catesby on the shoulder. She turned, startled.

'I say, would you care for a turn around the floor? Or is your dance card full?'

'It is blank,' Livia Catesby told him with searing honesty, and as she did so the hopeless look of a drowning kitten left her face and a really engaging smile replaced it. 'There is nothing more off-putting to young men than an empty dance card,' she confided, holding her dance card out.

'Then may I put my name in it for the next dance?'

'You will find Livia dances like a cart horse,' Consolata, her mother, announced to Valentine's open astonishment.

'In that case Livia and myself will make a splendid pair. I am famed for my large feet, so much so that when allowed, I wear a harness and horse brasses.'

Consolata fanned herself, unsmiling.

'Gracious, Consolata,' Opal Gaskell said, turning to her. 'How delightful to see Livia enjoying herself, and with such a well-set-up young man.'

The older woman fanned herself more vigorously.

'I think she is such a pretty girl,' Opal went on in encouraging tones.

'You may think as you wish, Opal dear.'

Opal turned away, and addressed herself to the lady on her other side, because Consolata seemed so determined on disapproval.

'Has Consolata always been as she is?' Opal asked Lily Stapleton in a lowered tone as, the polka having come to an end, Consolata stood up, and with a look of steely determination walked towards her daughter.

'Oh, she was much worse when she was younger,' Lily told her, cheerfully. 'Always known as "the inconsolable". Her deepest desire was to go into an enclosed order; but it seems that her father and mother determined that she *must* be married, so she *was* married, to Bede Catesby – usually known to his friends as Blessed Saint Bede Catesby. It was always rumoured that dear Bede died of the shock of siring his two children. My own mother said it was the cruellest thing to have Bede and Consolata marry. I should think it most likely that it *was* cruel. Oh, but do not look, I pray you, oh, do not *say*, Consolata is only marching Livia back here, poor child.'

Lily stood up.

'Lily, you cannot interfere, my dear, really you cannot.'

Lily looked down briefly at Opal. 'Neither can I stand by and watch, Opal. I have known Consolata for most of my life, and believe me, whenever possible, she must be stopped from her good intentions.'

Opal hurried off into the crowd, and before Consolata could march Livia back to stand once more behind the older women, Lily had commandeered her son.

'Pug?'

'Yes, Mamma?'

'Go at once to Livia Catesby and ask for the next waltz.' As her son gave her the kind of look that sons always give their mothers when they ask something of them other than what they would like in the way of wine, Lily rapped his arm sharply with her fan. 'Go on, go on, Pug, you will have to put your glass down some time during the evening; it might as well be now.'

Pug went up to Livia to ask her for the next waltz, but only just in time to deflect Consolata from her course. Happily Pug and Livia had been friends since childhood.

'What a frost, being made to dance with you!' Pug remarked, squinting down at Livia as he waltzed her gaily round, a movement that unfortunately made it impossible for his monocle to stay in place. 'Our mammas seem a trifle overheated, winging about like bats in a rectory garden.'

Livia knew that Pug affected to be a 'knut', a form of fashionable dandy. It gave him a distinctive air of vague arrogance, as it did all knuts.

'Dance the next one with me, Pug, do?' Livia begged. 'I think I would rather die than go back and stand behind all those mothballs waving their fans about and playing cat's cradle with everyone's reputations the moment they see someone so much as smiling at someone else.'

'Quite so,' Pug agreed, beginning to sweat from the unusual exertions demanded by the polka, or was it a waltz? 'This is more of a set-to than cricket, do you know that, Livia?' he finished, and puffing and replacing his monocle in his eye, he took her fan from her wrist and waved it in front of his face as they walked off the floor. 'Heigh-ho,' he continued in a warning tone. 'Here comes the old ferocity. Quick, let me put a host of names in your dance card.' He quickly penned different names on the card dangling from her wrist.

'Livia?'

Consolata had walked across the room to her daughter's side but now, noting the change in her daughter's eyes, she felt her heart quicken. It was as if Livia was a bird she had caught in her hands, but which, after just a few bats of its wings, had flown out of a nearby window.

'Livia, did you hear me?'

'Yes, Mamma?'

'You must return with me to behind the chairs.'

'Absolutely not, Mrs Catesby,' Pug put in cheerfully, monocle now firmly back in place. 'You see, Livia's in such demand,' he went on, nodding towards Livia's faked dance card. 'She will not be sitting out as much as one waltz before the end of the evening.'

Consolata was not given to vanity. She never looked in a mirror unless absolutely necessary, but nor did she ever wear spectacles to balls. She squinted down at the card. She could not make it out. She turned on her heel and went back to join the older women.

'You are a hoojah, really you are, Pug,' Livia murmured affectionately. 'But now what do we do?'

'See what you mean. Only beastliness is, I can't

go on dancing with you, or she will twig straight away. Better get some of the coves whose names I have imprinted here to actually dance with you, what? Follow me, old thing, and I will have whole teams of dudes lined up to trip the light fantastic with you.'

The result of Pug's ruse was that Livia had the ball of her life, and went home not just in love with Valentine Wynyard Errol, which was more or less a racing fixture as far as they were both concerned, but with the whole of life.

She was not the only one to make a success of the evening. Kitty was so much in demand that she ended the evening feeling vaguely guilty, for most of her dancing partners were Partita's admirers.

Not that Partita seemed to mind, only teasingly remarking once they had returned home to Bauders, been undressed by their sleepy maids, and retired to bed, 'I think you may well end up becoming my sister-in-law!'

It was a remark that embarrassed Kitty into silence, as it was perhaps meant to do.

'How many dances did Al beg from you, Kitty?' Partita called, having, as was now their habit, left the intervening doors open, the better to gossip until they fell asleep.

'I cannot now remember.'

'Yes, it must be difficult for you to remember, since there were so many. You might just as well have reserved your whole dance card just for him. He never dances, not usually, you know.

He vastly prefers almost anything you care to mention more than dancing at balls, and yet there he was at your side at every possible moment.'

'Partita—'

'Should you like to be a duchess?' Partita continued ruthlessly.

'Partita—'

'I have to warn you, life at Bauders is dreadfully old-fashioned and draughty, but it can be fun when it is full of people.'

'You danced with Peregrine Catesby several times,' Kitty retorted.

'Yes I did, but – Perry does not see me except as his little sister,' came the forlorn reply.

'Everyone is in love with you, Partita,' Kitty reassured her. 'They queued to dance with you.'

'Oh, yes, everyone is in love with me except the one I wish,' Partita agreed. 'Except Perry. But I will make him love me, one of these days, truly I will.'

'Certainly you will,' Kitty agreed, and fell to silence.

This satisfied Partita, and shortly after, they both fell asleep, filled with that particular warmth that the whole-hearted admiration of the opposite sex always brings, knowing that whatever lay ahead must be good. They were both, after all, young and beautiful.

Maude Milborne was convinced that their New Year's Eve ball had been a great success, until she saw her husband's face at luncheon the following day. Cecil's face was not like thunder, it was like stone. It was a mask of icy cold fury, which, as everyone knows, is the worst kind of fury.

'Is something the matter, Cecil?'

Cecil looked down the table at his wife with obvious reluctance. His marriage had brought him an aristocratic wife, a large fortune, and no happiness. He blamed Maude. He should never have left the army. He had left the army at her instigation and encouragement, both of which now, over the distance of the years, seemed to him to have been less like encouragement and more like insistence. At least he had managed to stay on the reserved list.

'Bertie has lamed me best hunter,' he stated baldly, and he speared the food on his plate and positively threw it into his mouth. Behind him, some yards away from the main dining table, Cheeseman, their butler, shuddered. 'The beast is now as lame as your conversation, Maude,' Cecil went on.

Maude winced. She hated people to witness Cecil's unkindness to her. However, patience as ever came to her aid, so she sighed inwardly, took a pull, and started again, speaking slowly, because she knew that Cecil's intake the night before had been huge, magnificent, foolhardy, or hideous, depending on your point of view.

'Bertie did not hunt on Boxing Day, Cecil.

There have been no days out since Christmas, on account of the weather. You may remember that. It was you yourself who took Almonds out. Bertie went to Castleton to see that poor boy who subsequently died – Mrs Thorncroft's youngest son. Yes, poor Alfred died, you know, and Bertie stayed over to comfort her and her family – Alfie and Bertie being such friends in the old days.' She went on as if speaking to herself, 'Always ragging each other, always fishing and swimming together.'

Cecil stared at his wife through bloodshot eyes. The fact that their asthmatic son, Hughie, was the heir to Maude's title had not helped their relationship; nor was it made any better by the knowledge that when Maude kicked the bucket, or, as she would put it, 'was gathered', Cecil himself would, more than likely, and equally promptly, be kicked out of the house, his wife's fortune having long ago been entailed on her sons.

'Where is *Cuthbert*?' he asked, using the tone of voice that he would sometimes employ in the training of one of his gun dogs.

'That is what I have been trying to tell you – Bertie, today, is attending Alfred Thorncroft's funeral, Cecil.'

'He is at the funeral of the Castleton grocer's son?'

'He is at the funeral of a dear friend—'

'He should be out with Daylesford, doing the rounds.'

'He excused himself to Daylesford. Daylesford understood. He is a gentleman.'

There was a small silence, during which Cheeseman stared at the space between the two protagonists. If it had been a cricket match and he the umpire, he would have raised his arm to indicate that her ladyship had hit a six. However, one look at Mr Milborne told him that this realisation had not gone unnoticed by him, and that boded ill, so no one was really surprised when the door slammed behind Cecil, and both the footmen blinked as it rattled the decanters on the sideboard, taking up the sound and seeming to throw it across the room and from there to slip seamlessly out between the ill-fitting dining-room windows to join the icy weather outside.

'Would your ladyship care for some fruit?'

Maude looked up at Cheeseman. A few years ago after such a distressing moment, the eyes she now lifted to her butler would have had tears in them – but thankfully no longer. She had grown stronger with age.

'Yes, I would care for some fruit, Cheeseman. Thank you. Such a pity that the dining-room door will keep slamming, do you not think? We must ask Daylesford to get Jeffryes to see to it, when things are back to rights.'

'Yes, your ladyship.'

Cheeseman took the grape scissors and carefully cut Maude some grapes grown in her own hot-house, and placed them on a gold and blue decorated fruit plate, itself resting on a wrought-silver server in front of her.

'Thank you, Cheeseman.'

Cheeseman retired back to his original position in the old, shabby dining room. All the servants at Milborne House would do anything for her ladyship. Such was certainly not the case when it came to Mr Cecil, who was known as 'the Kaiser' below stairs, and, secretly, to his sons too.

'A bully is born every minute,' Cheeseman's mother used to say, 'and it's up to us to stand up to them, George my boy.'

How right she was. Ever since he had taken up his position at Milborne House, Cheeseman could honestly say that he had made it his business to stand up to Mr Cecil, if only by his silence. Silence could not only be deafening, it could be defeating – at least he had always found it so. It said much more than words. More than that, silence was ominous; it threatened. He could honestly swear on the family Bible that he had hardly addressed a look to Mr Cecil in many a month. He knew Cecil did not like it. Cheeseman, on the other hand, greatly enjoyed it. It was this enjoyment more than anything that had kept him from leaving Milborne House. He had had offers from guests who came to stay at the house and were impressed by his work, naturally, but his devotion to her ladyship was one hundred per cent. While her ladyship was at Milborne House, Cheeseman made it his business to stay put, refusing more lucrative offers, even turning away opportunities to become a butler in a royal household. In his view her ladyship was a heroine out of a book, not that he would ever be caught reading one, but if he did, he would certainly have expected it to star someone such as Lady Maude Milborne.

Maude stood up, only too glad luncheon was over, yet already dreading dinner, and when the time came she was only too glad of the company of her sons. She appreciated that Hughie and Cuthbert made it their business to miss as many meals as possible when their father was in residence, making sure to come to breakfast at dawn, and remain out of doors all day, and only reluctantly appearing at night for dinner, which they now did if only to support their mother. The meal dragged on, and on, and on until at last they were able to follow Maude out of the room, their faces showing understandable relief that dinner was over, but perhaps because the weather outside was crisp and clear, Hughie's asthma was at its worst, as a consequence of which he was in no mood to see Cecil bully Maude. But he was determined to be strong, which made it all the more difficult when he announced that he was going to America, because on hearing the news his parents seemed to change roles instantly. His mother fell silent, and his father brightened.

'Doing something at last, are you, Hughie?'

Cecil took up his oil lamp from the drawing-room table, swaying a little as he did so – the port that evening having been unusually good.

'Yes, Papa, doing something at last.'

Inwardly Hughie cursed the noise from his chest, knowing that at any moment his father was quite likely to make a derisory comment about it.

'Perhaps your brother will be tempted to follow your example? No trouble following you – your chest makes enough noise for ten men!' Cecil went on, laughing heartily.

Hughie smiled at this. He and Bertie had made an agreement when they were quite small that they would smile, no matter what the Kaiser handed out to them.

'Have you any particular ambition that you wish to pursue in America, Hughie, dear?' Maude put in quickly.

'Yes, Mamma, I have been offered a position in a bank.'

There was a ghastly silence. It was a silence that, in a novel, would be described as 'the silence of the morgue'. Seconds turned into a full-blown minute, until at last a voice was heard.

'You have been offered a position in a bank?' Cecil turned to Maude. 'Did you hear that, Maude? Hughie is all set to become a *snob!*'

Snobs, as anyone employed in charging interest on money were always called, were looked down on, as was *anyone* who made money on the back of some other person's wealth. Cheeseman knew this, as did all the servants. Bankers, stockbrokers, folk from the City would never expect to be invited to places such as Bauders Castle or

Milborne House, being all too aware that old families considered usury to be one of the root causes of evil in their society. The lending and making of money by the exacting of percentages was considered base; so, if Mr Hughie had suddenly announced that he had just been out to the stables and shot his pet spaniel, his news could not have been more terrible.

'When are you due to depart, Hughie, dear?' Maude put away her handkerchief and shut her reticule with a snap.

'From Southampton, as soon as there is a sailing.'

Cecil turned to Maude, a triumphant look in his eye. 'I always told you that Hughie was no good,' he said, taking up his lamp. 'Do not,' he said, turning round at the drawing-room door, 'do not ever expect me to address another word to you. As of this minute, if you pursue this ambition, you are no longer my son.'

Bertie waited until the door had been closed behind his father, and then he looked across at Hughie.

'Well, that is a relief for you, Hughie, at any rate,' he said, going across to fetch his own oil lamp, preparatory to going to bed.

Maude turned to Cheeseman. 'You may all go now, Cheeseman.'

'Thank you, my lady.'

Cheeseman withdrew with dignity, followed by a sleepy footman.

Outside the drawing-room doors, and having

made sure that the master of the house had indeed retired to bed to be undressed by his valet, Cheeseman let out a vast sigh of relief, and his step towards the green baize door that separated the world of the servants from the world of the masters, was lighter than it had been for weeks. One son down, now only one to go. Whatever Mr Hughie's life in America might turn out to be, it had to be a great deal better than that which he had not enjoyed at Milborne House.

Chapter Four

Comings and Goings

With the thaw that had started two days earlier continuing to take the frost out of the ground, it was decided that hunting could be resumed on New Year's Day.

Naturally the house party at Bauders Castle was, as always, divided between those who wanted to shoot and those who preferred to ride to hounds. After a late night many of the young men usually chose to shoot rather than ride, preferring the noise of their shotguns to a line of fences on board a keen hunter. This New Year's Day, however, found most of the bloods electing to follow hounds, which was quite understandable once the rumour was abroad that Partita and Kitty were to make their appearance, which they duly did, riding sidesaddle on perfectly turned-out matching greys.

'What a sight to set before a duke!' Pug Stapleton murmured as all eyes rested on the two young ladies, their shiny top hats and veils at just the right angle, their impeccably cut riding jackets and tailored skirts showing off their tiny waists and perfect deportment. Partita was in a velvet habit of the same dark blue as her father's personal hunting livery, with a matching hat worn to the front of her perfectly coiffed blonde hair, while Kitty was wearing a superb hunting skirt and tailored jacket in lovat green, once the treasured property of Aunt Agatha.

Top hats were raised to the ladies, caps were doffed and forelocks touched as the two lovely young women rode into the heart of the restless and excited horses, all ready for the off, highly polished hoofs dancing restlessly over the gravel of the forecourts as stirrup cups were handed round, to the accompaniment of the sounds of bits rattling and leather slapping against gleaming coats steaming gently in the crisp air.

The Duke sat apart from the throng, as still as the handsome horse under him. The only part of Barrymore Boy's body that was moving was his head, his huge dark brown eyes seeming to be swivelling under frowning brows as if checking on the behaviour of the younger equines in his charge, his large ears moving backwards and forwards, seeming to be listening in two directions, as his reddening nostrils slowly flared until he snorted a light warning to his master that, as far as he was concerned, they were ready to go and do the day's business.

As if prompted by his horse, the Duke nodded to his huntsmen, his Field Master and his whippers-in, an ancient silvered hunting horn was raised and the call to move away blew out across the park. At once all chatter stopped as girths were given a final check, reins were gathered, and glinting spurs dug into horses' sides and the field moved off. Everyone tried to contain their excited mounts at the walk or the trot, not all of them successfully, as several of the more highly strung animals, resisting their bits, attempted to break into a canter, their riders managing to rein them in tightly, so they were forced to dance on the spot, the steam rising from their bodies adding to the mist that had not yet cleared.

Behind them the great house stood empty, deserted except for all the family's pet dogs, lying stretched by the fires, while below stairs the servants regrouped and planned their next attack on the rooms above them.

Wavell sat at the head of the table in the servants' hall, his mid-morning cup of tea nearly empty, his eyes on all the members of his company as they wearily conversed, some grumbling, some laughing, the younger ones, fresh to the household, still amazed by the pageantry they had seen over the Christmas holiday, the glamour, the decorum, the beauty.

Finally their commander rose from his position at the head of the table and with a nod to Mrs Coggle, his second in command, he went to do battle once more, his troops rising behind him, preparing to arm themselves with mops, buckets, dusters, polishes and brushes. Moments later there was a frenzy of activity as they went into action, sweeping, cleaning, washing and tidying, returning the state rooms back to normality, so that by the time their superiors returned, their quarters would be warm, clean and orderly, with fires lit, brasses shining, leather glossy, and woodwork gleaming. Nothing would be out of place and nothing would be missing. Sets of clothes would be laid out for tea, shoes polished and paired ready, undergarments ironed, hairbrushes washed and put back in place, fresh soaps unwrapped and laid in hand-polished basins with shining taps, decanters filled, bottles wiped and set, glasses bright, and fresh cigarettes and cigars placed in silver boxes in the smoking room. After which Wavell, at some silent signal, would begin his inspection, finishing with a check on the settings for dinner, making sure the places were laid at exactly the correct distances from each other, the knives, forks and spoons correctly ordered, and the glasses placed within perfect reach. Then hands would be washed and inspected, fresh gloves would be taken, shoulders would be brushed, uniforms checked and straightened, and final orders issued for the next phase of the campaign, the body of household troops signalled into action by bells calling them to their various posts and finally by the sonorous boom of the great gong as it summoned all to the table. By midnight once again, the house would fall quiet, the nocturnal silence broken only by the melodious call of Birdie, the nightwatchman, as he made his rounds, calling out the passing of another hour in the life of Bauders Castle.

'What did you make of the hunt meet then, Miss Malone?' Tully asked Bridie when he found her. 'Quite a sight, eh?'

'It was a lovely sight,' Bridie sighed. 'As beautiful as the dawn, and as fair as the summer, as my grandmother used to say.'

Tully stared at her. 'I wish I could talk like you, Miss Malone, I do truly. You have a way of talking . . .' he shook his head in admiration. 'Where are you from?'

'Timbuktu,' Bridie replied, eyeing him and deciding she liked what she saw. 'And where are you from, Mr Tully?'

'You're not from Timbuktu,' Tully laughed, putting his cap back on carefully as if it was the most expensive hat in the world. 'You're from Ireland, I know that – as I am from here. Here's where I was born and bred.'

'And I'm from a part of Ireland sure you'll never have heard of ever. Did you ever hear of Galway?'

'I did,' Tully nodded. 'His Grace had a fine racer by that very name. Won four races in a row. A jumper. Lovely horse he was, and he was called Galway Boy, because that's where he was bred, and it's in Ireland. See?'

'And that's where I'm from. Now if you don't

mind, Mr Tully . . .' Bridie stopped by a door into the side of the house.

'Just Tully, Miss Malone. Tully's my Christian name – Tuttle's the surname. Tully Tuttle is my name in full.'

'And sure how old are yous, Tully Tuttle, when you're at home? You don't look an hour over sixteen.'

'I'm eighteen and a bit,' Tully replied hotly. 'I shall be eighteen and a half in two months' time.'

'Well, I'm much too old to be talking to you. Sure am't I old enough to be your elder sister, so?'

'There you go again!' Tully exclaimed. 'I never met a girl who could make me laugh the way you do!'

'So you think I'm funny then?'

'You are. Old enough to be my elder sister! I mean to say!'

Tully shook his head in delight, his eyes closed. When he opened them Bridie was gone.

'Miss Malone?' he called after her, running into the house and down the long dark corridor into which he saw her retreating fast. 'Miss Malone? You're not upset, are you?'

She slowed her pace to allow him to catch up, turning round to look at him with a prim and quite straight face.

'No,' she said. 'No, I'm not upset now. But I well might be in the future if you continue laughing at me.'

'I wasn't laughing *at* you, honest, Miss Malone.'

Tully looked sheepish.

'So that's all right then,' Bridie replied, gathering up her skirts. 'Not that you'll have the chance.'

'What do you mean?'

'I mean, Mr Tully, that my mistress and I leaves for London town tomorrow by the train so you won't be getting any more of your grand chances to find me so definitely amusing.'

'You're going back to London?'

'What else would I mean?'

'I meant – I meant to say that what you just said was interesting news. That you were returning to London. I hope you enjoyed your stay at Bauders.'

Now it was Bridie's turn to laugh. 'God bless us and save us,' she said. 'And aren't you the polite one? As well as the funny one. Yes, thank you, Mr Tully Tuttle,' she continued, imitating the manner of her mistress. 'I have enjoyed my stay greatly and look forward to many more such grand occasions.'

'There you go again.'

Tully tried not to smile and they both fell silent for a second or two, Tully looking at her so hard that Bridie dropped her eyes. Finally Tully cleared his throat and took off his cap once again, to hold it and twist it in his big hands.

'Bridie,' he asked nervously. 'I don't know whether you have a lot to do at this very moment, but I have nothing to do for a while – I've done morning stables.'

'I have our packing to do, so I do.' Bridie didn't look at him. She stood staring at the ground, suddenly unsure of what to do next.

'I have to go out in half an hour to do second horses. But if you could spare perhaps ten minutes?' As Bridie looked up at him he continued, 'I could show you round the stables. I'd like to show you my work. Would you like that? That is, if you can spare ten minutes.'

Bridie found herself thinking that she would like that very much indeed, so she spared him more than ten minutes.

Tinker and Tommy Taylor were nearly caught in a fond embrace by Mrs Coggle, the housekeeper.

'Who's that in there?' they heard her call, even though, once they had been made aware of her approach, they had been as silent as mice – which was what gave Tommy the idea for their salvation, since, were Mrs Coggle to discover the sweethearts, she would have absolutely no hesitation in demanding their instant dismissal. 'Is there someone in there?' she demanded. 'Because if so—'

'It's all right, missus!' Tommy called back in the broadest of Midland accents. ''S only the ratman! Need have no fear there!'

Pulling a hopeful face, he held up crossed fingers to Tinker, who by now had taken refuge behind the debris at the back of the cupboard, a sanctuary she knew would be only too short-lived if Mrs Coggle opened the door and found Tommy standing like a lemon with his cravat undone and his hair all mussed.

'Oh Lawd!' to their great relief they heard the housekeeper exclaim. 'We not got the rats again?'

'Just caught two o' the brutes!' Tommy returned cheerfully. 'Would 'ee like to see 'em?'

'Would I just!' Mrs Coggle all but shrieked. 'You don't know me and vermin!'

A moment later she was gone and the coast was clear, allowing Tinker and Tommy to slip out unnoticed and make their way to a now deserted part of the sculleries where Tinker tidied Tommy up and Tommy did up the top buttons of Tinker's uniform.

'Do you really think your brother will take you on in his garage, Tommy?' Tinker whispered to him, brushing the last lock of his brown hair back into place. 'It's not as if you knows anything about motor cars.'

'Dick says it don't take much learning, Tinks,' Tommy replied with a grin, unable to resist giving her one more kiss on the cheek. 'You got such soft skin, do you know that?'

'I should do, Tommy. You're always telling me. But look – look, suppose Dick does take you on and all, and we was to get married—'

'Which we will, my girl. Make no mistake about that.'

'I'm not marrying you nor no one, Tommy, unless I got the future sorted. Catch me ending in the poor house. I'd rather stay here until I'm too old to do my duties than starve to death on the streets. Least they'd look after me here.'

'Yeah? For how long, you reckon? Till your knees give in from all the scrubbing you did as a housemaid, or your fingers get all gnarled up like Molly Crabbe's did from all the sewing and stitching, till she weren't no use for anything. There's not much use to be had from a servant who can't do nothing, Tinks. So better by far to be married to me who'll look after you till your dying day, and that's a promise.'

'Yeah,' Tinker suddenly agreed, smiling at him with real affection. 'Yeah, who gives a fig about all that, Tommy? Long as I got you.' Reaching up, she put her arms round his neck and kissed him briefly but sweetly. 'I do love you, Tom,' she whispered. 'Honest I do.'

'And I love you too, Tinks,' Tommy whispered back. 'And I always will. Till my dyin' day.'

Now Tom put his arms around Tinker to kiss her once more, which he did equally sweetly.

"'Ere!' came a stern voice from behind them. 'And what you think you two lovebirds is playing at?'

Jumping apart like frightened rabbits, they found themselves face to face with a grinning Tully.

'You do that again, Tully Tuttle,' Tom warned him, half amused and half furious, 'I'll pull your stupid ears off.'

*　　*　　*

'Sit up,' Cecil growled down the table at his daughter, who was sitting looking down into her soup bowl rather than up at her father. He then addressed his wife. 'I have told you time and again, Maude, I will not have children of mine round-shouldered. It's particularly unattractive in a girl, especially a girl such as her, who is going to need everything in her favour if she's going to find a husband. Sit *up*!'

Elizabeth sat bolt upright, pushing her shoulders back in an exaggerated fashion.

'And where the devil is Cuthbert?' Cecil continued, using his usual dog-training voice.

'I did tell you, Cecil, he is seeing Hughie off at Southampton.'

'This soup is almost as painfully thin as you, Maude,' Cecil bellowed back, determined to ignore any reference to Hughie's departure. 'Take this soup away,' he commanded one of the servants. 'This is fit only for the poor house. And you can tell Cook I said so.'

'Cook is indisposed, Cecil,' Maude called down the table.

Cheeseman took his master's soup from the footman, rolling his eyes behind his back, while Cecil waited for the second course. Nodding to the footman to help him to more burgundy, Cecil turned his attention back to his luckless only daughter.

'What have you been doing? Sitting in an attic teaching a parrot to speak, no doubt.'

'I don't have a parrot, Papa.'

'Still sitting about like a wet Wednesday.'

'Elizabeth has been helping to repair the church vestments, Cecil. She is a fine needlewoman. The vicar is most grateful for her hard work, I do assure you,' Maude stated.

'Needlework!' Cecil snorted. 'Maid's occupation, sewing – that's what that is, a maid's occupation.'

All of a sudden he drained his glass of burgundy, flung his napkin down, preparatory to storming out of the dining room.

'You have not finished your dinner, Cecil?' Maude called to him as he passed her by.

'Have something sent to my study,' he replied.

Elizabeth looked down the table at her mother.

'I wish I could go with Hughie to America, Mamma. Then I should not annoy Papa so much, should I?'

Her mother was silent for a second. 'I wish we all could,' she finally agreed.

'Maybe we all should, Mamma. Maybe we could run away together?'

They smiled in sudden sympathy at each other.

'One day, darling,' Maude murmured, while Cheeseman busied himself at the sideboard, pretending not to have heard.

The following morning, Jossy drove Partita and Kitty to the Halt for Kitty to catch the 10.30 train to London. The two friends bid each other the fondest of farewells.

'I wish you were not going, Kitty. I shall miss you so.'

Partita was wearing her lost-puppy expression.

'It won't be for long,' Kitty assured her. 'After all, the new term starts in two weeks' time.'

'Yes, and after that you can come back up again for Easter.' Partita's voice was becoming lost as a whistle from up the line signalled the arrival of the train, which steamed into the little station, clanking and spewing as it signalled its arrival, brakes screaming and protesting, until it finally came to a stop.

Kitty climbed into the Ladies Only carriage, followed by Bridie, who immediately took out her rosary beads and started tolling them.

Partita stood waving to the departing train long after it had left the station.

'Come on, Lady Tita,' Jossy grumbled. 'You can't spend yer whole life at the Halt.'

The two girls were not the only ones to be happily anticipating the new school term. Now that all the excitements of the Christmas balls were over, and her house guests had returned to London, Circe was once more looking forward to going back to town, to enjoying her little circle of artistic friends, to attending the theatre and the new art exhibitions. While she loved her garden in the summer, in the winter, once a Bauders house party was at an end, there was really not quite enough to occupy her intelligence, as a result of which she had often felt at a loose end in the early part of the year.

The Duke knew this of his wife and although he would have dearly liked to have her join him three times a week in the hunting field, imagining as he often did just how beautiful his Circe would have looked turned out to within an inch on a spanking dappled grey gelding, nevertheless he contented himself with the fantasy rather than the reality. This year, however, his sense of unease was such that he wanted her to stay at home with him, if only so that he could catch a glimpse of her moving through the routine of his life.

'I was thinking,' he announced suddenly, before Circe had time to think of packing up her portmanteaux, of making sure of her London clothes, hats trimmed, furs cleaned. 'I was thinking, dearest, that it would be a very pretty idea if you were to mount a musical entertainment here this year.'

Circe, who was busy noting that since Kitty's departure Partita had been wearing an expression of unadulterated gloom, looked round at her husband with sudden interest.

'A musical entertainment, John? But how original of you to think of such a thing. A musical entertainment – say a play with music?'

'You could do it so well, my sweet,' the Duke went on, not quite looking Circe in the eye. 'You know how musical you are, and it would be capital fun to see all our friends on stage, don't you think?'

Circe started to look excited. 'So many of them *are* so musical, and so many love the theatre.'

'Exactly my thoughts, my dear, and it would keep all the maids and the rest busy, sewing costumes and I know not what. Such a grey time of year otherwise, this time of year, so grey.'

Circe stood up and went down the library to where her three daughters were seated, dutifully sewing.

'Papa has had such a capital idea. We are to put on a musical here at Bauders, for the entertainment of the neighbourhood and for everyone who wants to take a part. Isn't that a splendid idea?' she asked of each of them, but paying most particular attention to Partita, whose face by now had become a study in misery.

'I was thinking about *The Pirates of Penzance*,' the Duke announced, coming across to join them. 'One of my favourites, you know. I would, I would be a Pirate King,' he murmured.

'*The Pirates of Penzance*!' Partita exclaimed, her depression lifting at once as she flung down her stitching. 'I love *The Pirates of Penzance*.' She started to hum 'Take a Pair of Sparkling Eyes'.

'That's *The Gondoliers*.'

'Oh, yes, so it is.' Partita went on humming the tune nevertheless.

Circe moved away, her mind already filled with the thought of the excitements ahead.

'We have the Great Hall here; it will make a most splendid theatre. We can have the estate carpenters build us a platform, and the orchestra can be on hand for full rehearsals. We must send to London for the musical parts at once.'

Partita stood up to follow her down the room.

'But, Mamma, what about school—'

Before she could go on, Wavell entered the library with a telegram, which he presented to the Duchess on a silver salver.

'This is not for me, Wavell,' Circe remarked, on seeing the name on the envelope. 'This is for Miss Rolfe.'

'Miss Rolfe has left for London, Your Grace.'

'Then – then I dare say – I dare say that I must open it *in loco*.'

Circe went to Partita as soon as she had read the message: 'Order your immediate return. Papa.'

'What does this mean, Tita? Do you know what this means?'

Partita stared at the telegram, feeling suddenly ashamed that she had always thought it such an adventure to have a notorious father. Kitty must be very brave to live with such a man. But why would he be ordering her home as if she was a flunkey?

'It must be something horrid for her father to send such a telegram,' Circe said, looking troubled.

'Something really horrid,' Partita agreed.

They stared at each other.

'We will soon know, when we return to London.' Circe folded the telegram, and then stopped. 'But of course. We won't *be* returning to London now, will we, John?'

'What's that, my dear?'

Circe went up to her husband. 'If we are to do a musical here, we won't be returning to London, will we?'

'It might be difficult,' the Duke agreed, looking both kindly and vague at the same time.

Circe frowned. 'Partita will have to go back to being schooled here. We will have to find someone new for her.'

Overhearing this, Partita started to protest.

'Now, darling,' Circe told her firmly, 'don't be foolish. Do admit we will have the most tremendous fun here helping stage *The Pirates of Penzance*.' The Duchess lowered her voice so that the Duke would not hear. 'More fun, I am sure, than you would ever be having in London at Miss Woffington's Academy, which you were already finding a little on the dull side – so many spelling bees your head span, you said.'

'But what about Kitty?'

'Kitty can come here. I am sure she is musical, and even if she is not, she can help with everything and when that is at an end, well, she can stay on, or do as she wishes. Never mind about her father and the telegram, it is of no matter. I will explain everything to her mother.'

The Duchess patted Partita on the arm and moved swiftly away from her. She did not like her children arguing with her. Not that Partita was arguing, but she was fussing her.

'I will write to her mother at once.'

Kitty stared at her father, unable quite to take in what she had just heard him say.

'What was that you said?'

'I said – your mother has *bolted*,' Evelyn stated for a second time. 'She has run off somewhere and with someone. When I find her I shall wring her neck like a chicken, that I promise you.'

'I don't understand, Papa,' Kitty said blankly, sinking down into a chair while trying to collect her thoughts. The idea that her mother might have run off with another man was a nightmare. Her mother was a pillar of strength, virtuous to a degree. She would not do such a thing. Kitty's eyes strayed to the decanter at her father's elbow.

'I was at Biddlethorpe for Christmas and the New Year and so on; now on my return in the New Year what did I find? I found a note. Like something in the music halls. *Here's the very note – this is what she wrote.*' He waved a letter in his daughter's direction before continuing. 'Left it on the mantelpiece your mother did – hadn't even the courage to tell me face to face.'

Kitty took the letter, wondering whether her father was really stupid, or just drunk, or both? He must know that if her mother had dared to tell him face to face that she was leaving him after nearly twenty years of marriage, she would have been carrying the bruises for months.

'You'll see from that note you're to contact some solicitor or other,' Evelyn Rolfe said, pouring himself another large whisky. 'Don't know what the hell's going to become of you, but that's not my business. No doubt the solicitor has instructions or some such because this is all your mother's doing and I dare say you've long had wind of it.'

'No. I can quite truthfully say that this is as great a shock to me as it is to you.'

Kitty put out a hand to the back of a nearby chair, feeling all at once sick and faint. As she did so, she dimly heard her father saying, 'I doubt that you are shocked. Mothers and daughters. You two were thick as thieves.' His tone was sarcastic.

'I knew absolutely nothing about this whatsoever, I promise you,' Kitty stated absently as she read the letter and discovered that she was to proceed to notify some solicitor or another at his offices in the Strand, as soon as she returned home.

'As I said, I have no idea what is to become of you. Never had any intention – never had the slightest idea what to do with you at the best of times, let alone the worst of times. So it's up to your mother to sort all this out,' Evelyn concluded, draining his glass, throwing his finished cigar into the fire and standing up. 'When the divorce papers are through I shall be selling this house so perhaps much the best thing is for you to find some employment or other. You certainly will not be returning to that ridiculous forcing house for young ladies, whatever it's called – Miss Willington or Wolfit, or whatever it is, that is for certain. If you need me for anything leave a message at White's.'

'I take it I may continue living here for the present?' Kitty asked a little formally, wishing she had the courage to pick the poker up and hit him.

'Do what you wish. I shall be using the house from time to time, until other arrangements are to hand, so do as you please. A lot will depend on what your mother has in mind for you. As I said, Katherine, you are entirely her business. I didn't want you in the first place.'

Later that day Kitty arrived at the offices of Collingwood, Skells and Rathbone. The doubtless worthy firm of solicitors were housed in cramped offices in an alleyway off the Strand.

'Whom may I say it is?' demanded a clerk, wiping his beaked nose slowly on a large handkerchief, which he promptly pushed into a shiny trouser pocket.

'Miss Rolfe,' Kitty told him quietly.

Eventually he returned.

'Follow me, Miss Wolfe.'

'Rolfe.'

'Just as you wish.'

He pushed open a door at the end of a short dark corridor and Kitty walked through it straight into her mother's arms.

'I am sorry, dearest. I had to ask Mr Collingwood

to write to you so that I could be here to explain. I could not let your father know of my whereabouts.'

For a second it looked as if they might both give way to tears, but finally Violet held Kitty away from her for a second, and then walked to the window of the office. Kitty found she was watching her mother as if she was watching someone she had never known. Part of her was admiring and appreciative of her courage, and yet another part of her was ashamed. How could her mother run off with another man? And who was the other man?

'Dr Charles and I . . .' Violet began, knowing that Kitty was waiting to know, wanting to find out, more than anything, whom it could be that had given her mother the courage to leave her father.

Kitty went to say something and then stopped. She could not imagine anyone less suitable, to her mind, than Dr Charles. Her mother hated even a mention of disease, was terrified of germs, and although kindly enough if you were ill, most reluctant to visit the sick room.

'Dr Charles? Dr *Charles*?'

'Yes, Kitty, Dr Charles.'

Richard Charles had looked after Kitty since she was born. He was like an uncle, certainly like a member of their family. It was almost horrible to think of her mother and her doctor together, kissing and fondling each other, perhaps even lying in each other's arms.

Violet turned away, not wanting to see her daughter's shock.

'He is such a decent, honourable man, Kitty, so different from Evelyn.'

They both knew how different, but still Kitty found herself at a loss for words, for now not only did she have to digest the fact that her mother had left her father for another man, but that the man in question was their *doctor*. Doctors were meant to be like vicars: they were sacred, full of kindly wisdom, practically without sin. It seemed to be such a breach of trust that all the time he had been attending them whenever their health required, he had obviously been availing himself of the chance to become acquainted ever more intimately with her mother.

'Richard will be here any minute,' Violet went on. 'He will explain.'

Kitty wanted to run out of the office, but not back to her father – that would indeed be from the frying pan into the fire – anywhere, back to Bauders, perhaps, back to a life that she knew was decent and honourable, not complicated and bitter-making. The last thing she wanted was for her mother to put out her arms to her again.

'No, Mamma.' She turned away from her mother. 'I can't go to you, really I can't. I have to have time to think.' She turned back to her. 'And where is Mr Collingwood, or Mr Skells, or whatever they are called, or even the other one? Where are they, may I ask?'

Violet straightened herself. It was not like Kitty to be so vehement.

'They very kindly lent us this office, Kitty. They are very kind men, truly they are. Mr Skells is so kind, why he could almost be a vicar,' she added quietly.

It was with some relief that the sound of feet approaching in the corridor outside put an end to their really rather futile conversation.

'I think I can guess at what you are thinking, Miss Rolfe,' Dr Charles said, sitting her down in a large comfortable leather chair in the corner of the office while he pulled up an ordinary wooden one to sit before her in his accustomed style. 'But I must stress that from the outset of my acquaintance with your mother, right until this present moment, there has never been the slightest impropriety. Our feelings for each other were never stated, not until the New Year, when I had to attend your mother suffering a fit of nerves at the prospect of your father's return. It was then that I felt it imperative that I make my long-held feelings clear to your mother.'

'I see.'

Kitty still couldn't, of course. She still felt that Dr Charles should stay as he was to her – a doctor, not her mother's lover.

'What will happen now?'

Violet turned at the window. 'What will happen now, Kitty, is that I will call in Mr Rathbone and he will discuss everything with you.'

'I will leave you at this point.'

Kitty watched Dr Charles picking up his hat. She had watched Dr Charles picking up his hat just like that for so many years, but now she was watching him in a different way. She was not sure that she liked the way Dr Charles picked up his hat. It was perhaps a little prissy, a little bit too like a valet would pick up a hat, a little bit too like a professional person, not like her father would pick up *his* hat. But her father was a drunken bully. He had betrayed her mother and squandered her money; he had behaved like a cad.

Mr Rathbone was next into the room.

'As the only child of your parents' union, arrangements must now be made for your immediate future, Miss Rolfe,' Mr Rathbone said. 'Your mother will be seeking a divorce from your father on the grounds of extreme cruelty. Divorce is always difficult, particularly from the wife's point of view, but nevertheless with the testimony of the maid of all work and so on, I feel sure that we will be able to prove cruelty.'

From the look in her mother's eyes Kitty guessed this would not be as easy as the lawyer was trying to make it sound. Women were still in effect, despite the law, the property of their husbands, and any money a woman had was her husband's unless she had earned or inherited it herself. Besides all that, as everyone in the room well knew, once divorced, women were considered unacceptable in society.

'We feel confident your father will not oppose

the proceedings, Miss Rolfe.' The lawyer leaned across his desk, removing his spectacles as he did so, in order to issue his caveat. 'But it must never be supposed that your mother and Dr Charles here enjoyed anything other than a perfectly proper relationship, as indeed is actually the case.'

'What a good thing you only have one daughter to worry about, Mamma.'

'How do you mean, dearest?'

'I mean that a whole clutch of daughters such as the Duchess has would be a bit of a headache, especially when it came to finding work for them.'

'You are not going out to work, Kitty. I will not allow it.'

Kitty looked from her mother to Mr Rathbone. 'Mr Rathbone knows what you do not then, Mamma. Mr Rathbone knows that work is all I can have ahead of me now.'

Mr Rathbone shook his head. 'This is, once again, in the strictest confidence, Miss Rolfe, but Dr Charles is insistent. He wishes to make you a small allowance, so that you can continue your education.'

'I would rather not accept.'

Violet shook her head. 'You must, Kitty.'

'I must not.'

'You must, Kitty.'

'I do not wish to accept anything from Dr Charles.'

'No, but if you wish for my happiness, you must accept.'

Kitty turned away. What could she say to that? After all her mother's sufferings, how could she hurt her more?

The following day, her father having left for a house party in Scotland, Kitty and Bridie started to pack up their belongings in almost unnatural haste. It was as if they expected Evelyn Rolfe to change his mind and return home at any minute.

'We must stop looking over our shoulders, Bridie!' Kitty said finally, after they had both started at the sound of a door slamming unexpectedly.

'Sure, how can we?' Bridie's hands were shaking. 'How can we do anything but live in fear? And with your mother gone, what protection have we?'

'Post.'

Mary was calling from the hall. It was a letter for Kitty. Kitty saw from the crested envelope that it was from Partita. Yet another ill-spelled letter. But she was not interested in the spelling, only in the message. Partita was sending for her to share her lessons at Bauders. She was not able to come to London any more, she wanted nothing more than for Kitty and Bridie to return to Bauders. They all wanted it. Her mother and her father too wanted it. She enclosed a letter from the Duchess to Violet as proof of this. They were to put on a musical. She must come back to Bauders. *'Plees, plees, plees!'*

Kitty sat down on the bottom step of the

139

Regency staircase. Upstairs she could hear Bridie banging about with hat boxes, and heaven only knew what else. Downstairs Kitty stared ahead, knowing that the doors of her cage had once more been flung open. She and Bridie could now fly off back to Bauders, where life would be beautiful once again, beautiful and kind, everything that her life with her parents had never been.

Chapter Five

The Pirates Club

Kitty's return was not the only one of note that month. Two weeks after she had settled down into a place that, despite its great size, she now felt to be her second home, the Duke and Duchess's debonair younger son, Augustus, often known as Gus, had returned from a long sojourn in Austria and was at the castle briefly before dashing up to London.

'They really feel their Empire is being threatened,' Gus explained to his family as they sat at dinner in the family dining room that night. 'They make that clear at every turn. They speak of nothing else.'

Circe smiled down the table at her younger son and fairest offspring, for Gus was, if anything, even blonder than Partita, although a great deal less pugnacious, possessing the easiest of natures, which was probably why everyone was listening to him, feeling as they all must, that if Gus, of all people, had noticed political unrest in

Austria, then there must indeed be cause for worry.

'They've outgrown their strength, Gussie,' his father replied, carefully removing some shot from his pheasant breast. 'Sneaking their way into Italy and Hungary, and heaven only knows where. A great many people think, although they are a small nation, they've been asking for trouble for quite some time.'

'Couldn't the same be said for England, Papa?' Almeric wondered. 'Look at the size of our Empire.'

'Take your point,' the Duke replied, finding another piece of shot. 'And we're running into the same trouble for the same reason – and I dare say we'll run into a lot more before the race is run.'

'Everyone is making everything so difficult for people like us,' Circe murmured.

The Duke stared at his plate. 'This bird is all shot and no bird. Must have been a foreigner that brought it down.'

'I often wonder what people in the future will make of us when we are just paintings and photographs on walls like our ancestors,' Almeric said, turning to his younger brother.

'They'll think we were beautiful, educated and irreplaceable,' Gus returned, straight-faced. 'All true, of course.'

'Just remember history's never fair,' their father reminded him. 'People think that history is a way of understanding the past, but that's not it at all. History's a way of understanding the present, and that's its value.'

'So how does that answer my earlier question exactly?' Partita wondered, looking round the table. 'I wanted to know about women taking a part in running the country . . .'

'It doesn't,' her father said. 'But it does express what I believe. We are a much more liberated society than we used to be, and more confident.'

'Even though women don't have the vote?'

Everyone stared at Kitty. It was a bold statement from a young guest.

'Yes, even though women do not have the vote, Miss Rolfe.'

'So how will people understand that, if women are still not proper citizens of their own country?'

'With difficulty,' the Duke agreed. 'The rights of women are a continuing blot on our country, I do believe that, Miss Rolfe. There can be no true democracy when one half of the population has fewer rights than a common thief.'

'Do we have a little tittle Liberal in our midst?' Almeric wondered, smiling across the table at Kitty.

'Or maybe even a secret suffragette?' Cecilia suggested, eyeing Kitty.

'*I* would *love* to be a suffragette,' Partita said, hiding her deliberate provocation behind a sigh. 'In fact, Kitty and I were thinking only the other day we might join the movement.'

'Don't be silly,' Allegra retorted. 'Suffragettes are becoming more dangerous by the day.'

'I thought that was the point, Allegra?' her father wondered quietly, nodding to a footman for some wine.

'No, Papa,' Allegra insisted. 'They have gone from being tedious to being dangerous. One only supposes they do what they do because they're all so wretchedly plain.'

'Stuff and nonsense,' Partita said hotly. 'Mrs Pankhurst is a beautiful woman.'

'Mrs Pankhurst is the sort of woman who does things purely for attention,' Cecilia stated coldly. 'The movement has got out of hand, and everyone knows it. They have lost the sympathy of the country.'

'This is true,' the Duchess agreed. 'But sympathy or no sympathy, the truth is the same. Women should be allowed a say in the running of their country. American women have been enfranchised, why not English?'

'Mamma,' Allegra replied, 'why should we need to have the vote in England? We don't have the need.'

'You don't. But other women do, Allegra. In America,' Circe continued, 'women are *considered*. They have so much more freedom, are more cherished.' The Duchess looked troubled. 'One has to ask just how much do Englishmen dislike women when in the *Morning Post* the other day they actually suggested in all sobriety that suffragettes should have their heads shaved and be deported. How can people be living in this day and age and be allowed to express such opinions? You do not want that, do you, John?'

'Most certainly not.'

The Duke shook his head and sighed. The question of women's suffrage was beginning to become wearisome to him, if only because he himself always took care to defer to Circe on matters where he knew her to be more knowledgeable than himself, while she seemed to leave other matters to him. They worked in tandem, in harmony; so much so that he found it difficult to understand why the rest of the world could not do the same.

'Your father is in favour of suffrage,' Circe continued for the Duke. 'He is in favour, but not for the *usual* reasons. He has seen how capable the women on his farms are; how very clever at managing their books, their land, and last but not least their men.' Circe smiled round at the girls, hoping that they were listening, while knowing that they were not. 'I wonder at politicians sometimes, really I do,' she ended a little lamely.

'And I am wondering about the next course rather more than politics at this moment,' the Duke gently reminded his wife, looking round for Wavell.

'Your father also maintains that no right-thinking man who admires women could possibly wish on them the same kind of dreadfully dull responsibilities men have to bear,' Circe continued. 'He says that women, particularly young

145

women, instead of worrying about such mundane matters as politics, should be allowed the full rein of their natures. Women, he says, should be concerning themselves with the beauty of life, and not the mire of politics.'

'What's for pudding, Wavell?' the Duke asked in a loud aside. 'Chap's getting ready to eat his napkin.'

'A jam roly-poly, as you requested of Cook, I believe, Your Grace,' Wavell replied.

'Your father says that no man who loves women wants them to be concerned with such a desperately tedious and dull business as deciding which dull and half-brained dimwit should be elected to Parliament to try and tell us how we all should behave,' the Duchess continued, by now seeming to be talking to herself. 'He says it is utterly inconceivable that any man who loves women should wish such a fate upon them.'

'That is very considerate of the Duke,' Kitty put in, straight-faced, as the footmen quickly removed their plates, making ready for the pudding, while Partita and her sisters' faces registered boredom and disinterest.

Kitty, however, knew it was a serious subject. Besides, she thought the Duke had a point. Politics were dull, and perhaps more the preserve of men, while children and the house, the real politics of life, were in women's hands. It was up to them to change a nation, to influence it for the good.

'I can't really see you as a suffragette, Kitty,' Almeric murmured. 'You would be utterly wasted. Besides, you would simply hate those dreadful prison uniforms covered in little arrows.'

'As a matter of fact,' the Duke spoke up suddenly after not appearing to be listening, 'if I were a woman, I would want the vote and for a very good reason – so I could help abolish taxation!'

'Quite right, but most of all, John,' Circe prompted him, 'you want the vote for women because you think Asquith completely wrong in his attitude towards these brave women. We must understand that by imprisoning and force-feeding these poor creatures we are horrifying Europe *and* America. Do admit, everyone,' Circe looked round the table, 'do admit that looked at from the outside, our behaviour towards these poor women is not that of a civilised nation.'

'Damn good roly-poly, tell Cook. Tell her she gets my vote any day,' the Duke announced from nowhere, which more or less put paid to the discussion of women's rights.

'That's one of the few good things about being a duke,' Partita confided to Kitty when the ladies had withdrawn. 'You can demand your pudding in the middle of the first course, wear togas in the evening if that is your wish, or a wig and lipstick just like William Frimleigh, or a cricketing shirt with evening clothes, as Papa sometimes likes to do. It makes up for all the other dull things you have to do.'

Kitty was left to wonder what all the other dull things might be – but not finding an answer she left it at that.

'You haven't been back to see the new things they've done in the theatre they're building in the Great Hall; so ravishing,' Partita announced one afternoon when, tuition being over for the day, she and Kitty found themselves with nothing much to do. 'Come along – it really is worth seeing what they have done – and on the way I want you to tell me what you *really* think of our governess, Miss Danielle – now that we have broken her in.'

As they made their way through the great house towards the theatre, the two young women discussed Miss Danielle, whom they discovered to their surprise that they both liked from the moment they had met her. Partita was especially astonished since she had an unreasonable aversion to anyone trying to teach her anything at all, preferring just to pick up her education as she went along.

'After all,' she had argued, 'Mamma speaks French, German and Italian, my father knows history backwards, my brothers ride, play tennis, fence and swim, Wavell is a walking encyclopaedia as far as etiquette and manners are concerned – and who on *earth* needs to know how to do more than add and subtract, which is something Hawkesworth, our estate manager, can do in his sleep? I do wonder sometimes, Kitty, what on earth is the point in sticking us up in the attics to be taught things we can pick up just by being around the place, really I do.'

Yet the pretty and good-humoured Miss Danielle, an Englishwoman, despite her continental-sounding surname, utterly con-founded her patrician pupil and delighted Kitty, managing to interest them both in the subtleties of poetry and literature, and best of all, drama. Within days of being under her tutelage the three of them were enacting scenes from every sort of drama, so much so that, to her astonishment, Partita found that learning could be exhilarating rather than a trial; while Kitty, used only to Miss Woffington's polite but unambitious style of teaching, never wanted her lessons to end.

'So we would now consider her to be a friend, wouldn't we, Kitty?' Partita wondered, as they finally arrived in a small, beautifully panelled hallway that served as an ante-room. 'Something which I have to admit is so much easier than having someone so awful coaching one that all one does is spend the whole time thinking up ways to get rid of them. Mind you, that could be quite fun as well. Now then – the theatre. Here we are. The Great Hall has been transformed, I think you will agree.'

Partita threw open a pair of magnificent double doors and when she saw within, Kitty fell silent. She had imagined a theatre that was housed within a house would be a very simple place; something constructed by the estate carpenters with a raised platform and perhaps some sort of simple proscenium, with homemade curtains and equally simple wooden seating, very like the sort of stages and auditoriums Kitty had sometimes visited in small halls to hear concerts and recitals with her mother. But even though it was dark and unlit at the moment, illuminated only by late winter sunlight that filtered through two large arched windows, Kitty could see enough detail to be impressed. The Great Hall was suddenly a magical place to be, a fairy-tale site where all at once the turmoil of the outside world became forgotten as those lucky enough were transported to the land of the imagination, a voyage of escape fuelled by dreams and fantasies, by play acting and pretence. Here was a world where bad things went punished and virtue was rewarded, where those who were wrong were put to right, those who fell in love lived happily ever after, and those who fell in battle rose again as soon as the curtain fell. More than that, there was this wonderful and strange aroma that hung about the place – a strange and cloying smell to which people became addicted: theatre.

Partita was up on the stage now, having arrived there by way of the wooden steps to one side of the orchestra pit, indicating for Kitty to follow, which she did, only to see Partita disappearing behind the curtains.

'Kitty? Come and give me a hand, would you?' she heard her friend call from behind the tabs. 'Kitty?'

Finding her way through the heavy velvet drapes, Kitty went to help Partita raise the curtains. Once they were up and the rope attached to its safety hook, they stood together onstage while Partita pointed out the hand-painted scenery that was still in place. The light was too dim to see the flats and the backdrop properly, but even in the half-light Kitty could see the standard of the art work that was being done for the scenery.

'Everyone on the estate has been called in to help with this,' Partita said proudly. 'They're all off having tea in the servants' hall at the moment, but they'll be back soon, working all night to get it perfect. They love it, of course. Makes a change from all the everyday things they have to do.'

On their way back up to their rooms Partita talked non-stop about the forthcoming production of *The Pirates of Penzance*, explaining that since both Sir Arthur Sullivan and Mr Gilbert were acquaintances of her parents and visitors to Bauders, they were perfectly happy to allow a private performance of their work, always provided, as Mr Gilbert had apparently declared to the Duchess's amusement, *they were not invited to witness it.*

'I take it you want to be in the production, Kitty?' Partita asked her. 'It really will be a *lavish*

151

production, and Mr Roderick St Clare is coming from London to produce for us. So we really are lucky.' She stopped, assuming a purposefully mischievous expression. 'Mr St Clare is musical.'

'Just as well,' Kitty said, after a short pause, 'if we are to do Gilbert and Sullivan.'

She turned to look at Partita, who was laughing in such a manner as to suggest that Kitty had made a really funny remark. Kitty frowned at her, not understanding, which only made Partita laugh all the more.

As always there was fierce competition for who was to play who in the forthcoming production, not to mention who was to do *what*. The rivalry might be decorous and above board, but that did not stop it being intense, particularly as far as Allegra and Cecilia were concerned. They had obviously decided to take against Kitty's now permanent presence at Bauders, whilst being too well bred to make their feelings obvious. As it happened, they did not have to. Kitty was only too well aware of how they must be feeling and, wishing only to keep the peace, she made it plain she did not wish to appear in the musical.

'I will tell you what I'll do, Partita,' she said. 'I shall help in every other way possible, I promise you – and I shall learn from the experience. Then perhaps next time, maybe I could take a very small role.'

'You're being frightened off by Allegra and

Cecilia. If it's any comfort, Kitty, they're quite the same with me.'

'Yes, but you are their sister.'

'Anyway, it isn't up to you,' Partita went on airily. 'It's really up to Mr St Clare.'

'He can only select those who want to be selected.'

Partita looked at her for a moment, about to argue with her, but she was prevented from doing so by a footman announcing the arrival of Elizabeth Milborne.

Knowing that whenever Elizabeth arrived at Bauders there was a limit to the amount of time she would have at her disposal, instead of bullying Kitty into appearing in the opera, Partita at once set about organising what had to be done.

'I would love to know why there is such a hurry,' Kitty gasped as she returned to the music room with all the sheets of music she had run to fetch from the Duchess, who had been marking up the parts. 'Suddenly everything is in double time.'

'I should have explained!' Partita called back, in the middle of directing two of the footmen, who were repositioning the grand piano in the best light for Elizabeth, who was already sorting out the sheets of music handed to her by Kitty. 'Elizabeth is forbidden to practise in her house since her father cannot stand the noise – which is perfectly absurd because Elizabeth is a quite wonderful pianist.'

'My father doesn't like wrong notes,' Elizabeth explained, with a quick embarrassed glance to Kitty. 'Or repetitions. If I have to go over and over some passage in practice he comes in and starts banging the piano with a stick.'

'You should see their piano,' Partita laughed.

'Is Elizabeth going to play for the production then?' Kitty asked.

'No – just for rehearsals. We can't get the orchestra until the last minute for rehearsals.'

Once the piano had been set in a favourable light, and with no more time to waste, Elizabeth sat down and played right through the entire score of the opera with barely a wrong note. With other things to do for her mother, Partita took herself off, leaving Kitty the job of sorting all the part music into sets for each of the characters, as well as books for the chorus.

As she set about her task, Kitty listened attentively to Elizabeth's playing.

'Do you play much at such events as this will be?' Kitty asked when Elizabeth took a short break between songs. 'You must do.'

Elizabeth shook her head, and smiled ruefully. 'That – I am very much afraid – would most certainly not be allowed,' she replied. 'My father, you know – he would have no time at all for such a notion.'

'Doesn't he appreciate your talent?'

'My father sees my playing the piano as a beastly nuisance.' She laughed almost gaily. 'He has absolutely no interest in music, and it was only thanks to Mamma's determination that I managed to learn the piano at all.'

'People who play like you don't learn the piano,' Kitty replied. 'You are surely born playing it.'

'That is true actually,' Elizabeth agreed, finding the music for 'Ah Leave Me Not to Pine'. 'I could play from a very early age, and it is also true that when my mother heard me playing she insisted I had lessons, but since they could not take place at home, I had to be taken to my teacher by pony and trap. I had to travel ten miles there and back every time I had a lesson.'

Kitty stared at Elizabeth, feeling ashamed. Cecil Milborne sounded much worse than Evelyn Rolfe.

'I'm so glad you can play for us,' she said, trying in some silly way to make up for how she was feeling.

Mr Roderick St Clare was a small, quick-speaking man with a shock of long fair hair that kept falling over his eyes, only to be quickly and impatiently tossed back overhead or brushed from his eyes in a gesture of irritation. He conducted proceedings, from auditions through to rehearsals, dressed in a loose flowing white shirt and ancient velvet trousers, held up with a multicoloured sash tied around the waistband.

'An otter,' Partita murmured with some satisfaction, her eyes taking on the kind of look that Kitty was already beginning to recognise. 'He reminds me of an otter.'

Mr St Clare had cast Partita as Ruth, which delighted her, Livia Catesby was to play Mabel, with Cecilia as Edith, and Allegra as Kate. Kitty was to lead the chorus.

As for the males, Almeric had been cast to play the Pirate King, Bertie Milborne the Major General, Valentine Wynyard Errol the Police Sergeant, and best of all, as far as Partita was concerned, Peregrine had been selected to play Samuel, the Pirate King's lieutenant.

Harry was cast as Frederic, the youngest pirate, a choice that caused considerable debate in the servants' hall.

'This is the sort of thing that's the thin end of a very large wedge, Mr Wavell,' Mrs Turton, the cook, opined in the servants' hall. 'Your boy will not just learn to strut and preen this way and that, he will learn to lounge. That is what bein' in a play does for young men. It teaches them to lounge, and that's all before they start to preen.'

'It really is not for me to say, Mrs Turton,' Wavell replied. 'This is no affair of mine and I have no jurisdiction one way or the other.'

'He's your boy, Mr Wavell, ain't he?' Mrs Turton persisted.

'This is Her Grace's business, and His Grace's idea, not mine, Mrs Turton. I am not consulted in such matters. Mr St Clare requested Harry about this entertainment, on the authority of Her Grace.'

'It will only make trouble for others, Mr Wavell, you mark my words.'

Mrs Turton eyed Wavell over the top of her teacup, an item she always had so much in hand that Wavell had come to imagine that she had actually been born with its handle wrapped tightly around her fingers. Wavell set down his own now empty teacup and rose gracefully from the table, leaving Mrs Turton and lesser members of staff to continue the debate as to whether or not his son should be allowed to partake in the forthcoming entertainment. Privately Wavell considered that Harry should not be allowed, but not for the reasons put forward by Cook. Wavell knew what he wanted for his son and that did not include what he classed as artistic *folderol* – in that way Mrs Turton was perfectly right to be critical.

But he also knew what was best for him and what was best for him would in the end be best for Harry as well. If the Duchess wanted Harry to sing, sing he would.

In common with every other young man who had grown up on the estate, Harry loved the Duchess with the whole-hearted devotion with which someone might love a star of the stage, or some society beauty whose postcard image could be bought in souvenir shops around London.

Now a small but complete silence had fallen in the Duchess's morning room, for the simple reason that Harry had just fallen and twisted his ankle monkeying about on stage. It was nothing really, just a bit of a twist, a bit of swelling, but the Duchess insisted on having her doctor, who happened to be passing, make sure that the ankle was not broken.

'It's as Her Grace says,' Harry told Dr Jones. 'I have twisted it, not broken it. It is truly nothing.'

The Duchess gave Harry a kind look, but Dr Jones's expression did not match that of Her Grace. The good doctor's face reflected restrained impatience.

'We cannot always be sure of the diagnoses of others. As I remember it, Harry, last time you broke your leg it had to be re-set, once by me, and once by Her Grace.'

'The last time was a hunting accident,' the Duchess put in. 'Everyone has an accident or two out hunting, Dr Jones.'

The look in Circe's eyes was not as benevolent as it was usually, since she did not like Dr Jones's attitude. To her mind, Dr Jones was an ignorant inebriate, and not good for the estate, whatever the Duke and Hawkesworth might like to pretend. Jones could not even deliver a baby. Indeed, when a baby was on the way in any of the villages, it was the midwife who was sent for, never the doctor. The only birth he had ever attended had ended in disaster, and the graveyard.

'I am minded, Your Grace, that when this young man broke his leg, it was not as a result of a hunting accident, but as a consequence of galloping one of His Grace's horses over rough

158

country with no saddle or bridle and only a harness to steer, and a cabbage stalk for a whip. That is not what I would call a hunting accident, but a foolish, careless unnecessary accident,' Dr Jones intoned.

'Master Harry's race that day was as a result of a wager laid between His Grace and the rest of the house party at the time, and the money won was given to the cottage hospital at Welton,' the Duchess said, tapping an impatient finger on a nearby table to emphasise her point. 'Gracious, Dr Jones, there has to be some sport allowed around the estate, or there will be no visitors to the house; and if there are no visitors there will be no donations to the hospital. There has to be give and take on an estate of this size, and without sport these places do not survive. Henry hunted here, Elizabeth hunted here, Anne would have hunted here, had she not been so busy having babies, poor dear queen. Swings and roundabouts, Dr Jones, swings and roundabouts.'

Harry half closed his eyes. He always loved the way the Duchess referred to the kings and queens of England by their first names, just as if she had played with them as a child, but Dr Jones looked unconvinced by both swings and roundabouts. He turned away, shortly followed by the Duchess and Harry, and as he did so the sound of music being played came drifting towards the three of them. It was not just any music either, it was music with a distinctly cheerful sound and a song that Harry happened to know well.

'For I am a Pirate King! And it is, it is a glorious thing To be a Pirate King!'

'I think I can be trusted to bandage Harry's ankle in my own special way.'

'Very well, Your Grace, you bandage Harry's ankle in whatever way you think fit. I was actually on my way down to the kitchens, where Mrs Dewsbury has poured hot fruit juice over her leg when, if you remember, you called me in here, Your Grace.'

'Since you were passing, it was the least I could do, truly it was.' Circe watched the doctor leaving. 'Just remember not to put butter on Mrs Dewsbury's leg,' she murmured, a little too loudly. 'It will only fry it.' Then to Harry she said, 'Come on, I will finish your bandaging. We had to make sure nothing was broken, that's all.'

Circe bandaged the ankle in her own special way, and minutes later she watched with some satisfaction as, despite the fact that she knew he was in some considerable pain, Harry was able to make his way about the stage as if nothing at all had happened.

After which there was a sudden commotion at the great doors. The Duchess turned.

'Gussie? Back from London, so soon?'

'Mother.'

The Duchess smiled and held out her arms to her younger son. Gus gave her a quick

160

perfunctory hug while at the same time looking around at the busy activity that was beginning to make the whole place seem like the West End of London, while the Duchess looked Gussie straight in the eyes, her expression unwavering.

'Gussie, would you not, please, *not* call me "Mother", dearest? It makes me feel as if I should be serving you brown soup.'

Gus looked innocent, his large grey-green eyes widened, and he put his head on one side, pulling a mock-serious face. 'Oh, had you rather I called you something else, Mother, dearest?' Despite every effort on his behalf, Gus burst out laughing.

'Gus, you are just as naughty as when you went away. Austria was meant to have *cured* you of all that naughtiness. Why have they not cured you of your mischief, may I ask?'

'Austria has cured me of most things, Mamma, so it has, *Mamma*, so it has.' Gus looked round at the army of workmen busying themselves in every direction. 'But *you*, I see, have not been cured of your love of the theatre.' He looked back at her and grinned, at the same time lowering his voice. 'Anything to get out of having to join the hunting field, eh, Mamma?'

'Gus! *Ça c'est interdit!* Please. It is utterly forbidden.'

'I want to play one of the policemen – *a policeman's lot is not a happy one, happy one.*'

Gus looked round what was now a theatre,

and let out a sigh that was half contented and half filled with melancholy.

'I feel I am home just in time,' he confided to Circe.

The Duchess turned away. She hated to talk about anything too serious. She only wanted to talk about *The Pirates of Penzance*.

'How was the skiing, Gus, you never did tell?'

'Very white.'

'And how is your German?'

'Very Prussian.'

'So.' A small pause while his mother sat down and put her head to one side while rehearsals continued apace on the stage. 'So, what will you do next, I wonder?'

Gus also knew enough not to tell his mother that he had already chosen which regiment he and his friends intended to join, so he pulled another mock-serious face and said, 'I am going to become a pirate! I shall sail under the black flag, owing nothing to anyone, taking all and sundry prisoner – except of course those who are orphans.'

He was alluding to the story in *The Pirates of Penzance* when everyone whom the pirates try to take prisoner turns out to be an orphan, it being well known that pirates – in Gilbert and Sullivan operettas, anyway – never rob or steal from orphans.

As it happened it was just the right note for Gus to strike. His mother laughed as, rehearsals temporarily at a halt, everyone started to drift into the library, where drinks were served, after which they went into luncheon. Guests helped themselves from silver dishes, while Wavell directed the servants as a bandmaster might on a regimental parade ground.

As for Gus, the younger Knowle boy, of the sunny nature and the sweet smile, whom some newly arrived guests were now greeting with love and affection, hugging him delightedly, the thought occurred to him, and would not go away, that he was not really home at all, but on a roundabout horse, and the horse was going up and down, as roundabout horses do, and any minute now the music was going to stop.

But until that moment he was happy not to think of anything except that he was going to be a pirate, along with Teddy Heaslip, and James Millings, his sister Allegra's beau, and their neighbours on the vast Bauders estate, Pug Stapleton and Bertie Milborne, and, of course, Harry Wavell, who was now limping about with a bandage around his ankle. And of course there would be Almeric, and Perry Catesby, and no doubt a whole host of people roped in from around and about the house. Tully Tuttle would be hard to keep out, and old Coggle and Flint, who had both sung in the church choir since they were knee high to a grasshopper.

Oh, it would be a riot, would the Bauders' version of *The Pirates of Penzance*. He could not wait to hear the orchestra playing the opening chords of the overture, and watch the heavy red curtains being drawn apart by the tall bewigged footmen to reveal the audience seated, the women fanning themselves, the men prepared to be bored, only shortly afterwards to find themselves becoming enchanted.

It was a marvellous thing to be at home and part of this great, untidy band of good-hearted people all living and working together on the magic island that was called Bauders; all wanting nothing more than to make jolly music for the entertainment of friends and neighbours.

But first the costumes had to be completed. The Duchess had already set up a sewing room on the first floor. Here everyone's maids, once they were clear of their other duties, skipped along to help out with the sewing of the costumes. Twenty pirates' costumes were being cut from sundry materials retrieved from around the place. Black patches were carefully designed, together with fearsome beards, made and dyed from remnants of coarse sheep's wool.

All the ladies of the chorus were destined to wear the prettiest little crinolines, the silk cut to be spread about their swaying hoops, their parasols made to match or tone with the dresses, so that they looked as fetching to the audience as they would look inviting to a band of pirates.

'It's the policemen's uniforms we are going to be stuck for this year.' Browne, who as the Duchess's maid had naturally assumed the position of authority, was standing at the head of the cutting-out table, frowning round at Bridie and Tinker, and the rest of the maids, all of whom already had their heads bent and their sewing needles darting.

'My George is a policeman; I dare say we could ask to borrow some of the old uniforms from the station, Miss Browne,' stuttered one of the newest of the younger maids, looking up from her neat hemming, but only after having been nudged into having her hand held up for her by a neighbour at the table.

Browne looked down the table at the flushed face of the young maid. It was years since she herself had felt nervous of anyone, even the Duke.

'You are new, aren't you, Findlay?'

Miss Findlay nodded and blushed, frightened that she might have spoken out of turn.

'And none the worst for that, Findlay,' Browne told her in a purposefully kind voice. 'No, you may indeed go to the police station and tell the men that we are badly in need of help on policemen's uniforms – and singers, for that matter.'

Browne nodded and turned away. They must have some singers down at the station; at least half of them would have been in the church choir when they were small. It was part of the reason the Reverend Mr Bletchworth and the Duchess were such friends. He could provide a choir for the castle, and she could provide cottages for the parents and children in the choir. It was an arrangement that suited everyone.

'Very well, we will wait to hear from Findlay. Have you a bicycle?'

Mary Findlay nodded.

'Go at once then, and tell them we need to beg, steal or borrow uniforms.'

Findlay bicycled off down to the park gates. The drive to the castle was so long, it would take her an hour to reach the old police station where her George worked. She bicycled harder and harder, knowing that on her depended so much; but more than that, she could not wait to tell George that he might be asked to be in the Duchess's musical play, because if there was one thing that George Bite could do was sing. Not that he could not do other things, of course he could, but his singing voice was exceptionally strong. He might even get to sing the lead and make a name for himself. She pushed harder at the foot pedals, and then coming at last to a downhill section of the great tree-lined drive, she freewheeled all the way downhill to the police station where she knew George would be sitting twiddling his thumbs.

'I don't know what the world is coming to, really I don't,' George's sergeant was saying to George and his friend Billy Andrews as Mary pushed open the police station door. 'Last week Miss Ponting had Rosalinda, her pet goat, taken from out her front garden where she'd tethered same. Tied up to a ring near horse trough in the square is where she found her. Not withstanding that, yesterday someone decorated the top of the village post box with a chamber pot, if you would believe it.'

'It was a prank, Sergeant.'

'And a very nasty one too. Someone could have hurt themselves when they was posting of a letter. And as to that poor goat belonging to Miss Ponting, she needed milking – the goat did. Imagine that – a goat taken at milking time? The cruelty of it. Leathering, that is what pranksters like that need, a good leathering, and then we would have less crime here, and that is certain. Ah, now who is this, may I ask? Why it is Miss Findlay, if I am not mistaken.'

'Good afternoon, Sergeant. I am come to ask your permission for George here to come to the castle, on behalf of the Duchess herself, speaking through Miss Browne.'

'I see, Miss Findlay. And may I ask on what duty am I to send PC Bite?'

'He is needed for . . . singing, now you come to ask, Sergeant Trump, singing in the musical play, which is all about policemen. You will all be needed, I hear, uniforms and all, and Miss Browne says any old uniforms, borrowed, or not needed, she will be most grateful to you, Sergeant Trump.'

'And who will mind the station when we are all meant to be a-singing, may I ask, Miss Findlay?'

Mary smiled. 'Oh, I dare say some of the Duke's men from the castle could stand in for you at the police station when you are needed up at the castle, Sergeant Trump.'

'But will they not be needed for the singing?'

'Most of them, unlike you, Sergeant, are a little too – how shall I say? – too mature to be on the stage? After all, it takes young, fit men to sing in a musical play.'

Mary was not so naïve that she was not aware that flattery could get her everywhere, and so it proved, because she returned up the long, long drive to the castle with not one fully uniformed policeman bicycling behind her, but two.

Half an hour later the Duchess found herself staring from George Bite and Billy Andrews to Browne and a justifiably triumphant Mary Findlay.

'Gracious, Browne. I know we needed policemen's uniforms,' she said in a faint voice, 'but it seems that we have both the uniforms *and* the men.'

'It is not just their uniforms, Miss Browne. They can both sing too,' Mary told Browne in a proud whisper.

Browne turned to the Duchess. 'They can both sing, Your Grace.'

Circe stared at them and, realising that both men were looking petrified by the sudden turn of events, soon set about putting them at their ease, discovering as she did so when she sat down to play a few simple scales for them, that they could not only sing, they could *really* sing.

'Perfect. You are cast,' she told them, standing

up and shutting the piano lid, having followed up the scales with a number of standards. 'And if there are any more like you at home, spread the word, we need all the policemen you can find for us!'

PC Bite and PC Andrews cycled back down to the police station, their lives transformed. After all, it was one thing to sing in the church choir, but to sing up at the castle, and in one of the Duchess's plays, that was indeed an honour.

'Let us just hope that we can keep crime to the minimum, PC Bite, let us just hope that,' the sergeant murmured quietly as he did up the gates to the police station with the station handcuffs. 'We must pray that there will be no more of these chamber pot and goat pranks during the time we are needed by Her Grace.'

George nodded. He wasn't much given to praying, but it seemed quite a good idea none the less.

The rehearsal time for *The Pirates of Penzance* galloped, not cantered, through the weeks set aside for its preparation; so much so that it seemed to Kitty and Partita that no one would ever be able to get the production together, least of all their producer.

'Mr St Clare will not have the ladies' hoops swaying, in what he calls "a distressing manner",' Partita moaned to Kitty. 'But, as I just said to Mamma, how can the chorus dance if their crinolines are never allowed to sway? I mean to say.'

Kitty folded a letter she had just received from Violet and gave her mind to the matter. It was obviously serious.

'Perhaps we should remove the hoops, and then he will feel less distressed?'

'Kitty,' Partita sat down, 'that is the whole point of the chorus. We *must* cause *distress*, or else it will all seem so dull. That is the whole point of the chorus dancing – it is to cause some kind of distress, if possible to *everyone*!'

Partita laughed, and after only a small delay as the penny dropped, Kitty too laughed, realising what Partita meant.

'Oh dear, are we about to sink?'

'Our producer, Mr St Clare, is about to sink the whole operetta, not us.' Partita turned from her dressing mirror and faced Kitty. 'Mamma is trying to persuade him. She is not stuffy like him. I mean, either our crinolines cause ripples of excitement to go through the audience when we dance onto the stage, and they sway about showing our pantalettes, or they do not. Mamma knows what is wanted, and she is becoming irritated by Mr St Clare. Everyone knows the producer has to let us do what is wanted in a production of this kind. I mean, it is hardly the end of the world if someone glimpses our pantalettes.'

Tinker gave her young mistress a stern look. 'Pantalettes is to be worn, not seen, Lady Tita, and that's my last word on the matter.'

Kitty was busily pinning up her hair, preparatory to performing the first of the dress rehearsals while Tinker was redressing Partita's straw hat with small artificial violets.

'Gracious, Tinker, it's hardly the cancan.'

'Oh, I do not think there is much that is very gracious about the French cancan, Lady Tita.'

'No, but it is exciting, Tinker, and that's what *we* want to be.'

Kitty was hardly listening, thinking only of the letter that had arrived from her mother. It seemed that Violet was going away from London for a while. It would be better. She would write to Kitty very soon with all her plans. Meanwhile she sent her all her love. For a second and then a third time, Kitty now reread, 'I send you, darling Kitty, all my love.' She suddenly felt all too homesick for the mother she had once had, the one who had lived in South Kensington, whose whole life had been Kitty, not the one who was in love with Dr Charles and going away to the – where was it? – oh, yes, the Lake District.

She went for a long walk, alone in the park, returning later in time to watch Valentine Wynyard Errol performing.

There was no doubt at all he occupied the stage as if it was second nature to him, unlike the line of real and pretend policemen, marching and singing behind him, who all looked awkward, some of them smiling self-consciously at the few people who were making up the rehearsal audience, others trying to hide themselves at the back of the stage. Nevertheless it had to be said they all looked more or less authentic, whatever their stage presence, because somehow or another, someone must have begged, stolen or borrowed their uniforms, with the result there were now ten policemen singing and marching with only a very occasional dirty look thrown at them from the conductor of the newly returned orchestra.

The pirates were called next to rehearse their opening number, and in contrast to the policemen, they occupied the stage as if they were born to it, boisterous, exuberant, their only difficulty seemed to be in not falling over each other's feet, not because they were clumsy, or their feet were inordinately large, but from laughing.

Almeric, eye patch securely in place, was a magnificent Pirate King. He seemed to be born to the role, singing of his delight in sailing under the black flag and spurning a sanctimonious part in society in favour of sallying forth to sea as a pirate king to pillage and plunder.

Pug Stapleton, Julian Sykes, James Millings, Teddy Heaslip, Peregrine and Gus, not to mention Bertie Milborne, were, among others, all part of Peregrine's faithful band, but of course it was Harry Wavell who, bandaged ankle and all, was busily intent on stealing the show.

'If Harry does not stop coming on so much the *star*, mark my words, before tomorrow evening, he will be lowered into the moat and left there,' Valentine whispered to Partita, as the second dress rehearsal of the day began.

Partita laughed, making a strangely exultant sound, because quite suddenly the whole miracle of the production overcame her – the whole magic of it, the whole excitement – and she wanted to jump on stage and join the pirates and Livia Catesby, who was starting to sing 'Mabel'. Partita wanted to dance and dance because somehow, this morning and this afternoon, *The Pirates of Penzance* had begun to knit itself together. Despite some of the bolts of silk arriving from London for the costumes not quite matching other bolts of silk, despite the chorus – most of whom had been recruited from the servants' hall – having the most terrible difficulty with their musicality, despite poor Bertie making a dreadful muddle of his role and holding everyone up – something about which he was even now being teased, despite everything, Partita knew that the production was going to be thrilling, all except for Livia, who was even now starting to sing – and failing horribly.

As soon as he heard her Harry could not believe his bad luck. He stood up. The key love affair in the opera is between the bashful and beautiful Mabel and the noble and ever honourable Frederic, and features one of Gilbert and Sullivan's most beautiful and touching love duets, when, having learned that because of being born in a Leap Year, far from being twenty-one and thus free from his contract with the Pirates, according to the Pirate King poor Frederic is in fact only five and a quarter years

173

old. Mabel assures him she will wait for him to be twenty-one, even though that particular birthday will not fall until 1940.

Mr St Clare, realising the extent of the crisis, stopped rehearsals and Dr Jones was once more called, this time to pronounce Livia's throat badly inflamed and not likely to get better for days.

'What to do?' Livia asked hoarsely, tears in her eyes. 'Who can take my place?'

Harry turned to Partita, who turned to Kitty.

'She can,' Partita announced blithely. 'She sings like a bird.'

'Oh, I don't think—'

'Well, *we* do!'

'We don't have very long to get it done,' Harry warned Kitty as soon as they started to rehearse. 'In fact, we only have today and tomorrow.'

'I do learn quickly,' Kitty reassured him. 'I have been told it comes from being an only child – so much attention from one's mother, you know. I can memorise a page after only two readings.'

'I am more worried about me letting *you* down. You have a really exceptional voice.'

'Oh, no, you go too far. I have an average voice – I know because my father told me so.'

'Your father must be tone deaf. Or stone deaf. Lady Partita is right, you do sing like a lark.'

That was about all the time they had for conversation, since every waking moment for the

174

rest of the forty-eight or so hours left to them was spent in rehearsing, long after the others had all packed up and left.

'You have surprised me, Harry,' Roderick St Clare informed him the next morning, after the first rehearsal of the day. 'I had utterly despaired of you ever getting the remotest likeness to Frederic, yet here you are giving an altogether attractive performance of the young blade. I shall eat my words. Munch, munch.'

Roderick raised two perfectly shaped eyebrows at Harry, then, walking away with quick, light steps, went to start berating the chorus of policemen, whom he did not consider were cutting what he called 'the mustard'.

'I still feel woefully unprepared,' Harry confessed. 'My fault – not yours, I hasten to add—'

'Yes, but forgive me,' Kitty interrupted. 'Because you must remember as the leader of the chorus I'm familiar with all the parts. It is finally easier for me than for anyone.'

'You have already come up trumps, Miss Rolfe.'

Kitty tipped her head to one side and smiled at him. 'We'll see about that, Mr Wavell. After the curtain falls.'

Kitty need not have worried, although she did of course.

As if in a magical moment that had somehow been brought about by the mutual wills of everyone at Bauders, the young that night sang and danced their way into the hearts of their audience. Partita's dearest wish that the ladies of the chorus should prove *exciting* came true; and the voices of Almeric and Peregrine, Harry and Kitty could not be faulted, even by Mr St Clare. It was a rare and beautiful evening and one that promised to be repeated, time and time again, in the years to come.

'So much to look forward to with such talented young men and women,' was the agreed verdict of all Circe's friends.

'As good as anything you will see anywhere.'

'Without doubt that is the very best amateur production of *Pirates* that I have seen,' Ralph Wynyard Errol told the Duchess as he joined the enthusiastic applause that the packed auditorium was bestowing on the cast as they took their bows, their faces glowing in the warm colour of the footlights. 'The singing was first class, but the acting! The acting, which is usually so sadly neglected, it was simply first rate.'

'I agree,' General Sir Tommy Sykes, who was sitting on the other side of Circe, announced, clapping his white-gloved hands slowly but with great appreciation. 'In the wrong hands this sort of comic operetta can be most frightfully tedious.'

There was hardly a person present who was not thrilled by the performance, so much so that Roderick St Clare, while flattered by all the praise that was being heaped on him at the buffet party thrown for the audience and cast afterwards, found himself insisting that the evening belonged to the cast not him, which he later remarked to a friend must have been really quite a first.

'Don't know what Wavell's going to make of it all,' the Duke muttered to Circe as he, as the host, enjoyed a measure of reflected glory. 'That boy of his has talent. Can't see young Harry sitting stuck away in the estate office with a pile of ledgers in front of him now, really I can't, but I ain't his father, thank the Lord.'

It was proving too difficult for the guests to let the cast go. Such was their enthusiasm they kept calling for reprises of their favourite songs. So with Elizabeth once more seated at the piano, the cast duly obliged. To everyone's delight Almeric reprised the number the Pirate King sings when he takes leave of Frederic, thinking his apprenticeship is over.

Away to the cheating world go you – where pirates all are well-to-do
But I'll be true to the song I sing, and live and die a Pirate King!

Partita danced upstairs to her bedroom.

'How did you think I was, Tinks, how did you think Miss Kitty was, Tinks? Weren't we all brilliant?'

'I am sorry to tell you I fell asleep, Lady Partita,' Tinker announced, with some relish. 'Mind, I did wake up for the Major General's song. That was excellent; we all thought that he had his words off excellently well.'

'Did you not see *me* dance, Tinks? Did you not admire my wearing all the costumes you helped to make?'

'No, Lady Partita, the moment you came on I fell fast asleep and started snoring,' Tinker told her with a straight face. 'I was fair tired out from all that sitting up and sewing until the clock struck midnight, and that is the truth. We all were. Did you not hear all us ladies' maids snoring, and snoring, why we made such a din I thought we must have drowned the orchestra, truly I did.'

'Sure take no notice of Tinker, Lady Tita, of course she saw you. She saw all of you, we all did,' Bridie murmured to Partita as she bustled past her to reclaim the curling tongs from the girls' dressing room. 'She is just teasing you, Lady Partita. You know Tinker, she thinks if she says too much you will get a big head, which of course you will not because you and I know full well Tinker would take her darning needle to it, wouldn't she now?'

Partita turned back and, taking hold of Tinker's hands, she shook them up and down.

'I promise I will not get a big head if you tell me how wonderful I was, Tinks!'

Tinker freed herself, grinning, and then turning by the door, her arms full of the costumes she had just removed, she said, 'The star of the evening was Miss Kitty Rolfe, of that there was no doubt, Lady Partita, and nothing you will say will change my mind.'

Partita looked after the closed door, momentarily sulky.

'I suppose I must not mind?' she asked, turning to Kitty. 'I suppose I must give best, I suppose I must acknowledge that you are the star of the evening?'

'You were beautiful, Partita. As far as the audience were concerned, you could do no wrong. Even the pirates were at your feet.'

'The *pirates*? What would they know? They were all so busy getting their cues wrong, they would hardly have noticed if Dame Nellie Melba herself was singing.'

'They were all truly inspired by the end, though, weren't they? Most especially Harry Wavell.'

'Oh, Harry will end up going to America and making millions on the stage,' Partita agreed. 'He is a natural show-off, and nothing to be done.'

Kitty gravitated towards the open fire and Partita followed her, putting out her hands to warm herself as Tinker returned with a tray of hot drinks.

'This is the best bit of any evening, either after the ball is over, or after the play has been cheered to the echo; or after we have made everyone fall in love with us, over and over and over again. We can sit here and hold up our memories to the light and see everything in an even more beautiful way.' Partita sipped at her hot milk, and looked at Kitty over the top of her gold decorated cup. 'You never realised I was a poet before, did you, Kitty?' she finished, pulling a face.

Kitty stared into the fire. Partita was a kaleidoscope, her character made up of a cornucopia of colours. Kitty always had the feeling that she only had to turn Partita, or shake her, and she would turn into something so different Kitty would be left wondering if she had ever really known her; so much did the pattern of her personality change within seconds.

'You are so many things, Partita,' Kitty murmured.

'She is a scamp and a mischief,' Tinker said, giving her charge an affectionate and proud glance.

Partita stared into the fire, perfectly happy now that everyone was talking about her, but restless because she knew not everyone was *thinking* about her.

If only she could make Peregrine see her as she knew she could be – as clever and brilliant as Perry himself – then everything would be different. Perhaps when they all went to Waterside for Mamma's annual seaside holiday? Perhaps then Peregrine would see that she was not just a child, not just someone to whom he could give a *reading* list, not just Almeric's little sister? He must not love anyone else, she would not let him, however much she caught him staring at Kitty with a look that he never seemed to have for '*titty bitty Partita . . .*'

Downstairs in what was known by the servants as 'the bachelors' wing' Almeric swayed into bed, finally falling asleep, dreaming only of Kitty, while James lay awake thinking only of his beloved Allegra and wondering, over and over, as he always did, when he would have enough money to ask the Duke for her hand in marriage. Meanwhile, across the corridor, Bertie and Teddy started to talk about the change in Bertie's sister, Elizabeth. How she had changed so much since the start of rehearsals, blossoming into a young beauty before their very eyes.

'I had rather you didn't talk about her,' Pug blurted out suddenly. 'I know you're saying nice things, but I would still rather you did not discuss her.'

'She is my sister, old thing,' Bertie said sleepily.

'I know, Bertie, I know very well that she is your sister, but you see – it is very difficult for me, because I am in love with her, I'm in love with your sister, Bertie, and nothing to be done.'

Even to his own ears Pug's voice sounded strangely clear and sincere in the darkness of their shared room.

There was a small silence.

'Surely you can't be in love with Elizabeth so soon, Pug old thing?'

'I am in love with her. I will never love anyone

else,' Pug assured them, after which, the other two, feeling a little awkward at this announcement, made sure to fall asleep as soon as they could, while Pug himself lay awake, knowing that his life would never be the same again.

Chapter Six

Waterside House

Now that the warm weather had arrived, bringing with it thoughts of picnics and croquet on the lawn, Circe's thoughts were on her gardens, in particular one of the old and now half-forgotten walled gardens in which stood a fine medieval dovecote. Standing some way from the house itself, too far from the kitchens for the planting of vegetables, the old rose garden had slowly become overgrown and neglected, but not forgotten. For some time Circe had nursed plans for its improvement, and now, on Opal Gaskell's recommendation, before leaving for her annual family holiday by the sea, she was on her way to visit the famous gardener Miss Gertrude Jekyll and the architect Mr Edwin Lutyens at Miss Jekyll's house at Munstead Wood. She had heard of Gertrude Jekyll's work so often and learned so much about it that her advice on replanting the old garden would surely be seen to be the right one. The only difficulty, if it was a difficulty, was that Miss Jekyll did not come and visit her clients. However rich or grand they might be, they went to see her.

'Don't be looking for any favours, Circe,' Opal warned her. 'And don't expect her to be interested in, let alone listen to, any opinions or ideas. Miss Jekyll lives in her own world, no one else's.'

'I'm perfectly happy to pay her a visit, Opal.'

'And do not forget, dearest, do not forget that, sadly, Miss Jekyll is all but blind, but it does not affect her gardening.'

Circe's visit took place on a fine sunny morning. She was shown straight into the gardens, where she found Miss Jekyll in a straw hat decorated with fresh flowers, and Mr Lutyens sucking on an unlit pipe, both of them already at work, the plans spread out on a table before them.

'Loveridge, our head gardener, has drawn a map of the area in question,' Circe explained to Ned Lutyens, tactfully showing him the prepared diagrams, glancing at Miss Jekyll, who was busy staring out across the gardens, and thinking how sad it must be for such a wonderful gardener not to be able to enjoy the fruits of her endeavours.

'He's included the soil type, I see,' Lutyens remarked, 'as well as the ambient temperatures, prevailing wind direction and a compass too. Doesn't leave anything to chance, your Mr Loveridge, Duchess.'

'He is a very good gardener,' Circe explained. 'But he doesn't feel he can trust himself entirely when it comes to working from scratch. And I have to admit it made me more than a little nervous.'

'Nothing to be frightened of, Duchess,' Gertrude Jekyll said out of the blue, without turning in their direction. 'Plants are a lot more forgiving than one supposes. Plenty of light and not too much overcrowding is all they want. Like us all, really. More precisely, what are your feelings about this garden?'

Circe hesitated, remembering Opal's caveat about giving opinions.

'If I tell you what I don't want, perhaps that might be better guidance,' she replied finally. 'Much of the gardens I feel have become a little over-formal down the years, so I thought here perhaps was a chance to introduce an altogether lighter and brighter element. Something I know that you are both so famous for as a partnership.'

A good long silence followed Circe's statement, so long a silence that Circe was convinced that she had said the wrong thing. Happily, such was not the case for finally the great gardener walked slowly over to the table where Loveridge's plans were spread out, and peered at them. Another silence followed as Miss Jekyll simply stood staring.

'I dare say we can help you, Duchess,' Miss Jekyll finally stated, now staring back at her own garden through her thick-lensed spectacles. 'We shall not expect miracles, however. I'm sure you know the other secret of gardening. Patience.'

'That is something I find I learn the more I garden, Miss Jekyll.'

'Obviously there is much work to be done. But you sound as if you have a sensible person in your head man. If he is willing to follow a few simple instructions there is no doubt we shall be able to fill your space to your delight and pleasure.'

'I should be so pleased, Miss Jekyll, if that were the case.'

Once again Lutyens smiled to himself at the Duchess's tact, wondering whether it took a duchess to understand such a grand dame as Miss Jekyll.

'Perhaps you'd like a tour of the grounds, Duchess?' he enquired. 'Although obviously you're familiar with Miss Jekyll's style – otherwise you wouldn't be here, would you?'

Sticking his still unlit pipe back into his mouth, Lutyens led Circe round the wonderful gardens while at the same time guiding Miss Jekyll. The borders, at the height of summer, were full of the most carefully graded colours, the heights of every plant graduated, the hedges beautifully cut and shaped, and the entire planting a landscape in miniature. Here was the work of great vision and talent, born not just from a singular, but from a shared imagination.

'It would be wonderful if we can achieve even a little of this at Bauders,' Circe enthused diplomatically.

'Kind of you,' Miss Jekyll said, stopping as if to check her handiwork, her stick raised as she pointed out something to her companion. 'But it's Mother Nature's doing really. We certainly didn't invent flowers. We might make them stronger, we might give them a different colour, or change their size, but they were all here before us. All we can do is try and show Nature's work in the setting it deserves.'

'I am greatly looking forward to this adventure,' Circe told the two partners, as she was taking her leave.

'You rightly judge it to be an adventure, Duchess. All gardening is an adventure. Goodbye.'

Ned Lutyens saw Circe off, thanking her for coming to visit them. In return Circe told him what a pleasure it had been for her, before dreaming all the way back to Bauders of flowers, and flowers, and more flowers.

Hard on the heels of the Duchess's visit to Miss Jekyll and Ned Lutyens, the family prepared to decamp to Waterside House on the south coast of England.

Waterside House had been a present to the Duchess from the Duke many years before. He had presented it to her in deference to her love of the sea, although the seaside was not a place that he himself cared to visit, being reluctant as always to leave Bauders.

As her family had grown up, so the size of the house had gradually increased, although never to the sort of dimensions as those enjoyed at Bauders. Friends from London would always be asked to stay, carefully chosen guests, famous for their *joie de vivre*. Certainly after so many years of owning the house Circe found that the list of guests could be drawn up with such confidence that they were proud to be known as 'Watersiders'.

Sometimes Circe thought she was never really more relaxed or at ease than when she was on holiday at Waterside. Here she could abandon the formality of life at both Bauders and Knowle House, the family's London residence. At Waterside, she could do nothing all day long except listen to the suck and tug of the waves on the beach, hear the call of the gulls overhead, and the sound of children laughing on the beach; here she could forget her position in society and be herself.

Perhaps this affected the young too, for whenever they were at Waterside they found themselves behaving as they had when they were children; getting up early to throw back the curtains in the hope of finding another fine and sunny day, checking the tides and the height of the waves, ambling down before breakfast to the beach to spend time looking in the rock pools for crabs and tiny silvered fish, planning the day's sandcastle build, or playing hopscotch on a grid marked out in the glistening sand.

It seemed that at Waterside time did indeed stand still, and in order to keep that feeling, Circe had long ago ordered that no newspapers were allowed in the house and all talk of anything topical or political was strictly banned – anyone found breaking the rules being liable to a forfeit. In order to further this special feeling of intimacy and timelessness, the smallest staff was employed, chosen from the neighbouring village, to include only a cook, a couple of housemaids and a general handyman to see to anything that needed doing and to supervise the running of the house. Bridie and Browne, Tinker and the rest all being left behind at Bauders.

'The servants need a holiday from us too,' Circe always maintained, with which the servants were only too glad to concur.

This year the main body of guests was drawn, not unsurprisingly, from the main corps of the *Pirates* cast.

'I say we should ask Harry as well. Harry is as much a part of the Pirates Club as any of us,' said Partita.

'The Pirates Club? Is that like White's?' the Duchess wondered.

'No, more exclusive actually, Mamma.'

'I don't know that Harry would want to be asked,' Allegra said looking round at the others. 'It might be *embarrassing* for him, Tita. There won't be anyone else, well – like him.'

'Like him?' Partita mocked. 'Harry is like all of *us*; we are like Harry.'

'Does he get on with you in a new way, after playing in *The Pirates of Penzance*, Partita?' Cecilia enquired, all seeming innocence. 'Is that maybe why you would like to ask him?'

'Harry?' Partita widened her bright blue eyes at her sisters, to stare at them as if they had both lost their senses. '*Harry?*' she repeated, and then walked off, simply leaving it at that.

'I don't see any good reason why Harry shouldn't be invited,' Circe said, ignoring everything that had been said because she knew she had the casting vote. 'I know Almeric would like him to be here. The two of them get along splendidly, and I very much doubt if Harry will be getting much of a holiday this summer anyway. His father wants him to start work under Mr Hawkesworth as soon as is convenient.'

So Harry was included in the list of guests.

Wavell slowly and carefully packed the last of the cases in the hired cars the Duke had decided were suitable and reliable enough for the conveyance of his family and friends, while Tully and Taylor helped passengers, lifting dogs onto knees, and handing in rugs for a journey that would take them the best part of six hours.

'Still rather see Jossy with a pair of ribbons in his hand,' the Duke observed, watching one of his former coachmen take his place behind the steering wheel. 'Confounded contraptions, motor cars. They'll be the death of us all, mark my words.'

With a salute from the first of the newly trained chauffeurs in their equally newly acquired caps, and with waves from all his family, the Duke and Wavell watched the cars making their way down the long driveway, waving all the way.

The Duke looked on long after they had disappeared from sight, until, sighing to himself, he went round to the stables to find Jossy, while Wavell and the rest wandered back into the house.

'Couple of us were thinking of joining the army, Mr Wavell,' Taylor remarked cheerfully as they went down to the servants' hall. 'The other day when we was off, there was a lot of talk around the place about what was going on, and quite a few of the lads when they was asked said they wouldn't mind joining the army.'

'Not me, Mr Wavell,' Tully said quickly. 'Our Ben's in the army, and I know enough not to want to leave here.'

'Tully's right, Tom Taylor,' Wavell told the younger man. 'You can think all you like about joining the army—'

'And doing our bit, Mr Wavell. For king and country,' Taylor interrupted.

'And doing your bit for king and country, except that is exactly what you are doing here, Taylor. You are doing your bit here, do you see? Being in service in a great house such as this is its own form of serving your country.'

'It's hardly defending the Empire, though, is it, Mr Wavell?'

'In its own way it is, Taylor. This personifies what the Empire stands for, and while you're in service here you are helping to protect the interests of the Empire. Places like this represent England and all that she stands for. We all do, everyone who works and lives here. By working here we are all doing our bit to preserve what we hold dear. Don't ever forget that, Taylor – you neither, Tully. This is what your father fought for in the Boer War, Taylor – and your father, Tully. So that places like this, the very heart of England, should be safe. Don't ever forget that, either of you, and let's have no more idle talk about joining up and doing your bit – because you don't know what you're talking about.'

'No, Mr Wavell,' Taylor said with a frown after the retreating figure of the butler. 'Never saw it like that before, but I do now.'

'Catch me joining up,' Tully said once more. 'Catch me leaving here. Come on, dropped scones for tea.'

Kitty was relieved to see that Waterside House could almost certainly be described as cosy. Built in the early 1890s, the house had something of the style of an Arts and Crafts house, with its tall chimneys, and windows with the leaded-paned Tudor look. Its immediate charm undoubtedly lay in the fact that it overlooked the sea, with balconies outside all the seaside bedroom windows, taking advantage of the wonderful views.

Either side of the main house was set a smaller house, each also with balconies outside the upper floor to take advantage of the sea views. Both houses were designed for male guests, and there was also a small cottage for the handful of hired servants. The grounds of the house were made up solely of well-kept lawns, and mature trees, which had withstood the winter gales that swept in off the Channel.

Waterside was always referred to as Circe's 'little beach house', which, given its size, could have been more than irritating had Circe not been a Duchess who lived in a house as grand as Bauders. As it was, the people who came to stay understood that the little beach house was so called because that was how it appeared after life at Bauders, whose rooms no one of the present generation had yet been able to swear they had ever been able to count.

Once they had been welcomed to Waterside by Circe and her family, and after a delicious light supper taken in the dining room where everyone served themselves, *à la russe*, Kitty was astonished to find waiting in the room she was sharing with Elizabeth Milborne a whole wardrobe of summer clothes the Duchess had sent for 'her girls', as she now referred to them all. They were not just new clothes, they were fine new clothes; so fashionable were the dresses and so thin and silky the stockings and under-wear, that when Kitty and Elizabeth first held the dresses up against themselves, they turned to each other nervously, both suffering from a vague sense of shock as they realised not just how expensive the clothes were, but how revealing.

'Should we wear them, Kitty?'

'Certainly we should wear them, Elizabeth,' Kitty affirmed. 'After all, if the Duchess has sent for them then she must mean us to wear them, and after all, not to wear them would mean that we look as if we are questioning her taste.'

Kitty quickly undressed and held a dress up against her, standing back from the dressing mirror as she did so, her head on one side.

'They leave very little to the imagination,' Elizabeth announced, really rather unnecessarily.

'It seems that everyone has been wearing these dresses to Ascot, and everywhere else for the past year at least,' Kitty told her airily, although she herself was privately amazed at the revealing cut of the dresses, all of which sported little trains. 'Besides, what is the difference between wearing this in the evening, or at lunch, when we have all been spending the day in bathing suits on the beach?'

'Well, that is certainly true.'

Elizabeth started to undo her long, brown hair and brush it vigorously. The journey had been long, supper late, and she was ready to sleep.

'Ssh!' Kitty put a finger to her lips, and going to the door she opened it slowly to reveal the three Knowle sisters all dressed in their new frocks, and quite obviously determined to show the dresses off.

'Aren't they just too-too?' asked Allegra. 'Mamma has such exquisite taste.'

Allegra twirled in front of the admiring Kitty and Elizabeth, while Cecilia stared at herself in their dressing mirror and Partita, eyes half shut, did a tango with a non-existent partner down the full length of the bedroom.

Out of the three of them, Kitty quickly realised, Partita, because she was startlingly blonde, would always have caught every eye from first to last, and of course once Partita realised that everyone had indeed finally turned to watch her as her quite outrageous dance became ever more extravagant and exaggerated, until she finally danced up to the French windows, opened them, and disappeared onto the balcony outside.

'Mamma told me that she has chosen the most outrageous costume for Partita – is it in the wardrobe?' Allegra asked in a tone that was half affectionate and half jealous, because Partita, being the youngest, it seemed was always being singled out for special preference.

Kitty peered into the oak wardrobe, and thinking that she might have spied the outfit, she removed it.

'Would this be it?'

Allegra nodded, and sighed. It was, it had to be – Turkish trousers and an embroidered silk jacket. Partita would simply scintillate in it.

'It is worn over flesh-coloured tights and underwear,' Cecilia stated, taking the diaphanous outfit from Kitty and wafting it towards the dressing mirror where she held it up to her, before discovering, just seconds too late, that it did not suit her darker, heavier looks. 'Gracious,' she exclaimed. 'It would not suit you or me, Allegra. It would make us look like *Pirate* Queens!'

At that moment a cry of help came from beyond the French windows, followed by an eerie silence, during which only the sound of the sea pulling and sucking at the pebbles outside the window could be heard. The three girls ran to the balcony, only to find Partita, hand over her mouth, laughing silently as the stars above shone down on the jewelled confection in her hair, on the mischievous look in her eyes, on her beauty.

'Next time you do that, Tita, I shall slap you hard and long,' Allegra grumbled.

'You are really no fun at all,' Partita said, sighing and following the other three back into the room. 'That was meant to be funny.'

'What is meant to be funny can sometimes turn to tragedy, just remember that,' Cecilia opined, a statement so pompous that Partita started to giggle.

Kitty turned away, struggling not to laugh at the sight of Partita's helpless giggles, made worse by her sisters' solemn, patronising expressions of disapproval.

'Well, the boys have arrived at last, I hear, and are having a pillow fight in the bachelor wing, so all is set fair for the summer holiday.'

Allegra turned to go and left the room, closely followed by a dutiful Cecilia.

Partita was the last to leave.

'I wish I was in here with you two. The other two are too old for me, really they are. It's like sharing with a couple of governesses, truly it is.' She pulled a face before shutting the bedroom door behind her.

Kitty and Elizabeth stared at each other, but much as they both loved Partita, they were secretly glad to be on their own, for when all was said and done, Partita was more than a handful, she was a constant drama. She was always so intent on making everyone's life more exciting.

'Partita has such a generous personality,' Elizabeth said, speaking into the darkness of the room as Kitty and she listened to the rhythms of the sea beyond the windows. 'She is always trying to help everyone enjoy themselves.'

'She pretended to fly off the balcony only because she was sure that the relief that she hadn't had an accident would be perfectly marvellous.'

'She is perfectly marvellous, that is exactly what she is,' Elizabeth agreed in her gentle, musical voice.

'Elizabeth?'

'Yes?'

'If you were a flower you would be a white Elizabethan rose, but if I was a flower what would I be, do you think?'

There was a short silence before Elizabeth finally said, 'A sweet pea, ancient as the world, and blooming all summer with a subtle scent and a brilliant colour.'

Kitty smiled at the moon and the stars beyond the window, at the sea that was as calm as the night sky above it. She liked that. She liked the thought that she was a sweet pea, a cottage flower, not too exotic, but with a variety of colour. She drifted off to sleep, not to wake until morning when the maid came in and pulled the curtains.

Partita was awake long before Allegra and Cecilia, which was not unusual, for ever since she was quite young she had always been the first to be awake, creeping out sometimes to trot down the corridor and from there up to the maids' floor where she would slide into bed beside Tinker. She was too old for that now, and not so young that she did not have a real purpose to her early awakening.

She bundled up her clothes and, sliding out of the two connected bedrooms, which, as always, she shared with her sisters, she fled to the large marble bathroom where she quickly changed, after which, clutching her bathing suit and towel, she made her way determinedly down the garden, past the few crooked, ancient trees that lined the edge of the lawn, which reached down to the pebbled beach.

The family beach huts were quite isolated, and since the access to the beach was private the huts were always left open, so it took only a small tug at the door marked 'Ladies' for Partita to step into the friendly beckoning darkness.

Once inside, the aroma of seaside holidays came to her instantly, not on tiptoes, not quietly and secretively, as she herself had left the house and garden, but at full gallop.

Up above her, lit by small windows, she could see beloved family swimming items. Her mother's striped bathing hats and matching swimsuits. Her sisters' costumes in a variety of styles, hung on pegs. At the back of the hut there was a stack of striped bathing towels, and a large basket filled with swimming shoes made of canvas with strange woven soles of rope. She stripped off and pulled on a demure black costume, and a pair of the shoes chosen from the basket, before, towel in hand, she crept off down the beach – towards the desultory sea, which seemed to be in two minds as to whether it should be coming in, or going out.

She moved slowly into the deeper water before finally jumping into the middle of a wave that seemed determined to welcome her into its midst, urging her to start to swim through it. As she dived into its middle, only to surface a few seconds later, she knew that she had never been happier, or more at ease, so that as she swam it seemed to her that she was becoming the water, and the water in its turn seemed to be becoming her. It was as if the water, not to mention the blue sky above her, understood her need to be up earlier than everyone, to be alone, to be a minute part of the vast sea, of no more importance than one of the tiny grains of sand or the pebbles over which it was passing. She was, in short, satisfyingly unimportant, and by the same token, able to be as irresponsible as the self-willed sea.

She started to play about in the water, diving down to retrieve a stone, before swimming off once again towards the always distant horizon. As she swam she allowed herself to imagine that she was a child once more, heading out into the unknown, in the distance a gloriously uncertain future only vaguely discernible as a jumble of sparkling colours.

'I thought I saw you!'

The voice came towards her as she waded ashore and picked up her towel from a nearby sea break whose green surface was so thickly draped with seaweed that its texture fleetingly reminded her of some old fabric. On hearing the voice Partita looked up, puzzled, shading her eyes from the sun.

'I thought it was you,' the voice continued. 'And just when I thought *I* was going to be the first to take a dip before breakfast. Instead of which I find a water imp, leaping in and out of the waves, doubtless up long ago.'

Partita took off her bathing hat and shook out her long blonde hair. Too late she realised that the simple gesture might be deemed flirtatious, but she felt so well and happy, she could not have cared less. She felt beautiful, and was well aware that because of that she probably looked beautiful, and that was all to the good, considering who it was that was standing in front of her.

'Good morning, Peregrine,' she said, taking care to adopt a careless tone.

'Good morning, Partita.'

'So . . . so you were saying that you were watching me from your balcony? I might have known that no moment at Waterside is ever truly private.' She sighed with sudden and genuine regret.

'Had I known that you needed privacy I should have turned away,' Peregrine told her, feeling vaguely guilty. 'But as it was – well, as it was, it seemed to me that the sight of you swimming was one of the most delightful that one could wish for.'

Partita nodded, looking momentarily bored, which amused Peregrine. It was as if, because they both knew that she was beautiful, she found the subject of being delightful to watch a trifle tedious.

'You are just going in,' she stated, looking Peregrine in his one-piece costume up and down with feigned detachment.

'This very minute,' he agreed.

'The water is clear and cold, and beautifully agreeable.'

'Come in with me?'

Partita considered this for a second.

'Oh, very well,' she replied, making sure that he knew that she was doing him a favour.

She turned and went back down the beach, flinging her hat onto the ground as she did so, still shaking out her thick head of hair. Peregrine followed more slowly, since he was barefoot.

Once in the water he raced towards the horizon, jumping and splashing, until he was far further out to sea than she was, or had been. Seeing this, Partita realised that he was throwing down a gauntlet to her; he was saying, '*I expect you do not dare to follow me,*' so of course she had to follow him, swimming strongly against the tide, which seemed suddenly to have strengthened its purpose, and was now pulling towards the beach huts, and the walls at the top of the shingle, which edged the gardens of Waterside House.

'I can't swim any further.'

Her voice, even to herself, sounded genuinely panic-struck. In a few seconds Peregrine had swum back to her and, turning her, he pulled her, he doing backstroke, she happily helpless in his arms, until they reached the shallow water once more, and she stood up, laughing.

'I always used to do that to Al,' she told an

indignant Peregrine. She put on a mock helpless voice. *'I can't swim any more!'*

Peregrine leaned forward and gently shook her, laughing as he did so.

'You are a very naughty little girl,' he said. 'You deserve to be stood in the corner.'

Partita became purposefully helpless in his grasp, but he did not seem to notice this, only went on laughing as she allowed herself to be shaken.

'Careful, I am not a cocktail.'

Peregrine stopped shaking her and let go, but he was still slightly breathless, and laughing at her deception, which was probably why he did not seem to notice Partita closing her eyes and raising her face to his, so he only turned away, reaching for his beach towel and burying his face in it.

'You have always been an imp – do you know that, Partita? Always. Ever since you were a little girl, you have been an imp.' He rough-dried his hair and then, pulling off the towel, he smiled around him at the still quiet scene. 'Aren't we lucky, to have today, in a place like this, and everyone here such friends? We must be the luckiest people in the world.'

'All the pirates are here now,' Partita agreed, walking up ahead of him as if he had ignored her closed eyes and raised face, while all the time comforting herself that he had perhaps not ignored her so much as not noticed. Peregrine, after all, was hers. She had been in love with him ever since she could remember. He was hers.

No one else can have him, she repeated silently to herself.

'Shall we all be meeting on the beach later?'

He stopped outside the men's bathing hut and looked down at Partita with his usual brotherly affection.

'I expect we shall.'

Partita shook out her still damp hair, but, despite this really rather abandoned movement, there was nevertheless a set expression to her eyes. She was not so young, nor so stupid, that she had not noticed that Perry still had that irksome, detached brotherly look on his face. Well, she would pay him back for that, if it was the last thing that she did.

'Is everyone – I mean, are both your sisters here?'

'You know they are, Perry,' Partita told him in a bored voice, pulling open the beach-hut door.

'And Miss Milborne, and Miss Rolfe?'

'Of course. Al would not forgive us if we did not invite those two, would he? Especially Kitty, with whom Al is madly and passionately in love, and whom I think is madly passionately in love with *him*.'

She did not know why she had said that, except she did. She had said that because she did not want Peregrine to love either Elizabeth or Kitty, and because she knew that he had never loved her sisters so she had not bothered to include them.

She also said it because she wanted Kitty to marry her brother Almeric. As she saw the expression on Peregrine's face Partita could not help feeling satisfied that her inference had hit home, but she also saw that it had made him unhappy, because he turned away from her quite suddenly, and went into the men's bathing hut, saying nothing more.

Partita stared at the closed door, realising that her victory was not really a victory at all, because if Perry felt nothing for Kitty why would he have turned and left without a word? Why would he not have stayed to enjoy their usual banter together? Because – it dawned on her quite quickly – because he did not want Kitty to be in love with Al.

She walked slowly back up through the garden, past the monkey-puzzle tree, and other strangely shaped specimens planted long, long ago. She stopped briefly, staring around her, imagining the moment when the trees had been first planted, perhaps by someone who, like her, had been in the habit of getting up early and going down to the beach for a swim. She imagined the delight that the person who had planted them must have felt at just the idea that they would grow tall and strong, as they had indeed done, and how delighted they would be if they could see how well the trees had endured, how they had somehow managed to protect each other from the violence of the sea winds, from the salt air and the storms that could sweep so suddenly in from across the Channel, bringing with them that sense of helplessness that is at the same time both satisfying and frightening.

Partita sat down on the bench, staring around her at the terrace with its empty furniture waiting for the guests, at the lead urns planted with her mother's favourite white roses. She thought she would wait for Peregrine, that he would shortly follow her up the garden, but then she realised that he had not followed her at all, but was once more picking his way back down to the sea's edge, before striding into its initially calm surface, and, as soon as he was able, starting to swim, moving steadily towards the horizon until his head became just a tiny dot.

She stood up. She knew why he must be swimming out to sea – because she had upset him, because she had pretended to him that she knew all about Kitty and Al. She felt panic-struck, but helpless. If she made a fuss and dashed down to the water's edge and called or waved to him it seemed to her that it would be tantamount to admitting that she had fantasised about her brother and her best friend. She sat down again, her eyes fixed on the horizon.

Could it be possible that Perry loved Kitty, and not her, and that now he was intent on drowning himself in the most gentlemanly manner possible? She felt herself grow dizzy, but quickly put it down to the increasing warmth of the morning. She hated herself, and loved Perry, both too much, and too little.

Still, she could not love Perry so much as to allow him to love Kitty, and she could not hate him enough to want him dead. Nevertheless, she should never have implied to him that she knew all about Al and Kitty's feelings, when she knew nothing of the sort. It was not true that Kitty loved Al. It might be true soon, but not at that moment. Partita stood up again and as she did so she thought she saw the swimmer turning, and realised after a second or two, that she had *actually* seen him turning. She sat down again, thanking God, in whom, most unfortunately, she only seemed to believe in moments of crisis.

Perry was turning. He was coming back to her. He was swimming slowly and steadily back to the beach, and then walking up the beach towards the house, with his towel slung over his broad shoulders. The handsomest sight that she was likely to see that day, that week, or that month. She loved him so much, nothing would ever stop her loving him, she was sure of it.

A little while later, changed into casual clothes that set off his tall figure so well, he strode slowly up the garden towards her, but such was her relief that he had not drowned, that he had not swum out to sea never to come back, Partita stood up and ran down the garden and flung her arms around his neck.

'I was so worried for you! I thought you would never come back.'

Peregrine held Partita away from him, smiling. He had swum off his confusion of emotions. He had swum off the hurt he had felt at the idea that Kitty could love Al. He was now sure that he was quite back to his normal self. He looked down at Partita. He should feel grateful to her. His feelings for Kitty were not something that should be entertained. There would be a war soon, he was sure of it, and what place had love when a young man was about to go to war? No place at all.

'Hallo, Mischief,' he said, still holding her away from him, and reverting to her childhood nickname. 'What are you still doing here, Imp? Should you not be at breakfast?'

Partita wrinkled her perfect nose and shook her head, covering the disappointment she felt as she realised that the look of brotherly affection in Perry's eyes had not changed, but had, in some strange way, actually increased, and for no reason she could discern.

'I never have breakfast until it is too late,' she said, turning away and walking up the lawn. 'I like cold coffee, and food that is too cooked, or too cold, and toast that is all twisted, and butter that is runny, and no one else around to see me enjoy it.'

'That is so like the Mischief. You have not

changed at all, do you know that?'

'Oh, but I have, Perry, really I have,' Partita pleaded with him. 'I have changed so much. I am a grown-up now, and I will be doing the season next year, if there is not a war. I shall be going to balls and dancing the night away endlessly.'

'But not pointlessly, I hope, Mischief. You will break hearts, of course,' he stated, not looking at her, but staring ahead of him at the house, hearing the increasing sound of breakfast noise and laughter drifting towards them through the open French windows. 'But however many hearts you break, you will still always be an imp.'

'Oh dear.' Partita turned away, and she caught her bottom lip with her small, white teeth. 'You sound just like Jossy.' She did an imitation of Jossy with a pretend pipe in her mouth. 'Ooh, Lady Teeta, you're that much trouble, and always have been, I'll say that for you!'

Perry laughed, not seeing the hurt in her eyes. He walked up the garden after her. The Mischief would always be the Mischief to him. Then feeling himself being watched, he looked up at the house, and seeing Kitty at her bedroom window, he waved to her, and she waved back to him, kissing her hand quickly and carelessly to him, before finally turning away from the window.

Just a glimpse of Kitty, in her flimsy-looking dress, caught at Peregrine's heart, and for a second he allowed it to, before walking back into the house and the friendly gaiety of the party.

As for Kitty, she walked back across her bedroom and, pausing for a second in front of the dressing mirror to check her dress, she stared at herself. She must not, *must* not allow her heart to dominate. Peregrine Catesby belonged to Partita. He probably always had, and that would not be surprising since they had known each other all their lives. If she did but know it, they had probably been childhood sweethearts. Certainly seeing how Partita had flung her arms around Peregrine's neck, Kitty had no doubt at all that Partita loved Perry with all her heart.

She walked slowly down to the hall, and was reaching out for the dining-room door handle when Almeric opened it.

He smiled at her.

Kitty smiled back at him, and as she did so she knew exactly what Al's smile was saying, and that there was nothing to stop it. It was a runaway horse of a smile, a speeding motor car of a smile, it was a smile that was saying openly and happily, '*I love you, Kitty Rolfe, on this beautiful summer morning, with the blue sky, and the blue, blue sea, and the sun shining. I love you, and you must know it.*'

Kitty knew she should stop smiling back at him, that she should discourage him, but she felt helpless to do so. He had said, and only that morning, that everyone they knew was sure that there was going to be a war.

If there was a war Almeric might die; they all might die. This might be the last time they could all be young and in love, for better or for worse. Seconds later, Almeric leaned forward and kissed her briefly on the lips, and Kitty let him, because not to seemed somehow really rather selfish, particularly if there was going to be a war. Besides, wars were always rather romantic, weren't they? Knights going off to battle with a girl's favour tucked into their battle-dress, and so on. So what was a kiss?

Ever since she was a child Elizabeth had always dreaded mealtimes, but since being invited to Bauders Castle she had come to realise that food and wine, taken in the company of friends, was not just a matter of eating, but a time to be entertaining. The Duchess told her that she must never allow herself to feel shy.

'The unwritten rules of luncheon and dinner are to make the men feel flattered, warmed, and finally, of course, entranced by encouraging *them* to talk,' Circe went on. 'If you are facing a blank, or worse, disinterested face, always start with childhood. It is, without fail, a very safe subject.'

Circe had also insisted that conversation did not come naturally to the opposite sex. They needed to be *prompted* into talking.

'If you go into a room and listen to men talking, they never chatter and laugh, confide or advise as women do. They do gossip, of course, but in such an uninteresting way that, quite honestly, it is not until you are left to yourself that you realise that they have brought you something of any kind of interest. It is important, from the outset, to try and find out your dinner companions' subjects. For instance, the Duke's subjects are Bauders Castle, his regiment, the Royal Horse Guards, and, er – Bauders Castle. My subjects are music, light opera, the theatre, and, just occasionally, the history of surgery in the modern age.'

But of course at Waterside House, Elizabeth found that none of this now mattered in the least. Down by the seaside everyone was expected to get on hugger-mugger, with the result that she found that she was holding on to every minute of every hour, probably because she had never *been* on holiday with young people of her own age before. She had never before changed in a beach hut and followed friends down to the waterside wearing only her bathing suit. It was as if by being released from the constrictions of her parents' moribund relationship she could at last become herself.

Besides, there was always some new excitement. For instance, the new guests from London that the Duchess had invited to join the house party were certainly not from Elizabeth's, or even Kitty's, sheltered background. They wafted into Waterside House smelling slyly of sophistication and tango teas. Roses and sweet peas would not be the flowers to which anyone would want to compare them. If anyone should wish to choose flowers to which Lavinia Ponsonby, Emerald

Bickford and Mollie Hanley Montague could be compared, it would be orchids and wild flowers, although which would be which was not something either Elizabeth or Kitty would find out, for the three new arrivals soon sequestered themselves with Allegra and Cecilia.

'They are old now,' Partita said factually, 'so they will all be worried about whether or not they are to be engaged by the end of the summer, or whether or not their younger sisters will be engaged before them.' She looked mischievously from Kitty to them and back again. 'How about if we all become engaged before any of them? Wouldn't it be too-too, my dears?'

'Oh, I don't think anyone wants to be in a race to be engaged,' Kitty began, while Elizabeth said nothing.

Partita pinched her lightly on the arm. 'We all know who is in love with you, my dear.'

'No one – truly, no one,' Elizabeth stuttered.

'No one,' Partita stood back and laughed gaily. 'No one, indeed! We all know that dear Pug becomes a pool of devotion the moment you come within three miles of him. As a matter of fact he goes precisely the same colour as you are going now. It is too, too sweet.'

Kitty frowned at Partita.

'You know how I feel about Pug?' Partita continued.

Elizabeth stared at her, dreading what she might be going to say next, and yet knowing that nothing, and no one, could stop her.

'I feel that Pug should have as his bride the sweetest girl in the whole house party, and it just so happens that it is you, Miss Elizabeth Milborne.'

Elizabeth turned away. She had no idea that everyone knew, or even suspected, that she thought the world of Pug, and she could not bear the thought that Pug might, in his turn, be teased about her, that she might be causing him embarrassment.

Seeing how upset she was feeling, Kitty put an arm around Elizabeth while continuing to frown furiously at Partita, who promptly turned away, pulling a little face. Really, Elizabeth had not just one skin too few, but a dozen. Everyone had to be teased. She should try being the youngest sister of three. Partita could not count the times she had had her plaits tied to the bottom of her bed, or Tinks had found her locked in a cupboard. Jossy even found her one day shut in with the pony stallion. Happily Partita had carrots in her pocket and a riding crop to bang on the door, or, as Jossy said, she might have been there all night.

'You must not take any notice of Partita, she is just ribbing you,' Kitty begged. 'Besides, everyone knows Partita is in love with Peregrine.' Kitty looked defiantly across at Partita.

Partita turned very slowly back to face Kitty, hands clenched, mouth set.

She was just about to order Kitty and Elizabeth from Waterside House, and run and tell her mother she never wanted them to come and stay again *ever*, when she remembered just how few friends she truly had, and how lonely she had been, how much in want of company of her own age, until she met Kitty at Miss Woffington's Academy. Not only that, but nowadays Kitty was so much Circe's favourite that Partita knew that her mother would give her daughter short shrift if she complained about Kitty.

After a short pause, during which the other two stared at Partita's murderous expression in silent fascination, she finally declared 'Of course I am in love with Perry, I have always loved Perry ever since I was five years old and he used to take me riding on a leading rein in the park here. He would let me jump logs long before I could even sit to the canter.'

She sat down on the edge of the bed and the other two sat down on the chaise longue, silenced, as girls always are when a confession of love has just been made.

'Does he love *you*, do you know?' Elizabeth asked her in a low voice, her face so serious that Partita started to laugh.

'No, of course not!' She shrugged her shoulders, suddenly looking sad. 'He thinks of me as being just like Livia, except younger. He thinks of me as being his younger sister, and nothing to be done about it.' Partita tossed her head and gave a great long shuddering sigh. 'It is awful to love, and not to be loved back. That is why you are so lucky. Pug loves you back.'

'Oh, I doubt that . . .' Elizabeth stammered.

Kitty and Partita looked at her and then each other and laughed.

'*We* don't,' they said together.

Elizabeth turned away. She knew that poor Pug was considered a bit of a joke, but to her he was quite simply head and shoulders above everyone else. She saw reflected in his dark eyes not just amusement, but sensitivity and kindness. Very well, he did fancy himself as a fashionable knut, but that was just fun. He had told her that he thought it very likely that he would soon be joining the same regiment as Al, and there would be a bit of a dust-up, and then he would come back and go on farming. It seemed such a perfect plan.

'You are not just a knut, Pug, you are a bit of a dude too, and all the girls think so,' Harry kept teasing Pug that night before they all sloped off to the bachelors' wing, but not without making sure to accept the girls' invitation to join them for a midnight swim.

'I doubt that any of the girls will stay awake long enough to hear the chimes of midnight,' Almeric announced as they all started to remove their top clothes, before lying down on their beds and waiting for the appointed hour. 'It's the sea air,' he went on. 'It makes you so sleepy.'

'I have banged the old head twelve times on the pillow and will let you know how or if it works,' Pug announced to no one in particular.

'Very appropriate for a wooden head,' Bertie joked.

'I will stay awake,' Harry volunteered.

'You will not be able to stay awake for a second, Harry.'

In the event Harry did not let them down. Instead, he stared into the darkness, thinking of the wonder of being on holiday, of being part of all of the fun, of being with so many beautiful girls. Of course, he had every idea whom he thought was the most beautiful, but no good would come of his paying any special attention to *her*. Just as no good would come of his falling in love with any of the others. He was different, and always would be, not one of them – himself, Harry, their friend. Eventually he got up off his bed and went over to the window where he held up his watch to the moonlight. It was midnight.

He went over to Almeric's bed.

'Al?'

'Oh, don't wake him, I beg of you,' Gus called from his bed over by the window. 'There is no one so frosty as Al when he is woken, that I can promise you.'

Almeric opened his eyes and, seeing Harry's face bending over him, he let out an over-dramatic yell, and they both started to laugh. Pug woke up shortly after, and went to the window.

'I doubt that they will come,' he said. 'Miss Milborne, everyone, they said they were so

217

sleepy they could hardly keep awake during the whist.'

'If they don't come out, then I will climb in their window and wake them,' Almeric stated, pulling on his beach dressing gown with an air of determination. 'Midnight swims are part of the tradition of Waterside House, and always have been. Besides, I gave – I can't remember her name – but at any rate I gave one of the maids a few bottles so that they could have a party, and she has put eiderdowns and pillows and flasks in the beach huts, not to mention cakes and all that kind of thing. Everything is ready and waiting for us, nothing to do but sally forth.'

'That is all very well, old thing,' Bertie put in, 'but if any or all of the other girls are like my sister, Elizabeth, mark my words they will be asleep as soon as heads hit pillows, really they will.'

'And yet,' Pug announced proudly from his viewpoint at the window, 'guess who is the first to come outside, and is even now looking round for us?'

He turned back to the rest of the room with a look of triumph. The others promptly joined him at the window, staring out into the moonlit garden, hoping against hope that it would be filled with the lovely sight of a group of the opposite sex waiting to run down to the water's edge with them.

'Bless me, Bertie, if you're not made an ass of,' Gus told him, at the same time nudging him.

'There your sister *is*, and here do come the rest of them and, all glory be to heaven, they *are* all standing waving their bathing things up at us!'

'Right, first down, first in, wins the pot from cards last night!'

They all raced down the stairs of the small house and out onto the lawn, each elbowing the others out of the way in his haste to be the first to be at the side of the girl of his choice.

'You are all late,' Allegra informed her brother as James Millings promptly attached himself to her side, and Almeric went straight up to Kitty, who was swinging her bathing hat from one finger, her swimming costume neatly rolled up in a large towel under her arm.

'Does your sainted mother, the Duchess, know about this?' Peregrine asked Cecilia as, having changed, they all walked whispering and giggling through the garden down to the beach.

'Yes, of course she does. Don't you remember, we always have midnight swims at Waterside,' Cecilia reassured him.

Peregrine nodded. It was some years since he had holidayed with the Knowles at Waterside, and he did seem to remember there was some sort of tradition to do with swimming in the moonlight, but they had all been so much younger then, or had seemed so much younger. His eyes drifted ahead to where Kitty was walking beside Almeric, and then he turned to Cecilia.

'Isn't it strange how strictly we are all chaperoned, until we either go hunting, or swimming, and then it's just a free-for-all?'

Cecilia, who was watching Valentine Wynyard Errol slipping what he must have believed was a surreptitious arm around Livia's waist, looked up at him and knowing that she must distract him from what was happening, started to talk nineteen to the dozen.

'I say, Perry, you know and I know that there is sure to be a bit of a dust-up quite soon. There is no getting away from it, Papa says. I know Papa is always a bit of an old gloom-monger, but he says Sir Edward Grey is only interested in salmon fishing and shooting, and he can hardly be brought to London, let alone be got to put his mind to preventing a war, and that the King is so much at odds with his cousin the Kaiser that they can't wait to get at each other, and that is all before their navy getting as big as ours is driving everyone to distraction, because *we* are meant to own the seas, and everyone knows it.'

Cecilia was talking so fast and so furiously that Peregrine was beginning to suspect that she had some other motive. He started to look round, partly because he found the conversation inappropriate to the setting, and partly because he could not help appreciating the delight of the scene, and he really did not much care to talk about stuffed shirts like Sir Edward Grey.

'I can't see Livia,' he said suddenly, looking behind him.

'Oh, Livia is here all right, Perry. Just behind you, as a matter of fact.'

'Where?'

'Just there . . .' Cecilia pointed vaguely in the direction of a smaller group of people who were bringing up the rear.

'Oh, yes, of course.'

Cecilia had always loved and felt sorry for Livia, if only because it was so apparent that her mother did not love her. She wanted nothing more than to see her freed from her family. Behind her she could hear Harry being urged on by Emerald.

'Come on, old thing,' Emerald was saying, catching at his hand. 'No need to be shy! I have lived in Paris, even if you have not!'

Harry allowed Emerald to pull him along, and then she went to squeal and dance at the water's edge along with the other girls, who were all also holding hands with their chosen beau. Teddy had even managed to find Partita's hand, and since she had let him, had instantly become convinced that he was the happiest man in the whole world.

'Oh, Teddy, isn't this romantic?' Partita asked, her face all innocence as she held it up to him in the darkness.

'It is beyond the beyonds,' Teddy agreed. 'And you are an angel.'

'If only I were, but I have a dreadful feeling that I'm actually a devil,' Partita said in a purposefully tragic voice.

221

'Remember when you came to see us at New-brook all those years ago?'

'Mmm?'

'Nanny Heaslip always said, "Sure that Lady Teeta, she'll either become a plaster saint or a she-devil." So, which is it to be, Tita?'

'Oh, both, don't you think?'

'Can you be both?'

'I can be anything I like, and so can you, Teddy,' Partita called, jumping into a wave, only to disappear into it, and not reappear again.

'Tita! Tita!' Teddy called, diving into the same wave after her.

They both surfaced together, laughing, Partita doing her best to push him under just as the moon decided to appear from under its large, dark cloud, so that Teddy, who had leaned confidently under cover of darkness in an attempt to do what he had been dying to do since he was all of twelve years old, found he was kissing Partita in the full spotlight of the moon's brightest light.

Partita cared less, she liked being the centre of attention, so she kissed Teddy right back, not minding in the least if anyone was watching, which, of course, they were, because the moon was so bright.

Peregrine saw her first and at once felt a strange mixture of jealousy and relief before turning away and kissing Mollie; this meant that they in their turn were seen by Allegra and James, so that pretty soon everyone in that warm dark sea was kissing and laughing, and then swimming off, only to come back and repeat the whole exercise. Meanwhile, behind the men's bathing hut, Livia was happily surrendering to Valentine.

Chapter Seven

Love Affairs

The days passed blissfully. The sun remained high in a sky that only a dolt would describe as anything but azure. As the sea grew warmer by the hour, life at Waterside assumed a lazy, idle and gentle routine, of early morning swims, picnic lunches, long walks or rides along the strand and equally long lazy meals in the evening, followed by either parlour games or rounds of whist. No one there wanted it to end – why should they? It was an idyll because, quite apart from anything else, everyone seemed to be either in love, or on the very verge of it, so as the holiday grew to an end, it was not altogether surprising when Almeric invited Kitty for a walk.

'Valentine has asked Livia to marry him,' he announced after some minutes' silence.

'How delightful.'

'I hope they are allowed to marry, but it will be a miracle if they are. Her family are such dyed-in-the-wool Catholics.'

'Does that matter?'

'In the case of the Catesby family it most certainly does. They find it difficult to forget the hard times.'

'But that was all a long time ago, surely?'

'I agree, Kitty – but try telling Mrs Catesby. I wish Valentine all the luck in the world, because he will surely need it.'

'You really think she will forbid the marriage?'

'I have no doubt that she will, just as I have every doubt that you will refuse what I am about to propose to you, Kitty.'

'I think people should be allowed to marry whosoever they wish,' Kitty continued, sounding a little shocked at such old-fashioned prejudice.

'So do I,' Almeric agreed, finding himself as always mesmerised by the upward curve of Kitty's mouth. 'And that is precisely what I am determined to do. I'm determined to marry the girl I love. And I think you know who that is.'

Kitty turned away from him.

'Kitty? Kitty, is something the matter?'

'No. Nothing's the matter. Not really.'

'So why – why the worried frown?'

'Almeric – if you really are about to propose marriage, I'm not sure—'

'No, of course I'm not. I'm about to suggest a game of French cricket. That's why I am carrying this – for you.'

He produced a ring box from his pocket, but Kitty put a hand on his, preventing him from opening it.

'Almeric,' she said, 'surely you should ask your father first? I feel sure that he will not wish you to marry Evelyn Rolfe's daughter.'

'Your father is neither here nor there. Nor, as a matter of fact, is mine.'

'My father is notorious. I might have children like him.'

'Of course you won't. You're being absurd. And you're quite spoiling my proposal. I will start again.' Almeric cleared his throat. 'I love you, Kitty Rolfe. I have loved you from the very first moment I saw you. I do not care about anything else – or anyone else, come to think of it. It's you I love, you with whom I fell in love, and you who I shall love to my dying day.'

'Al—' Kitty began to plead, trying to stay determined to turn him down, but softening when she saw just how much she meant to him.

'If you could see your way to loving me, Kitty, then I shall be the happiest man on God's earth.'

He opened the little red box in his hand.

'This is an old family ring,' he said. 'It belonged to my grandmother. She left it to me for my fiancée, for when I became engaged.'

'Almeric,' Kitty said, transfixed by the beauty of the diamond, 'Almeric, you could marry anybody.'

'I know I could marry anyone, Kitty, but I don't want to marry anyone. I want to marry someone, and that someone is you, Kitty Rolfe.'

'I really wasn't born to be a duchess – Al, really I was not.'

'I have to disagree.'

'I really am not suitable.'

'It has nothing to do with suitability. This is to do with love, Kitty – and I love you with all my heart. I always will. I have never felt this way about anyone, and I never knew that I could. I never knew it was possible. So, Kitty? Kitty, darling Kitty – will you please, *please* marry me?'

Kitty looked down at the ring that the Duchess had given Almeric.

'But of course I will,' she found herself saying. 'However could I possibly not?'

Partita was sitting outside trying to paint a water-colour of the seascape when she learned of Almeric's proposal from her sisters, who had both hurried out of the house to break the news.

'But of course you knew about it already, so why are we bothering?' Cecilia grumbled, sitting down under a parasol.

'No I did not know about it!' Partita returned, splashing her paintbrush crossly in a jar of water. 'I had no more idea than you had.'

'Somebody must have known,' Allegra said. 'It certainly wasn't either of us—'

'Although it should have been,' Cecilia interrupted. 'Seeing as we are *older*.'

'Somebody must have known, because Al has given her Grandmother's engagement ring.'

'Perhaps Almeric told Mamma,' Partita reasoned, staring out to sea as she tried again to compose her painting.

'I think it's perfectly beastly,' Cecilia continued. 'The least Al might have done was wait for us.'

'It is so unfair that Al can propose when he likes, and James can't propose to me because he has no beastly money,' Allegra said sadly. 'Papa will not hear of me marrying until James has prospects.'

'I don't think Papa minds as much as James. He wants to keep you in a fitting manner,' Partita announced, washing some blue from her paint-brush with a flourish. 'But perhaps now Almeric's proposed it will spur the others on,' she suggested, tilting her head to one side to view what she had just painted.

'I don't think anything would egg James on,' Allegra replied, swatting at a fly that was pestering her. 'And the sky simply is not that colour.'

'It's my impression of the sky,' Partita told her firmly. 'This is an impression, not a likeness.'

'It's far too bright a blue,' Cecilia said, glancing at the watercolour. 'What might egg James on – and anyone else for that matter,' she continued, sitting herself well back under the parasol and out of the burning sun. 'What might egg him on is – a war.'

'There's not going to be a war,' Partita said quickly. 'And you'd better be careful, Cecilia, or you'll have to pay a forfeit.'

'I'm not discussing the news, Tita, I am simply commenting in the most general of terms. Conversationally – the topic being if there is a war

men are inclined to get married quickly in case –
you know – in case they don't make it back.'

'Cecilia is right for once,' Allegra replied.
'Everyone gets frightfully excited when there's a
war and they do all sorts of things like proposing
and getting married and having babies really
quickly.'

'How do you know?' Partita swilled her paint-
brush angrily once again in her water jar. The
thought that there *might* be a war was not something she wanted to contemplate on such a
lovely day when everybody was having such
a nice time. 'You're just guessing.'

'I listen to what people say, Tita. Unlike some
I know. And I read. For instance, I read only
recently that men never wish to marry anyone
unless they absolutely have to.'

'What on earth did you read that in?'

'Something or other. It really doesn't matter
what I read it in – what matters is the observa-
tion.'

'So you would like a war just so that you could
get married?'

'I certainly do not want to sit on the shelf,
thank you, Partita – which is what we shall all
look as though we are doing if Almeric goes
ahead and really does marry Kitty. No one wants
one's brother to marry first; certainly we don't.
Let us hope and pray for a long engagement.'

'Of *course* he's going to marry Kitty!' Partita
replied so angrily that both her sisters turned and
stared at her. 'Of course he is!'

'Perhaps Papa will say no because of that awful father of hers,' Cecilia observed to Allegra, ignoring Partita's outburst.

'Only if Mamma opposes,' Allegra replied. 'You know Papa as far as Mamma is concerned.'

Allegra and Cecilia looked at each other and sighed, before parroting together: '*Whatever makes you happy, dearest dear – whatever makes you happy.*'

'*Pas devant*,' Partita said, nodding at the gardener who was busy in the shrubbery to one side of the terrace. '*Pas devant le jardinier.*'

'The main thing is, I do not happen to think Kitty is suitable,' Allegra said in conclusion, getting up and deciding the topic was now exhausted. 'And neither of us do,' she added. 'And the sea most certainly is not that *awful* bright colour, really it isn't, Tita.'

Meanwhile Almeric was having to deal with a totally separate problem rather than whether or not his sisters considered his beloved Kitty was suitable enough to be his wife. In response to Almeric telling Valentine his own proposal had just been accepted, instead of learning similar news from his friend, Valentine had just informed him that Livia and he had decided to elope.

'But whatever for, Valentine?' Almeric asked, aghast. 'People like us don't do things like that, believe me.'

'We don't have any option, Al,' Valentine assured him cheerfully. 'Mrs Catesby simply will not entertain the notion of someone of a different faith marrying her daughter, particularly not the son of a theatrical manager.'

'Nonsense, Valentine. Maybe a hundred years ago – maybe fifty, say – but not nowadays, surely? People nowadays are far more liberal altogether.'

'In government perhaps, Al – but not as far as families such as the Catesbys go. It's not just her mother; I know my father thinks everyone gets married far too young nowadays and because of that they live to regret it, although what it is really is that marriage hasn't really suited *him*. He says it's because when he was a child he was always on tour with his parents, which made it difficult to settle down with anyone.'

'As far as I can gather, old friend, life in the theatre is altogether different from life elsewhere, but much as I don't want to sound like your pater, I really think you should take a pull and think all over again about what you intend to do – or not to do, more to the point. There are some things one doesn't do, old thing, and eloping happens to be one of them.'

Valentine looked at his friend affectionately. Almeric was the best sort of friend any young man could have, steadfast, loyal and honest, but due both to his character and his upbringing sometimes he was oddly remote, however forward-thinking and modern-minded he tried to be.

'You are absolutely right, of course, Al,' Valentine said to him finally, putting a hand on his arm. 'But you see, you are a son of a duke while I am only the son of a theatrical manager, and a philandering theatrical manager at that, and even worse, a philandering theatrical manager's son who is determined to be an actor. I don't really need the rule book. I can throw the rule book away.'

'You can't,' Almeric replied. 'No one can. We've had relations who have tried to do just that, and they always ended up in the soup.'

'Yes, but that is the difference, old friend,' Valentine replied with a smile. 'Given my circumstances I already have at least one toe, if not a whole foot, in the soup bowl.'

'But what about Livia? This really will put her beyond the pale, Val, believe me.'

'She's as determined on it as I am, Al. Besides – suppose the gloom merchants are right and there is going to be some sort of a war? Much the best thing to snatch at whatever chance we have of happiness, wouldn't you agree? Aren't your feelings just the same as my own, truly, are they not?'

Almeric looked reflective. Such thoughts had been circulating in his own mind only too recently.

'I love Livia, Al, and that's all that matters – and she loves me. We know her family aren't going to allow it, so we have no alternative. It won't be the end of the world, believe me. The end of the world is a long, long way off.'

Valentine gripped Almeric's arm hard, as if to convince himself of the truth.

'When are you planning on it, Val? Not before the end of the holiday?'

'Of course not. That really would not be the done thing; might upset your mother.' Valentine smiled. 'Not the done thing at all.'

'But nothing to be done before the pirates sail off?'

They both raised a hand in their pirates' salute. *'We sail under the black pirate's flag . . .'*

'And when you come to think of it, Al, when you really come to put the grey matter to work, deciding to run off with Livia is really quite a piratical act, is it not?'

Almeric agreed before raising yet another thorny subject.

'Are you all right for the necessary? I feel sure certain chaps up in Gretna Green, in Scottish land, might need their palms a little greased. One's heard some of these padres can take ruthless advantage.'

'You sound just like your old man,' Valentine laughed. 'The very double. But there's no need to worry on my account. I have a small inheritance from an old actress who shall we say was a *friend* of my father's.' They both smiled. 'For some reason or other she left me a tidy little sum a few months ago, and so I shall be well able to afford to keep Livia in some sort of style – whatever happens. Or doesn't happen.'

'Jolly good,' Almeric said. 'But whatever does happen, Val . . .'

'Yes?' Valentine prompted his friend, who

had come to a temporary halt. 'Yes? Whatever happens, what?'

'We'll still be pirates, won't we? Nothing will change that.'

'You bet,' Valentine agreed, with a smile. 'Till dee does us part, old friend. Promise,' he said in a passable Scottish accent.

Over the next days the burden of Valentine and Livia's secret weighed heavily on Almeric, because he knew what Valentine just didn't seem able to understand – that by running away with Livia Catesby, he would put himself and Livia on the outs with just about everyone that could possibly matter. It wouldn't seem very important to either of them at this particular moment, now their love had come into flower, but all too soon the honeymoon would be over, as his father was always fond of saying, and they would find out the exact truth about society.

It was not just that people would be lining up to cut him, but Almeric felt sure it would greatly affect all his business relationships, the dealings with his bank and his club – and as for the attention they would get from the popular press, it was too dreadful to contemplate. Everything would conspire to make poor Valentine and Livia objects of scandal and derision, unless, of course, there *was* some sort of war, in which case everyone would immediately forget about the whole thing because they would have other things on their minds, things more important than cutting some poor chap who had just wanted to marry the girl he loved. So it might not be such a bad thing at all if there *was* some sort of a war, because some sort of a war might allow a bit of a clean sweep. That was the sort of thing that appealed to Almeric, the chance for new brooms to sweep away some of the old cobwebs, particularly those heavy old cobwebs that still hung in certain corners of society, ready to trap and ruin so many innocent people. No, Almeric concluded at the end of his reckoning, a short sharp war might not be such a bad thing after all.

Meanwhile Pug had other things on his mind besides the growing crisis in Europe. He was aware that everyone, including Elizabeth, knew how he felt about her, but how to state it without coming out sounding a complete chump? This was what was preoccupying him, and to such an extent he was convinced he was getting a headache just from the thought of it all.

He had worshipped Elizabeth from the moment he had really become aware of her, sitting as pretty as a picture at the piano during rehearsals for *The Pirates of Penzance*, so much so that every time he was near her he started to feel quite faint, which was simply not him. To him, Elizabeth was an angel sent from heaven, a vision with the sweetest eyes, the most perfect slender figure, and the most endearing way of speaking and looking at a chap. She was like a heroine from a book, a fragile being with all the delicacy of a rose but without any thorns, the epitome of the perfect English gentle-woman.

In order to find out the best way to proceed, he sought out Bertie, whom he found sitting in the shade of the drawing room.

'Bertie, old fruit?' he began, clearing his throat nervously. 'Mind a word or two, old thing?'

'Not at all, Pug,' Bertie replied and, putting down his book, he smiled up at Pug.

'The thing is, Bertie,' Pug began again, clearing his throat once more.

'This is about my sister, is it not?'

'The thing is, as you no doubt have observed, I am somewhat smitten,' Pug continued obliviously, before juddering to a halt. 'What?'

'This is about my sister, is it not?'

'Absolutely, Bertie. I am totally mashed with your sister, as you might or might not know.'

Pug heaved a sigh of relief, having got through what he thought was the worst bit.

'Absolutely, Pug.'

'Now I know I will have to speak to your pater . . .'

''Fraid so, Pug.'

'But before I do so . . .'

'Yes, Pug?'

'Thought a chap might speak to you.'

'Absolutely, Pug.'

Pug swallowed, and then, taking out a hand-kerchief, he wiped first his moustache and then his forehead.

'I say, old bean – all right if I sit down?'

'Go right ahead, old boy.'

'I am rather beginning to feel a bit green about the gills.'

'You are beginning rather to look a bit green about the gills.'

Pug sat down. 'I shall never see this thing through, don't you know. If a chap's like this with his girl's brother, then what's he going to be like with the girl's pater? Doesn't even bear the smallest of thoughts.'

'No,' Bertie said, doing his best to keep his face straight, 'I suppose not.'

Bertie thought of his own father and closed his eyes. His father would make mincemeat of poor Pug, put him off Elizabeth for life, which would be a shame, not only as far as his sister went but for Bertie too, because he liked Pug and would welcome him as a brother-in-law. But his father had always had it in for Elizabeth from the day she was born. He wanted nothing more and nothing less for her than a life of misery.

'Pug – I'm Elizabeth's brother.'

'You most certainly are, old bean. Absolutely,' Pug replied with some relief.

'And I know her better than anyone, since, after all, I am her twin.'

Pug looked astonished. 'I never knew that, old boy. Good gracious.'

'Not many people know we're twins, Pug. Elizabeth was born half an hour after me and rather unexpectedly, I believe, which maybe

237

could account for my father's intolerant attitude to her. Her arrival so unexpected, and so on?'

'I see, poor girl, not her fault,' Pug concluded, getting up from his chair and beginning to pace the floor. 'All this only makes me all the more jolly well determined to win the hand of Elizabeth so that she can live safely away from such intolerance, as you call it.'

'You have won the hand of her already, Pug,' Bertie replied. 'At least, you have won her heart, and that is what matters. Perhaps you don't realise it because you're too much a gentleman to discuss such matters, but, Elizabeth and I being twins, she's the same age as I am and I am now twenty-one. So there is nothing whatsoever to stop you marrying my sister if you wish to – legally, at least. It's only etiquette to ask for her hand formally, you know. And so rather than face a drubbing from our old man, if I were you and if Elizabeth does want to marry you, I should fire straight ahead.'

'I say,' Pug said, staring at Bertie. 'I say.'

'Only one thing, Pug,' Bertie said with a smile. 'You have asked her, haven't you?'

'Er – no,' Pug replied slowly. 'No, I haven't actually. Least, not quite yet. Thought it best to get all the formal stuff out of the way first—'

'Pug?' Bertie interrupted kindly. 'Pug, be a good chap and do go and ask her first. Just in case?'

'Oh. Right,' Pug agreed. 'Righto. Yes. Jolly good wheeze, Bertie. Thanks awfully.'

Bertie watched with affection as his friend hurried away to find the object of his devotion. He was a chap in a million, even if he was a knut.

Elizabeth stared at Pug, wide-eyed.

'You want to *marry* me, Pug? But why? Why me?'

Pug stared back at her in equally blank astonishment.

'Because – because I want to,' he replied, putting his hands up helplessly in the air.

'You don't have to, you know. Just because we held hands – and because you – because you – because you kissed me.' Elizabeth stopped.

'I don't want to marry you because I have to, Elizabeth,' he stuttered. 'I want to marry you because – because . . .'

'Yes?' She looked up at him carefully.

'Because – because I do.'

Elizabeth looked down again but this time it was not from shyness, but in order not to smile because Pug looked so fraught.

'Don't you want to marry me?' he asked rather forlornly. 'I mean, I quite understand if you don't actually want to, but I do so hope you do actually.'

'Oh, Pug,' Elizabeth sighed. 'Of course I want to marry you.'

'You do?'

'Of course I do! I never thought anyone would ever want to marry me – particularly somebody

239

as sweet and as lovely as you, Pug – so of course I want to marry you.'

'You do? You *really* do?'

'Of course I do. It's just that . . .' She sighed, looking suddenly so disconsolate that it was all Pug could do to stop himself from taking her in his arms and embracing her. 'My father will never allow it.'

'But that doesn't matter, dearest!' Pug gasped, sinking suddenly to his knees. 'All that matters is that you want to marry me – and so married we shall be! You are twenty-one, I know you are.'

'Yes, I am twenty-one, Pug. A little too old for marriage, perhaps?'

'No, just the right age because there is nothing or no one can stop us now. We can just – just go and get married!'

'My father will do his best. You don't know my father. He will spoil anything, just for the sake of it.'

'I don't see what he can jolly well do,' Pug returned, after giving the matter thought. 'Not if we organise things properly. Not if we get the licence, and everything is proper and above board. I really don't see what he can do.'

'He will come after me—'

Pug took her in his arms and for once he forgot to be a knut.

'He can come after *me*, but I promise you he will find me a really hard nut to crack.'

Elizabeth stared up at him, and realising what

240

he had just said they both started to laugh, and all before they started kissing, which Elizabeth found she enjoyed even more than on the night of the midnight bathing party.

And so finally the holiday at Waterside House started to draw to its conclusion, and as it did, everyone did their best to pretend they really didn't mind.

By common agreement it had been the very best of all the holidays at Waterside, and to celebrate the fact as well as to try to rid themselves of the unspoken sadness that might otherwise overwhelm them, arrangements were made for a last night dinner and dance, the music to be supplied by Elizabeth at the piano and by records played on the Duchess's phonograph. Before that, however, the bachelors organised a sandcastle-building competition, to be judged by the Duchess, and open to everyone.

There had been many sandcastles built that month, ranging from the modest to the splendid, Harry proving himself to be the uncrowned champion to date with his enormous and elaborate sand fortresses, buildings that increased in complexity and grandeur with every one he built. His castles attracted admiration from everyone, from the family and friends as well as from other holidaymakers, especially two young boys who were also spending many hours of each sun-filled day building their own fortifications a hundred yards or so from Harry's.

They would come and watch him in silence as he constructed elaborate ramparts, towers and moats, lost in admiration and envy before running off to try to put into practice the lessons they had learned. Building sandcastles obviously obsessed them both, so much so that they had set themselves up in competition with each other.

'Why not enter the sandcastle competition?' Harry asked the little French boy, repeating the same suggestion to the German boy.

'Very well, monsieur.'

'Good.'

They both ran off, albeit in different directions.

The day of the competition dawned fine and dry, and work began the moment the tide began to run out, pitches being chosen by all the contestants and the start of the building works signalled by the Duchess dipping the large Union Jack Almeric had brought down from the house.

Four hours later, as the tide turned and began to wash back towards them, everyone's castle was nearing completion, and fine though they were, none could match the magnificence of Harry's latest creation, a fantastic fortress he had been planning in his head for days. But before he could put the finishing touches to the bridge across the second moat, he was distracted by the sound of sudden shouting and screaming to the west of him, from the pitches taken by the two boys who had been building fast and furiously without a break from the moment the flag had dropped.

Harry could see a scrap in progress, the two boys locked in combat, rolling around the beach accompanied by much yelling and shouting. No one from their families seemed to be taking any notice as Harry ran towards them.

'All right, all right!' Harry shouted, arriving on the scene ahead of anyone else. 'That's enough, do you hear? *Arrêtez enfin!*'

He pulled the larger of the two boys off the smaller, who was lying on the sand howling.

'What on earth do you think you two are doing?' Harry wondered, more for his own benefit than theirs as he surveyed the wreckage of the smaller boy's castle.

'Yes, what on earth?' Pug wondered, his monocle dropping out of his eye as he and Almeric joined Harry. 'This is meant to be jolly good fun, chaps.'

'What's happening, Harry? Do you want a hand?'

Harry handed the larger boy over to Almeric.

'*Il est allemand!*' the smaller boy cried. '*C'est ça qui est le problème, monsieur! Il est allemand!*'

'No zat is not it, you stupid boy!' the larger boy now said in broken English. 'What is wrong is that you want *all* the beaches!'

'Zat is really not so, monsieur,' a woman whom Harry took to be the smaller boy's mother called to him. 'Thierry has his bit of the beach, yes, but this brat is always trying to take it.'

'Nein! Zat is not zo!' the German boy yelled. 'Zis was mine first!'

'Oh, come now,' Harry sighed. 'Surely one bit of the beach is much like another bit of the beach?'

'Nein, nein!'

'It is mine!'

'Hang on,' Pug protested. 'It is everyone's, for everyone!'

'But see – see he has so much beaches and I am pushed against the rocks!'

'Well, it really doesn't matter much,' Gus said. 'Because Hans here has ruined Thierry here's castle, so I say we count your castle out of the competition?'

'I think that's fair,' Almeric put in. 'I'm afraid you're disqualified, Hans.'

'My name is not Hans! My name is Pieter!'

'Fine,' Harry said, shaking his head at him. 'Then Pieter is disqualified.'

The boy looked at him furiously, while the man Harry took to be his father shouted something at him in German, as the boy's mother led him away.

'Anyone know what Papa said?' Valentine wondered. ''Fraid I don't speak the Boche.'

'He said that we are stupid too,' Harry said with a shrug. 'All the English are stupid, according to him, most of all for siding with the French – something apparently we shall regret.'

The young men looked at each other and then at the wreckage of the French boy's castle, as the tide began to rush ever more quickly up the beach, only a matter of yards now from where the sandcastles were being judged by the Duchess, who was working her way methodically along the line before the sea flooded everyone's moats.

Chapter Eight

Cupid's Victory

The silence in the library at Bauders had lasted for much longer than Wavell would have desired, but since he could think of no way of breaking it, he took his quiet leave, signalling to the footman to follow him and to close the double doors before heading off to the kitchens with the footman in tow.

'One must always be aware of the times when a family wishes to be left alone,' he remarked to Tommy Taylor. 'This will be one of them.'

'Why? Whatever's up, Mr Wavell?' Tommy enquired. 'Not something one of us has done, I hope.'

'Why should it be anything to do with the likes of you, Taylor?' Wavell returned. 'This is a matter of far greater import. It is a moral dilemma, to do with the young people – the sort of thing that eats at the heart of any family.'

As they went through the pass door on their way to the busy rooms below stairs, Tommy

Taylor frowned to himself and wondered what he might have missed. His mind had been far too full of thoughts of his girl, Tinker, to have taken any real notice of the Duchess opening the telegram that had been presented to her, nor of her subsequent remarks to the Duke. Tommy's head had been in the clouds, remembering fondly the sweetness of his girl's kisses from the evening and wondering when they could steal another half an hour together, to have gathered anything about the behaviour of anyone else, although as he followed Mr Wavell on to the kitchens he wasn't too dreamy not to notice two pairs of feet below the curtain hanging in front of one of the many bolt-holes below stairs, one a pair of riding boots he knew to be Tully Tuttle's and the other a pair of sturdy, sensible shoes that could only belong to Tully's pash, Bridie.

It had to be something in the air, Tommy decided, grinning to himself. Everyone seemed inordinately determined to find their other half, everyone that is with the exception of the ever upright Mr Wavell. But then as Tommy remembered, according to Cook, Mr Wavell was long past it anyway.

In the room Wavell and Tommy Taylor had just vacated, silence still reigned, a quiet broken only by the crackling of the fire that burned in the hearth, whatever the time of year.

'This brouhaha is not going to reflect at all well on anyone, you know,' the Duke finally said, breaking the silence. He was standing where he always liked to stand at such moments of reflection, at one of the long library windows, surveying his beloved parkland, seeing the white deer moving slowly among the trees, grazing the lush green grass and occasionally trying to pull down one of the branches of his precious young trees. 'Least of all you, my dear,' he concluded. 'Not going to reflect well on Waterside.'

'I'm afraid you're right, John,' the Duchess replied, still holding the folded telegram she had just received and tapping it nervously on one elegant hand. 'Of course one had no idea . . .'

'Course you didn't,' John agreed. 'Boys will be boys, don't you know. Particularly when there are pretty young ladies about.'

'I don't think there was any *real* impropriety, John.'

'Don't doubt your word for a moment, my dear. Fact is, however, the two of them have eloped, and there's an end of it. People like to point their fingers and this is just what people will be doing. Should have kept a more watchful eye, they'll be saying behind their wretched fans. Should have kept an eye on the emotional weather.'

'You're absolutely right, of course, John,' Circe agreed. 'I'm most dreadfully sorry.'

'Quite sure you are.' John continued to stare out at the landscape while he considered the situation. 'Since it's fairly obvious we're about to go to war, then we can be pretty sure that when we do that'll scotch any such scandal that follows in the wake of this sort of thing. Most other times this would cause the gravest of embarrassments, but I suppose in light of what's about to happen, it will all blow over, don't you see? It'll prove to be small beer, at a time like this.'

'You are convinced about this, John?' Circe asked, putting the telegram at last to one side. 'You really do believe war to be inevitable?'

'No doubt about it, my dear. Put my shirt on it.'

'I do so hope you're not right, John. Trouble is, you invariably are. You have a way of reading the runes.'

'Any fool can see it, Circe. Don't have to be some kind of prophet fellow. The Kaiser simply cannot wait. He's dying to show us all how big and strong he is, and how weak and feeble we are. Can't be doing with the man, but there you are. That's Germany for you.'

'I simply cannot bear the thought.'

'Which of us can? But that's how it is. Grown men make wars for boys to fight.'

They fell to silence once more, the Duke to stare out over his estate and the Duchess to wish the Wynyard Errol boy had been born with more sense.

'Anyway,' Circe began again, bringing the subject away from the unbearable, back to what she now saw as the truly trivial: the subject of Valentine Wynyard Errol and Livia Catesby's totally unforeseen elopement. 'To return to the news this telegram has brought us: do you know how I felt when I read it? I felt as though I had been betrayed. Absurd, I'm sure, since young people do this sort of thing without any such consideration, but I couldn't help it, John. I felt betrayed.'

The Duke nodded, turning now to face his wife. 'Don't know what they thought they were doing,' he said with a puzzled shake of his head. 'Consolata Catesby is a bigot, it must be faced, and there's nothing to be done there. She'd never have given her consent to Livia marrying the Wynyard Errol boy. Quite apart from the religious side of it, there is the question of the Wynyard Errols being theatricals. You know how many of the Roman Catholics regard the theatre as a place of debauch and temptation, no more and no less.'

'No, I didn't know that, John. I know my mamma's friends were all happy to go to the theatre in New York.'

'Apparently a great many of the more backward of them still think it's sinful to go to the theatre.'

'Surely not nowadays?'

'The absolute sticklers I understand won't even stomach the Bard.'

'Gracious heavens.'

'I'm not being judgemental, my dear. Just factual.'

'I have to tell you that I can never quite understand the notions people have about religion,

John. No one can prove God likes to be worshipped one way more than another, after all, can they, dearest?'

'Rather not, Circe, and if He could tell us, would He? Absolutely not, because it would mean He would be favouring one lot over another, and He wouldn't do that. I have always found religions of all kinds a trifle baffling. On the other hand, Nature,' John said, nodding backwards to the parkland behind him, 'I have no trouble understanding, however red in tooth and claw, but religious feelings that insist on being right, I just don't understand them, truly I don't.'

'Why should you, John? You are by nature tolerant; it is one of your many virtues,' Circe assured him. 'But to get back to the subject of Valentine and Livia – the reason they have run off is obvious, wouldn't you say? They have run off because Livia knows that Consolata would never countenance the match so I suppose the only way open to them *was* to elope. I don't know what gets into people with their young, I really don't. You know about Elizabeth Milborne and Pug Stapleton, of course?'

'Understand wedding bells are in the air, yes.' John grunted. 'From what Al has told me, that is imminent, which is something to celebrate, at any rate.'

'If only it were as easy,' Circe sighed. 'I dare say Almeric has not told you that Elizabeth's father is refusing to give his consent.'

'The devil he is! What is wrong with that man?'

'What is wrong with him, John, is that he takes the greatest pleasure in putting every kind of obstacle in his daughter's way. It would appear the last thing he is concerned about is Elizabeth's happiness.'

'He can't have any feasible objection to young Stapleton? Young Stapleton is a thoroughly decent sort of chap. All right, he is a bit mannered, but there you are, that's only a phase – sort of thing a lot of young men go through, that sort of affectation of speech. But you couldn't meet a more four-square young man. Don't know what the devil is wrong with Milborne, I really don't.'

Circe smiled to herself, amused how, as always, John seemed to know everything that was going on without ever apparently taking much of an interest. She had long suspected Wavell as being the source of the gossip, yet she knew there was more to it than that, because John always seemed to know that little bit more than even a butler could possibly know.

'Just wish all these romances had kicked off somewhere other than your summerhouse,' John said, looking momentarily and uncharacteristically glum. 'I can hear all the gossips at it already.'

'Actually, John,' Circe decided, getting to her feet and going to her husband's side, 'I think we're making a bit too much fuss. What does it matter where or how these things started? They're not children any more – they have wills of their own and emotions the same too. And if what you say is right and there is going to be war, all these young men will be marching off to fight. When and if they do, that really is going to make all these obstacles that have been put in their way look even more stupid and pointless than they are already.' Circe slipped her arm into his, and smiled up at him, at her most beguiling. 'Now why don't we go for a long walk in our park, sweetest? Why don't we go out and enjoy this wonderful weather and talk about all the things we used to talk about when first we met?'

'What sort of things were they, my dearest dear?' John heard himself asking. 'Not sure I can remember that far back.'

'Of course you can,' Circe smiled. 'And what you can't remember, I shall prompt, because I can remember everything we said to each other when we were young and first in love.'

'Dash it, I suppose you can too, Circe,' John said with a sudden shy smile. 'So very well – let's take the air. I should like to hear all the things you said to me when we met.'

'And all the things you said to me,' Circe replied.

Besides recalling how they had met and how John had shyly but successfully wooed her, Circe suggested that rather than worrying about what society was going to say with regard to Valentine running off with Livia, they should do what they could to shore up the happiness of the young lovers, in particular Pug and Elizabeth, who having both reached their majorities were fully entitled to marry whomsoever they wished, regardless.

'Why don't we invite them to get married here at Bauders, John?' Circe suggested. 'If Cecil Milborne is going to be so intransigent about poor little Elizabeth, the least we could do would be to offer to let them marry here.'

'And incur old Cecil's undying displeasure, you mean?' John mused with apparent delight. 'Can't think of anything better. Good for you, my dear. What a good notion.'

'Especially in light of what you think is about to happen,' Circe added, putting her hand in his, which John promptly kissed. 'We could make it a most memorable day.'

When the invitation for Pug and Elizabeth to be married at Bauders had first been extended, Pug had naturally been thrilled and honoured, but now that the fateful day had dawned, and he found himself staring in his shaving glass, he felt the very opposite of all those previous emotions. Now he only felt frightened, nervous and un-worthy. He wanted so much to please his bride-to-be, but his reflection told him a different story. The mirror showed him what he considered to be a plain and unremarkable young man with very little in the way of character, and certainly of wealth, to offer the sweet-tempered and talented young woman who had agreed to be his wife.

'Touch of the collywobs?' Almeric wondered cheerfully as he walked through from his dressing room to discover Pug leaning over the basin supported by both his arms. 'Like me to get you a little shot of brandy, old chap?'

'No, thanks, Al,' Pug said quietly to his best man. 'Just a little nervous, that's all.'

'And only natural too,' Almeric assured him, putting his hands on Pug's shoulders while at the same time staring at his own reflection. 'A small cognac might be just the thing, you know, a shot from the stick at the first meet, eh?'

'Wish I had your looks,' Pug said gloomily, having stared at Almeric's reflection behind him. 'Bethy's getting a very short straw, I'm afraid. I'm the sort of chap cows bolt from in case their milk turns sour.'

'You are absurd, Pug,' Almeric replied sternly. 'You are a dashed good-looking sort of cove if only you let yourself be. Instead of hiding behind that ridiculous eye-glass that you do not *need* – and letting that hair of yours flop all over your eyes, you should drop all that, let people *see* what a good-looking chap you are, Pug. You know what my advice to you on your wedding day is? Give Elizabeth the best present she could have; stop hiding yourself away behind all these silly pretences.'

'Almeric—' Pug began, feeling more than a little hurt.

'Just try it, Pug,' Almeric urged, taking Pug by the shoulders now and standing him up straight. 'Brush your hair like this . . .'

Almeric took a hairbrush and swiftly reformed Pug's hairstyle, with the help of some of Mr Trumper's best dressing, before returning him to stand in front of the glass once more.

'Better already, old chap. See?'

Pug frowned at the stranger he saw staring back at him.

'I can't have that, Al,' he protested. 'I don't have the sort of looks that – no, I really can't have that.'

'Yes, you can – and to prove you can, finish dressing – without your old man's monocle – and if you're still in doubt we'll call Partita in – and Kitty – and get their opinions.'

'No, Al,' Pug continued to protest, as if being asked to perform the most embarrassing of tasks. 'Chaps will just laugh.'

'They will not, Pug, I promise. And if they do – tell you what? I'll foot the bill for the honeymoon.'

As Almeric prepared his friend for the altar he wished with all his heart that he was getting married in his stead, although not to Elizabeth, of course, to his beloved Kitty. He sighed inwardly, remembering his recent conversation with his father, held inevitably in the library at Bauders. It seemed that, like it or not, Kitty had been proved right. His father had reservations about his elder son marrying a Rolfe.

'I understand your point of view,' Almeric had found himself saying. He did not understand at all, but he did appreciate what his father was saying about Evelyn Rolfe, and Kitty's mother, both of whom were never now going to be received by what was known as 'polite society'. 'However, I have to tell you, Papa, no matter what her parents' marriage might be, my feelings for Kitty are not going to go away.'

'I am not asking for them to go away, I am simply asking for you to take a pull, have a year to think about it, only fair to both of you.'

'If I have to wait a whole year for Kitty, Papa, then I shall merely love her three hundred and sixty-five times as much!'

'I'm sure you will, my boy,' his father had assured him. 'It's not what's in your heart that concerns me, it is what is in the bloodlines of the Rolfes. We must all have time to consider, to adjust. A year is a very long time, and who knows how you may both feel at the end of it?'

'I shall feel more, not less, Papa. You will see, but I shall wait, because I would not want to upset you or Mamma.'

So Almeric, for the love of his parents, and perhaps too because Kitty had warned him that this was how it would be, had agreed to wait to be married. Had he not, he would doubtless be standing where Pug was standing, feeling as nervous and apprehensive as he.

'Come and see yourself, Pug,' Almeric beckoned to his reformed friend. 'Because if you are not the very picture of a dashing devil, I don't know what or who is, I don't really.' He turned Pug to a full-length dressing mirror and waited for his final opinion.

'I wouldn't have recognised myself,' Pug said, without affectation. 'I simply would not have given such a thing credit.'

'You look bang up, Pug,' Almeric assured him once again.

'I hope I can carry all this off.'

'There is nothing to carry off, Pug. What you are looking at is the real you.'

Pug nodded and, taking a deep breath, walked to the window, which enjoyed a magnificent view of the parkland. Very soon he would be walking across to the church, and waiting at the top of the aisle for Elizabeth to appear on the Duke's arm. Supposing she changed her mind? Supposing because she had changed her mind, she didn't turn up? Or worse – suppose she did turn up, then seeing what or who she was about to marry, turned and fled? Whatever would he do then? He might shoot himself. Or if his courage failed him in that direction, he would most certainly enlist in the army.

'I don't think I can do it, Al, old friend,' Pug announced, reaching for his monocle. 'Too much of a risk, old bean. She's used to seeing me like this, truly she is.'

'Poppycock,' Almeric said, taking his monocle away and putting it in his own pocket. 'And don't you *old bean* me. You look absolutely splendid and you are absolutely splendid. Now come on, or I shall leave you to flounder all by yourself.'

As they made their way out of the house and started on the short walk to the church, Pug's thoughts now turned nervously to his honeymoon, which was to be spent in a house he and Elizabeth had been kindly loaned on the neighbouring estate, owned by a friend of the Edens. Thankfully he was a little less nervous about the honeymoon than he was about the actual marriage ceremony itself, believing that if Elizabeth did show up at the church the worst part would be over, since one of his more enlightened godfathers had sent his two older sons and Pug to stay with a friend of his in Paris.

'Must further your education, boys,' he had insisted. 'Get to know how the French enjoy themselves, all part of maturing and so forth, go and visit their beautiful poodles in their parlours.'

They had indeed furthered their education, and in so many ways, and at the hands of such beautiful French ladies, that Pug and his friends had returned home not just mature, but enlightened.

'Do you agree with your father, Al?' Pug suddenly wondered as they neared the church.

'On what particular issue, Pug?'

'The situation in Europe.'

'Not now, Pug,' Almeric groaned.

'Your papa says—'

'I can't actually remember a time when Papa

259

didn't think some war or other was coming – or some new form of taxation to bring about his instant ruination. That's Papa. That's older men.'

'I think your father is right, Al,' Pug insisted. 'And if so – in the event of anything happening to me, would you look after Bethy for me?'

'Pug?' Almeric stood in front of his oldest friend and took him by one arm. 'This is just wedding-day nerves, old chap, really. Apparently some chaps become totally addle-pated on their wedding days, but once the deed is done, they're just fine. In fact, they return to normality just like that – so much so that they at once start sticking their fingers in their waistcoats, tapping their fobs if someone is a second late, and so on and so forth. So enough of gloomy thoughts. This is meant to be the day you will remember for the rest of your life, so don't go filling your head with such gloomy stuff, do you hear? Mine neither.'

Pug nodded. Almeric was probably right, and he probably was just suffering from wedding-morning nerves. Even so, once the wedding was over and they were back from honeymoon, he would bring the subject up again with his best friend and best man and get a proper answer out of him. He had to make sure his beloved Bethy would be cared for.

Once she had been given her cue that it was time to leave Bauders for the church, Elizabeth followed her flower maidens and pages down the great oak staircase, watched by every servant in the castle, as was the custom on wedding mornings at the great house, where every member of the household staff was invited to share first look at the bride and her attendants. As soon as they saw Miss Elizabeth, all the maids gasped or sighed in wonder at the beautiful sight, while the men all smiled, nodding their heads appreciatively as Elizabeth walked by them. One or two of the younger maids began to clap, only to be hushed back to respectful silence.

'I don't think I ever saw a bride more beautiful,' Tinker said, her eyes filling with tears, which they always did whenever she saw a bride.

'Is it true her poor mother has been forbidden to attend the ceremony?' Bridie whispered. 'It doesn't seem possible, does it?'

'From what I hear, Lady Maude fully intends to be there,' Tinker whispered back, dabbing her eyes. 'Though as Tommy told me, having had it from one of their footmen, Mr Milborne has washed his hands of both of them, all of them, and no doubt of it at all.'

'God help us indeed,' Bridie sighed. 'Imagine missing your own child's wedding day. What sort of person would do that, I wonder.'

The Duchess had lent Browne, her personal maid, to Elizabeth for the day. She now hovered in the background as Elizabeth and her entourage prepared to leave the house, her small brown eyes darting over every inch of the dress and the veil that she had so carefully arranged.

As far as she could see, her charge was looking

perfect. The silk gown flowed from Elizabeth's slender form, and the veil – a Knowle family veil lent by the Duchess, who had worn it on her own wedding day – billowed out in front of her face and was held in place on Elizabeth's dark hair by the ducal family 'fender' – or 'tirahara' as Bridie insisted on calling it. Behind the veil Elizabeth's face was as pale, white and cool as the alabaster figures in the church.

As the congregation awaited Elizabeth's arrival, the rhythmic waving of the ladies' feather and silk fans caused the Reverend Mr Bletchworth to imagine that he might be not in a church so much as out in the park watching a flock of swans about to arrive on the lake. Meanwhile the church bells in the tower rang out insistently, calling everyone on the estate to witness by their happy sounds the solemn occasion they were all about to celebrate.

It was a fine sunny July morning outside, and the church was packed with wellwishers, most of whom had risen early to procure good places in the little church and so were already thinking hungrily ahead to the sumptuous wedding breakfast that awaited them all. Among the packed congregation, Peregrine smiled happily to himself, and not just for the pleasure of knowing that Pug and Elizabeth were about to become man and wife, but because he was delighted with the present he had chosen for them from Aspreys. It was a little silver galleon whose main mast had been topped, at his insistence, with a small flag engraved with a skull and crossbones.

'For a pirate and his bride,' the note on the gift box read.

Not that Pug and Elizabeth, now they were turning towards each other at the head of the altar, looked at all piratical. In fact they looked every inch the perfect couple, and so obviously in love that it caught at Peregrine's heart just to see the way they looked at each other. He dropped his eyes. One day perhaps he would feel the same about someone, or, perhaps more importantly, one day someone he loved might feel the same about him.

Happily there was no sermon, no endless singing, and not too many readings, so that once the couple had said their vows and signed the registry and all the rest, they were down the aisle in no time at all, and out into the sunshine, swiftly followed by their all too hungry friends.

Elizabeth had no exact idea what a wedding night might entail, other than the fact that greater intimacy would take place than anything she had previously experienced, which had necessarily been very limited indeed. So all she could do as she prepared for bed was to pray very hard that whatever did happen would go well. Even so, once the baggage had been removed from their carriage and they had been ushered into the pretty drawing room, any fears she might have been secretly nursing were soon dispelled. Their honeymoon destination was a small and delightfully cosy Regency house, filled with charm, and so tastefully decorated that it seemed to Elizabeth to be holding out its arms to her, the way Pug was holding out his arms to her now.

'Not now, Pug.' Elizabeth nodded towards the drawing-room door that was now opening slowly to admit a footman and a blushing maid, both carrying trays heaped with all kinds of delicacies.

Eventually they withdrew so that the bridal pair were able to relax, drink champagne, and taste their first real kisses, before enjoying a similarly carefree dinner, so that by the time they were climbing the stairs to their marriage bed they were full of excitement and anticipation as to what the night might hold in store.

As he shaved the following morning, Pug regarded his new look in the glass but this time with a very different attitude. He might not be as tall nor as handsome as Almeric or Peregrine, nor as delightful and appealing as Gus, but thanks to his far-sighted godfather, of one thing he was *quite* sure – he knew how to please a woman. He knew that because he had just spent a great part of his wedding night doing just that, just as he knew from the look of delight and bliss on his beloved Bethy's face as she lay still fast asleep on her pillows that he had indeed succeeded beyond even his dreams.

Had he the energy or indeed the inclination he might well have taken to horse and galloped off to Yorkshire to wring his godfather's hand and thank him personally, but having finished shaving he found he had something infinitely more enjoyable to do for the rest of the morning.

Partita and Kitty, on the other hand, were feeling quite listless and dispirited, as is so often the case after attending the wedding of a friend.

'I think we might all go to town for a few days,' the Duchess finally decided. Noting how dejected the girls seemed to be, she went on in encouraging tones, 'We could go to the music hall and maybe even the circus too. We can send ahead for my London maid, for dear old Weigel to tell Monty to get Knowle House ready for us, perhaps next week. Does that appeal to either of you?'

Partita turned to look at her mother, but since the expression on her face was still so dejected, the Duchess quickly continued, 'We could go shopping for some new and pretty things. I do so need some new gloves, and we could maybe even go to Worth and order some few dresses for autumn. It can do us nothing but good, I imagine. Now that the excitement has died down, we need to have a little innocent distraction.'

'As long as we don't have to go shopping for another wedding,' Partita said in dread, with a look towards Kitty.

'No need for that yet, lovey,' her mother replied. 'Besides, you make it sound as if you have attended Elizabeth's funeral, not her wedding.'

Both Circe and Kitty could not help laughing at Partita, even though Kitty would rather the subject had not been raised. She and the Duchess had discussed the matter of her engagement to Almeric over and over again, and it had now been agreed by all concerned parties that in the circumstances it would be wise to allow for a longer rather than a shorter engagement. Although every time they were together Kitty found Al was chafing at the idea, she herself could see the reasons behind it.

'You are from a very important and distinguished family, Al,' she had told him. 'You must be quite sure that you really do want to marry me, to marry a Rolfe.'

Kitty went to the window and looked out at the park. She knew that she was now entering into that strange state that she had observed in other girls, that of being engaged but not married, of being loved but not considered suitable.

She tried not to let her heart sink as she realised she could still be engaged in a year's time, but then it lightened the moment she saw Almeric far below her in the park. He was riding Slippers, his favourite bay mare, and he looked so dashing and debonair, it suddenly seemed entirely foolish for her to be nursing any worries. What was time compared to love? And even if she was not completely sure whether or not she really loved him as a fiancée should, she knew that because he was such a good man and so fair-minded and attentive, in time she could, and indeed would, learn to love him.

'I've seen photographs of the new season's gowns, darling lovey,' she heard the Duchess telling Partita, 'and I must say they are truly . . .' Circe stopped, searching for the right description.

'Truly fearful?' Partita offered.

'No, Tita,' Circe laughed, standing up. 'Truly interesting. Now, why don't we all go for a walk in the park – after which – alas – I have to call on Mrs Catesby.'

'Poor Mamma,' Partita said, pulling a face. 'I'd rather eat an earwig sandwich than be in your shoes, calling on Mrs Catesby.'

'I should imagine after hearing the news about her daughter and Valentine she would find an earwig sandwich nothing short of a treat, Partita.'

This remark induced a fit of coughing from the footman as he opened the door for the Duchess. She threw him an amused, conspiratorial look, but said nothing.

The blinds all over Consolata's house appeared to be drawn down, Circe observed on her arrival, such was the air of funereal gloom that greeted her as a footman in a much-stained livery with a great deal of stale lard and flour on his malodorous and rancid ancient wig opened the door to her. As always, Circe had to make a special effort to cross the threshold of the house, but such was her determination to see her mission through that she made an even greater effort than normal and stepped into a house that seemed to all intents and purposes to be plunged in mourning.

'Good afternoon, Circe,' Consolata greeted her from the murky depths of the drawing room as the Duchess was shown in. She was standing by the unlit fireplace, dressed in black, wearing as usual the oddest of shoes: a pair of what looked to Circe at first glance very much like oversize galoshes, but which in fact turned out to be some form of medieval pump.

'Good afternoon, Consolata.'

Oblivious to the normal protocol and without inviting Circe to sit, Consolata then sank herself down onto a much worn and very faded brocade sofa, clasping a well-faded handkerchief to her mouth. Choosing a chair that appeared to be less damp and certainly considerably cleaner than anything else on offer, Circe sat herself down and prepared for battle, curbing her impatience at her hostess's self-indulgence.

'To what might I owe this visit, I wonder?' Consolata said from behind her kerchief.

'I have come to see you, Consolata, because I feel that you're holding me in some way responsible for the elopement of Livia.'

'I have no idea what you are talking about.'

'You have every idea, Consolata, of course you have. Now we've known each other far too long not to talk frankly and honestly, so I must admit that I do feel some responsibility as to what has happened, but only indirectly. I have enjoyed my holidays at Waterside for many summers now, in the company of friends both young and older, and nothing untoward has ever happened before. What I think may explain this sudden rush of romances and, I have to say, your daughter's elopement, is the fact that there seems to be a war imminent, and if this is indeed the case then it really is little wonder that young men and women would want to enjoy what time they may or may not have left together. Your daughter . . .'

Consolata's dark eyes regarded Circe with indifference as she interrupted her. 'I do not have a daughter, Circe. Not any more. A son, yes, but not a daughter.'

'Do you realise what sorrow you're building up for yourself, Consolata?' Circe enquired, with a sad shake of her head. 'For you – and for any grandchildren you may yet have? How in heaven's name will Livia and Valentine manage to tell their children that their grandmother refuses to speak to them simply because they married? What kind of loving or spiritual example will that be to them? All that is saying is that their parents' love is wrong, and if that is not misguided and unchristian, for the life of me I do not know what is.'

'I have no idea what you are talking about, Circe,' Consolata insisted. 'I have told you. I have a son, but no daughter.'

Circe took a deep breath, disappointed that the

deliberate mention of grandchildren had seemed to have produced absolutely no effect.

'If there is a war, Consolata, as John thinks there is bound to be,' she then continued, 'imagine how you will feel should Valentine be killed and Livia left a widow with children. How will you feel then? What will your intransigence look like in light of such a loss, I wonder. I can only imagine that an attitude such as yours will bring misery and bitterness, rather than love or consolation, in spite of your apparently tender name. Think to yourself how other people will regard you, a woman of breeding who works so hard for the poor and the dispossessed, who gives so much to others – how does it look that you can take such an attitude to your daughter?'

Consolata stood up at once, her eyes staring with a look that Circe could only later describe to her husband as madness.

'I have a son, Circe,' she all but barked. 'I do not have a daughter! I have a son. I do not have a daughter! Do you hear me?'

'Consolata, Valentine and Livia are married now. In the eyes of God – whose opinion surely matters considerably more than your own – in the eyes of the laws of this land, and, indeed, in the eyes of every fair-minded decent person, their union is legal and nothing you can say, do or think is going to change that.'

'Circe—' Consolata began in warning.

'I insist on being heard, Consolata,' Circe continued, her voice indicating that she was quite prepared to use her superior social rank to do so. 'It is important that you understand what the effects of your attitude might be on perfectly innocent young people. Valentine and Livia are married because they love each other, and they had to run off to get married because they knew that you would do everything you could to forbid it. You consider this was wrong of them, as do society's tittle-tattlers, but they only eloped because of your intolerance. They are almost certain to have children, please God – and if and when they do, you will cast such a terrible shadow over their young lives that you must be mad if you think God is going to reward you for that.'

'I have heard quite enough, Circe,' Consolata insisted, ringing a bell to summon her footman.

'You are a very stupid, stubborn and misguided woman, Consolata,' Circe said with sudden passion, abandoning all her resolutions to be tactful, at the same time rising to her feet. 'You are about to cause much unhappiness, but if you do not have the wisdom to see the folly of your ways, then all I can say is God help you, although I doubt very much that He will. And please do stop ringing that awful little bell. I would much rather see my own way out.'

Circe hurried from the house of gloom and into her carriage as if escaping from some dangerous infection. She had done her best for Livia and for Valentine, but the truth was that Consolata seemed still to live in a time when people considered that life was merely a short journey towards the inevitability which was death; when the virtuous went to Paradise and God's love and mercy, and the not so virtuous were committed to eternal hellfire and damnation. The atmosphere in the Catesby house was that of a place that denied that there had been any kind of Renaissance, a movement that had determined people to raise their eyes upwards and see the beauty of life. Circe herself stared out of the carriage window thinking how different Peregrine Catesby was from his mother and wondering at it, while also marvelling that Livia had finally escaped from the clutches of such a bigoted mother, who had clearly been utterly determined to turn her sweet and lovely daughter into a bitter old maid.

How Peregrine had happened to turn out as he had was a mystery to all those who knew the Catesbys. He was golden, enchanting, kindness and patience itself. Circe knew, as they all did, that it was Peregrine's brilliant and patient coaching that had got Almeric into Oxford, after which, far from considering his duty as coach as being over, he had spent many hours helping Almeric through his three years at university. All in all, how Peregrine had emerged as balanced as he undoubtedly had done from a union as ill sorted as that of Bede and Consolata's, was generally considered to be nothing short of wondrous.

That evening at a small family dinner in the

informal dining room, while the young gossiped, Circe told her husband of her mission to see Consolata Catesby.

'I really did it for the best, John,' she assured him, while knowing all the while that she was also trying to reassure herself. 'I really did try to talk Consolata round.'

'Must have been a bit like trying to talk Queen Victoria into wearing a red dress, I should have thought.'

'It certainly seemed as impossible,' Circe agreed with a smile. 'What a terrible thing to see a rift about to happen in a family, John. Something that might make generations to come so dreadfully unhappy.'

The Duke listened sympathetically, as he could do, since he had a habit of insisting at informal dinners such as this that his duchess sit beside him, considering, quite privately, that there was simply no point in being a duke if he couldn't flout convention and seat his wife where he liked.

'Have to say Consolata's timing isn't too good,' John sighed. 'This is not the very best of times to decide to take a stand against the young.'

The Duke picked up his glass of burgundy and drank it rather too quickly, glancing momentarily after Cecilia, who had hurried out of the room following mention of the fact it had been hinted that Livia might be expecting.

'Something up with your sister?' John asked Allegra.

'She says she's suffering from nerves, Papa,' Allegra replied in a bored voice.

'Hmm. Women's palaver, more like,' her father muttered to himself, nodding to Wavell to refill his glass, before turning to his younger son.

'Thought about a regiment yet, young Gus?' he enquired. 'Possibly high time you should be doing so.'

'I hadn't given the matter much thought yet, Papa.'

'Don't want to leave these things till the last moment, you know, young man.'

'Perhaps we should study some of the portraits in the gallery, Gus,' Circe said, coming to his rescue. 'See which regiment has the most appealing uniform. Why don't we do that?'

But even his mother's swift intervention failed to restore the colour to her younger son's cheeks. Circe knew that, unlike with Almeric, the military life would never appeal to Gus, unsurprisingly since he was the brother who least enjoyed shooting, hunting or indeed even fishing. At heart Gus was a gentle soul, far more interested in music and painting. His mother smiled reassuringly at him, wishing there was some way she could prevent not just Gus, but both her sons from going into the wretched army.

Beyond the pass door, down in the servants' hall, Wavell and Cook were drinking tea and discussing the latest news gleaned from the newspapers.

'Lord alone knows what is going to become of

us, Mr Wavell,' Cook said, putting down the *News Chronicle*. 'There's no going back now.'

Wavell looked up from the *Telegraph* to glance at the faces of the younger members of the household, who were all sitting either at the large table or in easy chairs arranged around the servants' hall, anxious as always to try to keep morale at its highest. He saw a look come into the young men's eyes every time talk turned to the war, and knew that however boastful their talk about how they couldn't wait to give the Hun a bloody nose as soon as they could be off, what they would all infinitely prefer would be for the Kaiser to stop his belligerence and for their leaders to come to their senses and put an end to all the rumours and unease. No one wanted to shoulder arms and be off to trade bullets with people who, to all intents and purposes, were no different from them; young men who at this very moment he imagined to be happily drinking their late night beverages somewhere, smoking their last cigarettes of the day, gazing into the eyes of their loved ones and hoping with all their hearts that tomorrow the world would awaken from what could well turn out to have been just a terrible nightmare.

'They say the enemy will be able to attack us in all these purely unimaginable ways, Mr Wavell,' Cook continued, oblivious of the butler's warning look. 'Not just on land and sea, but by air now, would you believe it? And with all these terrible new guns – and there's even talk of gas now. I mean, what is our world coming to, Mr Wavell? I ask you. All we can do, we people, is to think up some new hell, some new ways of killing each other, I ask you, I really do.'

'Is there any tea still in that pot, Cook?' Wavell wondered, hoping he might be able to distract her from her present train of thought. 'I wouldn't say no to another cup.'

'My sister,' Cook went on, pouring the tea while she spoke, holding the top of the pot in place with a stubby finger, 'my sister over at Leeds, now she's got one boy in Russia, wouldn't you know it? And another in the Balkans, of course, on his way back from India. Talk about being caught in the cross-fire. She wrote me to say she just hopes and prays she sees one of them home safe and sound.'

Sipping his lukewarm tea, Wavell knew there was no stopping Cook in this frame of mind, so he did his best to switch off from the stream of worries Cook was intent on expressing, trying to blank out images of all the young men gathered in the hall in khaki, marching off to war with guns slung on shoulders and packs on their backs; trying not to imagine them wounded, desperately trying not to think of them dead, yet knowing this would be the fate of some, never to return to Blighty, to their home – or to Bauders. Wavell knew what it was like, having fought in the Zulu wars, then been invalided out of the army for wounds received at Cetewayo, before returning safely home, and going thankfully into service. He knew what went through young men's minds when they were faced with making the ultimate sacrifice, just as he knew the only way to fight a war was to believe you would be one of the ones lucky enough to survive it.

Excusing himself from Cook's company, he rose and took himself outside to stand on the steps by one of the back doors, smoke a cigarette and look up at the stars in the summer sky.

And when he did, all he could see far up in the dark blue above him was the face of his son, Harry.

Chapter Nine

Off to War

By the time Circe, her daughters and Kitty had arrived and settled into Knowle House in London at the end of the week, which was also the beginning of the first week in August, it appeared all hope of peace had been abandoned and Germany was mobilising. By Sunday, news was announced that Germany had declared war on Russia and had also attacked the all but defenceless Luxembourg.

'I am so excited I can hardly sleep,' Partita told Kitty that night. 'Imagine being alive at such a time as this! With these simply enormous armies all marching through Europe, set on knocking the blazes out of each other! It's like playing toy soldiers except without the toys.'

'I'm afraid I don't find it as exciting as you do.' Kitty turned away to go to the window, as if by staring hard, she could stop the war. 'I find it frightening.'

'But something frightening is also quite

thrilling, don't you think? Do you know what someone said the other day? Someone told Papa that not *if* but *when* war does break out, there will probably be over fourteen million men fighting. Can you think of such a number because I can't. *Fourteen million*, Kitty! That's like the whole world being up in arms!'

'Fourteen million . . . ?' Kitty shook her head, unable to accept such a preposterous estimate.

But nothing could contain Partita's excitement, and to judge from the prevalent atmosphere in the city she was not alone. Everyone seemed suddenly to be in a hurry, rushing to buy newspapers that were becoming ever more scarce, congregating on street corners to share the latest news, getting up on soap boxes, either to predict the end of civilisation or the need for all fit and healthy young men to join up and help save France – France, once the oldest enemy, being now the latest, and most unlikely, of Britain's allies.

The Monday after the Duchess and her family's arrival saw everyone joining in the rush to the shops to stock up on what people saw as vital supplies, a particular run being made on gunsmiths who suddenly found themselves selling more firearms and ammunition than in living memory, due to the ever-increasing rumours of possible invasion. These rumours were greatly exacerbated by reports of a naval engagement having already taken place off the coast of Yorkshire.

All in all, by the time the party from Knowle

House and their guests took their seats in the Coliseum on the Tuesday evening for the variety show, it would seem that the entertainment everyone had paid to see was being really rather overshadowed by the news.

'Such a thing!' an acquaintance of Circe exclaimed to her after they had taken their seats. 'Armageddon in Europe! Can you imagine?'

'I have no idea what you can possibly mean, Edith,' Circe replied. 'Unless you mean that as a result of all this talk of war you are actually looking forward to the end of the world?'

'I mean, dear Circe, that what we have all been hoping for is about to happen,' Edith replied with great gusto. 'Namely, teaching Johnny Foreigner to mind his manners – and long overdue, I do say!'

'That is hardly Armageddon, Edith,' Circe insisted, her voice sounding a little more American, even to herself. 'And by Johnny Foreigner I take it you mean Germany.'

'Of course! Who else? And all those perfectly dreadful allies of hers! One only hopes this wretched wishy-washy Liberal Government doesn't go and spoil the party by declaring us neutral.'

'With that you would have to agree, Mamma,' Partita whispered from behind her theatre programme. 'It would be simply *awful* to desert poor little France.'

'Poor little France indeed,' her mother returned, raising her eyebrows at her youngest daughter. 'I may be American darling lovey, but as I remember it from my history lessons, France was neither poor nor little when Bonaparte was busy making his empire, and enjoying lying in it too.'

Even the orchestra striking up the overture for the evening's entertainment barely silenced the audience, who continued to talk and argue well into the music and at every break in the action. The atmosphere was unlike anything any of the audience had experienced before, and although the theatre was barely silent throughout the entire bill, the excitement seemed only to enhance both the performances and the general enjoyment. After the performers, led by the bill toppers, Charles Hawtrey and Fedorova, had taken their bows to enthusiastic applause, the theatre manager walked onto the stage and held up his arms for silence.

'Ladies and Gentlemen, I have to make an announcement! His Majesty King George has announced that we are at war with Germany!'

There was a brief moment of hush before the entire audience erupted into even wilder applause, greater than anything that had been heard that night. Cheering broke out round the theatre as men got to their feet and threw their hats in the air, while the women clapped and embraced one another, relieved that at long last the period of waiting and uncertainty was over and now the country could finally pick up its guns and get at the enemy.

'Everyone's off down the Mall,' Peregrine

informed them all as their party gathered outside the theatre. 'We're going to the Palace. Any of you girls want to come?'

Partita immediately volunteered, taking the reluctant Kitty by the hand as she sought her mother's permission.

'I don't think so, Partita,' Circe replied. 'I think there'll be a bit of a crowd and I'm not sure it will be quite the place for you.'

'Oh, no, please?' Partita begged. 'This is history being made, Mamma! Please, I don't want to miss a moment of this.'

'I know, lovey,' Circe replied. 'But I think just the boys must go on this occasion. In case things get out of hand.'

'We'll tell you all about it, Mischief,' Peregrine assured Partita. 'I do think it'll be a bit of a scrum and that your mother may be right.'

'Spoilsport,' Partita returned sharply, pulling her arm, which Peregrine had taken, away from him.

'Mamma is right,' Allegra said, taking her younger sister by her other arm to lead her to where their carriage was waiting. 'It really wouldn't be very seemly.'

'Well, war is hardly seemly! There are going to be far greater mêlées than a bit of a scrum outside Buckingham Palace!'

'And you're not going to be in those either.' Cecilia took Partita's free arm to take charge of her furious younger sister as she saw Allegra suddenly running after James.

'Now what's up?' Partita said, watching Allegra. 'I thought we were all meant to be going back with Mamma.'

'She thinks James is going to enlist,' Cecilia told her.

'Not tonight, surely. That's ridiculous.'

'As soon as he can. Allegra's sure she's seen that look in his eyes that men are supposed to get – you know – when their blood's up? Like out hunting?'

Partita frowned. It had never really occurred to her before, at least not in realistic form, that this was what was going to happen. Matters such as people volunteering to fight had all been in the abstract, all part of her imaginings and although she had taken in all the talk about suitable regiments for Gussie, and Almeric returning to his own regiment in the near future, somehow she had managed to avoid thinking of them actually leaving the shores of England, crossing the Channel and fighting where fighting was to be. Now with mention of Allegra's fiancé possibly enlisting just as soon as he could, reality started to make itself felt. War was actually about those you loved going away, perhaps for a long time, perhaps for ever.

'Can we go home now, Mamma?' she pleaded, seeing James suddenly leaning forward and kissing Allegra tenderly on the cheek as the crowds that had collected already made their way past the couple towards St James's and on to the Mall. 'I really do think I would like to go home.'

Allegra joined them minutes later, silent and preoccupied.

'Anything the matter, dearest?' Circe wondered as the carriage began to head back to Knowle House. 'You're very quiet.'

'Now that war is declared, James wants us to get married as soon as possible, Mamma,' Allegra replied. 'By special licence.'

'I see,' Circe said, taking her daughter's hand. 'Then we must speak to Papa.'

Everyone fell silent now, each wrapped in her own thoughts, watching as the crowds hurried by outside, many of them running ahead to join the ever-growing throng headed for the Palace. It was as if, far from actually starting, the war was already over and the country was celebrating, for many of the throng were drunk, and the rest just high on the emotion of the moment, shouting and singing, thrilled, it seemed, at the thought of giving the Kaiser a bloody nose.

'I wonder what we shall all do?' Circe said, breaking the silence. 'We shall have to do something. More than anything we shall have to do something at Bauders.'

'What sort of thing, Mamma?' Partita wondered.

'We can't just do nothing, dearest one. It's all going to be so very different now. We must return to Bauders at once.'

'I don't see what we can do at Bauders that we couldn't do in London, Mamma,' Cecilia said. 'I suppose we could knit or something. I read the other day that if war did break out, what women can do to help the cause is to knit.'

'I think we're going to have to think of something more than knitting, Cecilia. We are all going to have to consider our talents, such as they are. We have to use our skills, our talents, our abilities. If the men are to fight—'

'But isn't that what men are for?' Partita wondered idly, earning looks from both her sisters. 'You know what I mean. Women can hardly go to war, can they? War isn't something women wage. I don't see what's so terrible about that. Women . . . I don't know . . . women cook . . . women knit as well. I know! Women nurse. We could all become nurses. Couldn't we? They're going to need nurses, and I have an even better idea. Seeing what a brilliant surgeon you are, Mamma – not forgetting your terrific interest in medicine – we could all become your nurses and turn Bauders into some sort of a hospital!'

'A hospital?' Allegra wondered. 'What do you mean, Tita – what sort of a hospital?'

'That is really a *very* fine idea,' Circe said, holding up a hand in warning. 'A hospital for soldiers, for recovering soldiers. We could never learn all the skills necessary to run a real hospital, but with some sort of training and the fact that Bauders is so huge, we could turn it into a recovery hospital for those unfortunates who get wounded in battle. That is really a *very* good idea indeed, Tita darling – and one we shall begin to act upon as soon as we get home – which we must do immediately.'

The following morning, as Circe was making arrangements to visit her London chemist, as well as the family gunsmith, she was nearly knocked off her feet by Gus, rushing precipitously down the stairs, headed for the front doors.

'Has the house caught fire, Gussie? Or have you perhaps caught sight of a particularly pretty girl passing by?'

'I'm off to meet Al, Mamma – don't worry,' Gus gasped, taking hold of his mother's hands and making sure she was all right. 'I have decided on his regiment, at last.'

'Gussie dearest?' Circe interrupted him, holding on to his hands. 'One moment—'

'Don't have the time, Mamma! I have to meet him at the Ritz! It's all arranged!'

'No, Gussie,' Circe insisted. 'It is not all arranged. You don't have to go rushing off to enlist now. There is plenty of time—'

'No, Mamma. You are wrong. There is not plenty of time! Nor am I too young! There was an appeal in *The Times* yesterday for all able-bodied men between the ages of eighteen and thirty to join the army, and there is certainly not all the time in the world because heavy firing has been heard from Margate and there is every chance of a snap invasion.'

'No, Gussie,' Circe insisted, keeping a firm

hold on his hands. 'Not yet, dearest – please. You must be a little more patient and a little less impetuous. If you are needed at a later stage, then so be it, but for now, please.'

'Mamma.' Gus eased himself free, and looked at her, suddenly serious, much older than his barely eighteen years. 'Almeric is to return to his regiment. James is enlisting this morning, and Peregrine too. I'm not going to stay back like some – like some milksop. I have to go with them. I shall be perfectly all right, Mamma. I learned all the drill, all our basic training at school.'

'No, there really is no need, Gussie,' Circe heard herself insisting. 'This morning, in the newspaper, there was every indication this is just going to be a storm in a teacup. The Germans have already been thrown back with very heavy losses at Liège – where apparently the Belgians were quite splendid and put the enemy to flight. People are saying that now Germany has been foolish enough to declare war on France, Belgium, Russia *and* ourselves, they have absolutely no chance whatsoever.'

'Excellent!' Gus laughed. 'Then if that's the case, Mamma, you have absolutely nothing to worry about!'

With that her younger boy prised himself free, blew her a kiss and was gone.

'Chloroform too, Mr Russell,' the Duchess told her chemist, after having inspected the mountains of goods that he had assembled on her behalf.

'Chloroform, Your Grace, most certainly,' the chemist replied, hurrying away to fetch the anaesthetic.

'For the wounded or for ourselves, Mamma?' Partita wondered, inspecting the ever-growing mound of medical supplies being assembled on the counter.

'Let us hope just for the wounded,' Circe replied, checking her supply list. 'I shall have all this sent on. We shall never manage all this ourselves.'

'If the war is going to be as short and sweet as everyone says, Mamma,' Partita continued, stacking the bandages into neat rows, 'shall we really need all this?'

'In the likelihood of it being surplus, lovey, we can always return it to Mr Russell here,' Circe said, with a nod at the now returned chemist. 'It is always better to be in hand than out of it. Now we must go on to Messrs Block and Sons before we turn for home.'

'What on earth Mamma wants with a gun and bullets I do not know,' Partita said to Kitty as they waited in the carriage outside the family gunsmiths. 'She has a small army at Bauders to defend her, and I don't think she has ever fired a shot from a gun in her life.'

'It's all this talk of invasion, Tita,' Kitty replied. 'I'm sure it's all an exaggeration, the way newspapers always seem to exaggerate things, but they do recommend that wherever possible

288

people should be ready to defend themselves, just in case.'

Partita shuddered. 'Imagine. Some horrid Hun rushing up the drive intent on raping us all. Imagine.'

'There would possibly be more than one, Tita,' Kitty smiled. 'Certainly if there was only one I don't think he'd have much chance of success.'

'Do you want me to shoot you if you're in that sort of danger, Kitty? Because I most certainly want you to give me the bullet if that sort of thing looks like happening.'

'It won't, Tita.'

'Just in case it does, promise me?'

Kitty looked at her friend and took her hand. 'It won't happen, Partita, it really won't.'

'If you won't shoot me, I shall shoot myself. I shall shoot both of us. Or I shall drown myself in the lake. I am not letting any Hun near me.'

Circe arrived back and climbed into the carriage.

'We have just decided to shoot ourselves if the enemy get to Bauders, Mamma,' Partita said. 'No Hun is ever going to lay a hand on any of us.'

'I dare say we shall leave all the shooting to the men, dearest,' Circe said.

'You've just been to get yourself a gun.'

'A four ten, Tita. On your father's orders. He says if there's to be a food shortage and we're short of men at Bauders, I must learn to shoot rabbits. Talking of which – your father, I mean – we spoke by telephone this morning and he has given his consent to James and Allegra to marry by special licence. I just hope they can arrange it before James goes off to France, but since he has already joined up I somehow doubt it.'

'How do you know he will be called to France, Duchess?' Kitty enquired. 'Isn't the war to be fought in Belgium?'

'Not according to the Duke, Kitty,' Circe replied. 'He doubts whether Liège will hold since apparently the Belgians are hopelessly out-numbered twenty-five thousand to one hundred thousand. As my husband always says, it isn't the best side that wins wars, just the one with the most soldiers.'

'But, Mamma—' Partita began.

'No more, Partita dearest. Let us just enjoy this little bit of peace while we may.'

'I thought it was all going to be over in a week, Mamma?'

'And so it might still be, lovey. We've only been at war for two days.'

A shock awaited Circe when she returned to Knowle House that morning where she learned from Kelly, the under-butler, that Weigel, her London maid, had met with some trouble.

'What happened to you, Weigel?' she enquired with great concern when her maid finally appeared in the drawing room, with cuts to her cheeks and a badly swollen eye. 'Who did this to you? How did this happen?'

'I vos in ze market for Your Grace's usual tasties from ze continental bakery – ze vuns zat you enjoy so greatly – and zis happen me! Zey throw zings at me. Zey call me all zese terrible names. Ze same peoples I have been meeting vith for years.'

'But this is terrible, Weigel,' Circe said, sitting her maid down. 'Simply unforgiveable.'

'Filsy Hun, they calls me,' Weigel sighed. 'Go back to your filsy country, zey say. A woman hit me mit her fist. So.' Weigel clenched her own hand and held it up in demonstration.

'You can't stay here in that case, Weigel,' Circe decided. 'If this is the way things are to be, then you must come up to Bauders.'

'Perhaps in truth I should go back to Germany, Your Grace. Perhaps zis would be ze best for us all, I am thinking.'

'That is entirely up to you, Weigel. If that is what you want to do then that is what you must do. On the other hand, if you wish to stay here then I insist you come with us to Bauders. I don't imagine for a moment the Duke will be keeping Knowle House as a private residence if the war is protracted, so if you don't return to Germany then you will have to come to Bauders anyway.'

'You are most kind, Your Grace,' Weigel replied. 'I must suppose ze same sing is happening in Germany to any English zat are zere.'

'I'm dreadfully afraid it might be, Weigel. Once peace is gone and war has broken out, then we must expect a lot of visits from the Lord of Misrule.'

Perhaps because she had been in England

291

since she was a girl, Weigel decided not to return home to Germany, but to accept the Duchess's invitation, after which Circe prepared to leave London, only to find matters such as keeping a German as a maid were not as easy as she had thought.

'You won't be allowed to bring Weigel here, Circe dearest. She is due to be interned, as a foreign national.'

'I've never heard such a thing – where did you hear that, John?' Circe stared at the Duke.

'Friend from the FO, my dear.' Despite frequent reminders that it was not necessary, John was in the habit of shouting down the telephone. 'Tom Bailey told me at the club yesterday. All German nationals will be interned, no matter what. They've already uncovered half a dozen or so spies – stealing military secrets, that sort of thing.'

'Yes, but not Weigel, John. She wouldn't even steal a recipe.'

'Of course I'm sure you're right, my dear. But don't you see this is war now, and the rules of engagement make everything entirely different from how it was before. Nothing to be done.'

Circe was furious. Weigel had been with her since before her marriage, and a more faithful, kind, sweet-natured and diligent woman would be hard to find. Yet Circe knew there was nothing she could do about it, although she blamed herself for what was about to befall her maid; Weigel had stayed in London because of

Circe and now it seemed she was to be interned for her loyalty.

But that was not the only upset Circe was to experience before she finally left for Bauders. Allegra was waiting for her when she returned from the telephone room, pacing in a state of visible agitation.

'Mamma,' Allegra began, not knowing or even seeming to care whether or not this was a good time, 'I am not coming back to Bauders with you all. I've made my mind up, so there is little use in protesting or trying to dissuade me because my mind *is* quite firmly made up. I'm going to stay here in London and learn how to nurse. Properly, I mean. I'm enrolling at the London Hospital, and while James is abroad I shall learn how to be a nurse in case they're going to need nurses – which, according to everyone to whom I have already spoken, is almost certainly going to be the case.'

Circe nodded, took Allegra's hand, and sat her down beside her on the sofa.

'Far from opposing the idea, I completely embrace it,' Circe said. 'I think that is a very positive idea indeed, believe me. Did I not say last night that we must all play our part? So what is this but playing a very big part? Of course you must do this – and I know Papa will understand and agree with me.'

'Oh, thank you, Mamma!' Allegra exclaimed, hugging her mother. 'I really thought you would forbid it!'

'Perhaps if it had been Partita I might have had second thoughts, but not you. But you must take care. There are all sorts of forecasts being made – about what might happen in London, above all from the Zeppelins. Whatever you do, you must learn to keep a weather eye on the skies. Not that I think the Kaiser will allow his army to bomb innocent citizens, not if he is as civilised as he claims. But even so, you must promise always to be on your guard.'

'Of course I will, Mamma. I promise.'

'I don't believe for one moment the Kaiser would allow such a thing,' Circe said again. 'It's not the sort of thing a gentleman could possibly condone, least of all someone who prides himself on being an aristocrat.'

But Allegra was not listening. All she was thinking about was that by staying in London she would be nearer to her beloved James when he came home, which of course she was certain that he would.

Chapter Ten

Goodbye to So Much

Harry, having learned of the family's return from London, took it upon himself to be particularly visible in the hope one of the younger members of the family might see him and bring him up to date. Of course he had to be tactful, for despite the fact that he had been born and raised on the Bauders estate, he still felt shy of simply presenting himself at the house. No matter that he had been in *The Pirates of Penzance* and had been to Waterside House for the holiday, rather than foist himself on the members of the family, especially the young women, Harry much preferred to be invited. So it was that as he busied himself in the stills room, where the Duchess had famously removed the shot from the beater's backside, Kitty came across him shortly after the family's return.

'Harry? Goodness, how delightful to see you.' Kitty stopped. 'What a stupid thing to say, why wouldn't I see you? I don't know why but just at this minute I hardly expect to see anyone of our age at all, everything being so awfully topsy-turvy.'

Not unnaturally, the ensuing talk was mostly of the war, once the social niceties had been observed. Harry was intrigued to learn of Partita's excitement over the declaration of war, and the scenes of jubilation that followed the announcement when they were at the theatre.

'People become so excited by war; they always have,' he said, not looking at Kitty in case she felt quite the same sense of euphoria.

'I hardly dare say it,' Kitty confessed, 'but I feel nothing but a sense of awful dread, quite different from everyone else. It's not that I'm not patriotic, because I am, but I keep remembering Waterloo, and – and, well, you know, battles like that. They were not very pleasant.'

'At the famous ball before the battle, the young men drank lemonade.' Harry turned and gave Kitty a rueful look. 'It doesn't bear thinking about, does it? Going into battle against the French with nothing to give you Dutch courage except lemonade.'

'I don't suppose the French were asked to muster a fighting spirit on lemonade. I expect Napoleon brandy was *their* refreshment. You know Almeric, James – oh, and Gussie – have joined up? Almeric has rejoined his regiment, and the others have volunteered.'

'My father is set against me volunteering,' Harry said as, having finished in the stills room, they went outside to sit on a still unrepaired part of the wall, where a few of the estate gardeners were now hard at work, starting to create the Duchess's new garden. 'I suppose my father's stance is perfectly understandable, what with him being alone in the world except for me as family. Not that he hasn't his other family here at Bauders, with all the servants and everyone. But I'm my father's future and I don't think he can see beyond that. Much as he loves working here, he doesn't want me to follow in his footsteps—'

'I can understand that – sorry, I didn't mean to interrupt.'

'That's perfectly all right.' Harry paused, and smiled. 'I don't mind.'

'I was just going to say that obviously things never stay the same, and even if there hadn't been a war, one can sense there are changes in the air already,' Kitty finished.

'It's got a lot to do with this government, obviously,' Harry said, nodding his agreement. 'You can sense they want to cut everyone down to size, to level things off as it were, and if that's the case, then all this' – Harry gestured around them – 'will be very different, and we have to imagine an awful lot of changes around here, nothing quite the same.'

'And particularly now we're at war, Harry. The men were all saying at dinner the other night – and this was before war had actually been declared – that there would be changes coming, social changes – that they had to happen.'

'Yes, but that was because everyone knew there was going to be a war, Kitty.'

'Just as much as everyone hoped there wouldn't be.'

'I don't know about that. You should have heard some of the talk round here. People were getting pretty shirty about the government because everyone had sort of got to thinking that Asquith wouldn't fight – that he wouldn't go to Belgium's aid, and France's. You get the feeling that when we're at peace, all an awful lot of people are waiting for is the chance for another war, for all sorts of reasons.'

'As long as they don't have to fight it. One does notice really that most of this belligerence comes from the older people who know they won't be the ones shouldering arms.'

Harry turned and looked at Kitty, appreciating as he always did the brightness of her mind and the economy of her thought. Kitty caught the look and smiled at him, something she had not intended to do.

'Come on,' he said, suddenly dropping his gaze and hopping down off the wall. 'Let's go and walk by the lake, and imagine it's all frozen over again as it was at Christmas.'

Kitty knew she should be doing busy things, but instead she found herself walking side by side with Harry along the path through the ancient bluebell woods and on towards the lake where only a few months before they had all been skating.

'Anyway, to return to the subject in hand,' Harry was saying, pretending not to mind that she had politely refused the offer of his arm. 'My father says that if I am to join up then I should only do so when there really is no danger whatsoever. So I suggested that perhaps I should volunteer after the war is over, that that would be the best time,' he joked.

'So what are you going to do, Harry?' Kitty wondered, her heart growing heavy since she already knew the answer. Much as she disliked the thought, she knew that any young man of merit and virtue had no alternative but to join up. It was called duty. Yet Kitty knew it was something more than that. People could not be, and were not, simply dutiful, not when the cause was wrong or unjust. But when the cause was right and proper, young men were willing to sacrifice their lives in order to save the lives of others. It might be imagined that it is a very beautiful and proper thing to die for one's country, but what men really died for was *other* men, for everyone they knew and loved, and since she also knew Harry, she was less than surprised by what he said next.

'I'm going to join Al's regiment,' Harry told her. 'Al said he'll look after us all and that there actually is less chance of something happening to all of us if we're in the same regiment, and we'll have a hell of a party.'

'Is this something you intend to do soon?'

'I'm going to see the recruiting officer tomorrow.

Al has already put a word in for me, so that's that, really. Anyway, from what I gather from the news, the Germans are not finding it as easy as they hoped. Liège still holds – in fact my father told me word has it that twenty-five thousand Germans have fallen there.'

'That is awful,' Kitty said quietly. 'Twenty-five thousand . . . I know they're the enemy, but twenty-five *thousand* . . .'

'They want a truce so they can bury their dead, but it's not been granted, which is despicable.'

'What nation can sustain losses like that? Twenty-five *thousand* – in just one siege.'

'I don't think any nation can, Kitty,' Harry said, skimming a flat stone skilfully across the placid waters of the lake. 'Then two German warships more or less committed suicide by leaving neutral waters with us in full pursuit. They chose to go down with all guns blazing, apparently, rather than surrender. After which there's a very big rumour that Japan are about to come in on our side, so really perhaps this *is* the best time for me to join up!'

Harry laughed and threw some more stones across the lake, handing Kitty some for her to try her hand. But Kitty declined, standing instead by the water's edge and imagining it to be the sea.

The following day Harry took himself off into town in the hope of enlisting in Almeric's regiment, his application being considered by a stern recruiting officer whom he considered to be about the same age as his father.

'Wrong regiment, son,' the officer said when he was halfway through taking Harry's particulars. 'No can do.'

'It's the right regiment, sir, if you'll excuse me,' Harry replied politely, his natural good manners sharpened into deference by the smartness of the man's uniform and general demeanour. 'I'm absolutely sure of it, sir.'

'You might be sure of it, son, just as sure as I am that it is not the right one.'

The recruiting officer put an end to the matter as far as he was concerned by defacing Harry's application with a huge pencilled X.

'I don't understand, sir,' Harry said. 'Is there something wrong with my – my credentials?'

'You could say that, son, although if it was up to me I'd have you in like a shot. A likely lad such as you, just the ticket for the army – but not this regiment I am very much afraid.'

'But – but I have a personal recommendation, sir, from one of the regiment's officers. The Duke of Eden's son, Lord Almeric Knowle, he's a friend, and it was he who said I should apply.'

'Very impressive too, son, but, with all respect, your friend the marquis, or whoever, should pay attention to the regimental mandate. Were he to do so, son, he would discover that you do not qualify for the regiment.'

'I don't qualify?' Harry looked at the hardened

old recruiting officer. 'Then tell me what I have to do to qualify, sir, and I'll set about it at once.'

'Very well, son. If you want to qualify for your friend's regiment, you will have to go back to school.'

'What? I need – what? – I need better examination results, do you mean?'

'I mean nothing of the sort, son. I mean you will need to go back to school but not only will you need to go back to school, you will need to go to a *different* school. A school as itemised and delineated here in the regimental mandate.' The recruiting officer opened a handbook at the relevant page and handed it to Harry. 'The regiment does not admit young men what have been to a grammar school, son.'

'That's ridiculous,' Harry muttered, his confusion now turning to anger. 'How can it matter where I went to school when it comes to joining the army?'

'I do not make the rules, son. My job is to see they are obeyed. To the very letter. The regiment what you wish to join has very strict rules as to whom it may recruit and admit, and grammar school boys and lesser are not included. But don't let that put you off, son. There are plenty of other regiments – fine ones too. Here's a list of the county regiments, for a start, and if you want I can go through them with you, and mark your card.'

Harry took it but didn't bother either to read it, or to ask for guidance. He simply stuffed it in his pocket and, excusing himself, left the room to wander the town until he could see the sense in what he had learned: that while the army, in its munificence, was quite happy to take you into its ranks and throw you on the sacrificial pyre, certain members in its serried ranks would rather not have you fighting and possibly dying anywhere near them if you had been unfortunate enough to go to the wrong school.

He found such prejudice almost impossible to believe, even after a couple of bottles of the local strong ale taken in a pub not far from the recruiting office, where several young men were busy arming themselves alcoholically in order to have the courage to present themselves for recruitment. They were local boys, for all the world like so many of the young men working at Bauders in the house or in the grounds, young men of open countenance and seeming high spirits, well-built lads with strong hands and limbs, some of them good-looking, others plain, but all of character, all of them what his father would call 'sons of the earth', many of whom Harry knew would soon be returning there to be buried, perhaps full of lead and shrapnel.

While he sat watching them laughing and joking, as they sank their pints until it was generally decided amongst them that they had drunk enough to go and take the King's shilling, it was as much as Harry could do not to go and bang on their tables, send their pint pots flying and tell them all they were going to waste their young lives – that it simply wasn't worth it, that much as they would be flattered and cajoled into joining some glorious old regiment, all they really were – young men like them – was cannon fodder; more bodies to make up the numbers, another half-dozen lads to fall among the other twenty-five thousand at the next siege, or in the next battle.

But of course he didn't do any such thing. He just sat drinking his beer in the knowledge that when it was finished he too would find his way back to the recruiting office, re-present himself and seek advice as to which of the local regiments would take him, which one would accept a lowly grammar school boy, which one could find it in themselves not to mind what your social rank might be as long as you could swell its numbers and willingly go to your death with the best, and the worst, of them.

'Wavell?' the examining medical officer called to him from the door to his surgery. 'If you would be good enough to come back in here, please?'

Harry put down the magazine he'd been reading, wondering why he had been asked to stay in the waiting room, rather than be given a quick and clean bill of health like the half a dozen young men who had gone in before him. Silently he joked to himself that he might yet again have chosen another wrong regiment, whose MO had only just discovered Harry hadn't been to either Eton or Harrow, or at the very least Winchester.

'Now then, young man,' the medical officer said, 'I'm afraid it's not good news.' He cleared his throat. 'You've failed.'

'I beg your pardon, sir?' Harry returned. 'I've failed what? I don't quite understand.'

The officer sighed, tapping Harry's papers into order on his desk. 'I mean you have failed your medical,' he said sadly.

'I can't have done.'

'You just have, *let* me assure you – you have.'

'There must be some mistake,' Harry said grimly. 'This is some kind of a bad joke. First of all I can't join the regiment I wanted to join, and now—'

'It isn't a bad joke, Wavell,' the officer interrupted kindly. 'Alas. Although I have to say normally when I fail men they all but jump for joy, but it seems you really want to fight.'

'Why else do you think I'm here, sir?'

'Mmm. Well, you're certainly not like most of the others I've examined today. Mainly they've been too drunk even to take off their shirts without help. They're the traditional type of recruit – the ones who wake up to find themselves in uniform. However, much as I'd like to pass you for your sake – not mine – alas I cannot, because you have a problem with your heart.'

'My *heart*? There's nothing wrong with my heart, doctor. If there was anything wrong with my heart—'

'I'd be one of the first to find out, young man. It's one field I happen to know rather a lot about, and you have what is known as a murmur. And any young man who has anything even remotely wrong with his heart, I fail. Those are my orders.'

'There is nothing whatsoever wrong with my heart, sir. If there was I wouldn't be able to do half the things I undertake, let alone all the things I do,' Harry protested. 'I'm as fit as a fiddle.'

'You have a heart murmur, Mr Wavell,' the doctor replied, consulting Harry's forms. 'It won't kill you, it won't incapacitate you, not unduly. But it will have to be monitored regularly in case of deterioration. When I say it won't kill you, it won't, not under normal circumstances – but war isn't what we regard as a normal circumstance and under the stresses and strains of battle, even the stresses and strains of training for battle, you might suffer a sudden deterioration, or to put it another way, some sort of heart attack, and my instructions are not to pass anyone with this sort of weakness. The army does not consider it worth spending money on any soldier who will not return their investment in full.'

Harry stared at the doctor and the doctor regarded him back just as unequivocally. It was obviously a time for rules, and Harry had just been on the receiving end of two of them. Not socially good enough for a top regiment and not physically sound enough for an ordinary one. He had begun the day in high hopes, proud of himself for having the courage to go and enlist at a time when it appeared, due to recent heavy setbacks, that the war was not going to be as easy nor as short as initially hoped, and confident that he was well and truly up for the hard training he knew he would have to undergo in order to make a good infantryman. Now he had failed on two counts, the second one not even allowing him the alternative of choice that his first failure had permitted.

'So what now?' he asked the doctor after he had heard the full details of his medical condition. 'Isn't there anything I can do?'

'Plenty, I imagine, if you're that keen, which you obviously are, Mr Wavell. There are all sorts of auxiliary jobs, you know – ambulance driver, stretcher bearer, medical orderly. Even useful and important jobs in civvy street. So don't worry – your determination to help won't go to waste, young man. Now, if you'll excuse me, I have an awful lot of young men to examine.'

'How long does it take to train to be a doctor?' Harry wondered suddenly.

'Too long, Mr Wavell,' the doctor replied with a frown. 'You want to be a *doctor*?'

Harry nodded. 'How long does it take to train?'

'Far too long. A minimum of five years, in peacetime. But in wartime . . .' He stopped and regarded Harry. 'You're obviously very determined, which is admirable, I can see that, but what I can't see is you having enough time to qualify as a proper doctor.' He stopped again. 'We're going to need all the ambulance drivers we can get. And stretcher men. And orderlies. If you're prepared to undertake any of those duties they require very little training.'

'I see. Well – if you think that's what I should be doing—'

'I think it's what you *could* be doing. It's not up to me to say what you should be doing.'

'Of course,' Harry said. 'Thank you. I think that's good advice. Thank you.'

'Have a word with the chap at the desk in the office out there. He can steer you in the right direction. And – good luck.'

Harry nodded and left, his spirits partially restored after his disappointment. He might not have the enemy in his sights directly, but he did have something positive now at which to aim; and if that was the only way he could help in the war then he would just have to give it his very best effort.

Cecil Milborne slowly descended the staircase, watched all the way by Maude, who was standing in the hall.

'You're in uniform, Cecil,' she said, in her surprise stating the obvious.

'Goodness me,' Cecil replied, staring at himself. 'So I am. I wonder how that happened.'

Maude looked at her husband and wondered

at his ability to be sarcastic even at this point in their lives.

'Is there a particular reason, Cecil?'

'I imagine even you, blessed though you are with only a tiny intelligence, can work out why I should be wearing my uniform, Maude.'

'Aren't you a little old to be thinking such things, Cecil? They are asking for the services of men between eighteen and thirty.'

'I am a reservist, Maude, remember? And now is the time for men such as I, trained officers, experienced in the field, to put themselves forward for active service. There are many men of my age all ready to go. Personally, I simply can't wait to have a go at the Hun.'

'I can understand that, Cecil,' Maude sighed. 'You are, after all, something of an expert at having a go.'

Cecil eyed his wife with his usual practised malevolence.

'Show them a thing or two,' Cecil said, checking his appearance in the hall mirror, 'our so-called sons. Hughie busy enjoying himself in America and Bertie idling about the place as usual. Show them a thing or two to see their father off first. I'm taking the matching bays with me – be just the thing. And I'll find myself a batman *en route* no doubt – don't see any problem there. Odd, having to take off without one's valet, but then ever since the declaration, Werner is nowhere to be seen.' He turned his face to one side to check his profile now he had put on his officer's cap. 'Another good thing about uniform, Maude,' he added. 'Makes one look even younger.'

'Werner's gone back to Germany, Cecil,' Maude said, eyeing him. 'You can hardly be surprised. Cheeseman has always been convinced your valet was a spy, and that whenever he said he was at the cinema he was actually spying on the local camp at Wynorth.'

Cecil now checked his other profile. 'Wouldn't have learned very much at that camp, Maude, except perhaps some new English swear words, and a most odd recipe for bully beef.'

'He left yesterday evening. I thought Cheeseman would have told you. He slipped away when you were up in town, seeing to whatever you had to see to.'

Maude knew perfectly well that Cecil kept a mistress in London, and could not have cared less.

'Plenty to do when one's off to war, Maude,' Cecil told his mirror image. 'Sort of thing you wouldn't understand. Goodbye, dear. I'll keep you posted, don't worry.' He nodded to his wife and made for the door.

'I hope you have a good war, Cecil. If there is such a thing.'

'Course there is,' Cecil assured her. 'Long as you know what you're doing.'

So Cecil departed to fight his war, and Maude returned upstairs as Cheeseman opened the front door to allow his master to go out to the waiting car.

Maude closed her bedroom door and, going to her yellow satin Regency chaise longue under the window, watched Cecil being driven off. As he went she realised she might not see him again. And while it was an odd thought she found it was not a deeply distressing one. In fact, she found it to be quite a relief that he had gone. How very different it would be if she had to say goodbye to Bertie or Hughie, but then she put such thoughts from her head, knowing that, like everyone else's children, if needs be, her sons must do their duty.

Sadly, she was not able to dismiss the thought for long.

'I suppose you know what I'm going to say, Mamma,' Bertie said to her that night at dinner. 'It's inevitable really.'

'I have absolutely no idea, Bertie darling,' Maude replied, feeling the blood chill in her veins. 'No idea at all.'

'Don't pretend, Mamma,' Bertie said seriously. 'Papa thinks the army won't have me and I won't have the army, but that just isn't so.'

'There is time enough for this sort of talk, Bertie, in the *future*,' Maude replied. 'Not now. Besides, we are not going to be looking at a war of any great length, so I understand – which no doubt is why your father saw fit to take himself off.'

'I don't like to disagree, Mamma, but the signs are the very opposite.'

'I do not believe so, Bertie. The Expeditionary

311

Force landed in France without a single casualty – and Japan is almost certain now to come in on our side.'

'Mamma, the Germans have taken Brussels with hardly a shot fired, Namur has fallen without any sort of a fight and the Allies have had to withdraw from the Meuse.'

'We have held Mons, Bertie. It isn't all doom and gloom, do you know?'

'The Germans are preparing to drop dynamite on our ports and our cities, Mamma,' Bertie insisted. 'This shoot is not going to be over by Christmas by any means, and I simply have to enlist. No, please don't look at me like that – and don't say anything. This is something I have to do – like everyone else has to.'

'Bertie—'

'Hughie will be back from America as soon as he can arrange it – he cabled me, which was decent of him. I couldn't look him in the face if I don't do this, I truly couldn't.'

Maude stared at Bertie. He looked so thoughtful and now, it had to be said, suddenly so mature.

'Of course, Bertie,' Maude said after a moment. 'You know, I was going to find all sorts of reasons why you couldn't and you should not join up.'

'Of course you were.'

'But I see it differently now. You have to be part of this, you simply have to be – otherwise after it's all over you'll feel you have been on the outside of it, and you won't belong to your generation. I understand that.'

Bertie smiled at his mother and put a hand on one of hers, once more wondering how on earth she had managed to stay married to his father.

'I shall enlist tomorrow, and if all goes well I gather I shall have to go to London and then almost immediately to camp to begin my training. But when finally I get sent over there, is it all right if I take Scrap? He could be rather useful, I imagine. I understand a lot of chaps are taking their dogs – the sporting ones that is. And Scrap, being trained to the gun, won't mind at all, even though he's a half-and-half.'

'Of course you must take your dog, if that's allowed.' Maude fell silent, regarded her food, and took a small mouthful.

'With you all gone,' she said finally, 'I shall have to find myself something to do. I certainly can't sit here and twiddle my thumbs.'

'Of course you will find something, Mamma,' Bertie replied, looking at his mother. Just as she had seen a new look in his eyes, her younger boy now saw a new look in his mother's eyes. It was as if she had been freed from a long prison sentence, and at last she could see the gates opening, the green of the grass beyond, the sun playing on the sea, and a sky that had suddenly lost all its clouds.

'I knew you were going to tell me what you have tonight, Bertie,' Maude said. 'I knew it.'

'I imagine you did, Mamma,' Bertie replied,

once more putting a hand on one of hers. 'Otherwise why are we having – my favourite – roast chicken, sausages and masses of bread sauce?'

It had all seemed to happen so quickly. One minute they had all been thinking the troubles in the faraway Balkans would all blow over, thanks to an endless succession of treaties, and the next moment it seemed as if most of the world was at war. Or, as the Duchess put it to Partita and Kitty, 'If our politicians hadn't made so many treaties we might still have been at peace.'

Even then, as the BEF, as it quickly came to be known, left the southern shores of England, a small under-rehearsed army of men sent to the docks in army lorries with no one to wave them off or to wish them well, there was still hope, however faint it might appear, that once the Kaiser saw that Britain meant business, the King's cousin would come to his senses and pull in his military horns. Yet the very opposite had happened. Seeing the size of the force Britain had sent to teach him this so-called lesson, the Kaiser simply laughed at what he called his cousin's *pathetic little army*.

So now, as the Duke and Duchess of Eden supervised the clearing of all treasures and valuables from Bauders, prior to it being prepared as a hospital for recuperation, even the small hope that the war would at least be short had faded, and John and Circe, like so many others with sense, prepared for a long campaign.

'Even Hawkesworth's gone to offer his services,' John told Circe as they took a break from supervising the storage of all the fine furniture and paintings, silver and other items safely in a wing of the castle. 'Told him he's far too old, but he's determined to be of some use, though I have to say, my dear, I shall not be too sorry if they send him back here, marked unwanted. If this place is going to be run efficiently we need his effort, so it's not as if he won't be doing his bit, do you know?'

'We shall have to keep some of the servants, John,' Circe replied, collapsing in one of the few remaining good chairs. 'And gardeners and groundsmen. We can't just let the place go to ruin.'

'We certainly can't let the farmland go neglected,' John agreed. 'Going to need all the food stuffs we can grow.'

'They'll make provision, surely? The government?'

'If they get their thinking caps on in time, I imagine they will. If the chaps have got any, that is. Thinking caps. Then there's the matter of the horses,' John added, unwilling though he was to broach one of the subjects closest to his heart. 'In the meantime, I say—'

'The meantime, John? What precisely do you mean by that?'

'Until it's been decided what to do, my dear,' John added quickly, clearing his throat as if to pass over it. 'Best to turn them away, I suppose.

315

Let them down, let 'em live out best they can. Except for the working stock – the shires, of course; any of them that's busy working, stays working.'

'You're not intending to turn all the horses out, John? Not with winter coming.'

'Going to have to, my dear.' John cleared his throat once more and, folding his hands behind his back, stood staring out over his land, trying not to think the unthinkable. 'They'll be perfectly all right, once they're roughed off, provided we give 'em plenty of hay – which we shall, always provided they don't requisition all the fodder. Anyway . . .' He fell to silence as did Circe, as they both pondered on the seemingly endless list of things they had to do. 'Anyway, Almeric's with his regiment, as you no doubt know, and so too, I have to say, is Gus.'

'I know,' Circe said, staring down at her hands. 'I know.'

'All the boys are off. Young Catesby. Stapleton. Although I gather young Wavell has been spun.'

'I wasn't aware of that, John.'

'Got something up with his ticker, it appears. Nothing serious, but enough to have him spun. Wavell tried to persuade him that was that, to stay at home. But young Wavell wasn't for that at all. Off to drive ambulances, I understand. Wasn't for staying at home at all.'

'He wouldn't be, John. None of them would be.'

'No,' John said slowly, still regarding the landscape. 'Don't suppose so. Dare say you're right.'

Circe stood up and went to her husband's side, taking his arm. 'It's going to be all right, John,' she said. 'Everything will be back to rights very soon, don't worry.'

'I shall have to join my regiment, you do know that, my dear.'

'No point in having your own regiment if you can't do that, dearest,' Circe teased him, smiling suddenly. 'Gracious, it's the Boer War all over again.'

'I was a bit more active then, Circe. Dare say the only thing I'll be armed with this time is a pen. But we'll see. We'll see.'

'Your experience will be invaluable, Colonel,' Circe said, this time seriously. 'When it comes to command, I imagine there are few better.'

'Didn't tell you?' John said, turning to her with a smile. 'Been made a general, so they say. Means a little bit more pocket money and that's going to be useful, what with Christmas coming up and all that. Now then – got to pop up to town for a bit, get things sorted. Sure you can manage all this without me?'

Circe nodded but refused to let go of her husband's hand.

'John?' she said. 'John – I don't think I tell you enough, truly—'

'Nonsense,' he said brusquely. 'Course you do. Course you do.'

317

'I don't, John,' Circe insisted. 'I really don't tell you nearly enough how much I love you.'

'No need, Circe.' John smiled. 'No need at all. Chaps have feelings, you know. I can feel things, you know. I can feel all that sort of thing.'

'You do make me smile, John.'

'I do?' John frowned. 'Why would that be?'

'Because you're so sweet, John,' Circe replied, kissing him gently. 'And so shy.'

'That so?' The Duke smiled, shyly.

'That is so.'

They looked at each other for a long moment, saying nothing, just remembering in a flash the thirty years they had spent together.

'You're my girl, Circe,' John said. 'Always have been, always will be my girl from across the ocean blue.'

'Thank you, John. That makes me feel eighteen years old all over again. Take care of yourself, John. I shall miss you.'

John kissed her sweetly, gently, then touched her cheek with one hand.

'Soon as this shooting match is over, my dear, we'll start going to the opera again,' he assured her. 'I know how much you've missed it.'

Wavell came in, attracting their attention with his usual discreet cough.

'Your carriage awaits, Your Grace,' he said.

'Carriage?' Circe laughed, pointing out of the window. 'Oh, that is just *so* good!'

John smiled as he saw what Circe was laughing at, although hearing her laugh made him feel suddenly sad as he realised how much he was going to miss that sound, as he was indeed going to miss all the sights and sounds of his family's lives at Bauders. He took a last look at the drawing room, now all but stripped of its treasures, one last look at the parkland beyond, then took his leave, followed by the still gaily laughing Circe.

The object of her amusement stood waiting outside, namely the new ducal carriage. In place of the usual fine conveyance with four matching chestnuts and gleaming harness stood the pick-up pony and trap with Tully's favourite pony, Trotty, between the shafts, brass blinkers burnished bright, hoofs polished, and tail and mane plaited, with Jossy holding its head. Since Jossy was to take the Duke to the station, even though he was driving a trap he had still dressed for the occasion, the buttons on his best coach-man's uniform catching the eye of the late August sun, his hat perfectly brushed and his boots spit and polished to a finish that would bring joy to the heart of even the sternest sergeant-major.

'Case of needs must, John, yes?' Circe enquired, as they made their way down the steps.

'Case of start as one means to go on rather, my dear,' John replied, going to the pony's head and pulling one of its ears. 'Looks like a three-year-old, Jossy. You do him proud.'

'Not bad for twenty-two, Your Grace,' Jossy replied, as Tully finished loading the last of the

Duke's cases into the trap. 'Enjoys hisself more'n ever, so he does.'

'Credit to you – and you, Tully. Do him proud, both of you.'

'Always been my favourite, Your Grace,' Tully grinned. 'Even though all he did when I was a nipper was dump me.'

'That's Welsh for you, Tully,' John replied. 'Got a sense of humour. That's what makes 'em distinctive.'

Tully handed the Duke into the trap. John was a tall, well-built man, and so a little out of proportion with the tiny trap, yet as always he managed to impart an air of great dignity to the proceedings, even when Boodles, his pet Parson Jack Russell terrier, had jumped up into the trap behind him, before clambering up to his favourite position on his master's shoulder, over which he draped himself as if to be able to watch his mistress waving his master farewell, which Circe then did, standing alone on the front steps of the great house, and waving until at last the little equipage had finally disappeared from her sight.

Somehow, even he did not quite know how, Almeric had managed to get himself a weekend leave to say goodbye to his mother and sisters, but more importantly, Kitty, before being sent off, so he at once took the train to London and from there to Bauders.

The weather was still fine so Kitty and he spent

as much time as they could away from the great house so that their thoughts and conversations should be private. All the time they walked they talked, and all their talk was about their future. Kitty understood this necessity at once, realising there must be no sense of *perhaps*, *if* or *maybe*, just *when*.

'When I get back . . .' as Almeric kept saying, and, 'When we are married, this is what we shall do and this is where we shall do it and this is why. And we shall have this many children and their names shall be this, and that, and we shall grow old together and I shall always see the love light in your eyes and you will always remember me as I am now, now that I tell you once again how much I love you and how much you mean to me, and how I promise you when this war is over once and for all, I shall make you the happiest woman in the whole, wide world. It will be my life's work.'

Everything Almeric said to her, Kitty memorised, knowing that she would always remember these walks and these words, yet when she went to bed each night, all she found herself doing was gripping her pillow and praying.

She no longer wondered whether or not she truly loved Almeric, because she now realised she had no right to ask such a question of herself at such a time as this. All she could do was what she knew she *must* do, and that was to return his love.

In answer to his questions she assured him, 'I

love you and always shall do – and I will wait for you. You will not just be in my thoughts every waking minute, but you will *become* my thoughts. I shall think of nothing else except you and your return and the life we are going to have together – and when I am at last asleep I will think only of you so that all my thoughts become dreams and all my dreams become realities until I see you again, dearest Almeric.'

He kissed her, somewhere away in the parkland, hidden by trees that had been growing for centuries, away in hidden pockets of land that had been grazed by deer before even the great trees had taken seed, and they held each other close and said nothing; and then they would walk again and laugh and fall silent and talk, then kiss again, so that even before he left for London on Sunday evening Kitty knew her heart was already breaking.

'I have some good news before I leave, dearest Kitty,' Almeric said, as he made ready to go. 'I have just spoken to my father on the telephone, which is something of a miracle in itself, seeing how much he detests the wretched instrument, and blow me but if he hasn't given his consent for our engagement to be announced. Now what a tonic that is, wouldn't you say? I shall do the necessary tomorrow when I am in town, before I have to get back to camp.'

'That is wonderful, Almeric,' Kitty agreed, getting ready to accompany him to the station in the ponytrap. 'I don't think we could have had a piece of better news before you have to leave.'

Circe too expressed her delight at the news and embraced them both, reserving an extra kiss and hug for her beloved elder boy, but diplomatically refusing to come to the station with the couple for reasons good enough for Almeric and Kitty. On the way to the Halt, driven sedately by young Tully, Kitty wondered among other things if it was such a good idea Gus joining up in the same regiment as Almeric?

'Should something happen,' she said carefully, 'should you find yourself in a tight corner, shall we say, isn't there a greater risk of both of you getting – getting hurt?'

'Of course not, my darling Kitty!' Almeric laughed, taking her hands. 'I shall look after young Gus and he will watch my back too, don't worry. Besides, we're pirates, remember? And nothing happens to pirates – at least not these particular pirates – nothing except they always get their girls!'

At the Halt the couple waited for their train, their conversation becoming slowly less animated until petering out altogether, silenced by the imminent arrival of the train, which now seemed to take on a great significance, Kitty imagining that once it had picked Almeric up it would steam at full speed non-stop somehow straight to France, its carriage doors flying open as it arrived at the battlefield to disgorge thousands and thousands of soldiers, young men who, like Almeric, had just kissed their loved ones farewell and goodbye and were now tumbling out of the train carriages, rifles already in hand, to be greeted not by more hugs and kisses, but by bullets and shells. Hearing the train at last approaching, Kitty flung herself into Almeric's arms careless who saw them.

Not that anyone would surely have minded, had there been anyone to observe them. As it happened, the Halt was deserted but for two loving young figures wrapped in each other's arms until the great heaving locomotive finally drew up, groaning and sighing.

As Almeric wound down his carriage window to lean out for his last goodbye, and as Kitty prepared to wave him farewell, all at once she saw herself in the company of thousands of women all over the country, all doing just the same thing at just that moment, the taste of their loved one on their lips, leaving their trace on his, the warmth of his embrace still enfolding her, the clasp of her hand still in his, the wave of her hand in the air, his kisses blown back through the smoke, the last calls of love shouted over the noise of the moving train and the blowing of guard's whistle, the late banging of carriage doors, the warnings of the station-master, the slow, sad exhalation from the train's whistle and the diminishing thunder of its departure, till all was oddly quiet. Silent, even though the back of the train was still visible somewhere down the line, an image pursued at first by those left behind as they took a few hopeless and pointless steps after it, as if to try to stop the impetus of war, as if perhaps they could just retrieve their love, just the one man, just one soldier less, the one who would never be missed, so that they could take him back to their beds for one last night of love and laughter, just one, just a few more hours spent in each other's arms before – before – before. But the train was gone and with it they all knew went their hope, even though the words they said in silence were now no longer words of love but words of prayer. *Please, God – please, God, please bring him home safe, please? Please let nothing happen to him and if You do I promise with all my heart I will love him and You for the rest of my days. Just please spare him, spare my man, my one, my love, please spare him God, please?*

Kitty stood there all alone in the company of ten thousand others, all of them silent, all of them watching until that train was no more, until it had vanished from their sight into the beginning of that late summer night, and then she turned along with ten thousand others to walk solely out of the station and return home, to a life where she and ten thousand others must pretend that life must go on as normal, when all the time a half of them was missing, soon, for so many missing, and presumed to be dead.

Once the notice announcing his engagement to Kitty had been posted in *The Times* and the *Telegraph* Almeric called in at Knowle House for a last look round before returning to camp. When he arrived the house was already half shuttered up.

'Already?' he said out aloud to no one but himself. 'This is quick work.'

He stared up at the fine façade of the family town house before letting himself in, there being no one on duty at the doors, everyone too busy clearing the house of its furniture and valuables.

'His Grace's orders, Lord Almeric,' Beaufort, one of the more senior servants, informed him, for a moment putting down a large chair he was carrying. 'Everything to be put in store at Barnes until peacetime, till the world comes to its senses, and that. Never know, could be looting and all sorts of things, milord. Now we're at war, who knows what we may expect? Who knows indeed, milord? But there you are, that's the world today, and that's the one we're stuck with.'

Almeric suddenly realised he had been far too preoccupied to consider the real implications of what was happening to them all, but now that he saw the family home being stripped and emptied, as he saw the servants crossing and recrossing the hall in their shirtsleeves, carrying furniture off to storage, coming down the stairs with fine paintings and gilded mirrors, carefully folding up the Persian rugs, taking beautiful, fresh flowers from their vases and wrapping them in newspaper preparatory doubtless to taking them to hospitals, taking down the superb curtains and drapes, and carefully wrapping glasses and decanters in yet more bundles of paper, he realised it was not so much that a great war was starting, but that everything else was stopping.

'The whole house is to be emptied, is it, Beaufort?'

'Those are the orders, milord. Everything is to go,' Beaufort replied, looking with milky eyes about a house he had known since boyhood. 'Everything. I only hope I lives to see it all back in place, so I do. My lad's over there already, you know. Not that he's a lad so much, more of a grown man now. Thirty-one years of age he is, and a good lad. Don't know whether you remember him, milord . . .'

'Of course I do, Beaufort. Tim Beaufort – he has red hair like – ' he stopped, realising that Beaufort's hair was as white as his shirt collar – 'red hair like his brother. Worked as a footman here for quite a while before – what did he go and do? That I can't remember.'

'Joined the Dorset Light, milord. Been in the army since he left here, and now he's over there. His mother and I, we give him a lot of thought, of course, a lot of thought. There's not a lot a soul can do other than give it a lot of thought, of course. But there you are, milord. That's the sort of world we've made for ourselves and, as they say, what you sow, you reap. I just hope we all see each other again. I just hope it all comes back into place. Now if you'll excuse me, milord, best get about my business.'

Watched by Almeric, Beaufort lifted the heavy red and gold Louis Quinze chair and carried it out to the back of the building where the carters were busy packing everything up into large green, immaculately painted wagons drawn by four magnificent drays, to be driven by men in smart green uniforms and buff aprons, waiting to head south across the Thames to the gentle countryside of Richmond, well set with park and common land, where the Eden valuables would be stored away in a vast furniture depository by the river, and where they would remain until such time, as Beaufort had said, that the world regained its senses.

'I thought you'd already left, Al,' a voice behind Almeric said, and turning, he saw his sister Allegra, putting on her coat and pulling on her gloves.

'And I thought you were learning to be a nurse.'

'I am. I had a couple of hours off so I thought I'd come and take a last look round.'

'We're not selling Knowle House,' Almeric laughed. 'Only putting it in storage, as it were.'

'Imagine,' Allegra said quietly, looking up the stairs. 'Does this mean one won't be able to stay here at all?'

'If you don't mind sleeping on the floor. Everything is to be stored, and the house made into a club for young officers home on leave. I gather Opal and Julie and a whole lot of Mamma's friends are going to run it. Good idea, don't you think?'

'That means it's going to go on, doesn't it, Al? The war, I mean. Papa wouldn't hand over Knowle House for an officers' club unless he knew it was all going to go on for longer than they're saying.'

'I'm inclined to agree, Allegra,' Almeric replied. 'Although I did hear Papa say that whatever happened Knowle House had to do its bit, no matter what the duration of the war. If there was a need, I seem to remember him saying, then they would make sure that Knowle was pushed into service. Good idea to have a place for young officers. Somewhere where they can come and relax. Put everything behind them for a while.' Almeric fell silent, all at once imagining himself to be one of their number, sitting in an armchair in his own family home, surrounded by companions putting everything behind them for a while. 'Right,' he said, returning to reality. 'Time for me to go and catch my train.'

'You're all right, aren't you, Al? You like this sort of thing, army and fighting and so on?' As Al gave Allegra a look as they walked to the door: 'What I meant was—'

'I know what you meant, Allegra darling. And I'm fine. I'm in altogether good shape.'

Almeric smiled at her and took one last look round. Never once had he thought that their whole life would be taken down and put away in storage, perhaps never to be reclaimed. Like so many he had imagined that they would sail across the Channel, give the enemy a bloody nose and come back to everything being absolutely and exactly as it had been before.

'What ho,' he said to his sister with a wink. 'What ho.'

Then he was gone.

Maude had left Cheeseman and a couple of maids in charge of the house, and taken herself off to London, determined to make something of herself at last, determined to join the growing numbers of women and girls who were offering their services for nursing. Bertie had already gone off to training camp, and Cecil, of course, could not wait to don a uniform, so there was only Hughie left, and since he was in America, there was nothing much more to be done about anyone.

My chest, you know, dearest Mamma – I am sure you will remember it – a bit noisy for running about the battlefield. Everyone will hear me coming! he had written from America. *If it got on the top brass's nerves the way it got on Papa's whenever he came across me, which happily for him was rare enough, they would order me to be shot at dawn.*

That had made Maude laugh, and she had read and reread the letter, before stepping out of the train, and looking up and down the crowded station platform. For the first time it struck her, as she saw the constant crowded movement around her, that not only was her country at war, but everyone in her country was going *off* to war. The young men that passed them with cropped hair and determined expressions were already giving the civilians in suits that had occupied the first-class carriage with her more than passing glances, glances that already held in them a vague disparagement, glances that told Maude, and them, that it was time for them to change out of their smart tailored suiting and join the rest of the world, who were busy climbing into uniforms. Her young footman, Jakes, had not been able to wait. He did so love a uniform, did Jakes. So off he had gone, could not wait to see himself in a smart new army uniform, the way he had not been able to wait to climb into a footman's uniform. Cheeseman, of course, considered himself too old to go, and that was only to be expected, and very practical from Maude's point of view, because it meant that she *could* go, leaving her house and grounds in his safe hands, bless him. And she did bless him. She sometimes felt more married to Cheeseman than she did to Cecil, which was hardly surprising, really.

'So you are staying in London while the war lasts, are you, Mamma? Off to join some splendid knitting circle, no doubt?' Bertie teased his mother when, having been given a pass for the day, he was able to join her for luncheon.

'No, Bertie, I am not good at knitting, I am happy to tell you,' Maude smiled. 'All that stitch counting, it does so preclude good conversation. Besides, knitting is for the women who are at home, and I am not going to stay at home. I am going to nurse; and if they do not want me as a

331

nurse, if they consider me too old, then I shall go into some other kind of war work. Perhaps making things for use on the battle front.'

In the event of having been turned away from nursing, Maude had actually put factory work second from the top on her list, which for a woman from her background, she knew, and was happy to know, would be considered unthinkable. If she was forced to admit this to Bertie, she fully expected him to be outraged, but happily he was far too busy fulminating about the treatment that had just been meted out to Victor Aldridge, his boyhood fishing friend.

'So, poor old Victor finds himself being confronted by this counter jumper with a list of schools pinned to the wall behind his desk, if you please. It seems that he hasn't attended the right school, so he won't be able to join our regiment. Victor could go up to Oxford tomorrow and get a double first with one hand tied behind his back, but this numbskull, who can only think in straight lines, tells him he is not officer material because – because he has not attended a public school, of all things!'

'Poor Victor . . .' Maude murmured in a vague voice as she stared round the dining room. On the surface, everything looked the same: people eating luncheon, talking to each other, no one scanning the newspapers, no lists yet published; and yet everyone knew, out there, over the Channel, on the borders of France and Belgium, everyone knew that the fighting had begun.

Somewhere someone's son, a Hughie or a Bertie, must already have been killed; some other mother would soon be grieving.

'I must go. I'm meeting Sister Agnes at two thirty, and she will not be grateful if I am so much as a second late.'

Bertie stood up. 'Goodbye, Mamma.' He leaned forward and pecked his mother on the cheek.

'You're not off now, are you, Bertie?'

Maude stared into her beloved younger son's face. Bertie was so handsome, but more than that, he was so decent; and yet the look in his eyes was sad, as if he already knew something that he would never tell her. Please God, he did not.

'I leave for Bovington at four o'clock,' he stated, but he was careful to smile, rolling his eyes in such a way that made it seem as if he was saying, 'So *dull.*' 'You know how it is, Mamma. They have to try and make something of us. All very jolly, sleeping under canvas, learning to teach the men something called "fearfulness". We are all nothing more than grown-up Boy Scouts really!'

Bertie had looked into his mother's eyes and seen how much she minded that he was going back to camp, that they were saying goodbye yet again, for perhaps – well, perhaps for quite a bit of time – so he was intent on pretending that he wasn't really off to war, wasn't really going to be shot at, might be going on a bit of a jolly to

France one of these days, but would soon be back to plague her, he hoped. He turned away as she left the luncheon room. He turned because he wanted to photograph his mother as she was that early afternoon in London, in her summer dress and straw hat, her gloved hands carrying some delightfully frivolous handbag, her long blonde hair looped up carefully, as it always was, under the hat, small drop pearl earrings, a thin gold bracelet over her glove, gloves whose buttoning she always slipped her hands through to roll back up her sleeve while she ate, and then slipped back again, once she was leaving. Yes, he had it all in the camera of his mind.

It was only a short walk to Sister Agnes's nursing home, but Maude was glad of it, and of the slight breeze that was blowing, hoping that as it danced past her it would take with it the picture of Bertie in his uniform, of his bonny looks, of his youthful expression, trying so hard to be brave the way he had always tried so hard to be brave when leaving for school, lifting up his face to say goodbye, his eyes blinking away the tears he did not want her to see. It was all hard, so hard, and knowing that thousands were going through the same thing did not help at all. What could help was to put herself to use. If only Sister Agnes, whom she had heard was a stickler, would not turn her away as useless, someone who knew nothing more than how to ring a bell for her maid, and draw up menus for Cheeseman to take to Cook.

As Partita followed her mother through the miles of corridors at Bauders, she found she was all too glad of Kitty's company. As the youngest of the family, to her, the whole of her life seemed to have been spent as an appendage to those of her older brothers and sisters, and apart from her mother, she liked to tell herself that, discounting the loyalties of people like Tinker, Tully and Harry, she had never really had a real friend of her own. Naturally, now everyone was gone, or nearly everyone, she felt even more sorry for herself, and at the same time more than ever grateful for Kitty's companionship.

'I just hope we'll be able to help all these poor fellows, the ones who are going to be coming here,' Circe fretted as she tried on one of several vast aprons that were awaiting her approval. 'It's all very well to plunge oneself into these ventures, but in the cold light of day one does suddenly realise what little one knows.'

'You will be wonderful, Mamma,' Partita reassured her. 'Firstly you have a natural understanding about medicine, and you always have had, and secondly, if you're not good with people I would love to know who is. One look at you and Tommy will be throwing away his crutches and dancing the grand fandango.'

Circe nodded, not really paying much attention.

'I do hope they don't find this place too bleak,

Partita. I mean, look, hardly a stick of furniture where it used to be.'

'I think there's still enough furniture here for most people, Duchess, really I do,' Kitty said, a little primly.

Circe nodded again.

'I suppose so, Kitty, but really one does wonder. After all, whoever comes here must be treated as a guest, not as a prisoner, and without so much of its usual fittings, poor old Bauders looks really rather bleak and medieval.'

'They're not coming here for a holiday, Mamma.'

'Or a lecture course on fine art,' Circe added, looking down herself and smoothing out her overstarched apron. 'What a perfectly ghastly piece of costume. I am not sure that I am cut out to be a matron, really I'm not, Tita.'

'Are we going to have enough hands, Mamma?' Partita wondered. 'Everyone seems to be leaving the old place in their droves – two more this morning, and seven yesterday, Wavell told me.'

'We hope there are enough of us left who are too old for active service,' Circe replied. 'I must say I was worried, just like you, and said as much to your father, but Papa thinks that we will have enough of an élite corps to keep the place going on all fronts.'

'Heavens, Mamma!' Partita stood back and stared at her mother. 'You not only look like a matron, you're beginning to sound like one!'

The Duchess sighed. 'All too true, Tita, all too true.'

She turned and nodded to the people who had carried her old gilt and inlaid favourite *bonheur du jour* down from her boudoir to place it at the top of what only a few days before had been her dining room.

Once Circe had decided on her apron and a dress appropriate for her duties, she returned everyone to the drawing room to help make up the beds, stifling any complaints from her daughter before they were joined by the maids she had designated to help them.

'We're all going to have to turn a hand to these things, lovey,' Circe told Partita, who was still looking amazed at the prospect of making up beds. 'Not only are we short-handed, but we have work to do, work that cannot be done by others.'

Partita pulled a face behind her mother's back and looked round the room, pulling an even more dismal face as she regarded grubby walls bearing only the outlines of where the magnificent Van Dyck portraits had been hanging, and bare floorboards stripped of their vast, faded oriental rugs. Gone were all the fine furniture, the silver, the china and the porcelain, the room being now furnished instead with rows of hospital beds and simple tables and side cupboards, ready to hold all the medical necessities of the sick and injured, newly acquired oil lamps, and piles of sheets and blankets ready to be made up on the beds.

'What on earth is that?' Kitty wondered as she saw Partita pulling on some sort of a bonnet. 'You look like a shepherdess.'

'It's the only spare bonnet I could find that was remotely suitable,' Partita said, tying the ribbons of the lace-trimmed bonnet under her chin. 'I got it from the dressing-up box.'

'Baa-baa black sheep,' her mother smiled when she saw her. 'All you're short of is a crook. Now come along, you two, we really don't have all day – especially since you both have to go off for your classes.'

The three of them took armfuls of bed linen, which they then placed on a set of as yet unmade beds. The Duchess looked at the bed, then at the pile of bedclothes, then at Kitty.

'Kitty will lead the way,' she said after a moment, smiling at Kitty for her to go first. Kitty also hesitated. She too had no idea how or where to begin, since she had never made up a bed in her life either.

'I suppose we start with a sheet,' she said with absolute uncertainty. 'At least I suppose we do.'

The Duchess frowned at the bed in front of her, pondering the dilemma further.

'Wouldn't that be . . . a little inadequate, I would have thought. All those bobbles on the mattress – one would feel those through just a sheet.'

'Perhaps this goes on first,' Partita suggested, holding up a tartan rug.

'I don't think so,' Kitty replied. 'That's a rug,

and if it's to go anywhere then I imagine it goes on top – it being a rug.'

'I know,' the Duchess said, in a moment of inspiration. 'Why don't we call one of the chambermaids? Or better still, why don't we go and see how they're getting on? After all, they're all busy making up beds in the dining room.'

The three of them hurried across the hall to the dining room where two of the chambermaids were indeed busily making up some of the dozen or so beds that had been installed in the great room where royalty had so often dined.

'Good,' Circe said, making for the nearest unmade bed. 'You're doing splendidly, you girls. Aren't they, Kitty? Partita?'

She nodded at where the youngest chambermaid was just starting to make up a fresh bed.

'Oh,' Circe said, observing. 'You put . . . I see, yes, of course.'

The maid looked up briefly at her mistress before continuing with her work, spreading the thick underblanket over the mattress before billowing a freshly starched and laundered sheet out over the bed.

'I do like the way you all do that,' Circe continued, nodding to Partita to observe the maid's handiwork. 'That's a very neat trick.'

'A hospital corner, Your Grace,' the maid replied. 'What they do on hospital beds. My mum taught us all that when we was little, 'cos she used to be a nurse, you see, Your Grace.'

'Rather like an envelope, of sorts,' Circe observed.

'Stops the sheet getting untucked,' the maid continued. 'Keeps the linen nice and tidy.'

'Then another sheet,' Circe smiled in private triumph.

'Then the blankets, Your Grace,' the maid continued, as if aware she was giving her mistress a lesson in basic housekeeping. 'And more hospital corners on them too, fold the top sheet back over the blankets, and turn the bed down so.'

'An absolute work of art,' Circe complimented her. 'Bravo indeed.'

Three-quarters of an hour later, the beds in the drawing room had been neatly made up, all with perfect hospital corners and top sheets folded neatly back and to one side, to await their patients. Their morning task completed, Partita and Kitty were dispatched into Stonebridge, the nearest town, driven there by Harry in a delivery van he had been lent by a tradesman friend of his father's.

'How long have you been driving, Harry?' Partita asked in delight as the van lurched away down the long drive from the house. 'Not just this morning, I hope!'

'Of course not,' Harry retorted, tongue stuck determinedly in one cheek as he searched for the next gear. 'I've had half a dozen lessons from Mr Burrows and he thinks I'm totally proficient – otherwise he wouldn't have lent me his van, would he?'

'Was that meant to happen, Harry?' Kitty asked, poker-faced, about the terrible tearing noise Harry had just extracted from the gearbox.

'Yes,' Harry replied blithely. 'It's called changing gears, Kitty.'

'Gracious me,' Kitty laughed. 'Sounds appallingly technical.'

'Give me a horse and cart any day,' Partita said. 'I agree with Papa.'

'*Rejoice that man is hurled from change to change unceasingly,*' Harry quoted, arriving triumphantly and at long last in top gear. 'Now we're motoring.'

'Pity those poor souls over there getting a lift from this driver,' Partita said to Kitty, eyeing Harry from the front seat as she teased him.

'When are you due to leave, Harry?' Kitty asked from the back of the cluttered van where she had done her best to make herself comfortable. 'Any idea?'

'No more than a week at most, I think,' Harry replied, wondering if he'd left enough time to brake for the road junction that was coming up in front of them, then jamming on the brakes when he decided perhaps he hadn't.

'Careful, Harry Wavell!' Partita screamed, laughing as the van slewed to a crooked halt. 'You are carrying the cream of England here!'

'I was about to say, drive carefully when you get there,' Kitty said, once she'd picked herself back up off the van floor. 'But on second thoughts that would be more than a little fatuous.'

'I'll be fine, Kitty, don't you worry about me,' Harry said, motoring on now that he had checked the roads were clear. 'I shall have a very large Red Cross on the side of what I drive and not even the Hun shoots at the Red Cross.'

'Even so, keep your head down and your window wound up,' Kitty advised him.

'If he does that, Kitty, he won't see where he's going,' Partita said scornfully. 'Will you, Harry Wavell?'

'No I will not, Lady Partita.'

'Will you please stop calling me that? You didn't call me that when we were at Waterside.'

'So stop calling me Harry Wavell then, like it's some sort of a joke.'

'It isn't meant as a *joke*, stupid. I was just teasing.'

'And I'd rather not be called stupid either, Partita.'

'Fine. Then I won't call you stupid, or Harry Wavell, if you stop calling me Lady Partita, because I don't know how you do it but somehow you manage to make my name sound sarcastic.'

'Just the way you make mine sound—'

'Pax?'

'Pax,' Harry shrugged. 'I wish it was all pax.'

'You two,' Kitty sighed. 'You're always squabbling.'

'No we're not!' Partita said.

'Yes we are.' Harry grinned. 'And we always have.'

Harry left the two young women outside the hall where they were to take their first practical nursing class, which had already started. The hall was filled all but to capacity, instilling in Partita an immediate sense of panic when faced with the noise, the heat and, above all, the smell of so many humans packed into such a badly ventilated place. For a moment she found herself considering slipping out the side door and finding somewhere quiet where she could wait for Kitty. Kitty, after all, could pass on to her everything she had learned at the class.

Partita began to work her way through the throng in search of a door that could afford her a swift exit, but was stopped when she heard a voice.

'You, please? You, young lady, yes you, making your way to the door. You look a likely sort,' a middle-aged man in a white coat was saying, indicating with one index finger for her to approach. 'We've gone through two mutton-heads here. Yes, mutton-heads – no other word for it,' he went on, nodding at the poor dolts whom he was insisting on identifying. 'Imagine! They think if you're treating someone with a cut throat you can use a tourniquet on them. Imagine that? About as likely as binding up a broken leg with cotton.'

This brought renewed laughter from all the women who thought they knew better, even as Partita went to the front of the throng.

'What would happen if one used a tourniquet

on such a wound, do you think, young woman?' the doctor finally demanded as she drew level with him.

'The patient would die from strangulation,' Partita replied in a calm voice.

'Shouldn't you be waltzing round some ballroom somewhere?' a voice called derisively from the back of the room.

'That's quite enough of that, thank you,' the doctor called back. 'We are neither at the hustings nor the music hall. This young woman is quite right – of course strangulation would be the result, so,' he turned back to Partita, 'what would *you* do if faced with a victim with a cut throat?'

'Call for help.'

'You think that sufficient?'

'I think it considerably better than killing the poor fellow with my ignorance.'

The doctor nodded, but remained straight faced.

'And if help was not forthcoming?'

'I'd use my hands, if at all possible,' Partita told him, remembering the time she had been out hunting and had had to stem bleeding when a young man in front of her had his ear torn off by a piece of wire.

'And?'

'And I'd make sure the patient didn't move.'

'Good.' The doctor nodded. 'And what would you do, say, for a fish hook embedded in the skin?'

'Are we likely to come across that in battle, Doctor?' Partita wondered in mock innocence, finally earning a shout of laughter from the audience.

'Answer, please.'

'I wouldn't make any attempt to pull it free, if that's what you're after. I'd cut it out with a knife,' she said, remembering now how, when Gus had been teaching her to fly fish by dry casting on a lawn at Bauders and had caught himself in the upper arm with a hook, she had in fact done that very thing, under Gus's direction, cutting the deeply embedded fly out of his flesh with his fishing knife.

'Mrs Forester here has broken her forearm in two places. Here.' He handed Partita a bandage. 'Let's see your bandaging skills.'

Partita looked first at the doctor and then at the mock-patient, who had now begun to groan overloudly, relishing her role to the full. Partita took the rolled-up bandage as well as two splints from a nearby table and proceeded to do a first-rate job of attending to the double fracture. When she finished, she threw the doctor a satisfyingly cool look, while at the same time earning a round of applause from the rest of the room.

'I would say that you have studied nursing at some point,' the doctor announced, looking vaguely disappointed.

'No, Doctor, I have done no nursing.'

'Your mother was a nurse perhaps?'

'Her mother's a duchess!' a voice from the back volunteered.

'And something of a doctor,' Partita admitted, edging away from the doctor with a smile to soften the blow that his failure to make an ass of her must have engendered.

Her victory complete, she went to find Kitty and see how she felt about the situation.

'I think you'd better take over this class.'

'I was actually wondering whether or not I could stick it,' Partita replied. 'But the good doctor made me see differently. Let's go and stare at him; try and put him off his stroke. I bet he knows much less about bandaging than I do. Come on.'

Kitty dutifully followed Partita, whose blood was up. They found two free seats in the front row, seats most of the other women were loath to take in case of being roped in as part of the many demonstrations. Once settled, Partita as promised did her best to disconcert the increasingly discomfited doctor as he lectured the hall on all forms of practical bandaging, and the initial treatment of more superficial wounds, before he brought the class to a close with a promise of a lesson on the means of containing infection and contagion.

'Just can't wait,' Partita laughed as they waited outside the hall for Harry. 'What a treat we have in store.'

'Look,' Kitty said, indicating a disturbance in an ironmonger's shop on the opposite side of the street where a burly man, still in his shop apron and shouting at the top of his voice, was being forcibly removed from his premises by two policemen.

Partita, her curiosity aroused, immediately crossed over the road to investigate, followed a little reluctantly by Kitty.

'He's speaking German,' Partita observed as the two of them stood by the Black Maria that was waiting for the miscreant. 'As I understand it, I think he's saying something about how he wants the streets to run with English blood. How sweetly kind of you,' she called back, in German.

Hearing this the young man turned, but Kitty, sensing what he was about to do, grabbed Partita and pulled her out of the way just in time as he spat contemptuously at Partita, before the police bundled him into the waiting car.

Despite the spittle missing her, Partita stared in horror.

'What a disgustingly girly thing to do,' she called after him, still in German.

'I didn't know you spoke German, Tita?'

'I don't, not really, only we all used to speak German with Weigel when we were small. Oh, there's Harry. Good.'

On the journey home, Partita was understandably quiet, leaving Kitty to do most of the talking to Harry.

'I say, Harry, your driving's coming on already. You've been practising while we were in class.'

'It's all in the clutch,' Harry called. 'I went up the lane and down the lane outside, must be fifty times – and hey presto! I suddenly got it.'

'So you'll be off soon then, Harry. Now you've got it. You'll be off driving ambulances with the rest of them.'

'I shall, Kitty. Can't wait to be of use. Faulty heart, indeed! I'll show them.'

Harry glanced at Partita but she was lost in thought, staring out of the van window at the passing countryside, so he glanced back at Kitty, only to find her equally lost in thought.

'I'll write to you both when I'm away. Let you know how many people I've run over,' he joked.

'That would be nice,' Kitty said, putting a hand lightly on his shoulder. 'And we will write to you.'

Circe laid out the new plans for the remodelling of the walled garden that had arrived in that day's post from Gertrude Jekyll and Edwin Lutyens. She leaned over them eager to identify each and every plant that had been carefully numbered or lettered on the drawings against the list of plants that had been contained with the plans. Once Circe had identified them she could visualise the colour and shape of each of the flowers the brilliant pair were proposing, plants in whose growth Circe saw the future, their petals and leaves seeming to beckon her forwards, giving her hope in renewal.

For springtime there would be first the green and half-white of Lenten roses, followed by the brilliance of many types of narcissi, then the pale cream and pink and mauve-hued bells of the fritillaria, before the blossoming of the spring and summer flowers, the delicate china blue of forget-me-nots, the gentle white of her favourite genus of foxglove, the columbines, the London pride, the begonias, the nepeta, and, of course, the roses – masses and masses of roses, all in the pale English colours that were Circe's favourites.

'I must take these out to the gardeners,' she said, after showing the designs to Kitty, Partita having excused herself to go up to her room to change her clothes. 'Will you come with me?'

'Of course,' Kitty agreed, wondering whether or not to say anything about the incident in town, then deciding against it since Circe had hardly seemed to notice Partita's abrupt disappearance, nor shown any real interest in how they had got on at their first-aid class.

There was no one in the walled garden, just several spades and forks abandoned, stuck upright in the earth where the gardeners had left them. Seeing the inactivity, the Duchess assumed they had taken a break for refreshment since their tools were still in the earth and several jackets and waistcoats were hung on the makeshift hooks on the old brick walls. While she waited for their return, Circe walked the plot with Kitty, plans in hand, explaining the

349

intended planting so that Kitty too could imagine the beauty of the finished garden.

Five minutes or so after they had arrived on the site, two of the more senior gardeners returned, caps on the back of their heads, pipes clenched firmly in their mouths. Seeing the Duchess, the caps were immediately whipped off and the still smoking pipes stuck in back trouser pockets, while Tim Scroggins and Bob Eldridge – known to all as 'Ole Bob' – greeted the Duchess.

'No, please, don't mind me at all,' Circe told them. 'I've only come down to show you Miss Jekyll and Mr Lutyens' plans. Yes, Tim, and Ole Bob, the plans have finally arrived. I wonder if there's somewhere we could spread them out? Don't you have a rather good table in that workshop of yours, Tim?'

As Circe was ushered into the big stone shed that served as an office, storeroom and resting place for the garden force, several of the younger men who had been grouped round the wall at one end of the room jumped to attention, nodded politely to their employer and hurried back to work. Then as Circe went over the plans with her two head gardeners, the papers spread before them on the large well-worn table up against a wall, Kitty became curious as to what all the younger men might have been up to when they were disturbed.

As she walked up to the wall she found the object of their activity. On the wooden panelling of the wall they had been busy carving their names below the previous gardeners' names, names which seemed to go back to the very date when the garden house had first been built.

The first name, a Thomas Goode, had written beneath it, 'Head Plantsman, Bauders Castle 1709–1740'. After him there came an increasing list of names, under which was written 'Head Gardener', or 'Head Plantsman', or more recently with the advent of John Eden's grandfather, always known as the Cricketing Duke, 'Head Groundsman'. Beside these, in a torrent of names, came inscriptions from all the junior gardeners, plantsmen and groundsmen, the latest being the young men who had just returned to work: 'Peter Nesbitt 1908–', 'Fred Welton 1899–', 'Nathaniel Thrush 1900–', 'Will Hickox 1892–', 'Jem Panter 1896–' and 'Albert Carroll 1903–'.

Those were the last names on a long, long list, several years below the names of 'Tim Scroggins 1875–' and 'Bob Eldridge', Ole Bob's starting date being given as '1874'. Above all the names, on a cream board fixed to the wall, someone had painted the legend:

We are nearer God's heart in the garden
Than anywhere else on earth.

'Do you think we can get this done, Tim?' Kitty heard the Duchess asking as she stood rolling up her precious plans. 'I know it's a lot to ask at this time, but if we could perhaps make a start, it might be a cheerful occupation, wouldn't you say?'

'We shall do our very best, Your Grace,' Tim replied, pipe back in mouth. 'It all depends on how many hands we got, if you understand me, Your Grace. Hands is getting fewer by the day, Ole Bob and I is finding.'

'Of course,' the Duchess said tactfully. 'There are other things a little more important than this going on, but if you can find a way to make a start, I should be eternally grateful.'

'We'll get it done one way or another, Your Grace,' Ole Bob put in. 'We'll get 'im done fer Your Grace, e'en if I 'ave to dig the blighter meself.'

That evening before dinner, Circe sat down to pen a letter to her garden designers.

Edwin Lutyens, Esquire
17 Queens Gate,
LONDON   31. viii. 1914

Dear Ned,

There is much to which to look forward in your and Miss Jekyll's plans for the old walled garden; and that I shall be reminding myself of this, over the next weeks and months, is not in doubt. Meanwhile, I shall put the plans on the Duke's desk, awaiting his return to Bauders. I know that whatever the future may hold for us, whatever comes to us, your garden will contain nothing but hope and beauty.

Yours truly,
Circe Eden

Kitty was sitting in the library, the one room the Duchess and the Duke had ordained should remain as it was, no matter what.

'Something so comforting about a book-lined room in times of peril,' Circe kept murmuring, as she bustled in and out.

As she put the finishing touches to a gift she was making for Almeric, Kitty could only agree with the Duchess. It was as if the thousands upon thousands of pages of writing that the books contained were reaching out to reassure Kitty that nothing she was going through now, or might be going through soon, had not been experienced, and written about, before.

Kitty was alone for once, Partita having taken herself off to practise bandaging and first aid on Tinker, of all people. It was so typical of Partita that, having said nothing to anyone about their experiences in nursing class, she had nevertheless decided that if she was going to be a nurse, she was going to be the best nurse of all time, leaving all the rest of them straggling behind.

'Where's Tita?'

Kitty looked up as Allegra came into the library, accompanied by her little dog, who promptly settled at her feet, once she had selected a book from the shelves.

'Tita is off practising bandaging on Tinker.'

'Poor Tinker,' Allegra murmured as she sat down and began to read.

'Yes, poor Tinker indeed. Tita's bandaged and rebandaged her so often, I think she's given her a sore arm.' As Allegra looked up, laughing, Kitty continued, 'You know your sister, she's setting her watch on it. I believe she's improved her time by fifty seconds already! Next thing, we will be having a bandaging Derby.'

'What on earth is that?' Allegra wondered distractedly, after a few seconds of watching Kitty.

'It's a sleeping bag, actually,' Kitty replied, stuffing the last piece of precious insulation into the lining, the wadding made up of a mixture of crumpled-up tissue paper and netting cut from the underskirts of old ball gowns retrieved from an attic by one of the chambermaids. 'Not a very romantic present, but one I think might be appreciated in the coming months.'

'I wonder what a romantic gift might be?' Allegra wondered, staring at Kitty with her head tilted to one side. 'What do you suppose a romantic gift would be under the circumstances?'

'I don't really have an idea,' Kitty replied, doing her best to ignore the cutting edge to her future sister-in-law's voice. 'I would like to have given your brother something nice to take away, but since he is going off to war and since winter is just around the corner I thought something practical might be more appropriate.'

'Hardly the sort of thing to give to your knight before he goes off to battle,' Allegra sighed, replacing the book of poetry on its shelf and taking out a book on nursing from a small valise. 'Still, as you say, under the circumstances . . . Heard anything from him yet?'

'Not yet,' Kitty replied, shaking her head as she stripped the end of the thread with which she had been sewing up the lining. 'But he's only been gone for ten days.'

'I should have thought you'd have heard something by now, really I would. Just something, seeing you two are now engaged. But knowing Al he's got too stuck in to remember to write to you, I dare say.'

Kitty put down the sleeping bag. 'I told him not to write to me, not to think of me at all. It would be weakening, I thought, to think of home when you are so far away, and in a battle. But he insisted he would.'

'You know Cecilia is coming to London. She is going to join me nursing,' Allegra stated, as if Kitty had not spoken. 'Proper nursing, that is – not Bauders-type nursing such as you and Tita have plumped for,' she added, with a falsely innocent look.

'I wish I could join you both, but your mother needs all of us to help her here.'

'Mamma loves pretending to be a doctor. She will soon be in her element.'

Kitty picked up the sleeping bag again.

'How is London nursing?' she asked after a minute's silence during which Allegra silently repeated something from her book.

'What did you say?'

'I said, how is London nursing?' Kitty said again.

There was yet another pause, this time longer.

'If you really want to know, Sister is a bugger,' Allegra announced suddenly, looking almost as surprised at herself saying such a word, as Kitty was at hearing it. 'If she says, "Well, *Lady* Allegra Knowle,"' Allegra continued, '"I never thought to see someone the likes of *you* wielding a bedpan" – if she says that *one more time* I think I shall probably crown her with one.'

Kitty laughed, both shocked and pleased at Allegra's outburst, as did Allegra, for the same reason, after which they started to chatter and cheer each other up, both grateful for some amusement, however trivial.

'Do you really think Tita and I should go to London as well, and learn to be bona fide nurses?' Kitty asked finally. 'Because if you do—'

But Allegra stopped her with a shake of her head. 'I was just being spiteful, forgive me. I'm just jealous, frankly, of you being here at Bauders – and Tita too. And even Harry.'

'There's no need – and Harry's gone, by the way. He went earlier today, off to drive ambulances.'

'I had no idea. I'm really rather out of touch. Good for Harry.'

'He failed his army medical, you see. He was devastated, really devastated.'

'Then even more good for Harry. He's come on a stone, he really has. But to get back to London nursing, you will be of much better use, both of you, if you stay and help Mamma, as you said earlier. I don't think she has any idea of what she is letting herself in for.'

Allegra shook her head, a worried look in her eyes.

'What do you mean exactly, Allegra?'

'It doesn't matter, Kitty,' she said. 'These things have to be done, don't they? And somebody has to do them.'

Kitty said nothing, resuming the folding of her now finished sleeping bag, while Allegra picked up her nursing book again, and pretended to study it, before looking up yet again.

'There is one more thing, Kitty. I wonder if you would mind looking after Jolly for me? It would be such a favour if you would take care of Jolly.' She lifted the still half-asleep little terrier up on to her knee to hug him. 'He's such a country boy I really can't possibly have him with me in town, and I really don't want James taking him with him, although he is quite happy to do so.'

'Almeric told me that a lot of his friends *are* taking their dogs, which I don't think is altogether fair, really I don't. So bewildering for them, don't you think?'

'I could not agree more. Poor dogs – why should they be subjected to all that noise and heaven only knows what else? And suppose he got lost – the French don't have the same under-standing of dogs as we do, so I would hate to think what might happen to him. So, all in all, if you wouldn't mind keeping an eye on Jolly for me . . . I notice he does so like you anyway, and I would be grateful.'

'I will take extra special care of him, Allegra,' Kitty reassured her and she touched her lightly on the arm as she saw the look in her eyes. 'I shall look after him as if he was my own.'

Livia was staring at Valentine, whom she was quite sure she still loved with all her heart, but whom, just at that moment, she thought she might not be going to understand as well as she might have once hoped.

'You don't wish to enlist, did you say?'

Valentine strolled over to the window and, drawing aside the net curtain, he stared out at the street below. Only a few months before, London would have been filled with impeccably dressed men and women making their stately way about the capital, their stylish clothes the envy of Europe. Now all he could see were uniforms, and more uniforms, and the figures of hurrying women, all of whom, for some reason he could not understand, seemed to be dressed in grey. Not that they were dressed in grey, they just seemed to be dressed in grey, dark grey.

'No I don't want to enlist, Livia, my beloved. It isn't compulsory – at least as yet it is not – and frankly what use would someone like me be in the army? I might make quite an impressive soldier on stage, but people like me, brought up in the theatre all our lives, what possible good would we be at the party?'

Livia stared at his back. She had heard what he had just said, she had just not taken it in.

'Valentine,' she said carefully, 'this really isn't a matter of role-playing, or whether or not you would be suitable for the part, you know,' she added, laughing. 'This is actually about defending your country, darling. You know hearth and home and all that.'

Valentine dropped the curtain and, turning, he walked across the room to her.

'I know you've given up a terrific amount to be my wife, and I love you for it. I love you and I know you love me, or else you wouldn't have done what you have done – but I must be honest with you, I think I would make a useless soldier, I do really.'

'Well, I think I can understand that,' Livia replied with some relief. 'After a life of being brought up in the theatre, I think I can perfectly understand that joining up would come as a bit of a . . .' She was about to say 'shock' but changed her mind, not wanting to sound either tactless or patronising. 'It would come as a bit of a change, after the life you have lived, that I do understand.'

'But then there is something else. My father doesn't believe that we can possibly win against

Germany, not with France, Russia, and even Japan on our side. He goes to Germany a great deal, as you know, taking the waters at Baden-Baden and all that, besides organising all his foreign tours – so he knows Germany and Austria pretty well, a lot better than most, I dare say. And what he says is that they have been training their armies, particularly the German army, for years now. They have been waiting for this day, for this eventuality. They train their sons the moment they leave school for two years and then they send them home as fully trained soldiers – so when the balloon goes up they can call on at least three million *highly trained young men*. And who have we got? Young men who've done a bit of square-bashing at school, and not a lot else besides, but who just now suddenly get sent off to some training camp somewhere – rather like chaps get sent to crammers if they can't pass their exams – and then off they go to fight the foe half trained and underequipped. It's laughable, Livia. I am afraid we don't stand a chance, not against a fully trained and mobilised army like the Germans have. We don't have an army, not a proper one. The Kaiser scoffed at the Expeditionary Force! You know what he said – he called it General French's *contemptible* little army!'

'I don't believe you're saying this, Valentine. At least, I do believe you're saying it, because I can hear you, but I don't believe you truly believe it, darling. You're just repeating what your father thinks. You're better than that. You don't need your father to think for you.'

'I am repeating what my father says, that I think is true, but it is also not the point, Livia. I *agree* with him, that's the point. I don't think we have a chance, any more than I believe we should have rushed in to defend Belgium.'

'What?' Livia gasped in astonishment. '*What?*'

'What did Belgium ever do for us? When did Belgium ever help us out?'

'Against Napoleon, for a start.'

'That was Prussia.'

'This kind of thing is not simply the return of favours, Valentine! Belgium is an ally! And it is a matter of your conscience that you should join up and fight for your country!'

'I don't really think you can speak for my conscience, Livia. My conscience is quite clear on the matter, which doesn't weigh heavy on it in the least. The fact is, I don't believe war to be an answer for anything. Nothing at all.'

'What do you believe in then? Sitting back and letting the enemy run all over us? Let them have what they want? Like your country? Like – like *me*?'

'That is not the point, Livia. All I am trying to say—'

'It's very much the point, Valentine! If you're not prepared to fight for me to defend my honour—'

'That is altogether different. That is a philosophical principle, and what it means is that I do not believe in fighting wars at all.'

'Or defending your country?'

'I am talking about fighting in a *war*, darling. I am prepared to do many things, but not mow down my fellow man. The Germans, the French, the Russians, whoever we have been talking about, they are just people. The sons of mothers who love them, and want nothing more for them than a happy life. They did not give birth to them to have some other mother's son kill them, because of some wavy little line in some piece of earth somewhere, or some tatty little treaty conjured up to enhance some conceited politician's place in history. I am immovable on this, Livia. Much as I love you, I am immovable.'

'I thought you felt the same as I did.'

'As did my mother. We all think everyone in a family will think the same, and we so often do not,' Valentine stated. 'My mamma is even now preparing to go out and sing to men and boys in village squares everywhere, to lure them into signing up, to deceive them into thinking that they are going to have a good time at the party. I do not agree with her. She does not agree with me. But we still love each other.'

A silence fell in the room as Livia realised that she too still loved Valentine, no matter what, and that she had to respect his conscience, no matter what.

'I am not a coward, Livia,' Valentine went on. 'This is to do with what I believe, and nothing at all to do with cowardice. I think war is wrong. I think we should always find another solution.'

Livia stood up and went to him. 'I understand, and I appreciate how you feel, Val. Truly I do. It would be quite wrong for me to feel otherwise.'

Valentine took her in his arms and they started to kiss, and how they kissed.

'I am so glad you understand how I feel, Livia,' Valentine said eventually, letting her go. 'I thought, as a matter of fact I *knew*, it would be difficult for you, but I so hoped that you would understand, darling.'

'Of course I understand. I love you, Val.' Livia put up a tender hand to stroke the side of his face. 'And I will always *love* you, always, but I also, like your mother, have the absolute right to follow what I believe in, to act in line with *my* conscience.'

Valentine frowned. 'Yes, of course.'

'I am going to be a volunteer nurse.'

'But you're married now.'

'I know, Val.' Livia smiled. 'But I truly can't sit by and knit scarves and socks while our boys are at the party. I feel I must do something more to help.' Livia stepped back and away from him. 'Sister Agnes says they need all the volunteers they can get hold of – at the Front. Tomorrow I am going to the Foreign Office for my *laissez-passer* to France.'

'But, sweetheart!'

Livia allowed Valentine to pull her back

into his arms, but as he did so she said, 'It's as you just said earlier, Val – all a matter of one's conscience.'

Valentine smiled ruefully. 'That is a hit, Livia, a palpable hit!'

Livia too smiled. 'Yes, Val, a hit but not a *war*!'

Chapter Eleven

Home for Christmas

'Almeric is quite convinced,' Kitty said, having read and reread yet again Almeric's first letter from the Front. 'He can't say much in a letter, of course, because of the censorship – even though he's written clear as anything "Contains only personal and family matters!" on the envelope – but he does say the way things are, they all expect to be home for Christmas.'

'You'd agree with that, Wavell, would you not?' Circe asked her butler as he served tea in the library, which he still insisted on, despite the fact that Bauders was now ready to receive its first patients and the whole place was in readiness. 'What was it that friend of yours in Milltown was saying? The Austrian army is finished, is it not, Wavell?'

'So they tell me, Your Grace,' Wavell replied. 'Not only is it now no longer a fighting force, but I am told the soldiers are starving and mutinous – and the Germans have had the stuff— the, er –

centre well and truly knocked out of them at Châlons.'

'Yes, that certainly *was* good to hear, was it not?' Circe asked generally. 'One more push, John said when we last spoke. For the life of me I cannot see how they can withstand any more – the Russians on one side of them, the French and us on the other. And they are most definitely running low on supplies.'

'And suffering from food poisoning, I hear tell,' Wavell added. 'My acquaintance tells me the Germans on both fronts are dying from a disease picked up from eating contaminated vegetables. It is, it seems, practically certain that the Austrian Emperor will be suing for peace and I further understand that the Kaiser is already preparing to flee.'

'So,' Circe turned to Kitty with a look of delight, 'dear Almeric could well be right, Kitty. They could all be home for Christmas.'

But some were home even earlier, the first of them arriving at Bauders from the Front at the end of November, forwarded from the hospitals that had tended to their wounds, those of them that were deemed well enough for recuperation being sent to one of the many large houses that, like Bauders Castle, had been converted to nursing homes, where they were greeted with open arms and treated as honoured guests.

And yet, strangely, quite against the tide of rumours that had been circulating, the war showed no signs of an early finish, for in spite of everything that had been thrown against them, including massive and punitive assaults by the Russians, and the predicted collapse of the Austrians, the Germans were fighting back and doing so with increasing success on not one, but on every front.

The first wounded that arrived at Bauders were welcomed personally by the Duchess as if she were greeting her house guests as of old, a protocol on which she had insisted as everyone had prepared to receive their patients. Circe told everyone working under her that since the people who were being sent to her had just spent a good spell in hospital, the last thing they would want would be to be treated as if they were in yet another hospital.

'We are having them to stay,' she insisted. 'We are to put Bauders and everything here, as well as ourselves, at their complete disposal, in order to help them complete a happy recovery.'

As a result of this careful and thoughtful preparation, even though there were fully trained nurses and two doctors in attendance, the wounded soldiers picked up visibly from the moment they were brought by ambulance to the still magnificent castle. There were fires burning in all the fireplaces, the servants' hall was turned into a warm and welcoming canteen where Cook and her team prepared nourishing meals and refreshments for those not still confined to their beds, and card games and simple entertainments were arranged to dispel any *longueurs* in the evenings. At first the authorities had tried to persuade the Duchess to receive only wounded and recovering officers, but she quite simply refused, pointing out that since officers and men fought side by side in the trenches why then should they not recover side by side? Bauders was open to anyone and everyone, she insisted, and if those with commissions wished to have an officers' mess to themselves, they would have to go and get better somewhere else. The authorities finally bowed, not just to her judgement, but to her implacable will.

But first everyone at Bauders had to deal with their initial intake: two dozen men back from the war, a third of whom had been injured and were still confined to their beds, leaving two-thirds to have their dressings changed, and many more intimate functions to which they could not attend themselves. Circe directed all such operations, however intimate, with a calm eye and a firm but kind voice, as necessary. But there was something missing. Some element that had always been part of Bauders' bustling life, something that they all loved now but had no time for. Music.

'We need Elizabeth,' Circe said one evening to Kitty and Partita. 'The men have spotted the piano and although one or two of them play with a couple of fingers, they haven't a proper pianist among them, and they're dying for a sing-song. Do you think we might recruit her?'

'I think we might,' Kitty said, with a look to Partita.

'What a good idea, Mamma. As it happens, Pug goes off tomorrow morning, so Elizabeth will be sure to be at a loose end with nothing to do but knit.'

Pug put his arms around Elizabeth again and hugged her close to him. She was so slim and slight; whenever he held her he had the feeling he was holding a young bird, and that he should be cupping his hands for her rather than putting his arms around her.

They walked round the garden, enjoying the last of the late autumn sun.

'There is one thing I have always meant to ask you.' Elizabeth stopped, looking up at him with shy amusement. 'Why were you called Pug when you don't even begin to resemble one?'

'A nickname from school. My mother had several pug dogs, as it so happened, at the time, and because there was another Stapleton at school, one of us became Pug for obvious reasons and the other became Fox because of his red hair.'

'Very well then, now I know, when the war's over I shall make sure to get a pug dog and call it Algie, after you, beloved Pug.'

'Time to go, time to leave, but only for a little while, eh?'

'Yes, of course, only for a little while.'

His mother waved at them both from the

window, reluctant to come out now that it was time for their farewells. Pug waved back at her. He had been so happy with Elizabeth during the past weeks that leaving her was almost too much to bear. The truth was, as he had once admitted to her, he had never thought of himself as anything but a bit of a joke, someone to cheer people up, so when he realised that Elizabeth really did love him for himself, just at first he had found it all but impossible to believe. Overnight the clown had become a knight in shining armour, and now, like all knights, what he had to do next was prove himself in battle. Like the knights of old he would go off to war, and he would prove to Elizabeth that she had been right to choose him.

A few minutes later Pug set off, taking with him two of the sturdiest hunters, and as a valet Pete Cooke, a young man from the village who had been helping out round the house and garden.

'It's going to be the most terrific adventure,' Pug told the young man as they prepared to take their leave. 'We're going to have a heck of a lot to tell everyone around here when we get back, but first we shall put the wind up Jerry, give him a bloody nose, and be back in time for Christmas.'

Pug gave a last hearty wave to his mother, a hug for Elizabeth, and then, complete with horses and dogs, he set out on what he hoped was going to be a really great adventure – a party to end all parties, as some of his friends were already calling it.

Inevitably, once Pug had gone, Elizabeth was only too pleased to be invited up to Bauders to help entertain the newly arrived patients. She had wanted so much to do something to help, but with Bertie having enlisted and Hughie still in America, she felt it would be unfair on her mother to leave her alone. But now Maude was off to London, and Elizabeth was free to fill her time as she chose.

It took a little time to collect all the sheet music necessary, but before long Bauders started to ring to the sound of song, a chorus of the wounded and the recovering led by Partita and Kitty and accompanied by Elizabeth in rousing renditions of favourites such as 'We Don't Want to Lose You', 'Little Grey Home in the West', 'Alexander's Ragtime Band' and 'The Sunshine of Your Smile'.

The sister looked up from her list and stared at Allegra.

'And for you, *Lady* Allegra Knowle, night duties, you have been put down for night duties.'

Allegra studied Sister's face. She had the look of someone who had never found anything in life about which she could possibly be cheerful. Why then did such a woman want to take up nursing the sick, who, after all, needed cheering, if nothing else? It might have been because she was so hardened to the idea of life being about suffering, and little more. Or it might have been because she sensed that by taking up a nursing career she could reach a position of power and importance.

'Thank you, Sister.'

No matter what Sister asked her to do, Allegra was always at pains to look and sound as if she had just been asked to do something quite lovely. She had accepted the strict discipline of the hospital, the unbecoming uniform, being called at six, and lights out at ten. She had not flinched at washing filthy bodies, or missing meals. She had accepted her ten-hour day as being something that was only to be expected. Yesterday, the hospital being short-staffed on account of an outbreak of influenza among the nurses, she and another young nurse had attended an amputation, not of a soldier, but of a man whose drunken neglect of his body had resulted in gangrene setting in. The other nurse had passed out after half a minute, but Allegra, used as she was to seeing headless chickens that had been left by the foxes, dead calves and culled deer, was proud to be able to write home to her mother that she had not flinched.

All in all, it was not difficult for Allegra to understand why she had been put on dreaded night duties. It did not feel like a compliment, but in truth it was.

'You may take early tea before you come back on duty,' she was told, but she did not feel like tea. Instead she took her letter pad and a pen, sat quietly in the corner of one of the common rooms and wrote to James.

She imagined that he was having quite a time of it at camp, sleeping under canvas, which he had always adored. It seemed, from what he had written to her the previous day, that when not going on route marches, having kit inspections and all the rest of it, he and Bertie and the rest went into Weymouth and enjoyed themselves. Allegra stared ahead of her, wondering how a soldier's wife should react to such news. Should she ask more, or leave it at that? She decided that she should leave it at that, and wrote instead of how she missed him, and wondered whether he would be taking off to France sooner or later.

The answer came back, and it was sooner.

It is all chaos here, everyone rushing about buying last-minute items that they very likely will never need. But we have all been determined to have as much fun as possible before embarking from Southampton for the show in France. We all want to get there before it is over!

As she took her place at the night desk, on the day she received this news, Allegra thought that there was something about the wards at night that made them seem not better, but much worse. The creaking of the beds, the indeterminate sounds emanating from every ward and building, and a weird and worrying chorus of noises that she had no wish to identify. The light she was using cast weird shadows over the floors and ceilings. And then of course she never knew what to expect. Would there be a sudden death? Or an emergency with which she could not cope, and which might mean calling for assistance?

The large area at whose head she sat on a raised dais was an all-male ward, one of the longest in the hospital. At night men of all ages slept and muttered, snored and called out from pain, or loneliness, or because they were having nightmares. She tried to concentrate on the books in front of her, studying the many aspects of hygiene, studying the right and wrong methods of bandaging, the proper use of morphine. Anxious as she was to concentrate, her studies all seemed strangely surreal at night, the weird shapes of limbs in her books, the men under their grey hospital blankets; she was frightened, but determined not to show it.

She stared into the strange shadowy scene below her raised desk. War seemed to happen very slowly, like a wave coming towards you on the far horizon, and then it crashed over you, and you had to swim as hard as you could. She thought of Waterside House, of everyone in the waves, laughing and kissing, and then for some reason, the sound of a slow waltz she had danced at the servants' ball at Christmas came into her head, and she could see the faces of all their servants and friends and neighbours passing her as she danced with Smart, the younger footman. Then came the sound of her brother singing 'I am a Pirate King'.

To have and to hold from this day forward. She longed for James, but knew in her heart of hearts that he would be too thrilled about the war to long much for her.

'If anyone gets out of bed, or attempts to get out of bed, you are to stop them at once, and call for assistance,' Sister had instructed her. 'Please have your eyes sharp about you.'

A sound distracted Allegra from her reading. She stared down the length of the ward, lit only by the occasional dim bulb. As she stared she saw a man getting out of bed and walking, not towards her elevated desk on its square platform, but off towards the end of the ward, which led to nothing but a wall.

Allegra stood up. This was exactly something of which Sister had warned her. She picked up her lamp and walked quietly down the ward, her sturdy walking shoes squeaking as she passed line after line of beds, some containing old men snoring, some young men with their heads hidden under their blankets, perhaps because they were as frightened as she. She reached the bed in question and held her lamp over it, but the man was still in bed, fast asleep, his face turned away, so she quickly turned and tiptoed back to her desk. Now she was convinced that she must have nodded off for a few seconds and imagined the scene which had just played out.

Dawn at last came, and then the sound of the milk cart arriving in the London street outside, and with it all came relief in the form of other nurses arriving on duty. Curtains were pulled, and the usual routines of the morning started up. Allegra, not wanting to seem unwilling, and despite the dozen or so hours she had been on call, did not take herself off but moved down the ward, helping men to sit up, helping others to the bathroom, doing all the usual duties expected of her and the others, until she finally came to the last bed, the inmate of which was still sleeping. The nurse she was accompanying went to the top of the bed.

'Mr Martin?' She touched his shoulder, understandably tentative because some of the patients could become violent if woken too quickly. 'Mr Martin?'

She pulled the pillow back a little, and then looked round at Allegra, trying to keep the expression on her face as calm as possible.

'I think Mr Martin's dead,' she stated in a low voice.

Allegra could now see from the set of his jaw that he must indeed be dead. She stared. She knew that it was the same bed, she knew it was the same man whose bedside she had visited in the night, she knew it for certain because it was the last bed down that side of the ward.

'Better tell Sister.'

They both turned and hurried back down the length of the beds, but when they reached the doors that led out to the corridor, Allegra stopped the other girl.

'Vera?'

The girl turned round and looked briefly at Allegra.

'I saw Mr Martin get out of his bed last night, I know I did. I went down the ward because I thought he might be sleep walking, or needing the bathroom, but when I got to his bed, he was still in it, as I thought at the time, asleep.'

Vera Logan nodded, and turned away. 'It happens all the time on night duty,' she said in an unsurprised voice. 'Just keep it to yourself. Everyone tries to explain it away, but you know what I think?' She raised her eyebrows and nodded back over her shoulder as they hurried on together. 'I think that was his spirit walking out of his body, and no one can tell me any different.' She lowered her voice once again, because another nurse was overtaking them. 'One night when I was first on night duty a woman I had only just settled down, walked straight past my desk, and when I went to follow her – quite cross too, I was, I can tell you – she walked straight through the ward doors without opening them. You can imagine. I was only new to the hospital and so frightened I was hard put not to scream. But then I realised that she must have died, and it was her spirit that had passed me, and so it turned out it was.'

Allegra frowned, and for a second she could not have said whether her colleague's firm belief in spirits made her feel better or worse, but realising that it probably made her feel better, she hurried on after her. She knew she was doing the right thing, she knew nursing was the only way to keep her mind off what was happening to James, but she also knew that come what may, as soon as she could, she would have to try to go to France. London was not the place for her. It was too far from James, too far from Al, it was too far from everything for which they were fighting. Yes, she would nurse, but no, it had to be in France, as near as possible to the fighting.

Later that day she met her father for lunch at his club. She knew he would not want to know about her nursing, about how proud she had felt that she had been able to get through helping with a major operation when the other girl had passed out, so she went straight to the point.

'I want to go to France – to nurse, Papa.'

It was always best to face her father with what you wanted head on. Any other approach would be a failure.

'I thought you might. London is not really the place for you, Allegra. You are like Boodles, you miss the open air. If he feels shut in, and I understand that, he starts digging up holes in the park.'

'No, Papa, I am not that desperate for Bauders!' Allegra laughed, but her father frowned, because he was not quite on to why she was laughing, so she stopped.

'Every time I take him out, Boodles starts digging up the park,' the Duke went on. 'The keepers are going to take a gun to him if he goes on. I should send him back to Bauders but there's no one there I can trust to keep an eye on him. Mr Tuttle has to take on every kind of task nowadays, and I am not sure that Wavell and Boodles get on the way I would wish.'

He stared ahead of him. His past life at his beloved Bauders seemed like a beautiful dream. He hated London, hated the traffic, hated the noise, hated the dirt, did not even much like his club. It was full of old bores reading newspapers and pretending to be busy when they were all just waiting around for news of the war.

'I shall have to stay here and try and contribute something,' he finished finally, his voice sad, his face a picture of misery, 'but if I were you, Allegra, and I know I am not, I should go to France, really I should, and as soon as you can. They will be needing nurses there, plenty of nurses, God help us, they will really.'

Allegra stared at her father, taken aback, not by his encouragement but by his melancholy.

'Do you not think it will go right for us, that it is going right for us?'

Her father shook his head. 'News is coming through. Not good, Allegra, not good at all. We shall know a little more soon, but do not expect it to be of the best.'

Her next evening on night duty, Allegra wrote to James,

Your evening out in Weymouth must have been a holiday after being on exercise, and now I wonder when it is you will be going over there? Do you have any idea and if so, can you tell me? I gather from everything you say that it's all pretty chaotic, and I know how anxious you are to get over there as quickly as you can in case it's all over before you get dispatched, but for me I hope you can stay a little longer so that at least I have the comfort of knowing you are still safe within these shores. People are still saying it will all be over by Christmas, and if that is the case, please God, you may not have to go at all. I know you'll be dreadfully disappointed, but I won't, because I love you, James, and can't wait for us to be together again.

She stared down the ward, remembering her father's melancholy expression, and as she did she started to see the war in France in terms of the ward with men of every race and creed huddled up somewhere under thick blankets, hundreds and hundreds of them in beds like the patients in her ward, but now not finding comfort in sleep or in the warmth of their beds, but finding only more suffering and even more fear, fear that they might die from their wounds before light, that they might slip away to eternity into the impersonal darkness of night. She frowned, trying to get rid of these nightmare images by thinking of Bauders. How she longed for home and how she longed most of all for James, and how she longed, now prayed, for this silly war about nothing at all to be at an end, soon, please, please God, soon.

A sound came from down the ward. She stood up, shading the light on her desk with a hand. Peering into the gloom of the ward, it seemed to her that she could see someone else getting out of bed. She was sure of it, she could see the figure quite plainly, heading not for her station but walking calmly in the opposite direction, with one arm of his pyjama jacket flapping uselessly by his side.

As the memory of Vera Logan's words came back to her, Allegra found it took all her courage to walk down the ward once more. It was Rory Jenkins! Was he too dead? Her mouth went dry as she put out a hand to touch his arm, but this time it was a proper pyjama jacket, and it was Rory Jenkins all right. He was sleepwalking.

Allegra could have laughed out aloud with relief as, holding on to his good arm, she led him back to his bed and settled him in once more.

'Everything all right, Nurse?' Sister asked as early morning dawned, and at long last it was time for Allegra to go off duty. 'Any trouble at all?' she asked, picking up the night duty log.

'None, except Rory Jenkins sleepwalking.'

'They do that, you know. Sometimes it's a sign

of getting better, I always think, trying to get out of the hospital, go home. Now off you go, Nurse,' Sister instructed her. 'Go home and get some sleep. We're expecting a big intake today, so we're all going to have to be on our toes in the next hours.'

Allegra thanked Sister and was about to take her leave, only to be stopped by a call from the bed of the patient sleeping nearest to where she had been sitting at her desk.

'Nurse,' he said in an even quieter whisper, indicating for her to come as close to him as she could. Allegra bent down to hear what he wanted to say.

'Yes – yes – Mr . . . ?' she said, searching for his name.

'Jim, dearie. Jim'll do just fine.'

'What can I do for you? Is there something I can get you?'

'Not get me, no – but there is something you can do for me.' He looked up at her. 'Write a letter to my mother for me? Tell her where I am, how I am, you see I can't—' He nodded at his right hand as if it was a person. 'He doesn't work right, see?'

'I know, I know.'

Allegra sat down by his bed and, taking out some of her own paper and a pen, she started to write the letter for him. Sleep, after all, could wait for just a few more minutes.

*   *   *

Maude looked up from penning her latest letter to Hughie in America. It was her last-ditch attempt to try to persuade him how unnecessary it was for him even to think of returning to England. The army would not want him; his asthma would mean that he would be passed unfit. It would be foolish to return. Even as she signed the letter she knew what his reply would be; it would be the same as he had said last time they had exchanged letters. 'No matter, Mamma,' he had written. 'I will be happy to take anything on offer.'

In fact, even before his mother had sat down to write to him on the subject, Hughie had undergone a medical examination in New York to ascertain the current state of his health and had been privately delighted to be told that his condition had improved dramatically. Neither he nor his doctor could understand the exact reason for his improvement.

'I can only think that it is the lack of damp here, or just being away, the change; that can happen to asthmatic patients. I have seen it before.'

Hughie smiled. 'Or it might be a well-deserved absence from my beastly father,' he volunteered.

The doctor laughed. 'Could be, Mr Milborne, could be that exactly, who knows?'

Hughie had, however, decided to keep the good news from his mother until he returned, when his intention was to enlist as soon as possible. He simply could not abide the idea of not going to the party along with all the rest. Bertie was going. He would go too, and that was all there was to it.

Later he sat down to write to his mother that as soon as he could wrap up his affairs in America he would be home: 'If the army won't have me, then I can always join a knitting circle!'

In the hurry that always follows a decision, he forgot to post the letter, and it sat behind the clock on his mantelpiece for some weeks. Finding it at last, just before his sailing, he quickly put it in what he had learned to call the mail with a PS on the back of the envelope: 'I might be home before this!'

It irritated Kitty that Partita was quite so good at knitting, particularly since she knew how much Partita hated it. But although she was still only learning the skill, she could knit as fast as anyone else seated round the library fire – a number that included both Tinker and Bridie, who could both already knit – with her feet up in front of her on an ottoman, racing through ball after ball of wool while sighing deeply with boredom all the while.

'I've always had this capacity to pick things up quite quickly,' she said between sighs.

'Quickly?' Kitty laughed. 'If there were an English Ladies knitting team you'd already be on it.'

'Oh, I don't think so.' Partita frowned. 'I may look as though I can knit but you haven't yet seen what I'm knitting.'

She held up her handiwork for assessment. It was greeted predictably enough with amazement from Kitty and laughter from the maids.

'May God help the poor lad who gets that,' Bridie grinned. 'Sure he wouldn't know whether to wear it or put it on his tea pot.'

'It is meant, I think, to be a body warmer,' Partita said gravely.

'Yes, but what part of the body is it meant to warm, Lady Tita?' Tinker asked, poker-faced.

'A foot, perhaps,' Kitty said helpfully. 'Or maybe an elbow?'

'If we're talking perhapses, then perhaps you all ought to wait until I've finished,' Partita suggested. 'At least it's a cheery colour. Guaranteed to bring a smile to the face – and actually while we're on the subject, you do wonder what the point of all this knitting is, if they're all going to be home for Christmas. What is the point?'

'Since it is now only two weeks away,' Kitty said. 'I don't *really* think that prediction holds any more.'

'No,' Partita agreed. 'I know it doesn't. But then it doesn't do any harm to keep thinking it – just in case of miracles. Have you any news more about Tommy Taylor, Tinks? Since he volunteered.'

'Didn't I say, milady?' Tinker replied, casting off her knitting and holding it up to appraise it. 'He come up from London two days ago 'cos he had some leave, and he looks so good in his uniform, I can tell you. He looks really smart.'

'He's bound to, Tinks. He always looked the part in his livery; took every eye.'

'And he looks every bit as smart as a soldier, milady. His battalion's part of Kitchener's Third Army, and he says once they get over there, look out, Jerry.'

'He's not going out before Christmas, surely?' Kitty wondered, looking up from her needles.

'Ah, no, surely not, please God indeed,' Bridie agreed. 'Surely they'll stick a white flag up for the Holy Season – please God so they will. They'd never be shooting at each other during the Nativity now, would they?'

'I understood that no fresh troops were to be sent out until the New Year,' Kitty assured her. 'But that's only hearsay. Something the Duchess said the Duke had mentioned.'

'Papa is still simply furious, being stuck behind a desk in Whitehall,' Partita reminded them. 'Said it's neither fish nor fowl, being a general and being given a pen instead of a sword. He told Mamma he had a very good mind to issue himself an order to go over to France and join his regiment, and when you think of it, it's not such a bad notion, because who could countermand him?'

'Tommy says his lot aren't going to be sent over till May,' Tinker said, casting on for a new garment. 'He says he heard if they were sent sooner Jerry wouldn't have a chance, but seems they're being made to wait so that when they do all go over, the New Armies this is, they'll be really certain of victory.'

'And now who needs the wireless or the newspapers when you've got young Tinker here?' Bridie wondered. 'She's a positive goldmine of information.'

'What about Tully then, Bridie?' Tinker wondered, glancing at her friend. 'Still not made his mind up?'

'He says he must see to the horses first, then he'll decide,' Bridie replied. 'All this requisitioning, he says it's a wonder they haven't been up here yet.'

'Tommy's brother, who lives down in Essex, he told Tommy they've taken just about every horse there is in Essex, so they'll be bound to be up here soon.'

'Just don't tell Papa,' Partita said. 'Can you imagine?'

She looked at Kitty, both of them knowing what a fell blow it would be if and when the purchasing officers finally came to call.

The Duke had failed to persuade the powers above him to offer him more than his present desk job.

'Anyone would think we were finished, Boodles,' he confided aloud to his boon companion as the dog streaked ahead of him across St James's Park. 'Truly, anyone would think one had lost one's marbles, instead of gaining a few more over the years. Still, might make it an excuse to kick on back to Bauders for a few days over Christmas, bit better than kicking one's heels in London.'

He was hardly home, and feeling once again oddly at a loose end, probably due to the busy nature of Circe's hospital routines, and one thing and another, when Jossy, having picked him up from the Halt, reappeared before him as he walked about the park, Boodles dashing in front, much as he had been earlier in London.

'Ah, there you are again, Your Grace. Sun's bin up more than a few hours, so doubtless we'll be going for a ride, won't we?'

'Will we, Jossy?'

'I'm thinking that's what Barrymore Boy just told me.'

'Oh, good.' The Duke nodded. 'Good idea, Jossy. Blow the London cobwebs away, eh? Come on, Boodles, time to change for a ride.'

When the Duke walked into his stable yard, Jossy had already saddled up Barrymore Boy, and was holding first his bridle by the saddling block and then the stirrup leather opposite to the mounting side as John swung into the saddle. Almost at once, and before they walked out of the yard, both horse and rider gave that particular sigh that men and their horses are wont to give when they are once more reunited.

Just for a second, before Barrymore Boy's hoofs started to touch the still damp grass, it seemed to the Duke that the park lay before them spread out as if on a vast table, with trees and deer merely toys. Yet they were real, just as his toy soldiers had been real when he was a small boy and playing on his own on the top floor of his father's house, wondering at the sights and sounds of the grown-ups below him in the same park through which he now began to trot and then canter.

The scenes through which horse and rider now cantered were those of winter, but a perfect winter in which the frost had hardly melted off the leaves of the magnificent old trees planted centuries ago by his ancestors. As Barrymore Boy started to canter, faster and faster, John knew that their spirits were as one, and as he flew over a wooden stile and increased his pace into a gallop, he happily surrendered thought for sheer sensation. It was as if all the worries and the cares of the past weeks had been pounded from under him, and he was ageless, a free spirit surrendering to the moment.

Finally he eased his mount back to the first halt they had taken, now they were back in the park, John taking the view from the last rise that overlooked his home, the ancient stonework of the great house illuminated by a great watery midday sun.

'Home, old fellow,' John said quietly, pulling one of his horse's big ears back gently. *'Dulce domum.* Home sweet home.'

They were waiting for him in the stable yard, standing idly smoking cigarettes, one of them seated on a water barrel, the other leaning over an empty stable door. Hearing the clatter of hoofs on cobbles and seeing the upright figure of the horseman and the scurry of the grooms to take the horse and attend to the rider, the two men had little trouble guessing the identity of the new arrival, and extinguished their cigarettes at once, straightened their caps and marched down the yard to introduce themselves to the Duke.

The purchasing officer, a small wiry man with an intense look to his eyes, a neat ginger moustache and prominent rabbit teeth, introduced himself officially to the Duke and stated his business.

'Name – Thomas Dyke. We are here to requisition horses, sir.'

The Duke eyed him. 'Yes?'

There was a way of saying 'yes', and another way of saying 'yes', and Jossy knew that way of His Grace's saying 'yes' after a bit of a pause – and it was chilling. However it did not seem to have much effect on this Thomas Dyke.

'We have already called on your tenant farmers, sir,' Dyke stated, moving towards the Duke to show him the list of horses already earmarked for service. 'You will be paid the sum of forty pounds for the ordinary horses up to fifteen hands three, and up to the top limit of seventy pounds for beasts deemed suitable as officers' chargers. The animal from which you yourself have just dismounted, sir – a good stamp of a horse mark – should fetch you the seventy pounds.'

'The horse to which you refer, sir, is already

spoken for and will not be going to you,' John replied, nodding to Jossy to take Barrymore Boy away. 'The horse has been loaned to Captain Harrington of the Dragoons, a neighbour of mine, and that is where he is to go.'

'That is a matter for debate, sir,' Dyke replied, regarding the Duke with a pair of singularly mean dark eyes. 'My instructions are to requisition all suitable beasts, after which they will be sent to the remount centre to be trained for service and to be allocated as the army sees fit.'

'You aware who you're addressing, man?' Jossy asked, stepping in between the two men, while still holding hard to Barrymore Boy. 'His Grace has made his wishes perfectly clear.'

'Horses away, Jossy, horses away.' The Duke nodded his appreciation and Jossy, taking the hint, moved off.

'Those are my orders, sir,' Dyke insisted, with a sly half-smile. 'I'm only obeying my orders, sir.'

'I am sure you are, sir, but no one questions my honour in my stable yard. I have told you – Barrymore Boy is promised to Captain Harrington of the Dragoons.'

'Can't disobey my orders, sir.'

'Your Grace!' Jossy muttered as he passed them once more.

'My horse is going to war under my terms,' John persisted. 'I don't wish to be paid. The army can take every saddle horse here that is sound enough to do service, but if I say this horse of mine is already spoken for, that is all there is to it.

He goes to Captain Harrington this afternoon, and if you wish for confirmation you may have it in writing. Is that understood?'

'The beasts must all go—'

'The *horses* that are not already on loan may be requisitioned.' The Duke turned to Jossy. 'Be so good as to arrange a parade of horses, please, Mr Jocelyn.'

'Aye, aye, Your *Grace*.'

The Duke watched as his horses were trotted up, one after another for the wretched Thomas Dyke, who stood with his corporal at his side, writing down sizes, marks and names. The Duke watched with a mixture of pride and heartbreak, proud at the quality and good temperament of the animals, most of which he had bred, and heartbroken at the thought of what lay ahead for creatures used to the best of lives, the kindest of treatments. Where they were bound there would be no great hedges and ditches to leap, no fine turf on which to gallop, no lush pastures in which to doze and graze. Instead, they would be hauling cannon, carrying men with guns, fighting their way through mud, deafened by the pounding noise of huge guns, terrified by the screaming of shells and explosions, fed on poor rations and made to sleep where they could, when not exposed to the winter elements and the never-ending scent of death.

His heart went out to the beautiful animals whose only real desire was to carry their masters for pleasure, pull ploughs and harrows, carts, carriages and buses for their labours, and finally to graze quietly in good pastures. He tried not to look in their eyes as they were trotted up. He knew that to them it was just another day, a time when they would be groomed, exercised, groomed again, fed, given fresh bedding and water and settled back in their boxes for another evening of equine contemplation, finally to fall asleep in a deep bed of fresh straw.

Doubtless this was the last day they would enjoy such comforts before being transported away from their homes, from a place they had always known to distant hostile environments, where they would become a number rather than a stable name, and where their only task would be to help slaughter innocent people whom politicians called 'the enemy'. It would be very different country to Bauders country, and it would be a very different form of hunting.

'These are fine animals, Your Grace,' the corporal, who up to now had remained silent, remarked. 'Wish we had access to more stock like this.'

'Kind of you. However, they were not bred for war.'

'Seen the stuff they sent us from Ireland,' the corporal continued. 'Had to spin near fifteen per cent of 'em.'

'You don't say.'

'You should have seen the state of some of 'em, Your Grace. Barely got off the boat, poor creatures.'

'Need to see the rest of your stock, sir!' Dyke interrupted them, calling down the yard.

'Those are my stock, sir.'

'Draught horses, shires and the like! Oh, and any ponies you may or may not have!'

'I dare say your children have grown out of their ponies, have they not, Your Grace?' the corporal suggested under his breath. 'If you get my meaning.'

'Perfectly, and you happen to be right, in the main, you are right.'

Jossy had been just about to say, 'We have no ponies,' when Dyke's eyes alighted on Trotty, standing looking over his box, a hay wisp hanging from his mouth, his large intelligent eyes taking in everything that had been happening, knowing, as horses and ponies sometimes sense when the routine of their lives was about to be shattered, that as Jossy would say, 'summat was up'.

Dyke turned to Tully, who was standing looking as if the earth had opened up under him and he had glimpsed hell.

'Let's have a look at him then, lad, and quick about it.'

Tully produced Trotty from the pony's box at the end, leading him up at the walk.

'He'll do us,' Dyke said, with a nod. 'He's a strong enough sort, and sound. No doubt of that, I'm sure. Lead him up at the trot.'

Tully took hold of Trotty's bridle and began to trot him up.

There was a long silence, which the Duke took care not to break.

'He's as lame as an old soldier,' Jossy announced, trying to keep the surprise out of his voice.

'So he is,' the Duke agreed, taking care not to look at Jossy. 'So he is. What a pity.'

'Put him away. He's no use to anyone except the meat man,' Dyke announced, turning away.

'Yes, sir.'

Dyke turned to the Duke.

'We'll have the manifest with you this afternoon, and the beasts off your hands by morning, payment as agreed.'

'These horses are on loan, as a gift from me, the Duke of Eden, to the army. They are to return here when their work is done.'

'I am empowered to procure animals by compulsory purchase.'

'And as a general, sir, I am empowered to tell you I am gifting them to the army. Is that clear? You do not have to pay a penny for these creatures!'

The Duke turned on his heel and walked off. He had produced his trump card when it was needed.

'Typical general,' Dyke muttered, remaining unabashed. 'Changes the rules to suit himself.'

He had hardly finished speaking when Tully led one of the older horses a sight too near him.

'Be careful, you idiot!' Dyke yelled, clutching his foot. 'Watch what you're doing!'

'I'd say it's you what wants to be more careful,' Jossy replied, without apology. 'You obviously

395

don't know your way round horses. Get too close to 'em and they're sure to tread on your corns.' He turned back to Tully. 'Same as what he's doing to other people, wouldn't you say?'

Jossy found his son in Trotty's stable, fixing the pony a fresh hay net.

'Want us to get the veterinarian, son?' he asked, going to feel the pony's leg. 'He's hoppin' lame, is our Trotty, and that's plain to see.'

'Thought you didn't agree with veterinarian, Pa?'

'I don't, son, but he is well lame, and seeing that—' He picked up the pony's hoof and stared at it, shaking his head. 'And seeing that—' He stopped. 'Ee, but that was lucky,' he murmured then, carefully removing a tack from the foot.

'Lucky, Pa?'

'Oh, yes, son, lucky.' Jossy straightened up. 'Lucky that the commissioning office didn't do what I just did. Long as no 'arm's done,' he growled, giving the pony a pat on the neck.

Tully had decided to join up long before the horses were led away from the yard.

'You don't have to go till you're called, son,' Jossy told him the following evening. 'From what I heard, army's not looking for recruits right now. They got men enough.'

'It's not the point, Pa.' Tully searched within himself for a minute to express what he felt. 'I – I just feel if they've gone, if horses have gone, and

396

this in't their quarrel, then most I can do is go as well. Maybe I can join a mounted regiment with horses and do my bit that way. Else – I'm just going to be idle here, and with most of my friends volunteering, it just don't seem right to stay behind.'

Jossy could not look at him, could not reply, could not say what he wanted to say – that it was enough that Ben, his younger boy, had gone; it was enough that all the horses – setting aside Trotty and the old carriage horses – had been taken; and now he had to lose Tully.

'As you wish, son, as you wish. Nothing a parent ever said could stop their children doing what they want, Mother used to say. Not a tear, not a cry, not a pleading, nothing – that's what she used to say. And wasn't she right?' He stood up abruptly.

'Where are you going, Pa?'

'Out to Trotty, lad. Out to Trotty. Nowt like burying face in horse's mane to bring a body to rights.'

Bridie knew Tully's mind was made up before he even told her, but she was careful not to let on.

'We had this letter only this morning, Bridie, from Ben, would you believe? Yes, it's from Ben all right. After all, he's got himself into position to write. Listen to this.

'We was barely settled down for the night when we hears a shot – so up we all got

397

thinking it were Jerry, all set to take the horses on. Next we hears – one of ours, and this bloke comes back who'd been sent out on patrol then they forgets about him and take a pot shot at him when they hears him. He was just having a smoke and nearly had his brains blown out. We all didn't half laugh and him too. No idea where we is, so all I can say is wherever we is is a whole lot bigger than England so it is. Exciting too being with all these other blokes and knowing the enemy is over there somewhere about the distance of a stone's throw, someone says. They is so close when we moves the horses up at night we wrap their bits in cloth, stop them clanking like, you knows how they do, sort of noise give you dead away – that's if they're bridled up cos sometimes we just lead them in collars like if we're just moving camp, say. But being on the move all the time means we got to lug all the fodder and forage and all, which in't something we does out hunting like. All we does is lead up second horses so it's hard work, I can tell you. First few nights we slept in barns and sheds like where ever we could but now we getting near the front it in't so easy and last night I sleeped with my two outside and near froze to death, I can tell you.

'That's it now. All the best to all still there at Bauders. Be home soon, everyone says. I say again all the best to everyone,

'Our Ben

'He always puts that,' Tully said with some pride. 'Always did.'

'If they're all going to be home soon, no doubt—' Bridie began.

'Yes, Bridie?' Tully replied, folding the letter back up as carefully as he had unfolded it.

'I was just thinking that's quite soon,' Bridie finished lamely. 'Sure that was all I was thinking, Tully.'

'And so I won't be gone long, Bridie. It's Christmas now – nearly – and so if I join up in the New Year, by the time I'm through training it'll probably all be over.'

Bridie stood up, not looking at him.

'I don't know what gets into yous all with this war business. You got a good job here, you and your da, *and* your grandda, you all got a lovely cottage so you have – there's no real *need* for you to go and join up yet, but then who am I to stop you? I'm just nobody, somebody who'll just wait for you and pray for you, and light a candle for you and wait till you're back home safe and sound again.'

'You're dreadful when you do all the mournful stuff, Bridie!' Tully laughed, taking her hand. 'You're so Irish.'

'So what do you expect me to be? French? I am Irish, Tully, and that's all there is to it – I can't help what I am.'

'I love what you are, Bridie. You know that.'

'So stay at home then.'

'You wouldn't love me if I did that, Bridie.'

'And who said anything about me loving you, may I ask?'

'Got it wrong again, have I?' Tully grinned. 'I must be hearing things again.'

'Go on – off you go. Go and join your pals and play soldiers,' Bridie said, but leaving her hand in his. 'And I'll get on with knitting yous all socks. And body warmers. And scarves and gloves and all that.'

Now she tried to pull her hand away from him, but Tully would not let her go. He just looked at her and shook his head, never taking his eyes from her face.

'Bridie,' he finally said quietly. 'No, Bridie, don't.'

'Don't what?' Bridie retorted, still trying to get her hand free. 'Let go of me.'

'Don't make something even harder. It's hard enough, Bridie, that's what.'

'I'm trying not to.'

'Yes, well, try a bit harder.'

They were silent for a few seconds.

'I'm sorry,' Bridie finally said quietly. 'Forgive me, Tully. I'm sorry.'

'There's nothing to forgive, Bridie,' Tully replied. 'And don't ever be sorry. Ever.'

Christmas came, but this year it came to many houses where no waifs called for sixpence to help with the family feast, and no decorations hung. All the young men had long ago gone to war, leaving no cause for family celebrations. Few gave presents that year, and fewer played games, but the churches were fuller than ever and the good wishes everyone exchanged with friend, neighbour and family seemed more genuine and heartfelt than perhaps ever before.

It was different at Bauders, a place that every year had been full of family, friends and relatives, and had resounded to the music of carols sung in the Great Hall and dance bands playing in the ballroom. All that, to those left behind, now seemed more like a century ago than only a year. It seemed as if that had been another age, when hearts were young and full of song and a strange haunting innocence. Now none of the young was home for Christmas except the lucky ones who had got leave, or the unlucky ones who had been wounded in the first of the battles, some of whom found their fortunes suddenly reversed as they were sent up to Bauders Castle to be cared for by the Duchess of Eden.

'We must make Christmas as beautiful as we can for our wounded,' Circe told everyone as they sat down to plan the decorations. 'We will put up a tree, as we always have done, in the Great Hall.'

No one could look at her, not wanting to ask the question, '*Who* will put up the tree?' Besides Circe and Partita and Kitty, there were so few of them left now. Just Jossy and Tully and a few old gardeners outside, and a few women from the village inside.

'I dare say we should be given the footmen's

country liveries. They would be a great deal warmer when we are doing this kind of work,' Partita grumbled as she and Kitty, hindered not helped by Bridie and Tinker, struggled to put the tree up straight, and then stood on ladders to decorate it.

Their breath made circles in the cold air of the hall, and their arms and legs were much scratched, and their faces too, when they were finally able to stand back and view the tree.

'Well, it's not much compared to the old days,' Tinker opined finally. 'But at least it's a tree, and at least it's got something on it other than its branches.'

Partita sighed. 'It looks more like something in Whiteleys than Bauders, Tinks, but it's the best we can do.'

'Very nice, dears, really – very nice,' Circe said bravely, a little later. 'I am sure all our brave wounded will appreciate what you have done. I am quite sure they will.'

Everything was to be, as much as possible, as it had been before, which of course was not at all possible. Nevertheless, there were some things that could go on as they used to. For instance, a carol concert was to be given in the house, although not by the servants for the servants, but by the church choir so that those still bedridden could enjoy the traditional music of Christmas. And also there was to be a banquet thrown for patients, staff and family around a vast table set in the servants' hall. A yule log had been brought up to the castle by Jossy and Tully to burn brightly in the servants' hall, and Circe, Partita and Kitty had even manufactured the hand-made crackers that were now such a tradition at Bauders, filling each one, not with some cheap novelty, but with generous gifts of watches, pens, silver key rings, gold tie pins, and jewelled cufflinks, presents that amazed and stunned the patients.

'This has been the very best Christmas I have ever had,' young Jack Wilson told Circe, bowing extravagantly and at the same time kissing her hand gallantly.

Although the subject of favouritism was never aired, it was silently accepted that Jack had become everyone's favourite. No one could resist Jack.

He had been wounded at Mons in the chest and back, but from the moment he arrived, he was determined to cheer up all his fellow patients, despite the fact that he himself was in constant pain. Jack was the lead singer, Jack was the gamesman, Jack was the spirit of recovery.

'Jack, you are a terrible old exaggerator!'

'No, I mean it, Duchess. You have given us all the best Christmas ever, certainly my best Christmas ever,' Jack insisted. 'This has been a day of days. The day they come to claim you – which, God forbid, will not be for a hundred years or more – you will go up there in a cloud of pink glory, surrounded by all these lovely angels all blasting away on their trumpets and shouting whatever it is angels shout. 'Cos you're a right angel, Duchess, and all your lovely staff.'

'You're tipsy, Jack,' Partita laughed. 'Your eyes are spinning all the way round in your head.'

'I am not tipsy, Lady T,' Jack told her, looking very serious. 'I am very slightly squiddly-diddly. Now, if I might have a Christmas kiss . . . ?'

Partita leaned over his wheelchair and kissed him on the top of his head.

'You're a bad lad, Jack Wilson, and we all know it. Don't forget we've got our eyes on you.'

'I think we should all have a Christmas kiss!' another of the patients called, picking up the thread. 'Because Jack's right, this is the best Christmas ever!'

'Oh, very well,' Partita agreed. 'Come on, everyone – kissing time!'

Every patient got a Christmas kiss from all the young women and from the Duchess too, a kiss on both cheeks and a tap on Jack's cheek from Partita for trying to pinch an extra one. After which, all the patients sang 'For They Are Jolly Good Fellows!' to the Duchess and her team before everyone prepared for bed. But as they moved to go, an older patient, a man called Michael, who from the moment of his arrival had hardly been heard to utter, sitting most of the time staring out of a window at the parkland and the winter skies, now suddenly began to sing 'Silent Night' in a light, lyric tenor. No one tried to join in. How could they? He had the voice of an angel.

'Odd, isn't it?' Kitty said to Partita as finally they made their way to their beds. 'That beautiful carol that poor Michael just sang,' and as Partita turned to look at her, 'it's German.'

Chapter Twelve

Letters Home

Letters were the hope of everyone, telegrams the dread, even in a house such as Bauders, where they had been commonplace once it was discovered they were the best and most efficient way of communicating the needs of such a vast household. Telegram boys could be required to deliver as many as half a dozen a day during busy times of the year, increasing to over a dozen when weeks such as Christmas approached. If the Castle stretched the patience of the Post Office, the Post Office quickly learned to economise once it realised just how many telegrams were being sent to Bauders, collating them into just one or two deliveries, the boy being dispatched to deliver them on pony or bicycle.

But now there was war, the significance of the telegram altered almost immediately. Far from announcing the arrival of a guest, or the birth of a relative's child, or any other such urgent but not fateful news, the telegram now generally meant only one thing, which was why Partita, having taken Kitty into her confidence, had decided that they should keep a constant telegram watch.

'I don't want Mamma receiving any bad news on a silver salver,' Partita explained to Kitty. 'Or even by chance, should she be near the front doors when the boy arrives. If one does come with a black border then I think it best if the news is broken gently. So what I propose is a series of shifts, rather like a fire watch. Whoever is free is to keep an eye out front. Since you and I are always up so early now, we can keep the first lookout for any post – and I shall instruct Wavell that telegrams are to be brought straight to me, or you if I'm not to be found, so that we can read the contents before Mamma.'

It soon became second nature, not just to the girls but to everyone, to watch for the post, but as the New Year matured and winter turned to spring, no telegrams arrived, only letters – letters for the patients, letters for the Duke and Duchess, letters for Partita from just about everyone, and for Kitty from Almeric – and her mother.

Violet did not write often, because she too was nursing, this time in the Lake District where she and Dr Charles had decided to settle before war was declared and he was called abroad, first to Switzerland, then to France. But although mother and daughter wrote dutifully to each other, the truth was that their time of intimacy was over. It was not that Kitty did not love Violet any more, or that Violet did not love Kitty, it was just that once Violet had chosen Dr Charles, she had effectively severed her relationship with Kitty. It was just a fact. Nothing would ever be the same again and, truthfully, the polite tone of their letters to each other reflected this.

In the mornings the wards and sitting rooms would be full of cigarette and pipe smoke but silent as the patients opened their letters from their chums and families and read them over and over again. After they had fully digested their contents, first they would read interesting or amusing bits out to each other and then there would be a general discussion on the state of the war according to what they had learned from their chums' letters, which, due to censorship, was of a very limited scope. That was of no consequence since they had the newspapers to keep them generally abreast of developments, while the letters they received were to boost morale and keep hope alive, just as were the letters they wrote and sent each and every day to their comrades in arms. Having already served in the theatre of war, they knew how important it was to get letters, so they would write to their comrades whenever they could, even if they had little to say. What hadn't happened they would invent in the hope that it would raise a smile somewhere in the trenches, and bring a little light relief to their men.

As for the family, Circe would take her letters from Almeric and Gus off to read in her bedroom. She would read them once as soon as they had arrived – unless she was busy with her duties, when she would set them aside until there was a free quarter of an hour – and then she would reread them slowly and carefully at bedtime, trying to guess at what Almeric, in particular, was saying between the lines, which she knew very well would be something that he was not meant to say. Gussie's letters were not perused in the same way. Gus being Gus, he sought only to amuse and reassure, a character trait that Circe found most endearing.

Partita and Kitty, on the other hand, would save up their letters all day, storing them up for bedtime, which was necessarily much earlier than they had been used to, thanks not just to the patients but also to the cold of the castle. Partita would get letters from her brothers and, eventually, even from Peregrine, who had joined up without telling anyone in September, and was now fighting with his battalion near somewhere they were not meant to know, but one of the newly arrived had whispered was called Ypres.

They all knew from newspaper reports where the fighting was intensifying but other than that it was left to guesswork and information filtered in carefully by the Duke in London, who let Circe know a certain amount of privileged information without breaking too many rules.

What he did not tell her was that Almeric was also fighting in the same area, not a dozen miles from a hill that was to become notorious. The impression those at home received was that victory was in the offing, although, as John pointed out to Circe on the telephone after the victory that never happened, after all the optimism that preceded and followed the engagement at Neuve Chapelle, there would be no celebrations until they had the Germans sitting round a table ready to negotiate.

Circe was delighted to receive a letter from Edward Bletchworth, the vicar of Bauders, who had volunteered to go to the Front as a chaplain the week after Christmas. Ranked as a captain, the official status initially of any priest who volunteered as a chaplain, he had not only surprised himself by his enrolment in the army but most of those who knew him in and around the environs of Bauders. He wrote:

This has been nothing short of a salutary experience, I can assure you. Not because of the behaviour of the men, which I have to say by and large has been exemplary, but because of the behaviour of many of my brothers in the cloth. When I arrived here one of the men said to me that he supposed I was yet another stay-behind chaplain, as they call us, meaning that when the men go to the front the chaplains stay safely behind, usually in easy reach of a mess or a canteen, reappearing only to offer the troops bromides and cigarettes, or to read aloud the letters the less literate have just received from home. The shame of being included in a band of such pusillanimous men haunted me for days and days, and I determined at once that I was not going to be that sort of a chaplain, and that I would go wherever necessary, wherever God called me to go or wherever I was needed by the men. Some of them still do not find it easy to have a chaplain sitting amongst them at times when they are not engaged in battle, and to be honest, listening to their language, their songs and their humour, I can understand why they feel inhibited. But after the initial shock of hearing mouths as vulgar as one could not even imagine (!) I have tried not to make my presence felt as if it were judgemental, but just to be there in case any one of them may need me, which from time to time they have, seeking me out for a quiet word or some consolation before they face the enemy again. I cannot begin to understand how so many of my brethren have chosen to play it safe, although that is not at all true when I come to consider it. They are doing so in order to save their own skins, and so it does not take a very great deal to understand the ready criticism that, while we are prepared to talk about the Kingdom of Heaven, very few of us seemed prepared to enter it. To say I am not frightened would be an unholy lie and mischief. Only the other day I was administering communion in what I can only describe as a hellhole below ground while all the time the most mighty shells were exploding around our small band. The noise was so great that I had to shout the service out at the top of my voice, and the ground shook so much that I thought we must all be sucked down straight away into its very depths – yet thank God to whom we were all praying I must say very mightily, we were spared, and as I spoke the Blessing the gunfire stopped as if on cue. Two of the men were crying, a sight I am now becoming well accustomed to, and understand that they do not cry from cowardice or from fright, but simply because they must. Here we all are, trying to hang on to the very thread of life, and while they try to kill us we fight or we pray or we hope – but when it is over, when the bombardment stops, some of us cry from relief, or perhaps from the joy of still being here.

As I write today, I and Father Joseph from County Mayo (the Catholic priests, by the way, are courageous beyond belief) are sitting side by side in what they call a funk hole, each with a tin mug of lukewarm tea that tastes like champagne, all we can hear, of all unlikely things, is the song of birds sitting in blasted trees. They know it's spring and while it's unlike any spring they have so far experienced, they do not know why it is different. We do, which is why we thank God for our life and pray to Him that we will be spared. It is all a very long way away from the warmth and safety of Bauders, yet when I think of it and all my little congregation back home I realise I am only next door.

Yours truly,
Edward Bletchworth

There were letters from Harry to Kitty, which included notes to Partita. There were letters from Tommy Taylor to Tinker, from Tully to Bridie, and notes to Kitty in Peregrine's letters to Partita. There were letters also to Jossy from Tully, from Harry to his father, and there were letters from Peter Nesbitt, Fred Welton, Nathaniel Thrush, Will Hickox, Jem Panter and Albert Carroll to all their friends and loved ones at Bauders, none of them failing to enquire after their particular interests back at a place that they all knew now was their home, and how the great place and its gardens were looking now that the spring sun was warming the earth and the plants and trees were beginning to come back slowly to life.

There were more letters too for all the patients, letters for everyone in the house, except for Michael, the man from whom nothing much had been heard after his unforgettable performance of 'Silent Night'. No one ever wrote to him and no one ever came to see him, however much he watched at the windows or stared down the drive.

'Someone must know him, surely to goodness. He must have family somewhere surely,' Kitty said to Partita.

'Maybe, or maybe not,' Partita replied. 'Perhaps he's completely unknown. Perhaps he's an unknown soldier.'

Kitty decided to make Michael her sole concern. She knew it would be useless to push him too hard, so she concentrated instead on gradually drawing him out, but even she, employing all her charms as well as genuine interest, could get nothing from him. Michael just sat there, listened to what she had to say and attended to the questions she asked, to which he would nod thoughtfully as if giving the matter his full consideration, before turning his head away to stare once more at the sky or the landscape. If she pressed him further he still would not respond, choosing instead merely to close his eyes and rest his head wearily on the back of his chair.

'It's no good talking to 'im, Miss Kitty,' young Frank told her one day, wheeling his chair over to where Kitty was sitting apart from Michael, who by this time, by way of variation, had simply opened the French doors in front of him and walked outside as Kitty was in mid-sentence. 'You might as well squeeze a stone for blood. We've tried everything, truly we have. We tried to get him playing whist and pontoon, we offered to read to him, we told him jokes, offered to write his letters but he never says a thing. He smiled once, but we don't know what at. We wasn't talking to him, no one was. We were playing a rubber of whist and when we looked up he was sitting there smiling. Like a bloomin' great Cheshire cat, except he had tears rollin' down his face and all.'

So Kitty gave up, deciding instead to leave him in peace, tending to his needs, which, naturally, had to be guessed at.

Michael's wounds had been multiple but miraculously only light, shot through both of his hands as if at the point of surrender an enemy had put two bullets through them, and shot once in his side, again a flesh wound, a gash that had now healed perfectly to form a scar. Apart from those three bullets he had suffered only minor abrasions, but Kitty, Partita and the Duchess all knew he had far greater wounds, injuries that no amount of medicines or surgery could remove; only time might effect that cure, but even of that there was no certainty. As Frank said to Kitty one spring day when she was wheeling him around the grounds, they thought he must have seen things no one ever wanted to see.

Then came the news that Almeric had been injured. No one knew with any certainty at first how bad his injuries were, just that he was wounded. His father, still in London at his desk job, at once set the wheels in motion, learning via the War Office that he had been hit while taking a hill near Ypres that, although an essential gain, had been the subject of very heavy casualties. Examining the lists and seeing how many fatalities there were, John found himself in the Guards Chapel thanking God that his son had at least been spared, even if he had been wounded.

'He's to be sent home,' he called down the telephone to Circe, as if he was speaking to her from across a battlefield rather than down a perfectly good connection. 'Been shot in the wrist, nothing more, thanks be. Apparently you can expect him to be with you by the weekend. I shall come home myself soon as possible.'

Kitty drove herself to the station to fetch Almeric. Jossy had taught her how to drive Trotty in the trap, a skill Kitty quickly picked up and greatly enjoyed exercising, all too thankful sometimes to be able to escape from her labours at Bauders. It was not that she lacked resolution but simply that, like Partita, she was finding looking after the patients a greater strain than she had at first imagined. It was not just their wounds, their dressings, or their other needs that was exhausting, it was keeping up their morale. Not that, with the single exception of Michael, the men themselves did not do everything in their powers to put on cheery faces, so much so that they were all agreed that a better bunch of men could not be found; it was that their very good nature, their determination to overcome all their pain and suffering, was almost unbearable. And then to watch them grow better, knowing that in making them better, they were bringing them nearer and nearer to having to return to the trenches – that was a thought neither she nor Partita could bear even to talk about. Seven of the first intake who had made quick recoveries had already been sent back to the Front just after New Year, and although everyone was sad to see them go, there had still been a very strong hope that with their departure the war really was coming to an end and so, with the necessary luck, those who returned would survive what people were firmly saying had to be the last two months of the war.

So as Kitty drove to the station warmed by the spring sunshine and delighted by the pink and white of the apple blossom, she was more than ever pleased to be out of the confines of the castle, and to be going to meet their beloved Al.

The train was over twenty minutes late, which made Kitty start to wonder if she was really going to see him again, if he was really going to be on the train, and finally if she would recognise him after what now seemed to be an eternity. She need not have worried.

He stepped off the train looking preposterously handsome in his immaculate uniform, and yet heartbreakingly vulnerable, with one arm up in a sling, his wounded left hand held high against his chest. With his right hand he took off his captain's cap, managing somehow to tuck it under his slung arm, while he stood and smiled at her, his eyes full of loss – loss of the time they could have been together and loss for the things he had seen. Kitty walked to him, her hand out to him, but he wasn't interested in hands. He wanted to feel her embrace, and to kiss her, which he did, holding her tightly to him with his good arm, kissing her sweetly on her lips.

'Your arm,' she murmured in genuine concern. 'You must mind your arm.'

'I could not care if it fell off, darling Kitty,' Almeric sighed. 'If that was a condition of kissing you once more, of holding you in my arms, I couldn't care if they both fell off.'

He kissed her again, as the train was drawing out, earning them both whistles and applause from other troops in the carriages, who whooped and waved their hats at them as the train disappeared in a cloud of steam.

'It is so good to see you, Kitty. I truly thought I might never, ever see you again.'

'I thought the same thing too,' Kitty replied as she took his hand to lead him out into the station yard. 'Yet here we both are, and guess what your fiancée has learned to do?'

Almeric stared at her and then at Trotty, who was being held by the porter.

'Not drive a trap? This is going to be taking my life in my hands!' He climbed into it. 'Sure you want to drive?'

'Positive. I am good, Jossy says. Among the best, he actually said. Hark at me boasting.'

'It really is about time my father bought a

motor car,' Almeric laughed as Kitty shook the reins and Trotty set off out of the station yard. 'Except if he ever did he'd probably drive it the same way as he hunts, so in that case perhaps it's best to stick to Trotty – if we're to stay in one piece.'

On the journey back to the castle they talked of everything but the war – of how the patients had settled in, how magnificently Circe was running the rest hospital and how Partita had become almost evangelical in her mission to mend the wounded.

'Partita?' Almeric said in mock astonishment. 'I would have thought she would have spent her time playing card games and flirting.'

'She does that too,' Kitty laughed. 'She wouldn't be Partita otherwise. But you know, Al, the men love her. She makes them laugh, of course, but the care she takes of them . . . She never stops. She doesn't fuss them, or patronise them, she looks after them and – most important of all – she keeps their spirits up sky high.'

'No need for that with me today,' Almeric declared, looking around him at the beauty of the countryside. 'Here today, with you, I am in nothing less than heaven.'

Once everyone had been fed and settled for the evening under the supervision of the two resident nurses, Circe, Partita, Almeric and Kitty took their dinner in the small family dining room, waited on as always by Wavell and one of the older maids, at the servants' insistence, not that of the Duchess.

There was more to Wavell's presence than met the eye, as everyone except Almeric knew. Not that there had been any kind of disagreement between Circe and Wavell, but there had been a difference of policy that had finally culminated in a small exchange.

'Well, Your Grace, if I am not to wait at table, and I am not to knit, and I am not to nurse, and I am not to help out in the stables, I am obviously going to be required to watch as the Lord of Misrule does his worst in the castle, rats run wild in the kitchens, Your Grace never sees or knows a hot meal, and what remain of the servants smoke cigarettes by the wine cellar doors.'

Circe saw his point at last. If Wavell did not wait on them, they would not be able to do what they did. So Wavell waited on them, and everyone was happy.

The next person to arrive home was the Duke, catching the late afternoon train from London and arriving at the Halt as darkness fell.

'What I want to hear, if I may, is what it really is like out there,' Partita demanded when they were at last alone with her oldest brother.

Almeric glanced first at Kitty, and then at his youngest sister.

'The thing that strikes you first of all, is the noise,' he replied, speaking slowly. 'The sheer volume of the din, the sounds of bombardments. Nothing can prepare you for this – nothing they tell you at camp, or in training. And even if they were able to prepare you, no one could give you the scale of the noise. It is quite literally stunning, and by that I do not mean wonderful, I mean it quite literally stuns your senses. I've seen troops arriving fresh at the Front and when their first bombardment begins they literally reel. They clasp their heads, they try to bury them in between their knees, they shout just in reaction to this terrible noise of the huge guns firing at them and the shells exploding yards from the trenches. It's been rightly compared to the noise of Hell – not that anyone knows what that is, but you can guess that's the sort of thing you would hear if you were unlucky enough to be condemned to eternal damnation, for that is the only comparison. It doesn't seem to cease either – it seems to be unending, until you wonder exactly how much longer you can stand it, and then it suddenly stops. But even when it stops all you can think of is for how long will it stop? How long before it starts up again? And now, of course, we have gas.'

'What sort of gas?' Partita wondered. 'How can they use gas in battle? I don't understand.'

'Not cooking gas. No, this is chemical gas – poison gas, in other words.'

'It doesn't seem possible.'

'You are not to tell Mamma. I don't want her worried. Papa will know already and I expect is keeping quiet about it.'

Partita and Kitty glanced at each other, knowing

as they did that, like all mothers and fathers everywhere in England at that moment, hardly a minute went by that John and Circe did not think about their sons.

'Whatever next?' Partita wondered, leaning back on her chair. 'It doesn't bear thinking about.'

'The men are taking it very badly, as you can imagine,' Almeric continued. 'They caught one of them red-handed – about to launch a canister. Brought him back and presented him to the CO. When he heard what the fellow had been up to he had a quiet word with his sergeant, after which they took him out the back, and that was the end of him.'

'I should think so too,' Partita retorted. 'I'd have thrown his wretched canister at him.'

At which point John and Circe came into the small sitting room to join them.

'Tell me how you got wounded, darling?' Circe asked as she settled down beside the fire. 'You haven't even mentioned it, not in detail anyway. May we know how you did that?'

'I was out mending wire in front of our trench. Some officers don't bother, as they think it's a waste of time and too dangerous an occupation, but I don't see why my men should be exposed to any more danger than necessary – so we mend our wire and I see that it's done. Anyway, we'd just popped out of our trench at what seemed to be a quiet moment, but they must have been waiting for us, had their sights trained on where they knew the ladders were, possibly, and as soon as we were out and at work they opened fire. I don't know how I got away so lightly. It was pretty intense fire and two of my men fell to rifle grenades. My brother officer, a junior lieutenant, he got hit in the face and I managed to get him back, and while I was doing that they took some more pots at us and I got hit in the hand that was holding him by the shoulder. They call it a funk's wound.'

'The last thing you are is a funk,' Kitty said quickly.

'I hope not – but that's what a hand wound is called, because some fellows shoot themselves in the hand in order to get sent home.'

'Not you, Al.'

'Is your fellow officer all right?' Kitty wondered, looking at Almeric. 'I mean – being hit in the face . . .'

'He's fine, Kitty. Remarkably, seeing the bullet passed right through both cheeks. But he's going to make it. We were in the same place being looked after, and when last seen he was sitting up and writing a letter home. I have the most terrific bunch of men under me. I'm very lucky. They have the foulest of mouths, and the bravest of hearts.'

Whenever they had the chance Kitty and Almeric went walking in the grounds, going where they always went, as if each walk was a form of ritual designed to keep them safe and bring good luck.

If Kitty began accidentally to walk in the wrong direction, Almeric would at once correct her, guiding her back on to the right track before setting off once more, talking of their future as they walked.

'If I come back all right,' he would often begin, which Kitty would correct.

'When you come back,' she would say. 'There are no ifs.'

And then one day Almeric had an idea. It was just after he had been given the all clear by the doctors and pronounced fit once again.

'I have had the most wonderful idea. I have already spoken to the parents about it.' As Kitty looked at him, wondering if what she was thinking was what he was going to say, he went on, 'My idea is for us to be married by special licence – before I have to go back to the party.'

Kitty stared at him. 'But, Al . . . ?'

'Don't you like the idea?' He laughed. 'You should see your face.'

'You just took me by surprise, that's all,' Kitty laughed, taking his arm. 'Nothing like surprising a girl.'

'It can't be that much of a surprise, darling. You know I want to marry you.'

'Of course, Almeric, of course I do. I just hadn't thought we could – that we might do this. I think it's a lovely idea, really lovely.'

'Then do it we shall. I'll make the necessary preparations.'

'You only have – how long? Three days. Less than three days – two and a half.'

'It can be done – and I shall do it.'

'But with the Reverend Mr Bletchworth gone, isn't that going to make it difficult?'

'There are other churches. I know how busy you are, darling – so just leave it all to me. It will be wonderful – believe me.'

Almeric made all the necessary applications on the telephone, assured by those to whom he spoke that there should be no problem, other than the fact that, understandably enough, there were considerably more applications for special licences at the moment, particularly now that spring had arrived.

'Don't know what it is, sir,' the clerk said to him on the telephone. 'Soon as Easter comes all folk seem to think of is getting wed. Leave it all to me, sir. We'll do the very best we can, sir.'

The next morning, the last full day that Almeric had before returning, Kitty prepared for her wedding, helped by Partita.

'This wasn't how it was meant to be, Kitty,' Partita grumbled, fastening the buttons on the dress they had both chosen from one of the many collections of gowns in the Duchess's ownership. 'It should have been a proper wedding. After all, you're going to be a duchess one day.'

'It doesn't matter, Tita,' Kitty replied. 'This is how it is going to be because of the war. We can always have another ceremony when it's all over.'

'If and when,' Partita continued to grumble. 'For once I was really looking forward to being a bridesmaid.'

'You're still going to be a bridesmaid. The only bridesmaid.'

'Oh, what a photey for the *Tatler and Bystander*!' Partita cried mockingly. 'The Lady Partita Knowle, sister to the bridegroom and bridesmaid to the future Duchess of Eden, now the Marchioness of Knowle, married today in the Church of St Hole in the Wall, Nowhere in Particular.'

'You are particularly dreadful, Tita. The whole point is Almeric and I are getting married.'

'I get the point, Kitty,' Partita said, suddenly a little sad. 'I was just trying to get around the point – so that we wouldn't think about it. I know why you're getting married, but I just can't bear to think like that, that's all.'

'Then don't, Tita darling,' Kitty said kissing her. 'Don't think that. I'm not. So don't you.'

'Sorry, Kitty,' Partita replied, breathing in deeply and pulling herself together. 'Don't know what came over me. A bit stretched, I think – probably a bit overcooked. Now. Let me look at you – oh yes. Yes, Kitty, you look, if I may say so? You look *ever so*.'

Kitty took one last look at herself in the glass, seeing an image so contrary to the one she had imagined she would see on her wedding day. The borrowed dress was old but beautiful, of that there was no doubt, as were her borrowed hat, gloves, shoes, silk underwear and stockings, but not being married in white, in a wedding gown of your choice, and not being led up the aisle clutching a wedding bouquet of fresh summer flowers in your hand while the man who was to be yours waited, hardly daring to look in case his bride vanished or he was turned to stone in front of a packed church, was not the same as hurriedly organising a special licence to be married in an unfamiliar church by an unfamiliar vicar in day clothes, however expensive and exclusive they may be, and spending one's wedding night in a room at a local hostelry. But as Kitty knew perfectly well, there was a war on. The plain fact was that the man she was to marry that day might never return, that this might be the only chance they would have to love each other before her bridegroom returned to the fighting line.

'The car is here,' Tinker told them, hurrying into the room and then stopping to look at Kitty. 'You look simply lovely, Miss Kitty,' she sighed. 'You look really beautiful.'

'Don't be silly, Tinks,' Partita said, making a last adjustment to her own hat and dress. 'She always looks beautiful.'

'She looks *particularly* beautiful, Lady T. Really.'

'As do I, Tinker,' Partita put in, pulling a little face.

Kitty turned back to the maid. 'Thank you, Tinker,' she said. 'And I think now we really ought to be leaving.'

It was to be a very simple service, with just Partita and her parents, Tinker and Bridie, Wavell and of course every one of the patients who was well and strong enough to make the five-mile journey to the church in the hay wagon, organised and driven by Jossy, who, of course, was also to attend the ceremony. Everyone arrived at the church at the appointed time, Almeric driving himself in the ponytrap, which had been specially bedecked with white ribbons and hung with cherry blossom, while the Duke and Duchess had been driven there in a hired motor car, much to the Duke's quiet disgust, two of the carriage horses being lame, and so ruling out his favoured form of transport. So too did Kitty and her retinue arrive on time, entering the church to the quiet strains of Bach being played on the harmonium by an earnest-looking woman in a heavy woollen cardigan and mittens, even though outside the day was mild and sunny.

The only person they were short of was the parson.

'Anyone seen the fellow?' John wondered at full volume. 'Hasn't slipped his mind, I suppose?'

'Perhaps he had another service to conduct,' Circe suggested. 'There is quite a shortage of parsons at the moment, you know, with so many going off to war.'

'And even more staying behind, if you ask me,' John grunted. 'Perhaps one should take a look in the vestry?'

Taking his cue from his father, Almeric went to

see if he could find the vicar, but the vestry was empty, although he did notice an overcoat hanging on a peg, which he took as a good sign. The exact moment he returned to his place the main door swung open and a small, rotund man dressed in cassock and surplice rushed in, his face red from his haste and his obvious anxiety.

'I am *so* sorry, everyone!' he cried, taking off his spectacles, which were steaming up on him, and wiping them on his surplice. 'I really am so frightfully sorry!'

'Perfectly all right, Vicar,' John replied as the vicar hurried up to the group waiting below the altar. 'Long as we get it done some time today.'

'Ah yes, Your Grace,' the vicar sighed, putting his glasses back on. 'But I'm afraid that is now not going to be possible.'

Everyone stared at him, unable to believe their ears.

'There is some sort of hitch?' John wondered.

'Obviously there is some sort of hitch, John,' Circe put in impatiently.

'What's the matter, man?' John demanded. 'This was meant to be done under a plain sail. We're all gathered, so what the devil can be the problem?'

'It really is not my fault, Your Grace,' the vicar sighed in return. 'This is really none of my doing.'

'What isn't? Out with it!'

'Alas, it appears they have sent the wrong

licence,' the vicar informed them all, with a long, doleful look. 'It is not only the wrong licence, it is totally the wrong licence. Not only is it made out for the wrong date, tomorrow to be precise, it is also made out for the wrong couple. A Mr Albert Hillier and a Miss Eugenia Nares-Pillow.'

'Nares-Pillow?' the Duke exploded. 'Never heard of such a name. This has to be someone's idea of a hoax. Or a joke.'

'I'm afraid not, Your Grace,' the vicar assured him, showing him the licence. 'It's not even for the correct church.'

'You've only just discovered this, Vicar?'

'The licence only arrived an hour ago, Your Grace. I telephoned the appropriate authorities at once, and they told me they would call me back immediately, which they did not. I then called them back again—'

'Yes, yes, yes, just get to the point, will you?'

'The long and the short of it is, alas, Your Grace – everybody – I am very much afraid the marriage cannot proceed until the correct licence is produced.'

'And when might that be?' Circe enquired, as Almeric took Kitty's hand in his. 'Later today, perhaps?'

'No, I am very much afraid not, Your Grace,' the vicar replied, taking off his spectacles again, this time to pinch the corners of his eyes. 'No, due to the volume of the paperwork on the authorities' desks and the demands for special licences at this particular moment in time, it would seem the best we can hope for is late tomorrow morning.'

'I shall be gone by then,' Almeric said. 'And I can't buy any time.'

'I am truly sorry, milord, but there is nothing I can do.'

'You can marry them, blow it,' the Duke suggested. 'You could go ahead and marry them and fill in along all the dotted lines later.'

'I could, but it would be neither proper, Your Grace, nor legal. We must have the proper licence or this young couple cannot be deemed to be married, whatever words I may say over them.'

'Ridiculous. Preposterous. You can say all our hail and farewells without a bit of paper in your hand, can't you? So why can't you marry this young couple, eh? That's what I want to know.'

'Because it would not be legal, Your Grace. And in light – in light of the – in light of the circumstances I fear it would not be in the best interests of the young couple here were I to pronounce them man and wife and that they should not be so. In the eyes of God.'

There was nothing that could be done, in spite of a dash by Almeric into town to try to get the damage repaired, only to find the necessary official had already left his office to travel to another twenty-mile-distant church in order to try to undo another of the mistakes that had precipitated this disaster. Finally it became clear that there was simply nothing they could do until the morrow, and even then there was uncertainty on the part of the registrar that the mayhem could be entirely undone in twenty-four hours, the party returned sadly and slowly back to Bauders to regroup and to decide what, if anything, could be done.

In spite of considerable resistance from Almeric, John did his best to pull strings at the War Office, but to Almeric's relief it was proved to be of no avail.

'Yes, what has happened is sad,' Almeric agreed when his father fulminated at the inefficiency, and the heartbreak it had caused Kitty. 'It's lamentable, but I really must say, sir, that I could not live with my conscience if I had to rely on a favour. The same rules must apply to everyone – officers and men.'

'I must agree with Almeric,' Kitty found herself saying, despite the fact that she had spent the previous hour struggling not to break down.

John sighed heavily, knowing as everyone else in the room knew, that Almeric and Kitty might not get another chance to tie the marital knot, just as much as he knew that there was no further use for his opinions, one way or another. Children did what they had to do, or what they should not do, or what they considered they must do, and that was that.

Before luncheon was served, leaving the men to have a drink, Partita took Kitty aside, and the two young women went outside onto a terrace, Partita moving them along to make sure they were out of earshot.

'What are you going to *do*, Kitty?'

'There's nothing I *can* do, Tita. There has been a mistake and that is all there is to it.'

'I don't mean that. What I mean is – what are you going to *do*?'

'Hope and pray Almeric gets another leave soon so as we can get it properly organised next time.'

'And suppose he doesn't? Or suppose he gets wounded again – or worse?'

'That's not the sort of thing I will let myself suppose, Tita. There's no point. You know that as well as I do.'

'Be sensible, Kitty! You are such a practical person, as well as a bright one – so think. Just suppose you won't get this chance again – I mean, you love my brother—?'

'Of course I do! I love him with all my heart, he is the best and kindest of men, and today I was to marry him.'

Partita shrugged and regarded Kitty a while. 'Not necessarily one and the same thing, Kitty – love and marriage. Except I've seen the way you look at Al, and I think I know the way you feel.'

'I hope you do, truly I do.'

'Maybe.' Partita kept looking at Kitty and waiting. 'Look, Kitty,' she continued, 'let's try and put it this way, shall we? This was meant to be your wedding day and this was meant to be your wedding night – and to all intents and purposes that's just what it is. Al's going back tomorrow, first thing – and you heard what he

433

had to say. He said he wouldn't ask for any favours, so it's only fair on him – and on you – I mean it's only fair all round if you – if you do what you were going to do anyway.'

Now it was Kitty's turn to stare at her friend in silence.

'You mean? You can't mean . . .' She petered out into a bewildered silence, still looking at Partita.

'Oh, don't be so – so old-*fashioned*, Kitty! You're a woman, in love with a man – a man who has to go back to the fighting. He might not come back at all, Kitty – and this is the twentieth century, not the Dark Ages! You must follow your heart, not your head! You don't have to slink off to that hotel – you can stay here! No one will know – least of all Mamma and Papa – and even if they did I dare say they would be the first to understand.'

'You're the one who doesn't understand, Tita,' Kitty replied quietly, turning away and walking further down the terrace to prevent Partita from trying to read her thoughts, something she knew Partita was particularly good at doing. 'I'm not like that. I couldn't. I'm just not like that.'

'How do you know until you've tried?' Partita insisted, following Kitty closely. 'Be sensible, Kitty – this isn't the time for any old-fashioned morality and all that fandango. You might never see Almeric again. Think of that – never, ever, ever.'

'I know!' Kitty rounded on Partita, suddenly hurt, not just by Partita's suggestion. 'You've just said I'm not stupid and I'm not! But this wouldn't be right – it just wouldn't! And because it isn't right, or proper, I can't. It wouldn't be right and so it wouldn't feel right – and it might ruin it! It might spoil everything!'

'I don't know what you're talking about. The way we were brought up – that doesn't mean anything now, not now we could all be killed tomorrow. Not just Almeric and Gus and Peregrine and Pug and everyone – but all of us. We could be in London and they could drop bombs on us! They're dropping bombs on Paris all the time and Papa said London is shrouded in complete darkness every evening in case of Zeppelins – so what does all the stuff we were taught to believe, what does it all *mean*? You heard Almeric. The Germans are gassing our soldiers! They're using poison gas – so what on earth are they going to stop at? Nothing! You have to! You have to *be* with Almeric before he leaves. You might not ever have the chance again.'

'Tita,' Kitty took Partita's hands, seeing how close she was to tears. 'Tita, I know what you mean just as I know how well you mean it. No one could have a better friend in the world than you, and normally I would listen to you and probably take your advice, but not on this occasion. I couldn't – I couldn't be with Almeric tonight because it wouldn't be right, for *me*.'

'I know, I know,' Partita said, turning away in despair.

'I'm sure Almeric feels the same.'

'Have you asked him?'

'Of course not. How could I?'

'You could ask him. I think you owe him that.'

'Now you're the one who's being stupid, Tita.'

'Don't speak to me like that.'

'I'll talk to you any way I please. This is something between Almeric and me – it has nothing to do with you.'

'He's my brother!'

'He's my fiancé.'

The gong sounded for lunch but they were going inside anyway, their argument done. Kitty knew Partita was right, but that what she proposed was wrong, while Partita knew that Kitty was wrong while what she believed was right.

Yet it was all academic because Almeric and Kitty never discussed it between themselves, even though they both knew exactly what each other was thinking. Instead – with Kitty having been excused all her duties for her wedding day – they spent the afternoon going for another of their long walks where they once again discussed everything – poetry, horses, friendship, anything and everything – except Almeric's return to war and the matter of their cancelled wedding night.

They had long conversations about their friends, they talked about the patients, they talked about the beauty of spring and the state of the gardens. They worried about the Duke and Duchess growing ever more short-handed as more and more people on the estate and in the house left to go to work in the factories. They even talked about the afterlife, and whether or not there might be one and if so, what it might be like. But it was a very abstract discussion, because neither of them really knew quite what to think.

In the evening they all had dinner together in the family dining room, the rest of the family retiring early so that at least Almeric and Kitty could have a little time alone together, leaving them sitting on the floor by a log fire in the library, the dogs curled up beside them.

Here again they talked into the small hours, sitting opposite each other at first, but ending up with Kitty leaning against Almeric, her head on his shoulder while they fell to silence, Kitty knowing that he would be gone in a few hours, and Almeric staring into the flames, watching as the life of the fire died and its warmth faded.

'Kitty,' Almeric said finally, when they had turned to each other and kissed passionately and in Almeric's case most longingly. 'Kitty, I'm not being presumptuous when I say this, only honest. I know what you're feeling – at least I think I do because that's what I'm feeling too. That bit's pretty obvious.' He took her hands and looked deep into her eyes. 'You know how I feel. This was to have been our wedding night.'

'I know, Al. And of course I feel the same as you – you know I do.'

'I want this more than anything in the world, Kitty. I promise you I do.'

'I want this too, Almeric, my darling. I promise as well.'

Yet she knew what he was going to say because it was what she herself was feeling. Had it been otherwise, by now he would have swept her up in his arms and carried her upstairs. If he had, she knew she would not have resisted or forbidden him, but simply have given herself to him, and tomorrow – in fact what was no longer tomorrow but today – in a few hours' time he would be putting on his captain's uniform and going back to war. But he had not. Instead he was standing with her still in his arms, talking to her and explaining why they mustn't, and she was listening to him and agreeing with him.

'We mustn't, my darling, not because it is wrong but because we feel it might be,' he was saying to her. 'And if that is really so, if that is what we both feel, then we must wait. It doesn't make any difference to the way we feel about each other, does it?'

'No,' Kitty replied quietly. 'Not a bit. Not even the tiniest bit.'

'And it will be something we can look forward to – on my next leave. When I'm gone you make absolutely sure that there are no more – sorry, I nearly got a bit military there.' He stopped and started again. 'You can make sure that all the arrangements are in place and if I can get a long enough leave then we can even motor off somewhere and stay there all by ourselves – somewhere really romantic.'

'Of course, Almeric,' Kitty agreed. 'I understand absolutely.'

The next morning they took the trap to the Halt and only just caught the train, it being right on time for once, their lateness caused by Trotty having to walk half the journey due to spreading a plate halfway to the station. They barely had time to say goodbye, both of them flying onto the platform as the station-master held the train back for them, seeing them arriving late and hearing Almeric's anxious call. Having found a seat for him, the station-master stood back, holding up his flag in readiness.

'Goodbye, my darling,' Almeric called above the sound of the engine and the slamming doors. He embraced Kitty, who kissed him back, holding her hat on with one hand. 'I'll write as soon as I can – take care of yourself.'

'And you take care of yourself too!' Kitty called back a little hopelessly, as Almeric closed the door, having pulled the window down to lean out and wave his last goodbye.

'I shall, my sweet!' Almeric laughed as the train began to pull out. 'I shall keep the old head well down and out of sight! I love you!'

'And I love you too!' she called, running up the platform after the train, before coming to a halt at the end of the platform as the train drew away, picking up speed, until it turned round the first bend and was gone.

Kitty stood at the end of the platform, looking into space, feeling the emptiness where warmth had just been and such a feeling of sudden desolation it was all she could do not to break into sobs. Instead she adjusted her hat, tying the bow back under her chin, and made her way to the station yard, wishing the porter and the station-master goodbye and wondering how long it would be before she found herself standing and waiting on the platform once again. And then she picked up Trotty's ribbons and, with a gentle flick of them, walked the pony on up the slight incline that led from the station yard to the road, and back to whatever the future might hold for them all.

There was consternation when Kitty returned to Bauders, some sort of a search party out in the grounds being marshalled by Jossy with some of the older grooms. Curious to see what was happening, Kitty redirected Trotty away from the stable yard to follow the line of men.

'One of your patients disappeared, Miss Kitty,' Jossy told her. 'Been told to organise a search of the grounds, like.'

'Do you know who it is, Jossy?'

'No idea, miss. Just been told to look for one of the patients – oh, yes!' he called, half turning back. 'Michael? Would that be right? Answers to the name of Michael. If at all – I gather.'

It seemed Michael's bed had been found to be empty when everyone was getting up.

'Not that there's anything unusual about that,' Partita told Kitty as she was putting her in

440

the picture. 'Lots of them get up early now the weather's so much better and summer's just around the corner. But as you know, Michael is not one of the earliest risers.'

'And nobody's seen him this morning?'

'Sight nor sound, Kitty. So Mamma thought it best to organise a search party.'

'Did anything happen yesterday to upset him, I wonder. It's difficult to know, since we were otherwise engaged, so to speak.'

They went to enquire of one of the nurses who had been on duty the day before, learning that Michael had indeed received a visitor, a doctor who had travelled from London to see him, accompanied by another gentleman. They had asked to be left alone with Michael, which they were, sitting out on the stone terrace while they talked for the best part of an hour.

'You say talked,' Kitty said. 'I take it Michael didn't do any of the talking, or weren't you aware of what was going on?'

'I was busy with my other boys,' Nurse Rose, a pretty little dark-haired Scots girl, replied. 'Although I did keep an eye on Michael from time to time, knowing how very sensitive he is. He wasn't doing any talking each time I had a peek, certainly not. In fact, he was sitting in his chair with his eyes closed, the way he does; that is his way.'

'Did you speak to the doctor who came up to see him?' Partita wondered.

'Oh, of course, Lady T,' Nurse Rose replied.

'He wanted to speak to us and of course we wanted to speak to him. He told us they were just checking up on his case because he had been so notably and badly traumatised by his – his experience, as they called it.'

'His experience?' Kitty glanced at Partita.

'Aye. He said they had to check his progress to see whether or not he could be returned to active service.'

'They don't usually send someone up from London to do that,' Partita remarked. 'They leave that to our team here – our doctors' reports. I find that jolly odd.'

'It was all done properly, Lady T,' Nurse Rose assured her. 'There's a full report awaiting the Duchess when she's a moment.'

'There's something happening down by the lake,' Kitty said, interrupting and pointing to the distant activity. 'They appear to have found something.'

'Let's hope it is something – rather than somebody,' Partita said, hurrying out.

They had a body on a stretcher, which they were carefully loading onto a long garden handcart, preparatory to bringing it up to the house.

'Is it Michael?' Kitty asked when she and Partita arrived breathless after their run from the house.

'Aye,' a soaking wet Jossy said with a grave nod. 'So they say.'

'Is he dead, Jossy?' Partita asked, direct as always.

'Not quite, Lady Tita, I'm happy to say. Got to 'im just in time, it appears.'

'You got to him, you mean?'

'Aye, Lady Tita. That's about the size of it. He were in that boat, see?' Jossy gestured to the rowing boat that was still floating halfway across the lake. 'Couldn't be seen from the house, like, because he'd taken the boat from its mooring where I were fishin' last evening. Must have jumped in straight from the boat.'

'How did you get to him, Jossy? You swam all that way and still managed to save him?'

'I can swim a bit, as you know, but he'd gone a couple of times when I got to 'im. One more dip and he'd have 'ad it. He's barely alive as it is.'

Someone threw a heavy towel round Jossy's shoulders and he began to rub his hair and face dry as he watched the rest of the party hurrying the cart and stretcher up to the house.

'Melancholy bloke, was he?' Jossy wondered, tipping his head on one side to shake some water out. 'Sort to do hisself in?'

'He was no talker, Jossy,' Kitty said. 'He hardly spoke at all.'

'Must have something dread on his mind then,' Jossy replied. 'Poor man. Shouted some'at as he jumped off the boat. You know how sound travels over water – heard it clear as anything. "It is done," he called. "It is done."'

Jossy shook his head, remembering the strange cry and wondering what bell it was ringing in his head, just as Partita and Kitty were doing as they

443

now hurried on back to the house to see what they could do for the victim. When they got there, they learned the duty doctor and Nurse Rose were attending to him in the surgery, but that Michael was now conscious and seemed on the way to recovery.

Circe was reading the report that had been left for her on her desk, both hands under her chin as she studied Michael's case history, having requested to be alone until she had finished it. Respecting her wishes Partita and Kitty went about their duties in a predictably subdued atmosphere as the men gathered into groups to discuss the day's event.

'He was at Mons, Nurse Kitty,' Jack said as Kitty was helping him do his walking exercises, her patient having now finally been released from his wheelchair to try his luck on crutches. 'And when he first come here word had it that he had seen the angel.'

'What angel's that, Jack?' Kitty wondered, concentrating more on Jack's tentative steps.

'You never heard tell of the angel, Nurse Kitty? You have to be kiddin'.'

'Why should I? And try putting that foot straight. You're turning it out too much.'

'It was in all the papers, weren't it? That's how you might have lemon curd.'

'Lemon curd?' Kitty laughed. 'It's all right – I've got it. How I'd have heard.'

'Or one of the blokes here might have told you. Don't know why I didn't mention it. Although I never saw nothing. I was at Mons too, remember?'

'I remember – and do concentrate on what you're doing, Jack. You nearly fell there.'

Jack took a few careful steps in silence, pondering about Michael and his attempted suicide.

'I don't believe I didn't tell you about the angel,' he said with a frown, shifting his weight from one crutch to the other. 'I told Nurse Rose, I know that.'

'Do you want to tell me now?'

'Like I said, I din't see nothing – and as far as I'm concerned it's a lot of hooey, but a lot of the old sweats—'

'The older soldiers, you mean?'

'The blokes who done service before, you know. The old sweats, as they're called. Usually pretty hard numbers and all, you bet – what they seen and done. I din't hear nothing about it while I was out there 'cos I got my wounds in action before we fell back, like. General French's fighting withdrawal.'

'You were heavily outnumbered.'

'And the Frogs had done a runner. Anyhow, I was invalided out of it all, taken off to hospital – but that's where I heard it first, all these stories. There were rumours buzzin' around about how this angel had been seen – although some say it were several of 'em – just when things were gettin' really hot, they said. And this was an 'eck of a lot of blokes what said it, Nurse Kitty. They said just as they thought that they saw these angels – the next thing they knew, Jerry was on the back foot and they were saved, like. I don't go for it meself, I think it's a lot of hokum, but all these blokes swear on the Bible that's what they seen.'

'And you think Michael might have been one of them? One of the soldiers who saw this?' Kitty asked, turning Jack round at the end of the room to walk him slowly back to his chair.

'I dunno, Nurse Kitty. All I know is he was at Mons, so he might have done. Somethin's done his head, and of that we may be quite sure.'

That evening after supper, which they had taken with the men, as was their custom when on duty, Partita and Kitty sat in a sad exhausted state, clinging to cups of cocoa in the underheated, underlit library, reviewing the events of the day with Circe and discussing what Kitty had been told, Partita confessing that she had never heard the angel phenomenon mentioned and, since she never really read the newspapers, had missed the story altogether. Circe, on the other hand, remembered hearing John remarking incidentally on some such thing, but was unable to ask him directly now since her husband had been summoned urgently back to his post in London that afternoon.

'He was more interested in the use that he said was being made of it, in propaganda terms, the powers that be being determined to show that the enemy is a pretty foul fellow and that God

446

is on our side – which brings me to Michael Bradley's case, which is really most intriguing. As you know, he was wounded in battle, at Mons, in fact, but not in the front line. I gather he was a sniper, and a very good one at that. But apparently when General French withdrew, Michael got cut off behind enemy lines, and was duly captured.'

'But if that was the case, Mamma, how come we have him here?' Partita interrupted. 'He'd be a prisoner surely, if he'd been spared.'

'Which he obviously was,' Kitty offered. 'But yes, yes, how did he get here if the Germans captured him?'

'It's a little gruesome, I'm afraid,' Circe sighed, with an eye on the young women.

'Mamma, there's hardly anything we haven't heard by now,' Partita returned. 'Some of the things the men tell us . . .' She opened her eyes wide and stared at her mother expressively. 'So please go on Mamma, please.'

'The enemy captured him but they didn't treat him very well, I'm afraid.'

'Probably because he was a sniper,' Kitty said. 'At least that's what I was told. Soldiers don't like snipers. They think in a way it's a cowardly act, shooting someone when they don't get the chance to shoot back.'

'They're afraid of them, that's why,' Partita said. 'And who can blame them? Being sniped at by an unseen gun, by someone up a tree, or a church tower.'

'Obviously this was what the soldiers thought who captured Michael, because they did the most dreadful thing to him.'

Circe stopped shaking her head and, unable to go on, she picked up the silver crucifix around her neck and silently held it out.

'That is what they did to him?' Kitty put her hands to her face.

Circe nodded, unable to speak.

'How despicable, how bestial! What happens to so-called civilised people?'

Circe cleared her throat. 'I would have to think that when war breaks out, Humanity goes and buries her head. The good part about it is that he was saved – rescued by a woman, apparently. At least this is what they gathered from Michael before he retreated into what appears to be eternal silence. A woman, who was some sort of camp follower it's supposed, a woman called Marie – she took pity on him and when the soldiers had gone and left their victim to die, she rescued him, and somehow – and I don't know the fine details – she tended his wounds and returned him to the British troops, to a field hospital where they learned what had happened to him, and duly sent him home to recover.'

There was more, of course, inevitably. Whatever the truth of the story, however embellished or imagined it might or might not have been, it seemed from the end of the report that those who had come to see Michael now wanted him moved, ruling that although physically he had recovered entirely from the wounds inflicted on him, his mental health gave rise to too much anxiety.

Everyone concerned with the welfare of the men at Bauders knew what this meant, that Michael would have to be transferred to some sort of mental institution, the sort of place from which he would have little hope of any immediate release.

Some, however, suspected there was more to it than that, Partita in particular.

'Seems to me from what one gathers that the politicos are at pains to step up the propaganda no matter what,' she heard her recently returned father saying as he and Circe sat by the fireside late one evening, while she herself, unknown to them, had fallen asleep in a large winged chair down the bottom of the room. 'It seems to me the idea is to turn the enemy into some sort of amoral fiend, sort of fellow who goes round ravishing the maidenhood of every country he conquers, who tortures and mutilates his prisoners and who will not rest until the entire world is under his yoke. I don't happen to think that it is quite so. I have had a lot of dealings and so on with some of these people who are now our sworn enemy – through no great fault of our own – and I hasten to add that I find most of them all too civilised. While one recognises that there are differences between us, just as much as there are differences between us and our allies, we are basically all very much the same when all is said and done. I'm not happy with all this propaganda machinery, telling our chaps things that simply are not true. There are fair tricks and there are dirty tricks. I think it is a perfectly fair trick to make it appear that there are thousands of Russian troops making their silent way through the heartland of England, preparatory to launching an offensive against the enemy from the South Coast, in order to draw as many enemy divisions away from the Front as possible for them to watch their backs – fair enough. That I call tactics. But I do not consider it fair to put stuff about concerning the appearance of God's messengers on the field of battle so that we might appear to have God fighting in our colours, nor do I consider it right and proper to – what's the word?'

'What word are you looking for, John?' Circe enquired, looking up from her knitting.

'What one does with information, that's what – disseminate, that's the word. The very thing, dissemination. No, I do not consider it correct to disseminate these untruths about torture and mutilation and make them out as being biblical in their veracity. This can only lead to an unfairly deep hatred of the enemy, and if that is the case, dearest dear, it will only lead to yet more wars of this kind of ferocity and size.'

'Don't you think we should be fighting this war, John?'

'What I think is that this war should never have happened. But now that it has, we have no real alternative. By the time the politicians had woken up and got out of bed, it was too damn late. That is what I think.'

'They want us to return one of our patients.' Circe put her knitting down. 'They want to move the man I told you about, Michael Bradley.'

'Yes, I happen to have found out all about that,' John replied. 'Been trying to put a stop to it. It's all part of the thing I've been talking about. I dare say they are planning to use the poor chap as some sort of tool against the enemy, all in the cause of propaganda. It's turning another nation into devils. All wrong, all wrong.'

'He's a sick man, John. I'm sure we can mend him here, finally, but we need time; and if they either lock him away or put him on parade as this freak show you're talking about, then I really see no hope for him. I want him to stay here, John.'

'See what I can do, my love – promise you that.'

'And if you can't? If you can't do anything?'

'Then perhaps you should,' John replied carefully. 'Although of course you didn't hear me say that. Or anything like it.'

'No, of course not.'

They both stood up, in complete agreement as always, and left the room, quietly shutting the doors behind them, leaving their youngest daughter still hidden behind a chair planning how best to help poor Michael Bradley.

*   *   *

'Mary,' Michael said out of the blue as Partita was sitting reading to him one summer evening. 'Mary – is that you?'

Before she could reply Partita was aware he was looking at her, but this time instead of looking through her or past her, he was looking directly at her and noticing her.

'You're there,' he sighed. 'Thank God. Thank God indeed.'

'It isn't Mary,' Partita said cautiously. 'I'm one of your nurses. My name is Partita.'

'If it hadn't been for you, Mary,' he sighed, 'what would have happened to me?'

'It's all right, Michael. You're perfectly safe now, and you're in good hands. You're here with us and we won't let anyone harm you ever again.'

'I knew that the moment I saw you,' Michael said with a smile, his entire look changed from that of a lost and anguished man to that of someone redeemed. 'I knew you were an angel. And where have you brought me? What is this wonderful place?'

'This is our home, which is also a hospital, Michael. You were badly wounded so you were brought here, finally, to recover from your wounds.'

'My wounds,' he said quietly, looking down at his hands. 'My wounds.'

'Your hands have mended so well, Michael, seeing how badly damaged they were. They don't open quite fully – ' Partita showed him,

452

taking one hand and gently stretching it as far open as she could – 'there, but they are much, much better.'

Michael studied his hands and fell silent again, the distant look returning to his eyes as he regarded his hands, and then once more the landscape beyond them both.

'My God,' he whispered. 'Why have you forsaken us?'

'He hasn't, Michael,' Partita reassured him. 'Everything is fine. You're going to be all right, and everything is going to be fine. Nobody has deserted anybody.'

'I died, Mary,' he said, now staring up at the sky. 'I died and I have risen again. I have come back to life and it is all because of you. Of what you did. Because of you.'

'How do you mean you died, Michael?'

'I was dead when you found me.'

'I didn't find you,' Partita said carefully, realising from what he had just said that he might be beginning to recover his senses. 'Some kind lady found you and took care of you.'

'Yes, Mary found me,' Michael interrupted, now looking at Partita with what seemed to be full recognition. 'She rescued me, and because of her I came back to life. I was dead, you see, Nurse. I saw the angel and I knew I was dead.'

'Do you know where you are now?'

Michael frowned. 'Not, not perhaps as I should. In a hospital, to judge from the nurses' uniforms. Although where that hospital is . . .' He shook his head again. 'I have no idea and it doesn't really matter.'

'I'm going to get Dr Watkins, Michael,' Partita said, smiling at him as she rose. 'He's a very kind man and I know how much he wants to talk to you.'

She actually went in search of Kitty, but when Kitty heard what Partita had in mind, she questioned her friend's sanity.

'Kitty!' Partita protested in return. 'Kitty, sometimes you are so – so – what *is* the word? Sometimes you are so *ordinary*!'

'Oh, thank you, Tita. Thank you very much for – that is not a really nice thing to say. Besides, what is *ordinary* about common sense? You cannot expect to hide someone who is still in the army! I may be *ordinary* but sometimes you are well – completely mad!'

'I overheard Papa and Mamma—'

'I know what you overheard and it doesn't make any difference. I'm sure that is not what your mother is thinking of doing. If Michael were to disappear then he would be classed as a deserter because he is still in the army, even though he is a patient here. He hasn't been *discharged* – he's still a *soldier*.'

'Very well, Kitty. I understand. But you don't seem to want to understand me. While Michael is still not in possession of his full senses – what do they call it? When the balance of his mind is disturbed, yes – he can't be held responsible for his actions. So he disappears for a while and, since you say he's coming back to his senses, by the time he reappears again he'll be perfectly sane and they won't need to lock him away! Don't you see? If he's come back fully to his senses then he's safe, we'll have saved him.'

'Where exactly are you thinking of hiding him?' Kitty wondered, less certain now that Partita had gone temporarily insane, since there was some logic to her argument. 'And how would we feed and look after him?'

'In a place this size? You think we can't find a bolt-hole somewhere on the estate or in one of the villages? Or even in the house? There are even two or three decent priest holes here, and if they were good enough to conceal priests safely during the persecutions, they'll be well up to hiding away one rather timid patient.'

'Let's see, shall we?' Kitty stalled. 'Let's see how Michael gets on and what sort of plans they have in store for him before we go doing anything rash. If we were to get caught—'

'There you go being ordinary again, Kitty. We're pirates, remember? Pirates don't get caught.'

While Michael continued with his recovery, Bauders received more visitors in the shape of Peregrine and Pug, simultaneously home on leave from France. Pug was joyfully reunited with his adored Elizabeth, while Peregrine, having dutifully visited his mother and found her in no more of a giving vein than when last he saw her, took himself off as soon as he could to visit everyone at Bauders.

'I'm astonished,' he told Kitty as she showed him around the wards and the dayrooms, 'not only at what you're doing, but how you're doing it.'

'You didn't think we were up to it, did you?' Kitty teased him.

'Of course I did. I just never imagined it being on such a scale – nor that Partita, of all people, should have stuck to it. Knowing the Mischief, I'd have thought she would have got bored of it all too soon, and taken off for London where, against all the odds, I understand there is still some sort of a Season.'

'One should never underestimate Tita,' Kitty said with some feeling. 'I sense that you still think of her as a mischievous young girl. She is very different from that. The war has changed her, as it was bound to change us all, and as far as hard work goes, she leaves us all in her wake – and, of course, the men just adore her.'

'Ah,' Peregrine smiled. 'Now I see why Tita has stuck to her guns, if she's being followed everywhere by platoons of adoring men.'

'That is mean-spirited, Peregrine,' Kitty returned. 'Not like you at all.'

'Sorry, Matron.'

'And that too is mean-spirited.'

'Do you not think you might be being a trifle starchy, Matron?' Peregrine looked sad.

'I'm sorry,' Kitty said, feeling suddenly guilty.

'It's been very hectic these last few months, especially now they're sending us even more patients.'

'Of course,' Peregrine agreed. 'It's just my high spirits – being back here. In one piece. Seeing everyone.'

'Now you're making me feel even worse. Here am I saying we're feeling the push, when you've been fighting at the Front. I am so sorry, Peregrine. That was very thoughtless of me.'

'You couldn't ever be thoughtless, Kitty. Not you.'

Seeing the look in his eyes, Kitty at once busied herself with what she had been doing prior to Peregrine's arrival: rolling and pinning up bandages, and cleaning up the medical trolleys that were loaded with a startling array of medicines, instruments and dressings.

'That one of Tita's special charges?' Peregrine wondered, noticing Partita sitting outside on the terrace, talking attentively to a good-looking dark-haired man seated in a chair by her side, realising with surprise that what he was watching had shot him through with a sudden feeling of jealousy. As he considered this, inevitably the higher part of his mind rejected such a notion as absurd, while the lower part of it made him realise that perhaps Kitty had been right in accusing him of never letting Partita grow up, at least not as far as he was concerned. 'She seems to be paying him a lot of attention,' he added, unable to stop himself from continuing to stare at the couple. 'Quite a considerable amount, really, not like Tita at all.'

'That's because he's a special patient,' Kitty replied, without needing to look at Partita and Michael. 'It's a very interesting case history – but not one that we should talk about, Captain, because I want to hear all about *you*.'

Kitty took Peregrine by the arm and walked him through the house, away from the terrace and Partita. She knew it would be quite wrong to interrupt Partita when she was with Michael. Every little step of enlightenment meant so much, and they were both so sure that he was climbing slowly back to some sort of sanity, although, given what had happened to him, that did not seem necessarily the right word to use. Nevertheless, as she saw Peregrine giving both nurse and patient a backward glance, Kitty could not help feeling that it would do Peregrine good to see how seriously Partita took her work, how involved she was with her patients.

'Would you like to come and have a cuppa with the men?' Kitty looked across at Peregrine, who was still glancing back, every few yards. 'They would love to see you and hear about the way things are going.'

'I'm sure that's the very last thing they want to hear about, poor chaps. They'd probably far rather talk about sport or girls or something.'

'I thought that, but when Almeric was home they couldn't ask him enough about how it was going.'

'Hell is what it is, Kitty. It's no good dissembling, not now, especially not now that things are going so badly for us. In fact, if you read the official German communications they're positively euphoric. You'd think it was all over, as far as they were concerned.'

'But it isn't, Peregrine, is it? Surely not?'

Kitty stopped and looked at him anxiously, genuinely worried for the first time that there was a real possibility that the war could and might be lost.

'It's just a bad patch, Kitty,' Peregrine reassured her, turning away from the true reality, which was that the war was taking such a toll, particularly on the young officers, that if it continued the rumour was they would literally run out of them. The latest casualty lists showed the loss of over two hundred officers in the battles that continued to rage around Ypres. On top of that, the much-vaunted Russians were in retreat, while the Germans, by their continued and universally condemned use of poison gas, were recapturing key positions, won at the cost of thousands of British lives. With all his heart Peregrine wished for the war to be over, but since he wished just as devoutly not to be on the losing side, he knew he and his brothers in arms must continue to fight until victory was assured, whenever that might be.

'How is Almeric?' Peregrine asked, switching the subject as Kitty led him to where the more mobile patients were taking their tea.

'Have you heard from him recently?'

'He's a very good letter writer,' Kitty replied. 'I had a letter from him only yesterday, as it happens, in one of these new rather odd green envelopes.'

'The ones where the writer has to attest there's nothing except private and family matters in it, so as the censor doesn't have to wade through details of what colour socks he wants, or how mother's bunions are going on?' Peregrine joked. 'As a matter of fact the new envelopes are really rather a good notion. Means when you're writing to girls you can say what you mean in a letter without feeling self-conscious.'

'Are you writing to a lot of girls?' Kitty teased.

'Masses,' Peregrine smiled. 'Including you.'

Pug went to visit no one other than his mother, who had tactfully vacated the cottage so that he and Bethy could be alone.

They talked little about the war, and when they did, Pug typically made light of it, telling her anecdotes about life in the trenches rather than a blow-by-blow account in gory detail.

'It's really very amusing, Tommy at war,' he told her. 'I doubt if there are any other soldiers like them in the world. And you should see what they do to their trenches. Every trench has a name – like streets, just like in towns – High Street, East Street, George Street, that sort of thing. Then there's Lucky Way, Wretched Way, Coffee Trench, Tea Trench – and others that are logical in quite another way, Petrol Lane leading to Oily Way, Scabbard Trench being ahead of Bayonet Alley. But it's all very sensible because it means you can find your way around. Not that I'm in any danger at the moment of getting lost because we seem to be stuck entirely in the same place. No, no, I tell a lie. Last week we moved ten feet on – only to have to move ten feet back again a couple of days later when Jerry gave us a shove.'

'What about your horses, Pug? You surely haven't got your horses in the trenches with you?' Elizabeth wondered.

'I gave 'em both to a chum of mine – fellow officer who'd had two shot out from under him.'

'And are they all right?'

'The horses are fine, Bethy,' Pug replied, sadness suddenly clouding his eyes. 'But sadly my chum bought it – shot in the back by a sniper.'

Peregrine accepted the Duchess's invitation to stay for dinner, even though she had warned him it would be a really scratch affair, just two or three courses taken late when the main tasks of the day had been done.

'I think it's wonderful what you're all doing here,' he told Circe as they finally prepared to go in to dinner. 'I was talking to some of the men and you should hear how they sing your praises. They can't believe how lucky they are to be at Bauders.'

'It is our privilege to serve them, Peregrine,

but, with all due respect, it's very hard to think of our guests as being lucky,' Circe replied. 'We're the ones who are lucky, to have men such as they to fight on our behalf. The good luck is all on our side to have that, and to have them here to recuperate. It's taught us all so much.'

'They're not going to want to leave here.'

'We don't want them to leave, but that is something we cannot fight. The great thing is it is never mentioned, on either side. If it was, Perry, it would be almost insupportable. But they know, and we know, that as long as the enemy is trying to break down our front doors then, if fit and strong again, they must return to the fight. Tell me,' Circe continued, accepting the arm Peregrine was offering her, 'I haven't heard a word about your sister, other than the fact that she has been working and training as a nurse.'

'She had hoped to work for one of the repatriation schemes. I don't know if you've heard about them?'

'I certainly have. I know Maude Milborne is working for the French one, she being a fluent French speaker.'

'Livia hoped she could do the same,' Peregrine nodded, 'also being fluent in French, but she was told you have to be twenty-five, I think it is. Anyway, they told her she was too young and so she's off to join the French Red Cross.'

'Good for her. And Valentine?'

'Apparently Valentine is a pacifist,' Peregrine replied carefully. 'He doesn't think it right to fight this war – for him, anyway. And now he's off somewhere doing errands for his father.'

'Yes, I understood as much in a letter which I received from Julia. Well, it's a free country, and that, after all, is one of the main reasons why we are fighting this war – so that people like Valentine can hold those sort of opinions.'

'Precisely, Duchess,' Peregrine agreed as they approached the table. 'I just wonder what might happen if they introduce conscription, as rumour has it they will. It will be a bit difficult for Valentine, as it is becoming for everyone who is not yet in uniform. People spit at you in the streets, you know, or kick you if you climb into their railway carriages dressed only in civilian clothes. There is so much anger about now.'

'Why should they want more men?' Partita wondered, having overheard the end of the conversation as they all took their places at table. 'Everyone says the one thing we're not short of is fighting men.'

'I'm not a politician, Partita.' Peregrine held out the Duchess's chair for her and she sat down. 'All I know is we've lost nearly half a million men, dead, wounded or missing, and the stream of volunteers for Kitchener's Army, so-called, seems to be drying up.'

'Because I suppose what everyone thought at the beginning hasn't come to pass,' Kitty observed. 'That it would be all over in weeks.'

Everyone stared at her for a few seconds, and as they did, Kitty found herself colouring. She had sounded angrier than she should have, and she knew it. Worse, she had sounded bitter.

It did not seem possible but there was worse to come when the news broke that the *Lusitania*, one of Cunard's most prestigious transatlantic liners, was sunk by a German U-boat off the south coast of Ireland, with the rumoured loss of over a thousand lives.

'A passenger ship?' Partita exclaimed, breaking the silence that seemed to have fallen over the whole castle after they had learned the news. 'They've sunk an innocent passenger ship? Why? Why? *Why?*'

'I simply could not begin to answer that,' Circe replied, trying to come to terms with the implications of what was in reality an atrocity. 'Except that it would seem nothing is either sacred or safe any more.'

'Well said, Mamma,' Partita agreed. 'Nothing *is* sacred or safe. You are right.'

'All I know is – from what I read in the papers – as the ship was about to leave,' Peregrine stated, 'I understand the German Embassy printed a warning in the *New York Times* – I think it was – saying that any ship that strayed into what's called the European War Zone would be a legitimate target for their submarines.'

'How can that possibly be?' Circe returned, standing up and starting to pace up and down as she realised that any number of her American relatives and friends could have been on board the luxury liner. 'A passenger ship, carrying only civilians? How can they *possibly* call that a legitimate target?'

'I suppose because they suspect we have broken certain codes, or might be as capable as they are in breaking certain codes.'

'What sort of codes, Perry?' Partita demanded.

'It would be perfectly possible to carry arms and armaments bound for the war zone, let us say, in the holds of passenger ships. I don't think the enemy simply wishes to target innocent civilians. The propaganda value of such a crime would tell against them too much.'

'They might do that sort of thing,' Partita said hotly, 'but not us. Never.'

'And certainly not a neutral country surely?' Kitty asked. 'What would be the point?'

'There could be all sorts of points, Kitty, and all sorts of possibilities. But it doesn't matter. What matters is hundreds of innocent people have lost their lives in the most terrible way, and whatever the reasons are for sinking the *Lusitania*, there cannot be one that could possibly justify such a wholesale murder.'

'Gracious heavens!' Circe suddenly exclaimed, rising from the table. 'I have just had the most terrible thought. Please excuse me, everyone.'

She hurried from the room without further explanation.

Those she had left behind fell to silence, with no idea what the thought might have been or what it was prompting but were too tactful to ask.

They all considered the latest grim piece of news. Partita watched Peregrine's face as he finally broke the silence the news had engendered. He was still as handsome as ever, his voice still as measured and mellifluous as when she had first known him, and used to slide down the banisters to greet him in the Great Hall. It was not fair. Part of her had hoped, so hoped that he would come back from the Front a changed man, not as changed as Michael Bradley, of course, but changed enough for her to stop caring about him, because the truth was she no longer wanted to have feelings for him. She no longer wanted to have her pulse quicken uncomfortably when she saw him; she no longer wanted to hope that he would see her as something other than this childish brat that he still called Mischief. She had found a new purpose to her young life. She was needed, if not by him, by her patients, and yet seeing him expressing his thoughts, watching his handsome face assume a look of compassion and understanding, she knew that strong as her will was, she could not suppress her feelings. She still loved him as she always had, would still pray for him every night, as she always had. In short, she would always love him, despite knowing now that he would never love her the way she wanted.

'Maude?' Circe was asking into the telephone. 'Maude dearest, this is Circe. I wonder, have you heard the news?'

Shortly after two o'clock that afternoon, just after the Old Head of Kinsale had been sighted on the coast of Cork, the first torpedo had been launched, hitting the liner right behind the bridge. It had caused an abnormally loud explosion for the impact of only one missile, followed almost at once by a very heavy smoke cloud, both the explosion and the cloud causing instant confusion and panic. The great ship listed quickly and began to sink at an angle that made a successful launching of the lifeboats all but impossible, the first loaded life crafts hitting the water far too hard and hurling all their passengers into the water.

Like most gentlemen passengers on board, Hughie's sole concern was to try to ensure that the women and the children got safely into the other lifeboats that were being prepared for launch, but the pandemonium and panic was so intense that he twice got knocked clean off his feet and only managed to save himself from plunging into the water by a last-minute rescue from one of the crew, who grabbed his hand as he was slipping down the decks to haul him back to safety. But his wellbeing was only temporary since the liner was sinking very quickly, taking with it hundreds of panic-stricken, screaming innocent people. Someone had thrown him a life jacket, but seeing a woman being loaded into a lifeboat without one, he sacrificed his last chance of redemption by insisting she took it.

He and another man, an American his own age whom he had met on the voyage, then looked for something on to which they might cling or somewhere safe where they might shelter until perhaps some miracle happened that might save them, because they both knew that without any such miracle they were most certainly doomed. As they clung to a steel post that instead of standing at one hundred and eighty degrees to the sea now stood at right angles, both men hung on for dear life, lives so dear they had both prayed at the tops of their voices for the miracle that would save them, knowing there was no chance now that their lives would be spared. As the liner plunged ever faster into the turbulent seas, he thought of two things, of the fact that he had only got a ticket on the liner at the very last moment, the holder of the passage being one of a handful of passengers to take heed of the anonymous telegrams many had received warning them not to embark on the liner, and of the fact that he had been anxious to avail himself of the opportunity simply because now that he had been freed by his employers he could get back to England as quickly as possible to enlist and go to fight, only now to drown helplessly and hopelessly before he could get in even one blow for the freedom of his country and of Europe.

Now, as the waters began to close around his feet, he closed his eyes and prepared himself for his death.

'God bless you, pal!' he heard his American companion yell. 'See you up there!'

And then they were gone, gone to the unforgiving waters of the ocean, gone to their graves with nearly twelve hundred other innocent souls, couples and lovers, single folk and hopefuls, old and young, civilians and merchant seamen, the rich and the poor, twelve hundred of them sacrificed for the bellicosity of one nation and the foolishness of its enemies, a number *of souls, which, though horrific at the time, would hardly merit consideration when the final tally was told.*

Maude had only known that Hughie was about to return home and that he had been unable to get a first-class berth due to the lateness of the application he had made for his booking. She had been unaware that he was in fact already under way until she got a cable sent on his behalf by an American friend: 'Surprise. Put out the flags. Sailing into Liverpool tomorrow. Hughie.'

And then Circe telephoned her.

'Have you heard the news, Maude?' Circe asked.

'News? What news, Circe dearest? I have been working day and night at Sister Agnes's nursing home, as you no doubt know.'

'The *Lusitania* has been sunk off the coast of Ireland. They believe she was torpedoed.'

'The *Lusitania*?' Maude repeated, trying to make sense of why Circe of all people should think it necessary that she be told this piece of news. 'The *Lusitania* is the pride of Cunard's fleet, isn't she?'

'Yes, my dear,' Circe said gently and carefully. 'She is. But—'

'She's a very safe ship, fast enough to outrun any possible danger,' Maude continued quickly, while in the back of her mind a terrible possibility was forming.

'So they said,' Circe agreed. 'I just thought I

should tell you because I wasn't sure on which ship Hughie might be making the crossing.'

Maude was silent, quickly realising, dread possibility having become an all too terrible probability, that Hughie might have been a passenger on the stricken ship.

'She sailed from New York, of course?' Maude asked suddenly.

'Of course, dearest. And was due into Liverpool tomorrow. I do so hope—'

But the telephone had gone dead. Hughie had to have been on board, or else why did the telegram say that he was due in at Liverpool tomorrow?

The reality spun round her and she gazed at the telephone that she had just dropped, and picking it up, she started to dial Circe's number at Bauders.

'Forgive me, Circe,' she said, sotto. 'The shock.'

'Do you want me to come to you, Maude? I can't bear the thought of you being alone,' Circe offered.

'No, I am all right, thank you, Circe. For the moment. Do you have any idea of the number of casualties?'

'The first reports are of several hundred dead, dearest,' Circe replied. 'The numbers have yet to be confirmed but it is understood the ship sank quickly, which leads everyone to suppose the casualty list will not, alas, be small.'

But no one knew with certainty until the following day, and those with relatives or friends on board had to wait even longer to have news confirmed or denied. Maude received the tidings by telegram, directly from the Cunard office.

'Deeply regret your son Hugo Milborne lost in *Lusitania* tragedy. Cunard representative to call.'

As she sat in her London house holding the rectangle of off-white paper that bore the strips of typewritten telegraphed information announcing in cryptic terms the death of her beloved boy, one of the maids came through to where she was sitting and placed the post in front of her on a silver salver. Maude gazed at it dully, and then her eyes caught sight of the American stamp. She turned the letter over and saw Hughie's postscript written in his generous hand.

'I might be home before this!'

Chapter Thirteen

Dawn Mourning

'It seems now that everything is sinking,' Partita said to Kitty as they walked around the grounds, trying to make sense of what they had learned, for once barely able to contain their emotions. 'That somehow everything we know and love went down with that poor ship. I keep imagining the terror of all those innocent passengers.'

'Fifteen hundred people,' Kitty said in a low voice. 'Fifteen hundred.'

'Fifteen hundred souls including poor, lovely, gentle Hughie Milborne.'

'Poor, poor Hughie.'

'Oh, Hughie, Hughie!' Partita cried out suddenly, leaning forward and clutching herself. '*Why* didn't you stay in America? *Why* did you have to come home? You didn't have to *fight*! You of all people, Hughie! You who was always so frail! They'd never have let you fight! They'd never have passed you fit!'

She collapsed into Kitty's arms, and started to

sob, her arms clasped round her tightly, Kitty's arms holding her up as best she could.

'Poor Maude,' Partita moaned. 'Poor Bertie.'

'Poor Hughie,' Kitty whispered, as Partita straightened up, getting a hold of herself.

'No,' Partita said, wiping away her tears. 'This will never do. This won't do at all. We have patients; they must come before our feelings.'

She detached herself, almost violently, from Kitty, walking away from her and from the house while she composed her emotions, Kitty remaining where she was for a moment before following her.

'What do you think, Kitty?' Partita asked as her friend joined her. 'What do you think everyone did to deserve this? This – this mayhem.'

'Nowadays I am afraid I think a great deal less of what we all did to deserve it, and more of what we all did to cause it,' Kitty replied, just a little tersely.

'You think we're to blame as well?' Partita regarded her with some wonder. 'But we didn't do anything.'

'Exactly, Tita. As a country we didn't do anything at all, not when we should have done, and now we are paying the penalty. Everyone intelligent is saying so; whatever nonsense is being put about, we all know it.'

'I can't even begin to understand what's happening. First of all it was all so exciting – and you can't deny it, because it was. Everyone was so excited by what was happening as if it was our chance to beat the bad men and reform the world. Our army was going to do it, and so easily. They were just going to march over there, fire a few shots, the enemy would put their hands in the air and that would be that. What fools we all were – what absolute dunderheads. And now we're going to lose everybody – and for what?'

'Don't say that, Tita. Don't.'

'Why not, Kitty? We know it's true.'

Partita looked with defiance at Kitty, challenging her to contradict her and knowing that she couldn't.

'Even if it were true . . .' Kitty shrugged her shoulders and stopped before starting again. 'Even if it were true, saying it isn't going to help anything at all, not one bit, and especially not at this time. How can we possibly go on if we start talking like defeatists? This is just the sort of thing the enemy wants. They want us to be demoralised because demoralised people start to wave white flags and then everything really *will* be lost.'

Partita regarded Kitty for a moment, then once more walked away from her, onwards towards the lake.

'I wonder what's happened to Harry?' she said once they reached the lake's shore, as if the lake had all at once reminded her of his absence. 'I doubt that anyone's heard from him in an age. You haven't had a letter from him, have you, Kitty?'

'No, of course not, why should I?' Kitty stopped. 'Although I heard his father saying to your mamma that he'd had a letter recently, but his handwriting was so bad he could hardly make out a word except that bullets appeared to be bouncing off his ambulance so effectively he thinks it must be made of rubber!'

'Sheer Harry,' Partita smiled. 'Impudence in the face of the enemy. Now come along, Kitty – back to our front, back to our party, shoulder to the wheel and all that.'

'Me come along?' Kitty retorted. 'You're the one who was just about to cave in.'

'Oh, I know, I apologise from the bottom of my heart. I was just feeling sorry for myself. Unforgivable.'

'No, you weren't. That's not you. You were feeling sorry for everyone else, as you always do.'

They both started to walk briskly back to the house and as they went along Partita explained that Michael was yet again in danger of being taken from Bauders and put in an institution.

'So what do you intend to do, Tita? Have you an idea?' Kitty asked, catching her by the arm to stop her walking so fast and furiously. 'Hide him in a priest hole?'

'No – it's much simpler than that, Kitty,' Partita replied. 'I'm going to marry him.'

She continued to walk on, but Kitty caught her by the arm yet again.

'That is simply not amusing, really it isn't.'

Partita shook off her arm, trying to continue to

walk, defiance seeming to emanate from every part of her, before she finally turned and faced her friend.

'Why isn't it amusing, Kitty? You are engaged already, so you can't marry him. I am not engaged, so I can become engaged. Besides, why would it not be amusing for me to become engaged to Michael Bradley?' Partita's expression changed from defiance to compassion.

'Because, as you very well know, Partita Knowle, poor Michael Bradley is already in love with you, and it would be cruel to lead him on.'

'Oh, you don't think so, really? You don't think he's really in love with me?'

'Of course. Gracious me, why *wouldn't* he fall in love with you? You're beautiful, patrician, and have given him your sole attention for days on end. He is bound to fall in love with you, as so many on the ward have.'

Partita sighed. 'Yes, but it is not love they are feeling, is it, Kitty? It's schoolboy crushes, that's all. At any rate, a kind of grown-up version, because they are so far from everything they know and love, as I imagine people at school must feel when they are locked away from everything they know and love.'

'Maybe, yes, maybe, but it is none the less felt keenly for all that, Kitty. Truly there is so much of which we must be careful, and people's emotions are of the most tender. Remember Michael has already made one attempt on his life.'

'I know, and that is why I am trying to think

up some plan to help him before they come and get him. If he could pretend to be engaged to me, nothing more, or if I just said to the authorities that he was, that would mean they couldn't take him away and put him in some ghastly institution where he certainly will want to take his own life. He is not mad, Kitty, truly he isn't. He has just gone away from life because of the terrible, terrible thing that happened to him. He has gone away, and we could get him back, we should get him back. We can't stop this terrible war, which I sometimes feel will never, ever end, but we can stop anything more terrible happening to men like Michael Bradley. Not only can we, I feel it is a sort of – well, duty to do so. Really, it is our duty.'

'But – but what will your papa and mamma say? They will never believe that you want to be engaged to poor Michael, never.'

'No, I know,' Partita admitted. 'But I think I can get Mamma to agree to my idea, and I think once she has agreed to it, it will have an effect on Papa.' Partita's mouth set in a stubborn line. 'If Papa thinks I am so desperate to help Michael Bradley that I will even marry him to stop the authorities taking him over – perhaps even taking him not into a mental institution but to some awful place where they experiment with gases and drugs on people whose minds have been destroyed – then he will act to pull the necessary strings to stop it happening. I am quite determined on it, Kitty.'

'I can see that.' Kitty smiled suddenly. 'And whatever you say about the war, with people such as you on our side, I don't think that finally the enemy have a chance!'

Nevertheless Kitty considered the plan wayward, to say the least, but she also realised there was nothing she could say to dissuade Partita. The only people who could possibly have talked her out of taking such a course would be Almeric, and even perhaps Peregrine. She determined to write to him at once on the matter, but no sooner had she done so than she found herself hurrying out to the front drive to greet a new influx of patients.

She stopped and stared first at the men climbing from the ambulances, and then at the other nurses.

'What in heaven – what in all that is merciful have we here?' Kitty's eyes met those of Nurse Rose.

'Shell shock, that is what we have here, Nurse Rolfe, shell shock.'

'They look as if they don't know where they are.'

'That is probably because they don't,' Nurse Rose replied crisply. 'They know nothing of where they are, at any time. They will hardly be able to eat, or talk, or light a cigarette, or write a letter, nothing.' She paused. 'My mother has been nursing some of these cases in a home in Norfolk. She wrote to warn me that they are more difficult to nurse than the openly wounded. Limbs heal faster than minds, Nurse Rolfe. So –' she nodded briskly towards what looked like a sea of crippled men staggering towards them – 'time to roll up our sleeves, and get going.'

'Have you both taken leave of your senses?' The Duke stared from his wife's face to that of his daughter. 'What are you all thinking? One simply cannot interfere with this sort of thing in this sort of way, d'you understand me?'

'No, Papa,' Partita replied. 'I think we have an absolute duty to our patients. We must stand by them in the same way that you would stand by your men. It is no different.'

Circe felt quite proud of Partita at that moment, if only because she looked every inch the daughter of her father; but also because she could see that John was looking at her as if he was seeing her as a formidably strong character, perhaps even as a young woman at last.

'Hmm.' Her father paused. 'So you are standing by your men, are you? You don't say.'

'I do say, as it happens, Papa. You know the last thing any of us wants is to take advantage of your authority and your position. What we want is for you to see what we're trying to do, and when you do, we know what your feelings will be because we know you are the sort of person who, in our place, would be just as unflinching in your determination. Michael Bradley is a victim of a terrible atrocity, but we have helped him, and we can help him further. What we cannot do is turn him back to those who will take ruthless advantage of his mental state, perhaps use him as a guinea pig, only to throw him into a mental institution where he will languish for the rest of his days.'

'That will not necessarily be his fate.'

'Not necessarily, no, but it could *well* be his fate, Papa.'

'You couldn't let them do that, John,' Circe put in, turning to him. 'Not if you knew the poor man.'

'Be that as it may,' John replied, his defences weakening, 'this is a matter for the medics. We can think what we like and feel what we like, but in the end this is a matter for the experts who must be allowed to do what they think best, surely?'

'No, please, it is you who will do what is best, surely, John?'

The Duke, seeing the steely look in both wife and daughter's eyes, realised that for once he was being outgunned.

'Very well. I will see what I can do. If the matter comes up—'

'But the matter will not come up!' Partita protested. 'Not unless *you* bring it up, Papa. Don't you see?'

'I do see. But I also see this is just one chap – albeit a soldier who has been subjected to an appalling atrocity, which, if proved to be true, will be dealt with officially. But it is just one soldier – one soldier who is part of a vast army of millions of men who are all being exposed to the greatest brutalities that man has ever inflicted on man. Now if we were to examine each and every one of these cases to ensure that no one was being exploited or used in any way that might upset them, where would we be? Every single one of those men who every day and every night are being ordered over the top are being exploited, if you look at it that way. They're certainly not doing these things because they enjoy it. They might believe in the greater good, and they might have volunteered to fight the good fight, but believe me every man jack of them would rather the whistle didn't blow for them to climb the ladders out of their trenches and go over the top, but that's how it is. In a fight like this there are bound to be sacrifices, and this is something to which we must all get used. Something we all of us must learn to expect to happen – or, if not to us, then to someone close to us. If we start trying to protect everyone who comes to Bauders – why, that'll never do, never do at all. We don't have the time for it and that's all there is to it.'

'But if the matter does arise,' Partita persisted quietly, although by now feeling more than a little forlorn, 'you will do what you can?'

'If the matter arises, Partita, I shall see what, if anything, I can do. And if it is for the best then I shall do it.'

'But—'

'But you are not to become engaged to this man. Is that understood? It would be the most terrible thing to lead him on in such a way, and I can't think what took possession of you to think up such a scheme, or for you to persuade your poor mamma to go along with it.'

'I do see your father is right,' Circe agreed, turning to Partita with a warning look, and then back to her husband. 'We must all be a little overwrought. Really, we must be, John.'

'Understandably so.' The Duke straightened his shoulders. 'I will do what I can, when I can, believe me, I will.'

'Thank you, Papa.'

'Good,' her father said to her with a nod. 'And don't think for a moment that your work here is going unappreciated, because it ain't.' He cleared his throat. 'You are all as much at the party as the men. Hearts and souls and wills, we will win. It is just taking a little longer than we all thought, that's all. A little longer.'

Although nothing was said again by anyone in reference to Michael, he was still in residence at Bauders at the beginning of June. The fact that his continued presence was not even remarked upon by any of the family, was as if they all believed any mention of him or his salvation might break the spell.

Plenty was said between Partita and Kitty, however, when next they received word from the Front. Kitty was the first to get a letter, a long, loving and intimate screed from Almeric from somewhere in Flanders. He wrote:

It seems to be so odd to be here as summer breaks. All I think of is home, of all Mamma's beloved flowers, especially her roses, and the fresh green of the trees – and now the most beautiful of all the flowers of home – you, my darling Kitty. How I would love to be sitting by the lake with you, or going on one of our famously long hikes. Do you remember the last walk we took when we got absolutely drenched in that sudden squally shower and I don't think either of us noticed?! I suppose we must have done so sooner or later because the next picture I have is of you and me in the folly, with you in my arms and me kissing you and kissing you. How I love you, darling Kitty! If I didn't love you so much I don't really think I could manage this very well at all. Yesterday we buried two young men killed by shell-fire while out mending cables for the telephones. That in itself is a terrible job but a necessary one because good communications are absolutely vital and practically nonexistent. Rumours abound concerning some of our recent fatalities not so far down the line – that they were killed by our own guns because of incorrect information. It could have happened, I suppose, but it simply does not bear thinking about. These young men were two particularly jolly types – never a moan or a grumble from either of them, and they both went about their dangerous tasks as if they were out gardening. Only three nights ago we were at a dance in the village just behind our lines where the locals all carry on as if whatever war is happening is happening in some other country! This in spite of the constant noise of the guns clearly audible from everywhere in the village – yet no reference is ever made. Drink and food are willingly fetched and carried as if we are all here on a holiday – hence the dance. They held it for us in the little hall with a typically French band – endless accordions, a fiddle, drums and a trumpet – and everyone danced with such exuberance you would think we were celebrating peace instead of preparing for yet another battle. I didn't dance – have no fear! Well, that isn't strictly true – there were many pretty – or rather *jolie* young ladies present but the only dance I had was with Madame who runs the café with her husband, a huge, sanguine man with a moustache like a walrus and a great capacity for *le bon vin rouge*. The two young men we have just buried danced all night. I can see them now, well and truly lit up and prancing and galloping round the smoke-filled hall like lads at a village hop. I was going to say, as if their lives depended on it, and I suppose in a way that would be true. They say people here get a sense of their destiny and act accordingly. I don't know what that sense is, dearest – but if I get it I shall look out!

It was only the briefest of funerals because any gathering attracts the eye of the enemy, but we did get the chance to read something over them while another of the boys produced his harmonica and played 'Greensleeves'. I have to say it was all rather moving. It's so very odd – while we hurried through the briefest of services the guns suddenly stopped as if orchestrated to do so. When they did, after only a few moments, the air was filled with a chorus of birdsong. There we were, deafened by the barrage one moment and the next we were all standing in a summer garden at first light (because it wasn't long after dawn) – serenaded by the sweetest sound you could imagine. Poor old Flanders – there really doesn't seem to be very much left of her – and you do have to wonder why.

Anyway, there's talk of a bit of activity soon so I'm not sure when I shall be able to write again. It has been fairly quiet here for the last week, besides the sound of the bombardment, which thankfully is not directed anywhere near our position, although a couple of stray shells dropped about five hundred yards behind us, killing a woman, so they say, who was out walking with her two young children. That is what is so hard to fathom, Kitty – we who wear the uniforms of our country's regiments are legitimate targets, but women and little children being blown to pieces? What sort of world have we made?

As I lie here at night or at day, whenever it is possible to snatch some sleep in my fughole, I think of you. I think of our times together, I think of your laugh, I think of your gentle smile, I think of your sweet kisses. Most of all I think of your love and I think of you and I expressing our love for each other when this war is at last over and we are reunited properly. It is that thought – the thought of you and how much I love you – that keeps me sane and inspires me to try to lead my men safely through the battles to come and to do my bit to get sanity restored to this mad world of ours. You are not just in my thoughts, darling Kitty – you are my thoughts – entirely, even when sleeping when all I see is your beautiful angelic face. How I long to be in your loving arms once more! Sitting by the fire in the library with the dark night enfolding us while I enfold you in my arms, kiss your hair, your face, your soft cheeks and your sweet, sweet mouth. Love me as I love you, which shall be for –

Always, as ever, yours,
Almeric

Kitty wrote back to Al at once, almost as if she knew she had to catch him before he moved on, before the push to which he had referred began and her letter might not reach him at his new position. She had no idea how the postal services worked as efficiently as they did, under such duress. Every time she sat down to write to Almeric, she wondered how her letters ever reached him, how letters from home ever reached any of the soldiers to whom they were addressed and yet they did. Somehow those bags of mail containing letters marked to hundreds of thousands of different men serving in different regiments, subdivided into battalions, subdivided yet again and yet again until they were platoons, until they were units, until they were individuals, the very individuals to whom the letters had been written at desks, at kitchen tables, by firesides, under blossoming apple trees, besides lakes, rivers or ponds, on knees, in railway stations, hotels, houses, cottages, flats, hospitals, wherever a loved one could sit and put pen to paper – to write to their lover, their brother, their father, uncle, cousin, lover or just friend, before dropping that small carefully written missive into a post box, trusting it to a mail service that somehow miraculously managed to put that letter – finally – into hands all too eager to tear open the envelope. And having found a quiet place to read, the recipient would sit, smoke a cigarette or light a pipe, shut off the seemingly interminable noise of war and read all the news from home.

But this letter of Kitty's seemed to have a different urgency. It was as if the words that Almeric had so lovingly and carefully written to her had made her even more aware of the necessity of writing the right words. Because of this she found herself hesitant, searching, always searching, for the absolutely right thing to say to the man she was to marry.

Because of the genuine depth of her feelings for him, finally she was able to write a letter to him that she hoped conveyed adequately everything she felt. She wrote that she thought of him always, that she remembered their walks, their talks and their kisses, and that all she could think of was his safe return and of their being finally united. Then she kissed the envelope and posted it in the box that stood in the castle hall.

The letter that was delivered to Partita several days later had a very different effect indeed on the receiver.

Partita saved it up to read in bed. It was the end of a particularly difficult day, which had been spent tending to a number of patients who had just been sent on up to Bauders to recover from the effects of inhaling chlorine gas, the chlorine deeply affecting their respiratory and digestive systems. Bauders had been forwarded the first few cases in the forlorn hope that recuperation in the fresh summer air of the English countryside would do the trick. But the first of the arrivals were still so dreadfully distressed when they arrived that they had to be sequestered away from the other patients.

It was yet another harrowing experience, and one from which Partita had not had time to recover when she opened the letter and started to read.

'What on earth do you mean by this, Kitty?' she demanded, bursting into her room, waving the letter dementedly. 'What on *earth* – can you have been thinking? Are *you* shell shocked now? What did you mean by this?'

Kitty, worn out by the disturbing events of the day, had been fast asleep, so she now sat up startled, trying to make out who was in her room and why, putting her feet to the floor, thinking that it might be a patient, before realising it was Partita.

'This is a letter from Peregrine! And it appears – it appears that what it contains is all your doing! How could you write to him like that? How could you?'

'Just calm down, Partita,' Kitty replied, picking up her gown and pulling it on, 'and tell me what's going on.'

'Going on? Going on! I'll tell you what's going on, you interfering little fool!' Partita was at her bedside now, flapping the letter at Kitty like a mad woman. 'I've just had this letter from Peregrine congratulating me on my engagement, that's what's going on! And all thanks to you, apparently! You wrote to him and told him I was getting engaged to Michael! And he's taken it to be the gospel truth! What did you think you were *doing*?'

'Try to calm yourself, Partita. If you don't calm down you'll do yourself harm, really you will – particularly after everything you and I have been through today.'

'Today has nothing to do with anything! This is what matters! This letter! Don't you realise what you've done?' She sat down suddenly on the edge of the bed. 'You have finally managed to put Perry off me completely!'

'You're not making sense – it's because you're exhausted.'

'He will never see me as anything but a piece of thistledown now,' Partita continued, brushing away Kitty's conciliatory hand.

'No – think sensibly, Tita – and do try and calm yourself,' Kitty advised, now managing to get hold of Partita by her shoulders and guiding her back to her own room. 'Why should I try and do something like that? No – no, don't say anything for a moment, please? Not until you've heard me out. I admit, yes, I did write to Peregrine, but only because he asked me to do so as a friend, that's all – and I admit I mentioned the fact that you were thinking about becoming engaged to Michael – that this was how far you were prepared to go for your patients. It was a joke, in the letter, that's all, a joke.'

'What sort of humour is there in that, may I ask?'

'No – listen, please? I only did that for your sake.'

'For *my* sake?'

'Yes, for your sake.'

'How for my sake?'

'So that Peregrine will see you in a different

490

way. See you as you are. I was praising you to him. And I also hoped—'

'Hoped?'

'Yes, I really hoped that it might make him a little – well, I must be honest – *jealous*.'

For once Partita kept quiet. 'Jealous?' she asked eventually, frowning. Peregrine had always seemed so far removed from petty matters, she could not even imagine him entertaining such a petty feeling.

'You should have seen the look in his eyes when he saw the attention you were giving Michael.'

'Is this true?'

'Of course it is! Why should I lie to you? I'm engaged to your *brother* so why should I try and spoil things for *you*? I don't think Peregrine quite understands his real feelings himself. Nor does he understand just what a golden girl you really are.'

'But all he says here is that he must send me his congratulations. He blithely congratulates me on being such an angel and hopes we'll be very happy.'

'That's Peregrine all over.'

'Yes, I suppose it is.'

Partita looked pensive, so Kitty continued, 'If you ask me, half the trouble – no, the whole trouble – with you and Peregrine is that he's always been determined to see you just as a little sister, Almeric's little sister. But you have grown up, you've changed, and maybe when he was here, seeing how sweet you were being with your patients, maybe he suddenly saw you in a different light.'

'Maybe so, but – I hardly think so. Oh, why did you have to write to him?'

'You're tired, Tita,' Kitty said, sitting down on the bed beside Partita and putting an arm around her shoulders. 'We both are.'

'Oh God, oh God, Kitty, will this war never be over? It seems that it will never, ever end.' Partita sighed in misery. 'Oh, for it to be all over and everything to be back just as it was.'

'I don't think that's going to be possible.'

'For the war to be over?'

'No, for everything to be back just as it was.'

If people at home were being told that things on the Front were meant to be improving, at the actual party there were few signs of them doing so, while at the Front there were stories of Zeppelin raids on London, rumours that soon proved to be true with the news of over ninety bombs being dropped on the capital. People began to talk about the chances of a full-scale invasion, but this rumour died an early death due to the realisation that Germany's armed forces were too stretched on all European fronts to be able to spare a powerful enough force for an invasion. Nevertheless, the threat of aerial bombing did not diminish, and British cities were dark and frightened places at night.

Unaffected by either Zeppelin raids or rumours,

the nurses at Bauders worked longer and longer hours, but they also determinedly trained on. Partita and Kitty diligently attended their nursing classes, learning more and more about the newer techniques that had come about simply because of the war. Every bed in the castle was now taken, and there was an ever-growing waiting list of invalids ready to be sent there for recuperation. Yet despite this, Michael Bradley still remained, continuing a more or less untroubled convalescence, his only real anguish now being caused by something over which no one, least of all himself, had any control. He had, as predicted, fallen in love with his beautiful young nurse.

'Michael has just told me that he has fallen in love with me!'

Partita hardly dared to look at Kitty, who started to laugh, almost hysterically.

'Stop it, Kitty! Please, stop it. What on earth shall I do?'

Kitty handed Partita a cup of much-needed tea.

'Humour him, dearest, just humour him, but keep away from any ideas of rings or engagements!'

'It's going to make looking after him so difficult. Will you take over? Perhaps that would be better.'

'Of course I will, but it won't do any good, you know it won't. I told you he was besotted weeks ago.'

'Yes, I know, I know, but I thought it was just you exaggerating.'

'Just charm him.' Kitty gave Partita a tolerant look. 'You know more about charm than anyone.'

'How do you mean?'

'Never mind what I mean, Lady P. I know, that's all.'

Partita tried to do as Kitty advised, making jokes, putting on funny voices, anything to distract her patient from his all too evident emotions.

'I hope you didn't mind me expressing my feelings,' he said to her a few days later. 'I hope you didn't feel that I was speaking out of turn, what with you being who you are and everything.'

'Me being who I am and everything has nothing to do with anything, Michael,' Partita replied. 'I'm simply me and you are simply you, and that is all there is to it. I've explained my situation to you, and you're never to think that you spoke out of turn. But I have time only for my work, Michael, and that requires all my attention and all my devotion.'

But of course, her devotion to her patients only served to endear Partita to Michael all the more, and he was not alone. Kitty could not help being moved by the change in her friend, who, once she had been reassured of Kitty's innocent intentions towards her, was back to being a positive Catherine wheel of activity. Her latest idea being to put on a home entertainment such as they had done with *The Pirates of Penzance*. It was to be performed by the fittest and most recovered of the patients, and anyone else working at Bauders who might feel so inclined.

'I think that is a perfectly splendid idea,' Circe enthused.

'I thought we might do a pantomime,' Partita replied. 'We don't have the time at the moment to get it all organised, but if we put aside a few hours each month, by Christmas we will be just the thing.'

'A very jolly notion,' Circe replied. 'And I want to play a part in it.'

'So you shall, Mamma,' Partita laughed. 'You and – you and Consolata Catesby – you can both be the Ugly Sisters!'

Circe sighed. 'That is very sweet of you, dearest, but you can be the one to tell Consolata.'

Not much later they saw two people walking slowly up the long driveway, their shoulders rounded, their hands held tight together. As soon as she saw them Circe knew they were messengers of the Fates and a chill ran through her heart. Sending Partita back to her work before she too noticed the sad pilgrimage, rather than instructing Wavell to see to them, Circe went herself to meet the visitors in person.

They were possibly about the same age as she, Circe thought as she got closer sight of their faces, yet they seemed centuries older, their ashen faces shadowed with grief and despair. The man, tall and gaunt, took off his hat slowly when he saw the Duchess to nod his head respectfully, while the woman whose hand he had been holding made a small curtsy.

'Your Grace,' he said, 'we have met but I dare say you might not remember.'

'I remember your face very well,' Circe replied. 'But if you might be so kind as to remind me of your name?'

'Taylor, Your Grace,' he replied. 'Sidney and Margaret Taylor. We live over Blenham way, and I did work in the factory there. The linen mill.'

'Please come in,' Circe said, standing to one side of the door, knowing at once why they were there. 'You must be tired after your journey.'

'Thank you, Your Grace, but we don't wish to put you out,' Mrs Taylor said. 'We'd heard the fine work you were all doing here.'

'Thank you, Mrs Taylor, but I insist you come inside and let us give you some refreshment.'

Mr Taylor looked at his wife and nodded once, then thanking the Duchess again for her kindness, they walked through the front doors into the Great Hall.

Circe took them through to the library, while Wavell hurried away to make tea and sandwiches.

'I think you know why we're here, Your Grace,' Mr Taylor said.

'I think I do, Mr Taylor,' Circe replied. 'And if I am right I can only tell you how deeply sorry I am for you at this time.'

'It's our Tommy,' Mrs Taylor said, at which point her husband put a hand on her shoulder, as if to ease the pain.

'Yes, Mrs Taylor, I was afraid this was so.'

'He's dead, Your Grace,' Mrs Taylor continued, looking at Circe with the saddest pair of eyes Circe could remember seeing. 'Our Tommy. He's dead, I'm afraid. Killed in action.'

'They'd just gone over, you see,' Mr Taylor explained. 'The second time that very day. They'd survived one raid, then they was sent out again.'

'It were a direct hit, apparently, so they say.'

'I am so sorry, Mr Taylor,' Circe said gently. 'We all thought the world of Tommy. He was like one of the family.'

'He loved it here, Your Grace,' Mrs Taylor said. 'Never happier. That's why we has come to tell you in person. We wanted to tell you in person because we knew how happy he was here.'

'I'm glad you did, Mrs Taylor, although I only wish you had not had the occasion.'

'He was a lovely lad,' his father said. 'A very happy boy. What he liked best of all was to laugh. He liked nothing better.'

'He was a fine boy,' his mother said, still looking steadily at the Duchess. 'You understand we are not just here for us.'

'Of course.'

They had come to tell Tinker in person, but it seemed that Tinker already knew the moment she saw Wavell, the moment she saw the expression on his face. He walked her through to the library, holding her arm, already supporting her, knowing what was to come.

Livia was in Flanders, working in a Red Cross hospital run under the direction of Nurse Florence Cadell, a quiet-spoken Scotswoman who showed little emotion whatever the circumstances and seemed imbued with apparently endless energy and drive. Livia herself had been in the hospital for a few weeks, working under her maiden name of Catesby, when the realisation came to her that she had never yet seen Nurse Cadell off duty. Whenever Livia returned from her few hours of snatched sleep, Nurse Cadell would be still at work, quietly attending the wounded and giving comfort to men under her care, whom she was careful to keep from knowing that they were close to death. She seemed to inspire hope and courage in everyone, so much so that after the initial shock of working in a hospital so close to the front lines, inspired by the example of the woman running the hospital, Livia found herself capable of work she would previously have considered impossible. She also discovered in herself an ability to accept the terrible wounds she came across. Nurse Cadell, she saw, had the gift of addressing and treating each newly arrived patient as if he were someone very special to her, someone to whom she was prepared to give as much love and attention as was possible to ensure his survival.

As she worked alongside Nurse Cadell, Livia could not help thinking about Val, and about the stance he had taken on the war. Nor could she help wondering whether he had been right. Surely nothing, but nothing, was worth what these poor men were being put through? And then she saw him.

She had just come back on duty one evening after snatching a couple of hours' sleep, her first real rest in nearly two days, due to a sudden flood of badly wounded men, victims of a bloody engagement fought in the defence of some obscure ridge not fifteen miles distant, when through the half-glass door she saw what she was suddenly sure was Val. Whoever it was, at any rate, was in deep conversation with Nurse Cadell, the man talking animatedly while Nurse Cadell listened attentively.

Yet Livia held back until they parted, after which, her heart pounding with excitement, she started to run forward.

'Valentine?' she called, hurrying forward down the ward towards the office, some fifteen yards from her. 'Valentine? Val?'

He had not heard her the first time but when he did he turned quickly to stare at the figure hurrying towards him out of the half-light. Then, as Livia was halfway to him, he turned quickly and hurried out of a door to one side. By the time

Livia reached the door and pushed it open the figure she was pursuing had run down to the end of the corridor and was still hurrying through the double doors ahead of him. When Livia in turn reached the doors, finding herself in the busy lobby of the hospital, there was no sign of him. He had vanished.

She ran outside the building in the hope she might catch sight of him, thinking that whatever his hurry it could not have been precipitated by the fact that he had identified her because if that had been the case he surely would have waited to greet her or even hurried to her side, rather than running away. Unless, of course, she had been mistaken and it had not been Valentine. But there was no sight of anyone recognisable in the throng outside the building, so big a crowd of people – attendants, nurses and ambulance drivers – that any hope of catching him disappeared at once.

'I'm sorry to trouble you, Nurse Cadell,' Livia said, returning to the office at the top of the ward. 'That man who was in here just minutes ago ... ?'

Nurse Cadell looked up at her. 'What about him, Nurse?'

'I had the impression, the distinct impression—'

'Yes?'

Something in Nurse Cadell's tone and manner indicated that she neither welcomed this intrusion nor was she ready to impart any information about her caller. Certainly Livia was sufficiently deterred to stop.

'I thought I might have recognised him,' she said. 'For a moment I thought it was someone I knew.'

'Were you speaking about Monsieur Lacombe, Nurse Catesby?' Nurse Cadell replied, now consulting a list of her duties on her desk. 'Gerard Lacombe. He helps here in an advisory capacity.'

'Monsieur Lacombe?' the bewildered Livia returned. 'He's a Frenchman?'

'I would have to agree with that, Nurse. Now, if you don't mind, we have rather a lot on our hands today. They're still bringing them in from this latest engagement so I shall need all hands, please.'

Nurse Cadell had risen from her desk and was now at the door of the office, holding it open for Livia to leave.

'You know our Monsieur Lacombe, Nurse?'

'I was mistaken, Nurse Cadell. I didn't get a very clear view of the man and obviously my first impression was wrong.'

'Who did you think it was?'

'Just someone,' Livia replied quickly. 'Someone I knew from England.'

For a brief moment Livia was aware of a sudden inquisitive look in Nurse Cadell's eyes, but then she was gone, hurrying off to administer to the wounded who were being brought into the ward, with the still puzzled Livia in her wake.

*   *   *

Harry was also busy. It was up to him and his fleet of ambulances to deliver the wounded from dressing station to clearing station. From there, those who survived the initial traumatic journey would, it was hoped, be transported to base hospitals on the French coast, the luckier ones being sent home to recuperate in Britain.

Harry had been ordered to the grim, slag-heaped landscape of the heavy coal mining area of Loos only at the last minute. It was there where he learned a large-scale Allied offensive was planned. It was to be another battle that, if successful, was predicted would bring about a swift conclusion to the war. When he arrived he found nothing but chaos. No one either in or behind the lines had been prepared for the devastation of the conflict, a battle where the enemy machine guns were deployed with dreadful effect, their barrels raking at will along the Allied lines, each gun firing up to ten thousand rounds in an afternoon, killing hundreds and hundreds of the troops advancing steadily and unflinchingly into their deadly fire. Those who managed to survive found untouched barbed wire greeting them, entanglements the artillery had failed to destroy, an impenetrable obstacle that forced them to wheel about and retreat, whereupon they were once more subjected to a hail of machine-gun fire. In under four hours over eight thousand officers and men lay dead in the mud.

In all his time driving motor ambulances, Harry had never seen injuries like the ones he saw that day, nor had he seen such alarm and disarray in both the dressing and the clearing stations, the latter set up in huts, tents and sequestered local accommodation, the medical staff at both posts all but unable to deal with the stream of desperately wounded men being brought by stretcher off the battlefield and then transported by motor ambulance to the not exactly adjacent clearing stations. Because of the distance between the posts, and the uneven terrain, Harry and his fellow drivers found that they were unloading dead soldiers at the end of the journeys, prompting Harry to remark, as he had so often before, that the clearing stations were too far from the dressing ones and should be moved closer to the lines.

'Sir?' he asked when he found a moment to seek out the chief medical officer at the clearing station at which he had just arrived with all but one of his casualties now dead. 'Sir, don't you think we'd all save a lot more lives if these clearing stations were nearer the dressing ones?'

'I'm busy, damn you!' the officer shouted back at him over the mayhem. 'I don't have the time to answer questions!'

'Think about it, sir!' Harry called before leaving to return to his ambulance for his next dash. 'It makes sense!'

Amongst the wounded waiting for transport at

the dressing station, Harry saw the mud- and blood-covered figure of a young officer sitting on an upturned crate with his elbows on his knees and his hands supporting his battle-weary head. Normally Harry would not have looked twice at such a sight, since he would have considered a man capable of sitting up to be capable of waiting in turn for his ambulance ride, unlike the casualties lying on stretchers around him outside the tin shed spilling over with dead and wounded. Yet Harry stopped because he thought there was something immediately recognisable about the young lieutenant, and when he retraced his steps to take a second look he found himself staring into the all but blank eyes of Gus.

'Gus?' he said disbelievingly. 'Gus – Gus, is it you?'

Gus looked up at him for a moment uncomprehendingly until all at once he recognised him and the vacant look in his eyes became one first of identification and then pure delight.

'Harry,' he croaked, getting slowly to his feet. 'Well, I'm dashed – Harry Wavell.'

Seeing how unsteady he was on his feet, Harry sat him carefully back down on his crate and kneeled before him.

'I haven't got long, Gus,' he said. 'I have another run to do.'

'Another run?'

'I'm driving ambulances, Gus – and I have to get some more of you blokes back to the clearing station. Are you all right? Are you injured? Because if you are I'll see if I can shift you up the line.'

'I'm all right, Harry,' Gus replied, so wearily that for a moment Harry feared he might expire. 'At least I'm not wounded. At least I don't think so. Do you have such a thing as a cigarette?'

Harry produced a battered packet of cigarettes and lit them each one.

'There's blood coming down your arm, Gus,' he said. 'And a burn mark on your uniform. Looks to me as though you've been hit.'

Carefully Harry rolled back the sleeve of Gus's tunic as far as he could, to find a moderately bad flesh wound on his forearm.

'You're bleeding quite badly, Gus. We'd better get you into the dressing tent over there – come on.' Harry eased him back to his feet, put Gus's good arm round his shoulder and began to lead him across to the first-aid post. 'I think the bullet went right through – at least that's what it looks like, but I'm no doctor.'

'They heard us coming, Harry,' Gus said, barely above a whisper, forcing Harry to put his own head as close as he could to Gus's. 'After the first wave, we were attacking this redoubt – but they must have heard us long before we got there.'

'Don't speak, Gus,' Harry advised. 'I think you ought to save your strength.'

'There were only three of us left in the end,' Gus continued regardless. 'Then Sergeant

Blake was hit, just before we made it back to the trench.'

'Come on,' Harry encouraged the weakening Gus. 'Nearly there.'

'He needn't have gone to fetch him – at least not at once – not under that barrage of bullets.'

'Who? Who are you talking about, Gus?'

'But you know my brother – you know Al – he couldn't leave someone lying out there – not even for five minutes.'

'Almeric's here as well?' Harry said, stopping. 'Of course – you're in the same regiment.'

'I shouted at him to wait but he wouldn't, Harry,' Gus continued. 'You know my brother – others first. Always himself last.'

'Nurse?' Harry tried to attract the eye of one of the nurses, all busy seeing to the wounded in various states of distress. 'Nurse?'

'I'm all right, Harry. These other chaps are in far greater need.'

Finding a couple of empty wood crates to one side of the tent, Harry made Gus as comfortable as he could while he waited.

'Is Almeric all right, Gus?'

'Almeric's dead, Harry,' Gus said flatly. 'I was just telling you.'

'What? What did you say, Gus?'

'He was fetching Blake. Sergeant Blake got hit badly. Al went back to fetch him.'

'Did you say – you didn't, did you?' Harry asked, horrified. 'You can't have done.'

'I thought I'd told you, Harry,' Gus said, tears

rolling down his cheeks. 'Oh Christ,' he sighed, putting his head back in his hands. 'They shot him to pieces.'

John Eden saw the name of his first-born son in the lists from the battle at Loos and made immediate enquiries. Once the news was confirmed he made arrangements to return to Bauders at once. There being no trains running to the Halt, he commandeered a motor car from among those at the disposal of the War Office and was driven to Bauders. The English countryside was bathed in the late glow of a fine, hot September day, but he hardly moved, sitting in the back of the motor car with his feet firmly planted on the floor and both hands grasping his knees. Afterwards he remembered little if anything of the journey, other than thinking about how best to break the news to Circe of the loss of their resolute, brave and dashing Almeric. He could think of no possible way; could not imagine anything that could be said in any way to lessen the pain. He resolved to tell her only of their son's courage, and he would tell her of his valour on the day he fell, but knew that would bring little comfort.

But then as he drew near his ancestral home, as he passed through the gates and saw the deer and the sheep grazing peacefully in his parkland with the great house outlined against the pink of the evening sky, he knew there was nothing he needed to say because as he finally alighted from the motor vehicle and composed himself on the steps of his home he realised that Circe already knew. As soon as she had seen the official car she had known, and was already waiting for John, her arms outstretched.

Chapter Fourteen

The Pantomime

The show had to go on, if only to keep up the spirits of the patients, but how to tell the Duchess? It was something that preoccupied both Partita and Kitty.

'You really don't need me to tell you, my dears,' Circe said to them both when they finally plucked up the courage to go to her. 'We all know in our heart of hearts that the one person who would be truly delighted that you were planning another production would be astonished that you even thought of cancelling it. *We* might not feel like doing it, but then *we* are not the point of it. The point of it is these young men who are here as our guests to recover from their wounds and the infamy of war, men some of whom, I would remind you, might possibly be deemed fit enough soon to return to do more battle, and if that is the case the very least we all can do is to make this Christmas another one to remember in every possible way.'

'Well, I suppose at least we wouldn't have Mr St Clare telling us what to do and what not to do,' Partita remarked when she and Kitty were reviewing their feelings about the proposed pantomime. 'Mamma said he's working as a stretcher bearer.'

'Mr St Clare?' Kitty said in surprise. 'Good for him.'

'Let's just hope he doesn't see anything too *shocking*,' Partita joked. 'No lacy drawers or such like,' she finished with a smile, remembering Mr St Clare's sensitivity to the sight of female underwear during the staging of *Pirates*. They both fell silent, each of them once again struggling against the overwhelming grief that threatened them at every turn. The alternate bouts of tears – to be brushed hurriedly away – and sickness, the sleeplessness, where old memories came dancing back, faces, laughing faces, voices, music, only to disappear as if they had never happened, which of course they might not have. The nightmare of today making, as it did, hideous mockery of their joys of yesterday. All their joys seeming to have conflagrated, leaving only ashes, and tears. But tears could not be fostered, must be suppressed, sublimated to the cause of a war which they did not understand, which in their heart of hearts they knew had to be the result of old men's regret, of old men's conceit – old men's boredom even.

'It is very brave of Mr St Clare to go and do his

bit at the Front, don't you think?' Kitty said, eventually.

'Of course it is, Kitty. I was just teasing. Anyway, are we going to do as Mamma says, or defy her and risk being sent to the Tower? Or holed up in one of the priestly hiding places?'

In actual fact there had never been a good reason for not going ahead with some sort of Christmas show. It was simply that, fighting grief as they were, to the girls and the Duchess the organisation of the proposed pantomime had suddenly seemed a little too near home for comfort.

As Kitty said, '*Pirates* was so special. We were all in love with someone by the end of it. Everyone in love, and then – and then Waterside coming after it – it was all like some magical dream, a midsummer night dream of our own.'

As Christmas approached, suddenly seeming to be upon them before they quite realised it, they began to throw themselves wholeheartedly into the preparation and production of their chosen pantomime – *Cinderella*.

'You'll play Cinderella, will you not?' Jack turned to Partita, as in love with her, if not more, than Michael Bradley.

'No, I think you should, Jack,' Partita protested. 'I think you'd make a lovely Cinders.'

'Yeah, I might and all, Lady Partita,' Jack replied with a grin. 'But you'd be even lovelier. I shall play Buttons.'

'Pity we're not doing *Treasure Island*,' Partita

replied, poker-faced. 'You'd be better in that – as Long John Silver.'

'I shall be off me crutches by then, don't you worry,' Jack assured her, waving one at her. 'Thanks to Nurse Kitty I'm all but walking already.'

'Good,' Partita concluded. 'Then I shall look forward to it.'

'I wonder if we can get Michael to take part?' Kitty asked later of no one in particular, when they were drawing up a cast list. 'We know he can sing – and not many of this lot can. Jack can, thank heavens, but have you heard George Skellern? And as for Charlie Bennett – he has a voice like a foghorn.'

'I thought George and Charlie should be the Ugly Sisters,' Partita said. 'And it would be hysterically funny to give them a duet, don't you think? Bring the house down.'

'I wonder if we could get Michael to play Prince Charming,' Kitty wondered idly.

'You don't think that might be going a little too far, Kitty?' Partita asked with a glint in her eye. 'Because I do.'

'I think it's a way to get him involved,' Kitty replied. 'It's up to you whether or not you let it go too far.'

'Well, of course I wouldn't!'

'So ask him then.'

'It's just that he might get the wrong idea.'

'I don't think so,' Kitty maintained. 'It really won't make any difference to the way he truly feels – not about you, anyway. But it might make a lot of difference to the way he thinks about himself.'

'That's very clever of you, Kitty,' Partita replied. 'I didn't look at it that way. Very well, I shall ask him.'

'I think we should find a part for Tinker as well,' Kitty added. 'She's been so plucky. It might help her. She could be the Fairy Godmother.'

'I had you down for that part.'

'Tinker would be sweet – and funny, too.'

'No, you are going to be the Fairy Godmother – because the men have demanded that as well – so let's put Tinker down for Cinderella's kitchen maid.'

'Tita,' Kitty sighed, 'Cinderella *is* the kitchen maid. Not even at Bauders does a kitchen maid have a kitchen maid.'

'All right,' Partita said with a cross sigh. 'She can be the Fairy Godmother's *assistant*.'

'The Fairy Godmother doesn't *have* an assistant,' Kitty protested.

'She does now,' Partita informed her. 'And Mamma is going to be the Queen, and Papa – would you believe? – Papa has agreed to take his first acting part. He is to be the King.'

Canon White, only newly arrived to help cover many miles of neglected parishes, proved to be an invaluable help, once it had been discovered that he was a pantomime buff. Not only did he have full books and lyrics for the traditional versions of almost every pantomime, he also had costume and prop books and was only too willing to lend a hand with the production, even though it was not going to be a traditional panto. And, of course, Elizabeth was to provide the music, just as she had done for *Pirates*.

'Latest from Pug?' Partita wondered when they all met up one evening for rehearsal.

'Still in one piece, bless him,' Elizabeth replied, lowering her voice a little, as she realised how unfair it was that Pug should be in one piece, and not Almeric. 'He hopes he might be given leave some time around Christmas. But do you know, in his last letter to me he says he's practically in the same place as where he first started?'

'How come?' Kitty wondered. 'How do you mean?'

'It seems every time they *make* fifty yards, the next day or week or month, they go *back* fifty yards. He says he can't be more than thirty yards forward from where they were first engaged.'

'It simply doesn't make sense.'

'I don't think war ever does make sense,' Elizabeth stated sadly.

It was certainly not making much sense for Elizabeth's father, Cecil, who was now beginning wholeheartedly to regret volunteering. He had fondly imagined the war for which he had put forward his services to help fight would be nothing more than a brief skirmish, a chance to get away from Maude, renew old regimental acquaintances, and perhaps see a little bit of action from a decent distance. Few men of his age could expect to be thrust into the front line, but such had been the heavy loss of officers early on in the combat that the need for experienced officers was a more than ready one.

So it was that, after the failure of the September offensive, Cecil Milborne found himself dispatched to Maricourt, just north of the Somme, as part of the Fourth Army. Prior to this move he had already been for a short time in the front lines, but in a relatively quiet part along the Marne, where he had managed to survive, but – it was rumoured – at the cost of the lives of many of his men whom he frequently sent out on suicide missions, having waived any need for carrying out reconnaissance. Unsurprisingly Major Cecil Milborne was hated by the unfortunates who served under him.

In the end Cecil's cunning ability to stay away from danger rebounded on him when, as a result of his new commander's appraisal of his apparently spotless record, he was sent to the Somme. The commanding officer could be forgiven for thinking that he had landed on his feet with Major Milborne. For here, undoubtedly, was an experienced and first-class officer, just the sort of soldier he was looking for. He promptly added him to the list of men required for the forthcoming campaign planned around the Somme. As a result of this, Cecil was denied Christmas leave, forced to up sticks, and accompanied by a large body to make his way to Maricourt.

As a result of the dyspeptic mood he then suffered because of the backfire, shortly before leaving for the Somme, and acting in his usual bitter manner, Major Cecil Milborne ordered a detail from his brigade out on one extra mission.

After two and a half days and nights of fighting in the front line, the men were exhausted, but this did not deter Cecil, who promptly ordered them to retake a trench lost to them in the previous twelve hours. There was only one officer free to go with the party. He apologised to his men for taking them out again, making it perfectly clear that this was the sole decision of his superior officer. They reached the redoubt in question where he and three of his men were killed immediately by shell fire. Seeing the fatal trap into which they had been forced to fall, second in command, William Wilkinson, managed to fight his way back to the safety of the divisional trench, one of only three survivors. Once there he swore to avenge the death of his gallant comrades. No one who heard him could doubt his sincerity.

By the time some semblance of order had been restored in the clearing stations behind the lines at Loos, the medical teams could only wait for orders to their next destination.

In an effort to make some sense of what he had endured, as well as to distract him from what he knew must come, now that the Allies had been pushed back, during his free moments Harry decided to accompany the journal he had started with sketches. At first they were merely quick line drawings of desolate war landscapes, but these were soon followed by depictions of life in the dressing and clearing stations, pencil drawings of the wounded lying on stretchers in fields of waving corn, among wild flowers as they awaited transport to field stations, of surgeons operating under the most severe conditions, of fellow drivers at work and at rest, men exhausted by their labours, some sitting smoking, others reading letters, or writing home, many just sitting or lying where they could find comfort, staring blankly.

The battles fought round Loos had hit them all hardest of all, the ravages being caused by the almost unopposed use of the machine gun by the enemy. Until this point the wounded the ambulances had transported had been hurt by rifle fire, shrapnel from the guns – often their own – small shell fire, rifle grenades, provided they had not scored a direct hit, and bayonet wounds, the damage done to those hit by larger shells or blown up by mines being too devastating to survive.

'What's all this you're writing, Wavell?' Richard Charles, the senior medical officer, asked him, sitting himself down beside Harry and offering him a smoke. 'Every time I see you you're scribbling away, or trying to ask me awkward questions. Can I see that?'

Charles took Harry's journal before Harry

could stop him to read what had just been written, Charles reading the last two pages in silence while Harry smoked his cigarette.

'You don't mind, do you?' Charles asked quietly, as he turned the page. 'Say if you do.'

'I don't mind,' Harry replied, although he did.

'Hmmm,' Charles said, when he had finished reading the latest pages, and flicking back through the notebook to admire the drawings. 'You have quite a talent, Wavell,' he conceded. 'A considerable talent, if I may say so?'

'You may,' Harry replied. 'I don't mind at all. In fact, if you mean it—'

'I mean it,' Charles interrupted. 'And I know what I'm talking about, I assure you. My mother's an artist and my father's a publisher.'

'And you're a doctor.'

'The great thing about life, Wavell, is that it follows no logic. You can really write, you know, *and* you can draw.'

'And you can operate – quite brilliantly. I've seen you in action.'

'I would rather I wasn't practising my skills under these sorts of conditions. Wasn't quite what I visualised when I started training. Still – needs must when the devil drives, and all that sort of thing.'

'I've also heard you don't stay put,' Harry continued. 'That you're often out there in the field, tending to the wounded.'

'You don't want to believe everything you hear.'

'I also heard you got a roasting for it,' Harry grinned. 'Too brave to be a doctor, they said.'

'And no damned use at all to the wounded if dead,' Charles added, before returning to the matter of Harry's journal. 'We should find a publisher for this, the journal, drawings, everything. People should know what it's really like out here. Well, of course you do, otherwise you wouldn't be keeping a journal. They say everyone who writes one only does it so that it may be read. Look, tell you what. When we get back to Blighty – soon I hope – get in touch. Here.' He took Harry's journal back from him to write his name and address in the back. 'You never know. The old man publishes a lot of this sort of thing – by that I mean good writing, poetry, the better sort of prose. He's a bit of a bright man, my father – and my mother would be able to help you with the illustrations.'

'Thanks,' Harry said, meaning it. 'That's very good of you. I wish there was something I could do in return.'

'I'll think of something,' Charles replied, putting his cigarette out in the mud at his feet. 'In the meantime I have to say that your idea about moving the dressing stations nearer the field stations, and thus the front line itself is a good one. I've been giving it some thought, and as far as I can see the only minus is that if we move too near the front lines we could be vulnerable to capture. It's not that practical to clear a station in a hurry.'

'As against that, though, we would save a lot more lives.'

'Yes, indeed. We should balance these things up, make a judgement that would possibly prove that the one far outweighed the other. Which is why I've written a memorandum to a high up, one of the consulting surgeons, putting forward your idea – and giving you credit for it, I may say,' he finished with a smile.

'Thank you, sir.'

Harry offered Charles a cigarette and they lit up and smoked in silence for a while, both lost in their thoughts.

'Any chance of getting home for Christmas?' Charles asked.

Harry shook his head.

'No,' he said. 'But then who has?'

'Damn few,' Charles agreed. 'And it's funny, isn't it? I was getting more than a little indifferent to Christmas, but now – now I realise just how much I'm going to miss it.'

Peregrine was also thinking of Christmas and what he would be missing. He looked round his dugout. It needed cheering up with something more than the plate of bully beef and the mug of tea that he was holding. It was, however, a pretty good billet on the whole, and certainly well worth the work: half a dugout and half a hut, with the side that faced the enemy well sand-bagged. Peregrine had used up most of the little free time available to furnish it in the plushest manner possible. There was a table and four chairs – gifts from a local farmer – a small bookcase holding a variety of books and magazines, a case containing a large stuffed pike that he had found in an abandoned *gîte*, along with a small brass bed he had commandeered for his own use, a fine washstand, complete with china jug and bowl, an antique cabinet containing a supply of *vin ordinaire*, an umbrella stand with two umbrellas, a gramophone with a good selection of well-worn recordings, gas masks and powder bombs in case of a gas attack, and finally a working fireplace taken from the same farmhouse and built into the clay – and all this in a dugout no more than a hundred and twenty yards from the enemy.

What he needed now was a small Christmas tree, complete with decorations, but so far he had had neither the time nor the luck to find one, despite feelers having been put out by one of his men. The last he had heard, from Private Wilcox, had been a hint from one of the more obliging natives that he might – just might – be able to get hold of a small spruce with decorations for a consideration. Peregrine had dug deep into his savings only to find that due to one thing and another, more precisely wine, cognac, cigarettes, tobacco and English magazines, he was well short of the required tip. Happily Dick Huntley, one of his fellow officers, came to his rescue, only too happy to contribute to the costs, taking a cheque from Peregrine for the entire amount and some cash to spare on Peregrine's insistence that Christmas was his treat.

With the tree and its decorations promised within the week, plus some extra coal and milk thrown in, Peregrine rightly considered Christmas was now in order.

'Just need a few presents, eh?'

Peregrine looked at Dick Huntley, and then back at the tree.

'Mmm, not sure Harrods delivers this far,' he said slowly.

None the less, by further searches in forsaken dwellings he found some bric-a-brac that he promptly parcelled up, along with cigarettes and chocolate, cognac, and other small items, in pieces of precious brown paper saved from parcels from home.

Now, during a lull in the bombardments, Peregrine was able to put his feet up in front of the fire, light a cigarette and dream of Christmas at Bauders. He imagined it was as it always had been at this time of year, with the giant tree beautifully decorated, the local choir singing carols at the foot of the great staircase, the great luncheon for fifty, and presents for everyone, followed by the servants' ball on Boxing Day, and in the midst of it all he could not help seeing Partita, her lovely face lit by the library fire, her blonde hair shining in the glow from candles, and her blue eyes full of mischief.

'Dreaming of home, sir?' Private Wilcox

wondered as he prepared to brew more tea. 'That's the ticket.'

'Yes I was, Wilcox,' Peregrine replied, pressing his cigarette out in an old mess tin used as an ash can. 'Although to be truthful I was dreaming of someone else's home.'

'That so, sir. Wonder why that is.'

'Because that is where *she* is, Wilcox – which reminds me. We haven't had any post for some time. Know anything about that?'

'I shall make yet another enquiry, sir, soon as the kettle's boiled,' Wilcox replied. 'Rumour is, any moment now.'

Wilcox was as good as his word, returning with a box full of letters and a small sack for the parcels, all of which were opened by the recipients by the fireside to the sound of recordings of heavenly arias by Donizetti and other composers. Peregrine's post contained two letters from Livia, forwarded from home, recounting her nursing experience in Nurse Cadell's hospital and including her belief she might have caught sight of Valentine, of all people. There was also a long, mournful screed from his mother, making no mention of his sister or brother-in-law, a short letter from Kitty, and a very long, funny, warm and affectionate letter from Partita that he saved until last, and then read and reread, because she managed to put so much of herself into her accounts of life at the Bauders hospital.

'Quiet for the time of year,' First Lieutenant Toby Ferguson remarked in one of his many accents. 'I was saying to the wife only the other day, doesn't seem a bit like Christmas.'

'I was thinking of inviting Jerry over for Christmas cocktails,' Peregrine remarked as he finally put his letter from Partita away. 'Think he'll come?'

'I heard Jerry doesn't need an invitation to visit our trenches, Perry,' Toby replied. 'He's one of those perfectly beastly people who don't know when they're not wanted.'

'All the same, I thought we'd send him an invitation, make it formal,' Peregrine said. 'Fire over some empty canisters asking them for drinks in no man's land.'

'Black tie, of course.'

'Naturally.'

'And decorations?'

'Only the ones worn by Christmas trees. We'll get Wilcox to find us some suitable canisters, and I'll send the invitations to the engravers.'

'What ho, Perry,' Toby said, raising his glass of *vin ordinaire*.

'Here's to it,' Peregrine toasted in return. 'I really do think it's time we stopped all this shooting lark and got down to some very serious jollification.'

'Couldn't agree more, sir,' Wilcox added, putting some more coal on the fire. 'Just hope we don't have too many more sorties before the big day.'

'CO indicated things are going quiet everywhere,' Toby assured him, everyone listening.

'Just a bit of wire repairs to be done, and maybe a couple of recces, then that's it until the New Year.'

Peregrine tapped a fresh cigarette on his silver case, ready to light up, nodding as he listened. He had already had a good briefing from their CO. It seemed that the only real party that was being planned was a sortie on a farmhouse one mile to the east of them, which had already changed hands twice, the enemy recapturing it according to the latest reports on the previous afternoon. The CO had expressed the hope that the information was faulty, or if it were not, that at least HQ would not demand any attack on the farm until after Christmas Day.

'I can't see the need for any rush, I can't really. After all, the last time they had it we let them pitch up there for a week or two. I say let them pop a few corks, put their feet up and loosen their uniforms, then we'll stop by and say how do, once we have Christmas out of the way.'

Peregrine raised his wine glass in a private toast to that hope, watching the flames dancing in the fire, and then with a slow look at his surroundings found it impossible to suppress the thought that it was a pretty funny place to spend a holiday.

'Happy Christmas, everyone,' he said finally. 'And let's hope we'll be home safe and sound by this time next year.'

'No doubt about it, sir,' Wilcox said, his duties done. 'In fact, my money says home by Easter.'

'Reliable information, Wilcox?' Peregrine wondered.

'None better and never known to be wrong, sir. Said so in the tea leaves.'

'Easter it is then, everyone. And here's to it.'

The Bauders pantomime proved to be such fun and so entertaining in rehearsals that it was quickly decided to organise it as a charity event in aid of the war effort, in particular to help towards financing the Red Cross in their unceasing work in the war zone. Hardly able to believe how many tickets they had sold in the first few days they were marketed, thanks to the work of volunteers in every walk of life, the organisers realised that one performance was not going to be sufficient, so they planned an extra one, only to find that was all but sold out in three days, which meant that they finally managed to sell every available seat for three performances.

Thanks to the labours and enthusiasm of Canon White, who revealed himself to be a talented theatrician, the standard of performance for an amateur production exceeded all expectations, both young Jack Wilson as Buttons and Michael Bradley – who had taken surprisingly little persuasion to play Prince Charming – revealing natural talents. As for the costumes, due to Partita's extraordinary ability to make something out of nothing – and not just something but something quite unique – they were outstanding, most particularly since all she had at her disposal were two very old dressing-up boxes, some old clothes from previous generations that for some reason had been kept rather than passed on, and yards of fabric, shiny paper, Christmas decorations and papier-mâché, which she used with great skill for masks and props. As a result, the costumes alone all but stopped the show, particularly Cinderella's ball gown and even more so the golden coach in which she arrived at the ball, the coach having been painstakingly built by Jossy on the framework of the ponytrap, under the careful supervision of Partita, the ensemble being pulled onto the stage set up in the ballroom by a superbly turned out Trotty.

The audience demanded two encores for the Ugly Sisters' comic out-of-tune duet, and the same for Kitty's beautiful rendition of 'Cinderella's Dream', a song specially composed for the show by Elizabeth, while Partita's interpretation of Cinderella softened even the most unsentimental of hearts, enchanting everyone in the audience, but most of all capturing for ever all the hearts of her adoring patients.

As for Partita and Kitty, the organisers and co-stars of the panto, their own particular never-to-be-forgotten moments were Michael singing 'Bless This House' after he has discovered that Cinderella will go to the ball, and Jack, who, having insisted on playing Buttons on crutches, brought the show to a stop when having made a wish to the Fairy Godmother he found it had come true and that he could walk unaided. The moment Jack placed his crutches aside, and almost danced across the stage had a very special meaning to those who had nursed him for so long.

There was only one major difficulty to overcome and it was left to Circe to manage the diplomacy.

Shortly before curtain-up on the third night, as she was preparing for the evening, Circe was summoned to the telephone.

'I am so sorry to have to telephone you in this way, Circe,' Consolata began, 'but I have only just heard and I thought you should know.'

'Is it – is it Peregrine?'

'I am afraid so. I received a telegram an hour ago, informing me that my son is missing in action.'

'Consolata,' Circe said, 'while I don't know what to say, you must know that I do understand exactly how you feel.'

'That is why I rang you, my dear.'

There was a long pause.

'The telegram simply said missing, did it?'

'It just said "missing in action".'

'Then you must live in hope.'

'I think you and I understand what terms such as "missing in action" mean, my dear,' Consolata replied in a steady voice. 'While of course I shall live in hope, and will of course continue to pray, I must also prepare myself for the worst, the very worst, news.'

'I understand, Consolata. If there is anything I can do at this time . . . ?'

'You are most kind, as always, Circe,' Consolata assured her. 'Perhaps I might come to call after your pantomime is over. I should like that.'

'Of course,' Circe assured her. 'I shall telephone you and we shall make a suitable arrangement. In the meantime you are in our thoughts, and our prayers – all our prayers.'

Circe stayed in the telephone room, her mind rushing ahead as it always did, thinking of the practicalities.

It simply would not be fair to tell the girls the bad news before they went on stage. There was nothing they could do about Peregrine's disappearance, but then – just as she was about to put the finishing touches to her own makeup and costume as the Pantomime Queen, a voice inside her head wondered: but what if the news had been about Almeric? Or Gus? Would you still have kept the matter secret?

Circe looked at herself in the mirror as she made up for her part, and despite the laughter she could hear, the sounds of happy bustle all over the castle, she could not help recognising the sorrow in her eyes.

What would she have done, she wondered, if the young man posted missing had been Gussie? What in truth would she have felt and decided then? She had simply no idea, and for a moment she despaired at what she saw as her hypocrisy, until she remembered what John had said to her when she was trying to come to terms with the loss of their beloved boy.

'These are not normal times, dearest. And the events that happen to everyone are not normal events. Yes, they have happened before – people down the ages have lost their loved ones, but war is not normal, and the things that happen within its context are not what we would call normal, and so we must not expect our reactions to be any different. Different demands are being made on us for very different reasons. They make us search inside for the right thing to say or do, but there is no such thing, never has been, probably never will be.'

Circe finished her preparation, and then prayed for Gussie, and most especially for Peregrine. After which she checked herself one last time in her dressing glass before descending the great staircase and making her way to the ballroom for another splendid performance of the Bauders pantomime.

When Partita heard the news that Peregrine was missing, she fainted, and had to be revived in the stills room.

'I am so sorry, so sorry,' she kept muttering to Kitty, who kept wringing out cold flannels and pressing them to her forehead. 'It was such a shock, somehow such a shock. Poor Consolata, poor Livia, what will happen?'

'He has been posted missing, not dead. That at least is some comfort.'

Peregrine was not the only one to have vanished. Two other soldiers were included in the casualty lists as missing presumed dead, but that was all that was known. It seemed that the enemy had set a clever trap, making it look as though they had deserted a farmhouse, when in fact they were all hidden in the roofs and rafters of the outbuildings, the haystacks and the pigsties. Peregrine's squad was hopelessly out-numbered and his commanding officer let it be known in his report that in his opinion the sortie should never have been ordered, based as it was on a slap-happy and lazy reconnaissance.

But it was no good protesting, either abroad or at home, because Peregrine had disappeared and no one knew where. The loss of her beloved brother had been hard enough for Partita to bear, but now the reported loss of the man she knew she loved coming so hard on the heels of Almeric's death, and the agonising, unbearable moment of the return of his uniform and effects, made life seem like a living nightmare, and there was no other word for it. She would never forget the look on her mother's face as she saw all that was left of her son, all that had been sent back to them, which was nearly nothing at all – except for Kitty's letters tucked where his heart should have been.

Kitty herself was resolute. She had to be, because she knew how strong the Duchess and Partita were trying to be. She insisted that she knew that Peregrine was missing, he was not dead, and so long as he was only missing, that was how they would think of him, not as dead, but as lost for the moment.

Partita was also resolute.

'I have decided that I will go to France and find Peregrine, Mamma.'

Her mother was seated at the kitchen table in precisely the chair where Mrs Coggle had used to sit. She looked up slowly.

'They're short of volunteer nurses, and the closer I am to where it happened the better chance I have of finding out something more about what has happened to him. I will do it for all of us, we all loved Perry. More than that, I must do it.'

'You must do as you feel best, dearest,' Circe told her in a tired voice. She paused. 'Your patients here will miss you, but that is your decision, darling. As your father so rightly says, these are unusual times and the things that we do and decide to do aren't governed by the same rules as of old.'

'What do *you* think I should do, Kitty?' Partita asked her friend later. 'What would you do in my place?'

'I think I'd feel exactly as you do,' Kitty replied. 'But then I might also think it would be rather like looking for a needle in a haystack – mostly because all the men with Peregrine were killed, and those two or three that weren't are also missing, so I might think that no one would be able to tell me anything useful.'

'While here . . .'

'What you have achieved here is very special.'

'What we *all* have done here, Kitty,' Partita insisted. 'This is something we have all done. Everyone at Bauders.'

'Of course,' Kitty agreed. 'But in the end it is entirely up to you.'

In the end Partita stayed, and she did so because of the patients. At the back of her mind she knew that there was little if any chance of learning something about one missing man in a war where thousands were being killed, wounded and going absent believed dead, while at Bauders she was needed in a very particular way. In the field stations she would, of course, have her uses, but finally she would only be another pair of hands, whereas at Bauders she had specific work to do, work that was still unfinished.

Others left. After Christmas, celebrated in much the same style as the year before, at the next medical board, held to see which of their patients might or might not be deemed fit to return to either active or to home duty, among the many passes was Buttons, as Jack Wilson was now affectionately known, and Quiet Mike, now seemingly fully restored.

Naturally everyone remaining at Bauders was anxious to know where their friends were being sent, and were happy and relieved when they learned that, although passed fit, Quiet Michael was not to be sent back abroad but had been assigned a posting at home. Young Jack Buttons, however, was to return to the Front.

'Course I don't mind, Lady Partita,' he grinned. 'It's not as if I didn't volunteer, know what I mean? If I hadn't bloomin' well volunteered I mightn't be quite so anxious to return to the fray, like, but I did and I tell you, I can't wait to get back and have a go at the blighters what have done this to me – and to all my mates here, including Mad Mike.'

'You're not to call him that, Jack,' Kitty scolded him.

'I din't, Nurse Kitty! It weren't me that called him that, it was Mike his bloomin' self!'

'Yes, all right, Jack,' Partita sighed. 'But even so.'

'I do love you, Lady Partita – and your "even so's" and all. You're a right angel, and I shall always remember you. I shall remember you all, and that's a fact. What a cosy billet this has been, I can tell you – *and* I got the use of me Scotch eggs back, so I'm not grumbling.'

'You will come back and see us, Jack?' Kitty asked him as she gave him a last haircut. 'When it's all over, promise you'll come and see us all here?'

'You try and stop me. If I'm still in one piece, or even if some of the pieces is missing, I shall return!'

'And what about you, Michael? I hope you'll stay in touch?'

Michael looked at Partita. 'You know my

534

conditions, Lady Tita,' he replied gravely. 'Only if you promise to marry me.'

'And you know what I told you,' Partita replied, equally straight-faced, this being by now an old routine. 'I'm not the marrying type.'

'Neither am I. That's why we're perfectly suited.'

'Ask me again when the war is over, Michael,' Partita replied, taking his hand and leading him to the door, outside of which the transport waited for those leaving. 'Although I would bet a penny to a pound that by that time you will have been snapped up by the prettiest of girls.'

'I'll ask you to marry me every time I write,' Michael promised her. Then looking at his feet, he said, 'Thank you for all you've done, every-one. All of you. Every one of you.'

'It's us who should be thanking you,' they all chorused, and turning went smartly back into the castle.

It was a routine that Circe had devised.

'Don't want any lachrymose moments when they leave us; it will only weaken them. Lots of jokes, lots of cheery faces, that is what they must remember, before they go back to the party.'

Valentine knew nothing about Almeric or, as it happened, anyone else in his group of friends who were missing. Cut off from all sources of information other than his immediate under-ground contacts and most importantly Nurse Cadell, he simply worked at playing the part at which he had supposed he might excel. So far he had been proved right inasmuch as he had not yet lost one of his 'cast', as he liked to call those in his charge. They had all been safely rerouted and delivered to the right location. What happened to them afterwards he could not know, nor did he make it his business to find out. That was something he had very soon learned.

His role in the war had been his own idea, born out of a conversation with his father. Despairing of the European situation and holding out no hope for any war shared between chaotic Allies against a superbly organised enemy, Ralph Wynyard Errol had advised his son to stay uninvolved, at least until he saw how events were going to unfurl.

It was difficult for Valentine to go against his father's wishes, but he had finally protested, arguing that since all his friends were intending to volunteer, the very least he could be expected to do was to follow their example, and by doing so gain the respect, not only of them, but of his wife.

'Dear boy, you will make a hopeless soldier.'

'I must do something, Father,' Valentine complained. 'I can't simply sit at home and do nothing.'

'The theatre of war is very different from the theatre you and I know. Besides, we are keeping the home fires burning, making people laugh, making people cry in the theatre every night, cheering them on before they go back to the Front.'

'That is your role, Father. For my part I want something better – a part that I would enjoy playing in the theatre – a part such as the Scarlet Pimpernel.'

And that was precisely how father and son arrived at Valentine's role in the war. By appearing to be little other than a theatrical dandy, he would in actuality be working to help soldiers trapped behind the lines to escape. He was given a brief training before being dispatched to Flanders where he was to work, among others, with Nurse Cadell. Since he had been in the habit of spending all his holidays in Europe and was bilingual in German, and French was second nature to him, Valentine proved to be an ideal choice. It was only when a close comrade was caught and shot that he started to hope that while his current role would continue to be a success, the run of the play in the particular theatre in which he now found himself might prove to be for a limited season.

But against all his fervent hopes, the curtain still refused to fall.

Chapter Fifteen

Another Year Gone

'It's so hot!' Partita collapsed into a kitchen chair. 'It's so hot I could almost long for winter.' She stared dully at the iron bars that guarded the basement windows, iron bars placed there centuries ago to keep out, she suddenly wondered, what, or who? Certainly not bad news.

'Winter was long enough without you wanting it back again,' Kitty said crisply.

'How can it still all be going on? How can it?'

Kitty gritted her teeth. Much as she loved Partita, she had been saying precisely the same thing for the past week.

'The butter's all runny, the milk's sour, and there are not enough clean bandages. We'll have to wash some more out. Washing!' Partita suddenly kicked the chair in front of her. 'I hate washing. I hate washing worse than war.'

'You might as well get used to washing, Partita, because everyone is needed upstairs.

There are all too few of us now that half the nurses have a bug.'

'Why did they all eat that gooseberry pie, and get ill?'

'Probably because they were hungry.'

'I swear I made it to the right recipe.'

'Yes, but Cook's writing being what it is, who knows that you read it right? Besides, it's been around so long, people's tummies have probably changed.'

'People's tummies don't change, Kitty!' Partita started to laugh, half hysterically, half genuinely. 'People have the same stomachs as they have always had.'

'They do not. We couldn't eat what our ancestors ate, lark pie, and geese stuffed with seventeen different birds, and the like. We just couldn't.'

Partita stood up. 'Tell you what, Kitty, let's have a dance. Let's have our own little servants' ball down here.'

They looked at each other, remembering the gaiety of the servants' ball, the Duke leading out Mrs Coggle, all the fun of it.

'After all,' Partita went on, 'we are the servants now – why shouldn't we have our own ball?'

Kitty turned away. 'Maybe,' she agreed. 'We could ask the Duchess. Except it might make her sad, mightn't it?' She picked a newspaper off the kitchen floor and started to read it, and then another, and another, all old newspapers that were always put on the floor after it had been washed. 'When you see what has happened this year, it seems hardly credible. Zeppelin raids, Jutland, Ireland, forty-five thousand lost at Loos, and now all this talk of the atrocities that the enemy are inflicting on the villages and towns, on civilians everywhere.'

'Just more of our own propaganda. I wish they would stop. Why they think we will believe that in this day and age civilised nations would rape and plunder their way backwards and forwards instead of fighting fair and square, I don't know.'

'It hardly bears thinking about, if what they say is true.'

'It's not true, Kitty. Really, it can't be.'

Harry was on his way back from what was the last journey to the clearing station that day, the wounded having all been sent on to hospitals down the line, when he narrowly missed getting caught in a sudden barrage. Realising he must have lost his way to be that close to the action, he turned about and became even more lost.

Finally finding what he thought was a road that would lead him back to the dressing station, yet again he found himself lost and disorientated, driving through countryside devastated by the guns and scarred beyond recognition, until he came to a village that, despite the rain and the mist, looked like nothing less than a ghost town.

There were the all too familiar signs of occupation, but worse, more than anything there were what Harry understood at once to be the all too familiar signs of deliberate devastation.

At first he could see no sign of anyone. The population had obviously been put to flight by the enemy when their little village had been overtaken. But the enemy, instead of being content with billeting themselves in the un-occupied houses, which would have been perfectly understandable, had deliberately savaged the place. Everything was burned, razed or ruined. The streets were littered with smashed beds, chairs, dressers, chests of drawers, sofas, broken with what looked like axes. Even the gardens and orchards had been savaged – centuries-old fruit trees cut down, gardens that had once been bright with vegetables and flowers hacked to pieces. What had once been vegetable or flower gardens, tended lovingly for centuries, now contained beds, lavatories, baths and basins, ripped out from the buildings and hurled through windows. Everywhere Harry looked there was clothing, filthy sheets and blankets thrown to the ground, soiled and violated, curtains and covers given the same vile treatment, and the clothing of the people, most of all of the women, spread along the muddy streets and pavements.

Harry found himself searching everywhere for a sign of life but finding none he was about to leave when he heard the faintest of cries, which sounded like a child, or perhaps a baby.

He found them in the ruined church, hiding

under an altar that had been severed in two by a weapon that had then been plunged into the ancient oak of the pulpit. What he found was a mother and child, a baby that could have been born perhaps only twenty-four hours earlier, a tiny mite wrapped in a bloodstained altar cloth, in the arms of a young woman whose eyes were mad with terror.

She said nothing to him, only stared in panic, her whole body trembling while her baby continued to cry. Harry stretched out both his hands to her, speaking to her quietly in French, assuring her he was her friend, that he had not come to harm her, and that he would take her to safety. For a long time she refused to move, shrinking away from him and trying to hide further and further under the altar until Harry was forced to his knees. Finally and all at once she seemed to give in and passed him the baby as she extricated herself.

'Who are you?' she whispered as she straightened up, and he handed her back her baby. 'Why do you come?'

'I'm an ambulance driver,' Harry told her, taking her outside and pointing to his vehicle. 'I drive the wounded to hospital. I'm going to take you there now, to hospital where you'll be well looked after, I promise.'

The woman shrank from him as Harry led her to the ambulance.

'No harm will come to you, I promise,' Harry kept repeating to her. 'No one will harm you.

You must come with me. If you don't, I'm afraid your baby – and you – I don't know what will happen to you, but I'd worry for your survival. There's no food here, and you look – you look as though you've been hurt.'

By now he had seen the blood and reckoned if he did not get her attended to very quickly, she might die. As it was, she was as pale as death itself, and with the amount of blood she seemed still to be losing, Harry knew that there was no time to be lost.

'Please,' he beseeched her. 'You must trust me. Please?'

She climbed into the back of the ambulance where again he had to plead with her, this time to let him try to dress her wounds. He had a supply of field dressings as well as some analgesics and morphine tablets that he always carried in the back of the vehicle. She was terrified, sitting as far away from him on the stretcher as she could, her baby child clasped tightly to her, all the time begging him not to come near, not to touch her. But the sincerity of his pleading eventually prevailed, so that he was able to dress her wounds, and ask her the way to the little village behind Loos where the clearing station still stood.

It seemed that despite the odds he was somehow headed in the right direction. He drove as fast as he could along a road pitted with craters, a road so bad in places that it was barely passable, before at last he came to a relatively undamaged stretch where he could really push on, arriving at long last at the clearing station some forty minutes later.

Both the woman and her child were still alive when, with the help of a bearer, he decanted them both onto a makeshift bed for which he managed to find some clean linen. He then went in search of his friend Dr Charles, whom he found taking a catnap, but who was only too willing to come and attend his new patients.

'I don't think she has much chance of survival,' he told Harry who, alongside the doctor's nurse, was attending him in the makeshift operating theatre. 'She's lost an enormous amount of blood and her resistance is all but gone.'

'What could save her, doctor?' Harry wondered. 'More blood, obviously.'

'More blood? Yes, very good, Harry, we do need more blood,' Charles agreed, carefully suturing the worst of the young woman's wounds. 'As a matter of fact I was working on transfusion just before I came out here.'

Dr Charles stopped stitching for a moment and looked at Harry.

'The first thing that needs to be worked on is how to stop transfused blood from clotting. Appears the addition of sodium nitrate does the trick.'

'So why aren't we doing it?'

'Question of keeping it fresh enough. They might manage that in first-class hospitals, but not so easy out here – in these sorts of conditions.'

'What do you need to do to keep it fresh?' Harry wondered. 'Refrigerate it – of course!'

'Need power to do that, Harry.'

'Mmm, we would, wouldn't we?'

'Good,' Dr Charles stood back. 'I think she'll do.'

The following day the young woman was sitting up in bed, taking nourishment, after which Harry volunteered to take her and the baby to the nearest hospital.

A couple of days later found Dr Charles going in search of Harry.

'I need your help, Harry,' he said, as they sat smoking in a hut normally filled with stretchers bearing the wounded but for once happily empty of pain and suffering. 'It's not that you're wasted driving ambulances, but I think we might make better use of you.' He proffered him his brandy flask. 'You have been nothing but an asset here, but we desperately need someone to get our field stations up to muster, bring them nearer to the dressing stations here. You are right. If we can do this we shall save even more lives than we do at the present time, besides alleviating a great deal of unnecessary suffering. You were also right to point out that the journeys the ambulances have to make are far too long and men are dying unnecessarily. Will you give the matter some thought? I'd be delighted if you would.'

Harry gave the matter all the time it took to finish his cigarette.

'I'd be delighted. As you know, I have all sorts of ideas about this. When would you like me to start?'

'Tomorrow morning will be soon enough.'

As soon as he'd caught up on his sleep and finished his letters home, Harry started to prepare the plan for moving the clearing stations nearer the line.

One of Harry's letters was to Kitty. It was on the subject of Almeric.

I find myself so often saying of course we must continue without him, without our best friend, yet for the life of me I can't see how. He was my friend since childhood and a better friend a boy and then a young man never could have. He was head and shoulders above the rest of us, and always fair. But what I loved most about him – and I mean loved – was his resolution. It takes enormous courage to be true to yourself – to honour your resolve above all things and to stand up and be counted, yet he was a man of such principle, good principles, high principles, the sort of principles that gave him the vision he had. You heard him talk about his plans for Bauders and the future of the estate – and by that he meant the futures of *everyone* who worked on the estate – and those plans were visionary. He would have been a grand duke.

So when I think how are we meant to

continue – how are we meant to make some sense out of our lives now that this man is gone – all I can hear is him saying that he expects us to pick ourselves up and continue to do what we were put on this earth to do – not to fight each other but to try and save humanity, and above all to love one another. When I witness the terrible carnage of this war, what men are capable of doing to their fellow men, I sometimes doubt my own resolve – but then I remember Al and I remember his resolution and I have to say I feel pretty ashamed of myself. So I wash my face, brush my hair, strop my razor sharp and prepare myself for another day – this is all sort of metaphysical, if you understand me, Kitty – it's a bit like falling in the mud, then getting up, having a bath and putting on what my father always calls clean linen – and making a fresh start. That, I tell myself, is what Almeric would have wanted us to do. But then at night when the demons return, when it's been one long and ghastly day driving the wounded and dying to the next post, then I wonder if I'm not using Al for my own philosophical purposes; if I'm not putting words in his mouth, particularly knowing that now he cannot answer me back. How do I know, how can I *possibly* know what he would want of us? He might have changed his mind completely, seeing what he saw, and he might want us all to convert to some Eastern religion of contemplation and take no further part in this terrible war. How do I know? How?

I suppose I think I know because I knew Al so very well – as you were just getting to do and as you would have done even better than I, had he survived. Let us admire what he admired, and love what he loved. That is his legacy, and it is one I intend to keep, because I think that is what a loving friendship must mean. It must mean we should honour one another to the very best of our ability, and to live our lives for the benefit of those we love, so that what we cherish so very much doesn't once again get lost in the mire of bloody battle. You were lucky that Almeric loved you. He will love you even more for your strength, the strength I know you are going to show at this time for yourself, and for all who loved him. I think of you all constantly, and you in the most particular.

Your loving friend,
Harry

Kitty always thought that the moment she finished reading Harry's letter her life changed, that his letter was a turning point at a time when she, and indeed Partita, and everyone at Bauders felt at their lowest.

For some reason what Harry had said in his letter had taken away the anguish that she had been secretly nursing since Almeric's death, the feeling that she had finally not been worthy of his love, the guilt that she knew that he had loved her even more than she had loved him. Now she knew that if, as Harry had said, she tried to live her future life as Almeric would have wanted, she need not feel so wretched. She had a reason to go on, not just existing, but to try to go on living an ideal – Almeric's ideal.

'You're looking very jaunty, Wavell,' the Duchess remarked one morning. 'Can your smiling expression be due to some good news, may we ask?'

Wavell nodded.

Life below and above stairs had become very hard for a middle-aged man used, as he had been, to having an army of servants to do his bidding, but much as Wavell might have liked to have retired to his cottage on the estate, as he had been planning once he reached his fiftieth year, he could never let Her Grace down. He was a man of honour, and men of honour stood by their women in time of war, and if the Duchess was not 'his woman' he did not know who was. He had loved and served her from the time he was an underbutler, first in London, and now at the castle.

'As a matter of fact I am in quite a good frame of mind, Your Grace,' Wavell admitted, as he put down a tray of tea on the desk at which she now sat for most of the day. 'Harry, you know, Harry, my boy?'

'Dear Harry, and how is he, Wavell?'

Wavell cleared his throat, and pride shone from his shrewd grey eyes.

'He's quite a bright spark, though I say it myself, Your Grace.'

'Yes, yes, Harry is quite a bright spark, indeed he is.'

Circe was used to the conversational detours that her butler liked to take. They did not make her impatient, rather the opposite; she found that they were comforting, settling, as was so much that was gentle: her flowers, her dogs, and, yes, Wavell's way of speaking.

'Yes, Harry, being a bright spark, as I say, although I say it myself that perhaps shouldn't. He has been promoted. Quite a leg up, that is what our Harry has had.'

'Tell me more, Wavell.'

'Harry had this idea, Your Grace, that the dressing stations and the clearing stations were too far apart, and he put it to the doctor he was working under, and now – ' Wavell cleared his throat again, a hand going up to his really rather sadly under-starched collar – 'now he is being put to work on his own plan, bringing them together, coagulating all the stations, as it were.'

'I am a great believer in coagulation, Wavell,' Circe agreed, straight-faced. 'Gracious, where on earth would we be without it?'

'Not as far as we are with it.'

'Exactly so. His Grace tells me that there is fine work going on in the field, that doctors and surgeons are operating and stitching and so on, on the actual battlefields.'

Wavell nodded, thinking of Harry. 'I dare say, Your Grace. It's not easy work, but very rewarding, I gather, very rewarding, in the same way that our work here is rewarding, I am thinking, saving lives. Just a pity we keep having to send them back once we've mended them, I always think.'

Circe turned back to her paperwork. 'Thank you so much, Wavell.'

Wavell went down to the kitchens still walking tall, and naturally, since Lady Partita was busy preparing breakfast for a new arrival, he confided the same news to her.

'Well done, Harry,' Partita said, and she leaned forward compulsively and shook Wavell's hand. 'How proud you must be.' She turned back to her cooking pots. 'I don't know what it is about boiling an egg, Wavell, but it always seems to defeat me.'

'How long has it been in, Lady Partita?'

Partita frowned. 'About ten minutes, I think.'

'Probably best if I take that one for luncheon and we start again,' Wavell told her diplomatically.

As a fresh egg was lowered into water, Partita began a dissertation on the courage of the doctors and surgeons as compared to the Anglican clergymen.

'Some of the stories the men tell me, Wavell, really, they do make you wonder. The Catholic priests dash out and administer to the dying, no matter what, but it seems the most that the chaplains out there can do is make the occasional dash forward to offer the troops cigarettes and then dash back to safety again. Apparently it is known as the Woodbine Faith.'

'You can't *altogether* blame the clerics, Lady Partita,' Wavell murmured, watch in hand, his eyes on the egg saucepan. 'My Harry wrote to me that the Church actually forbids any of the clergy to go further forward than Brigade Headquarters. Thinks they'll get in the way.'

'How wretched,' Partita protested. 'What spiritual food is there in that? The Roman Catholic priests go right on to the battlefields to give Extreme Unction, while the battle's still raging. The chaps tell me that the people they admired the most out there were the Catholic priests, the medics, the stretcher bearers and the drivers.'

'Harry did say that a lot of the chaplains simply ignore the order to stay behind at HQ and get as far up front as they can.'

'The joke upstairs when Jack Wilson was here was that he said that one chaplain said to them, "May God go with you all the way – I shall go with you as far as the railway station."'

'I'm sure,' Wavell agreed, carefully removing the egg from its water and placing it in its cup. 'But there again, my Harry says there are some remarkable men of the cloth out there with him, including vicars such as our own Mr Bletchworth. I had another letter from him the other day and I understand he's been holding

Holy Communion in barns and farmyards and ruined houses – in fact where he can – and always at night so as his men will be safe from attack. He said that recently he even held Communion in an abandoned bar in some village or other, using the old bar as an altar and an old pewter beer mug as a chalice. Harry says that because of his ministry being under fire on so many occasions, Mr Bletchworth has been recommended for a DSO.'

'Mr Bletchworth?' Partita stared at Wavell, as she now picked up the breakfast tray. 'Gracious.'

'Long may he last,' Wavell said, opening the kitchen door for Partita to go through.

As he closed it he shook his head. Lady Partita might make a good maid, and an excellent nurse, but a cook she would never be.

'Out of wretched Flanders and into the Somme – at last,' Cecil wrote in one of his few letters home.

The change of scenery is most welcome and I must say the landscape here is very pleasant. Provided they send us up enough guns there is absolutely no reason to believe we shouldn't finally get Jerry on the run, and for good. The chalky ground here is ideal for digging in, the weather is good and all the men are of much better countenance.

Home soon, I have no doubt,
Truly yours,
Cecil

Tully was feeling a wave of optimism as well, as he and his fellow troops dug in and prepared for battle. As was his role, he had been in a gun party, using the horses to haul up the field guns and help position them as instructed, and now, as the last day of June faded into evening, he fed and watered his charges, paying particular attention as always to Sam, the battery's favourite.

Sam was a heavy horse with three white feet, a thick flaxen mane, which Tully kept knot and mud free to the very best of his considerable ability, two very small furry ears, which were completely out of proportion to the rest of his head, and the most enormous bright pink lower lip, which gave him a permanently good-tempered and well-humoured appearance. His favourite trick was to catch hold of soldiers' caps and hurl them as far as he could away from him. But the habit most enjoyed by the troops was the way he rolled back his upper lip into the most enormous grin when they fed him sweet titbits. As for his workload, he never seemed to tire, and although he was a big animal and took up more space, needed more grooming and ate more fodder than two smaller horses, he had become the gunners' fast favourite ever since he had stamped off the boat and set foot in France.

Now his work for the day done, he stood contentedly munching his hay and swishing his long flaxen tail to keep the flies at bay, while Tully, as always, settled in for the night in his sleeping roll under a side of canvas five yards from his charge.

Tully remembered little of the following day once the bombardments started. He had seen plenty of action but, like most of his fellow troopers, had never previously been exposed to the sheer weight, din and danger of the enormous barrage that was now exploding everywhere in the skies. Shells of every size and description screamed overhead, everything from the nick-named crumps and coal boxes to the menacing, screaming deadly whiz-bangs. All day the artillery pounded the enemy positions and all day the enemy guns pounded those of the British. Everyone dug in as deeply as they could, some in trenches so deep that not even the heaviest artillery was going to dislodge them.

At some point Tully was called to reposition a field gun, so, collecting Sam, he hurried forward under a fresh hail of howling shells, and the next thing he knew he was being crushed to death. He had no idea where he was or what had happened; all he knew was that he was covered in blood and finding it all but impossible to breathe. Managing to get a hand to his face that had gone completely numb he could barely recognise the feel of his features, while the rest of his body also seemed without feeling. Slowly, very slowly, some senses began to return both to his body and to his mind, and turning himself one way and then the other he found he was trapped beneath the enormous body of Sam.

They were lying in a crater, a hole obviously made by the shell that must have all but blown them both to Kingdom come, but he was alive, he was definitely still alive.

And so too was Sam, as Tully felt a great shudder heave the horse's body almost off him, followed by the deepest sigh and groan he had ever heard from an animal. Once Sam had moved, Tully found he could ease his flattened body out from under the stricken creature, sliding his way to the edge of the crater where he could get a better look at his charge. Sam was lying on one side with half one flank missing and both his hind legs smashed, but he too was still alive and unmercifully so, Tully thought, as he slid his way on his stomach to try to comfort his old friend.

He reached his head, which Sam had tipped to one side, one apple eye that used to be so bright and full of cheer now dulled and rolling slowly from side to side as if the horse was looking for something, or for someone.

'I know what you want, old boy,' Tully said in one small furry ear, cradling the horse's head in his arms as best as he could. 'Don't worry, I'll see to you. Tully won't let you down.'

He kissed the moaning animal on the side of his great head, then crawled his way back to the side of the crater, pulling himself up to the rim to try to get sight of what was happening. He could barely believe his eyes when he saw the sheer devastation that must have happened in such a short time. What had been a huge area of rolling land was now a scene from hell, and from what Tully could see through the smoke and the hail of flying earth and debris, it seemed as if the earth had exploded and caught fire. Vaguely he could discern the distant shapes of men, some running, some falling and some even flying through the air as explosion followed explosion, each seemingly bigger than the one before. Shells screamed over his head, some falling not fifty yards from him, making Tully leave go of the edge of the crater and roll back in agony on top of his groaning horse.

He had no gun. His pistol was gone, as was his belt and half his jacket, so there was no way he could help his dying friend to leave this earth. All he could do was wait and hope and pray: wait for help, hope that it came soon and pray that Sam would die quickly and be spared further agony. But no help came, and as Tully lay in the bloodstained earth he wondered why it should, since no one would know they were there. Everyone was too busy being killed or killing.

He had no idea how long he was in that hole in the ground – it could have been minutes, it might have been days, since Tully kept fading in and out of consciousness – but every time he awoke the first thing he did was check on Sam, who sadly seemed no better and no worse. He was just about alive, and it was in fact a miracle that he was, but so strong was his constitution and so great his determination, it seemed to Tully, not to leave his master and abandon his post, that the horse was simply clinging on to life. Then finally and mercifully, as the light seemed to be fast fading, Tully heard the fateful shot and the great horse was still, freed from his undeserved agony, released from his unearned torment. Looking slowly up above him Tully saw an officer from his battery slowly putting away his service revolver, before coming to the stricken Tully's side.

'Thought it best to see to the old boy first!' he yelled over the barrage of screaming, exploding shells. 'Thought his need was even greater than yours!'

'You can shoot me and all!' Tully yelled back, now feeling the terrible pain of his wounds. 'I'm done for, sir!'

'Like hell you are, man!' the officer shouted back. 'Chap who stays with his horse deserves only the best! Just hang on one tick! We'll soon have you out of here!'

At enormous risk to himself, the officer returned to the top of the crater and disappeared to get help. Minutes later, by some miracle, two stretcher bearers arrived, caked in mud and gore, their sleeves rolled up to the tops of their burly arms, their faces shining with sweat, to lift Tully gently and carefully out of the vast hole in the ground and to carry him to safety.

He remembered little after that, only vaguely recalling being on the stretcher before being driven fast down a bumpy road. After which it seemed he was in the middle of a field of the brightest summer flowers he had ever seen with the sun shining on him, then someone injected something into him, and it took away all his pain, and must have made him sleep for days, it seemed, for the next thing he knew he was lying on a bed, a proper bed in a bright white room, being nursed by what appeared to be an angel, someone who kept smiling at him.

'Please,' he croaked, 'will you look at me? Please, I'm so sorry, miss – will you ever forgive me? Will you just look at the state I'm in. I'm covered in mud and blood.'

The angel put a finger to her lips, and promptly gave him another injection.

After which all he remembered was that he was on a ship, he knew it because he could hear the drone of the turbines, feel the motion of the vessel, and he could even hear seagulls. He never had liked their sound, but now he loved it, because it could only mean one thing.

He was going home to Blighty.

Over a mile down the line from where Tully and Sam had been hit, the men under the command of Major Cecil Milborne were fighting a losing battle as wave after wave of them were sent over the top to meet shells that either hit them directly, or killed them in groups, until finally Major Milborne was left with a handful of soldiers – two of them nursing the sort of wounds that would induce another officer to call off the attempted assault.

Now they sat huddled in their trench as the bombardment seemed to increase in its intensity, staring at the major they had long ago nick-named 'Backside', since he was now infamous among the men for backing on to that particular part of his anatomy.

'Right, you lot!' Cecil Milborne suddenly hollered, raising the whistle he blew to signal them over the top. 'Over you go, and fast!'

He blew his whistle loudly. The men didn't move.

'You heard me!' Cecil screamed. 'Get going! Go on! Out!'

By what seemed suddenly to be tacit agreement not one of them moved.

Cecil undid his holster and in his customary manner went for his revolver, but he was too late. Before he had time to put a hand to his pistol, he was dead.

The man responsible looked round at his companions. As one they rose to stand beside him.

'Pity about that. But if you will stick your head over the top that's what 'appens, Major, that's what 'appens, eh?'

They all nodded.

'The way I feel about 'im he might as well be a Hun!'

One by one they took understandable pleasure in making sure that Cecil Milborne was dead.

The incident was reported quite simply. Major

Cecil Milborne was found dead in his trench from a rifle shot to his head – a sniper, naturally.

As for the soldier who shot him, as second in command, he led the rest of the men over the top, and by some miracle not only did they survive their passage through no man's land, but so did he, only to find himself on top of an enemy machine-gun position, a nest he cleared out single-handed with grenades, pistol and bayonet, before being blown unharmed by an exploding British shell into an enemy trench, which, as luck would have it, had just been taken by soldiers from his division.

For his heroism under fire, above and beyond the call of duty, Captain William Wilkinson was awarded the Victoria Cross.

Chapter Sixteen

When This Lousy War Is Over

Maude accepted all the sympathies extended to her for the loss of her husband, grateful for her friends' kindnesses while knowing that Cecil had been less than popular. She understood from his regiment that he had died in action at the Somme with a record of diligent if unremarkable service. 'Backside' earned no medals, and went sadly unmissed.

But while there was sad news about her husband there was good news about Bertie, who had not only survived the horrors of the latest battle but had apparently distinguished himself and was now in line for an MC. When she learned the news Maude found it all too difficult to possess her soul in patience until they could see each other again. Meanwhile, Elizabeth and she clung to Pug's letters, unable to quite believe that he had somehow remained unscathed, as had Scrap, and the two hunters.

*   *   *

I cannot tell you all how ineffably drear it is staring at the same old roots and branches of these wretchedly blasted trees and the same vast potholes in the ground. Some say we're oh so lucky to be in a safe salient, if there is any such a thing, which I have me doubts! But I say socks to that – give a chap a new vista and a new set of blasted trees to stare at before he loses his marbles! I'm not complaining because I'm still here, and where you read how many who ain't any more, you must get down on your knees and thank the Lord above us. We have the odd flurry of activity every so often. We rush out, shoot a few trees, and rush back again – only joking – we actually took two Hun trenches last week with no losses, only to lose them again two days later with one loss. Seems Jerry can't stand his land being took – soon as you take a yard he comes and snatches it back and yells That's Mein! (Good joke, eh?) Other things happen too, like just along the line from us there are some Taffs, a fine bunch of lads who've seen a fair bit of fighting so far (lucky devs) and they got moved up closer to the fray a few days ago. It was the most amazing thing because someone said a lot of them had been in a choir or somesuch – although I think that's a bit of guesswork – but I do know why and so would you if you'd heard them up the road. All the way back we heard them – and that's a fair old way. It was a beautifully still day with what little breeze there was blowing our way –

and we saw them, marching off with rifles slung and they were all singing – not like our rum bunch who can hardly sing the National Anthem so as you'd recognise it (you should hear them after dark sometimes – groan). These Taffs were amazing. They were singing 'Men of Harlech' and that other one – 'Bread of Heaven'? No – 'Guide me, O Thou Great Redeemer' to give it the proper name – and they were singing in this magnificent harmony. It just filled the air. I cannot describe what it was like. One of the men – one of the hardest men I've ever met and one you're *very* glad is on your side! – he was sitting there with these tears running down his stubble. He wasn't the only one. Up the road they went – and they ran into fire – maybe an ambush – I don't know what – and yet they were still singing – or so it seemed. This is a *very* rum business, this business of war.

Anyway, enough for now. My love to everyone – especially you Bethy, and Mamma.

Your devoted

Pug

There was news about Tully too – more news about the state of his injuries after Jossy had learned that he had been hit.

'And lucky to have survived and all,' he told Partita and Kitty when the three of them were catching up on the news with Jossy in the old tack room. 'Good thing is he's not lost no limbs –

least not yet, though they think he might have a bit o'gas gangrene in one of his legs. We'll see. He says t'medics are A1 and should have medals – and I must say I agree, havin' been to see him – and don't ask me 'bout London because I'll only tell you – except for that hospital. But I think he's done with scrappin' now. Leastways I 'opes so. Now there's only young Ben to fuss me head about.'

'And how is Ben, Jossy?' Partita wondered. 'Last heard of, he was doing great things with some gunners or other, was he not?'

'He is that, Lady Partita,' Jossy said. 'And just like Tully now, he's doin' his bit, he's seein' to the 'orses.'

'Tully seein' to 'orses? Some things never change,' Partita remarked, as they walked back to the house.

'Thank heavens,' Kitty said, adding with a smile, 'the more things that don't, the happier we will all be.'

'Nice day, Mamma. No one we know in the lists this morning,' Partita told Circe a little later.

Circe continued filling in patients' records without looking up. She was all too aware that Partita and Kitty were in the habit of keeping the morning newspapers from her until they had read through the lists for themselves, just in case. It was quite touching really, if a little exasperating, because she knew they were only trying to protect her, that they didn't want her perhaps finding out about Gussie that way.

Really no point in telling them it was quite unnecessary; she would always know if Gussie was dead. A mother always did know about her children without being told.

'How long when someone's missing, Papa, before they presume – you know – that the person is not coming back?' Partita asked her father the following week when he returned to Bauders for what he was in the habit of calling 'a bit of a refill'.

'Indeterminate, I am afraid, Partita,' he replied, carefully folding over his newspaper to study the accuracy of the war reportage. 'I am inclined to think they gallop at it. Son of a friend was reported missing the other week, then declared 'presumed dead' about a week later, only to be found to be still alive when a member of his family noted from his bank statements he'd just cashed a cheque the week before. Dash of a thing! He'd been taken prisoner and needing some things, cashed some money. Fair enough, but the WO still haven't made his survival formal, even though the family have had a letter from the poor chap from some camp or other. So all in all, no real answer to that, my dear. How long's a piece of string really.'

'You're thinking there's still a chance that Peregrine may be alive, aren't you, darling?' Circe wondered, looking up from her knitting, an art at which she now quite excelled, turning out socks and gloves by the half-dozen every week.

'Don't see why we should abandon all hope,' Partita replied. 'And it's funny really, because I had this dream last night – a really strange one.'

'Do tell.'

'Other people's dreams?' Partita smiled. 'Best way to put your audience to sleep.'

'Nonsense,' Circe said. 'Look at us rabbits.'

'Rabbits?' Kitty wondered.

'Family for all ears,' Partita told her. 'All right. Very well. See what you make of this. I dreamed Valentine was putting on a play but it wasn't here. In fact it wasn't in England at all. It was in this big white room that looked like a hospital ward except it wasn't, because all the people in the beds weren't *in* the beds but sitting on them, or lying on them, all fully dressed. Not in uniform, but in all sorts of costumes. Then Valentine was there and they all clapped him. He was completely disguised in some sort of dusky makeup and pirate clothes, would you believe? And he opened this trap door and Peregrine popped up – as someone would on a stage – and he was carrying a big heavy bag on his back that turned out to be coal. I know that because he asked me if I'd like some coal, and I said yes – more than anything. Then there was Harry, somewhere completely different, toting some sort of klaxon in a large bus that had a Red Cross on the side and he leaned out and shouted that everything must be written down – don't ask me why – but he kept insisting, shouting everything! Everything! Then Peregrine got on the bus, paid

Harry a fare and waved at me through a window.'

'What an extraordinary dream,' said Kitty, after they had all listened in silence. 'I wonder what it means?'

'It could mean that Peregrine is coming home,' Partita said, trying to sound as off hand as possible. 'Or not – I don't know.'

'Always stumped by dreams myself,' the Duke remarked, 'what they're trying to tell us – because they must be trying to tell us something – and where all the people come from. All these people one dreams up. You end up wondering who the devil they all are, really you do.'

'So let's just keep hoping, shall we?' Circe said. 'And praying. I still have every hope.'

'Not like Peregrine's mother,' Partita said gloomily. 'I hear she's now gone into official mourning.'

'Then she'll have to come out of it, won't she,' the Duke stated, returning to his newspaper, 'when young Peregrine comes marching home.'

At the end of the following week a letter addressed to 'The Lady Partita Knowle' arrived from abroad, not from any of the usual correspondents but in a hand that no one recognised.

'It could be from one of our guests, I suppose?' asked the Duchess.

'It's not what Al used to call a "greeny" – an uncensored letter – and it's not been through the censor either. In fact, it hasn't a military mark on it. So it must be from a civilian.'

'Abroad?' Kitty wondered.

'I know,' Partita said, looking deliberately mysterious. 'It's an ardent admirer, someone who doesn't wish to be known!'

'Well?' Circe demanded after Partita had opened the letter and was seen to be staring at it in some amazement.

'It is actually anonymous,' Partita told her. 'Signed "*A wellwisher*".'

'I wonder what this wellwisher wants?'

Kitty looked from Partita to the Duchess. 'It must be from one of the patients, surely?'

'Looks like it's someone who's off his chump,' Partita replied. 'It's all just gibberish.'

At first it appeared to be just two pages of absolute nonsense, yet it was all carefully set out in backwards-sloping writing and set in paragraphs as if it all meant something.

'Which it obviously does not,' Kitty put in, confirming the thought expressed by all three of them. 'So I suppose it's some sort of a joke.'

'D'you think so?' Partita wondered, taking the letter back to study it closely. 'Because I don't. Why would anyone go to the trouble of writing pure gibberish as a joke? Or even as an offence? If they wanted to be rude they'd just be rude, as it's anonymous; or if they wanted to be funny, there'd be some point. But for someone to send an absolutely *pointless* letter can only mean one thing – that it has a point, perhaps an important one.'

'So what do you think, darling?' Circe wondered.

'I think,' Partita said slowly, examining the letter even more closely, 'I think it's in code. Not only that – I think it is written in the dot code.'

They all looked at each other excitedly, while Partita fetched a pencil and pad from a desk, before explaining what the code was, and how it worked.

'Almeric taught me about codes years ago, and so did Perry,' she explained. 'Al learned it at Eton from a master who'd served in the Boer War and used to use it in his letters home. Apparently, some spies somewhere or other belonging to some country or other – Russia, I think it was actually – used it all the time till we cracked it. It's very simple – even simpler than the substitution code, you know – rot thirteen?'

'I have no idea what you are talking about, darling,' Circe laughed. 'Not a clue, and I'm quite sure Kitty doesn't either.'

'Letter substitution is the schoolboy's code really,' Kitty explained. 'Rot thirteen, for instance, is called that because you rotate the alphabet by thirteen – that is, if you want to write the letter A you write N, thirteen letters into the alphabet. So Partita would be – let's see . . .'

Kitty took a pencil and began working out the rot thirteen code for 'Partita' while Partita smoothed the gibberish letter out on the table before her.

'Kitty's right, Mamma. That's absolutely so about the substitution code, but this is infinitely more subtle and not easy to crack if the sender has done his work properly.'

'Partita would be CNEGVGN. Cnegvgn. Very Russian.'

'I've always wanted to be called Cnegvgn. What you do is you write your message by concealed dots, the dots being the full stops. Because it's that complicated it's best to keep the message short or else you have to write pages of rubbish – or something – so then you look for the dots and you join them up so . . .' She showed them what she was doing, tracing full stop to full stop. 'Until you get some letters. *Comme ça.*' She stared at the letter in front of her, the expression frozen on her face.

'What's the matter, Tita?' Kitty asked. 'What have you got?'

'P, so far,' Partita said slowly. 'The letter P absolutely, see? Then S then Λ, then an F, then over the page – an E.'

'P – S-A-F-E, P is safe?'

'Peregrine is safe? It has to be. Perry is safe!'

'Peregrine is alive?' Circe stood up, her hand to her chest. 'Perry is safe?'

'It has to be, Mamma,' Partita answered. 'What else could "P is safe" possibly mean?'

'Is that all it says, Tita?'

'Isn't it enough? Peregrine is safe!'

'But who sent it, darling?' her mother wondered. 'Who could possibly know this and who would know to send it in code, and why?'

Partita thought for a moment, then returned to the letter to examine it for further clues. 'I'll tell you who sent it,' she said. 'Someone called V.'

'V?' her mother said, already there. 'But—'

'Who else do we know whose name begins with V?' Partita demanded. 'Only Valentine!'

'Valentine? But how could Valentine possibly know that Peregrine is safe? He couldn't possibly know. Isn't he meant to be doing some theatricals for the troops somewhere or other?'

'Yes,' Partita said slowly. 'Perhaps that's exactly what he's doing.'

The three women stared at each other, all of them gradually seeing the debonair Valentine in a rather different light.

Peregrine's survival could not be confirmed, although none of them could resist clinging to the idea that he would soon make a miraculous reappearance. Nothing more was heard until out of the blue a postcard arrived for Partita.

Couldn't get in touch before and apologies. Had a good run but luck ran out just as I thought I was home and dry. You wouldn't recognise me now – unshaven and jolly grubby – and you wouldn't have known me then – ba eha nf zvare!

'On run as miner,' Partita translated. 'That's the rotation one.'

'So why does he need to use a code, when the rest of it is written?' Circe wondered. 'Or is he just playing games?'

'You'll understand when you hear the rest of it,' Partita assured her.

If you could get round to sending a parcel? Need shaving kit, warm clothes (really warm!) and some provisions if poss. Send to given address below – my new hotel! Miss you all and you most of all, P.

'Where exactly is he staying then?' Circe wondered with a frown. 'He's staying at some hotel?'

'Peregrine's joke, Mamma,' Partita said, handing her the postcard. 'He's in an officer's prisoner of war camp.' Partita turned away. Perry was alive. It didn't seem possible. She was going to write and explain her so-called engagement to Michael Bradley as soon as she could. She would make a splendid joke of it. Something to amuse him over the next dreary weeks.

'But he's safe,' Kitty wrote to Harry.

The wonder of it all is not only is he alive, but he is unharmed and safe. We're all sure he's absolutely furious at getting caught and we're all dying to know the details, but of course he can't write to us about it without giving the game away – so we shall have to POSIP, as the Duke has it. Possess our souls in patience!

But you can imagine the relief all round, now that we know bar some sort of accident of the fates, as it were, nothing should befall him before the end of the war. Partita is walking on air, as you can imagine, but of course, being Partita, she says nothing. When she writes to him, which she does almost every day, she shows him no mercy, and he rags her back no end – but then that's how it's always been with those two. It's quite touching, because it's obvious that they are gradually coming to realise that they mean more to each other than just friends. I am sure of it.

Any news about you having some leave? They seem to be working you dreadfully hard – or is it you working you? I suspect the latter, knowing you, Harry, but do try and find a little bit of time off to come and see us all here. I know you have vitally important work to be done and we must come down the list of priorities, but if you came up here, it would give us all a chance to catch up with your news. I do miss you – of course we all do – but I should dearly love to see you, and hear at first hand about what you have done and what you are doing.

You asked me for a recent photograph and although I don't think it's a very good one (Tita is not the very best of photographers!) I mean, it was such a sunny day and I had my hand over my eyes (q.v.) and squinting almost into the sun but Tita thought it was what she calls 'v. natch', so that's the one you're getting. Sorry! Write soon – I love your letters.

Kitty

Harry read and reread her latest letter, lying on his iron bed back in a tent behind the newest clearing station. The last time he read it through before turning in for the night he stared at the last line and mentally edited it, dropping the 'r' from 'your' and cutting the word 'letters' altogether.

After which he kissed her new photograph, smiled at the beautiful girl laughing back at him, hatless with hand shading her eyes and her dark hair seemingly being blown by a summer breeze, before carefully placing it in the pocket of his shirt, the side nearest his heart.

Allegra had long since won Sister over to her side, much against the senior nurse's better judgement, who up to now had always considered that all girls from Allegra's sort of background, when it came to nursing, were little more than dilettantes. But Allegra had held fast, working hard at both her duties and her studies, and now proved herself to be a valuable member of Sister's dedicated team.

'Have we heard any more from our young man?' she asked Allegra one night when they were sharing a well-deserved cup of tea. 'When last heard of he was on the Ypres salient, was he not?'

Allegra looked down at her teacup. She used to hate tea, most particularly this kind of tea, but nowadays, after a long day on the wards, it tasted like nectar.

'How strange you should mention it. It's a fortnight since I heard anything from him,' she said, after a pause. 'Until today. Then I got a letter from him, unfortunately it was dated over ten days ago.'

'That is worrying, but at least you know he was in one piece ten days ago.'

'At least he was when he wrote. But one does wonder for how long? The losses out there—' She stopped. 'The officers more than the men even, ten to one, I believe, or something like that.'

'If we hear nothing we assume the best until we hear otherwise,' Sister said crisply, but she sighed.

'The only thing I find that works at times like this is – work,' Allegra said. 'One can't dwell on things when one is busy.'

'I was the same when Fred was sent to the Dardanelles.'

Allegra stared at Sister. 'I had no idea.'

'And why should you?'

Allegra did not dare ask what the outcome for Fred might have been.

Sister shook her head. 'It was a slaughter. Altogether a slaughter. The boys lost there, doesn't bear thinking about. You have to think the people who organise these shooting matches

– because it seems to me that's how they see them – no offence, Allegra, but they do, you know – it's as if they're planning a few days out on the moors and wondering about what sort of bag they're going to have. It's the same mentality except God didn't bother teaching the wee birds how to shoot. But anyway, you have to wonder about their sanity. How they can go to bed at nights and sleep is way past me – and here we are. Those poor souls have to take the damage and us poor souls have to try and repair it.'

'Fred was . . . ?' Allegra wondered.

'He was my boy. He was my son.'

'I am so sorry.'

'I was very young. I hadn't even started nursing – and I fell, the way we girls do, you know. He was a soldier too, the father. A cavalry man, a Dragoon, and he's dead too, killed in the first month of the war in a mêlée somewhere between Mons and Brussels.'

Allegra said nothing, trying to imagine Sister, whom she had never seen out of her uniform, as a young girl *falling*. She struggled with a picture of her as a young woman falling for a Dragoon and having his baby.

'My mother brought Freddy up,' Sister continued. 'I went nursing. I had to earn my living, and with my father dead and my brothers all in the army, my mother could bring him up fine. Which she did and he was a very bonny, happy child. But there you are – that's who they send off to war – our bonny, happy boys. So let's just hope and pray you hear good things about your James. I'm sure you will. I have a feeling about these things.'

Sure enough, three days later Allegra got the good news that James was indeed alive, the bad news being that he was not exactly in one piece, having been badly hit by shrapnel, wounds that resulted in the amputation of his left arm. He had been transferred to a French coastal hospital in Calais and when the doctors considered him fit enough to travel he would be returned home and awarded an honourable discharge from the army.

'As well you're a nurse, my dear,' Sister said, smiling when she heard the good news. 'You'll know best how to care for him.'

Harry had been drowning in what he now called the Red Tape Sea, trying to get a bunch of stuffed shirts to understand the need to move the dressing stations, when, in answer to Kitty's invitation, he was able to borrow a car from a generous friend, and drove to Bauders.

Wavell opened the door to him, and for a second, it seemed to Harry that everything was as it had been. His father at the great doors of the castle, the hall beyond him, until he saw how much his father had aged, how crumpled and creased he looked, and a little bent.

'May I help you, sir?' Wavell asked.

'Father?'

Wavell stared at his only son, unseeing.

'Father?'

Harry grew closer. 'It's me – Harry.'

Wavell put out his hands and took Harry's. He started to pump them up and down, and as he did so Harry realised that his father's hands were no longer those of an upper gentleman servant, but of a groundsman, so much must the nature of his work have changed.

'The old eyes are going, you know! Or I surely should have known my own son. Her Grace advises some spectacles, but I haven't yet had time to go into Milltown.' Wavell stood back. 'You are handsomer than ever, Harry, my boy,' he told him. 'Now give me just a moment to change my jacket and we will go straight home.'

At home, in his father's estate cottage, Wavell prepared a simple dinner for them both.

'I've had to get good at cooking for want of Cook and Mrs Coggle and I don't know who else going off to the factories,' he told Harry, and the dinner he set before them both was good and tasty, and plenty of it.

He then ran Harry a hot bath, and left him to sleep the sleep of a returned hero before returning to the castle where there were still plenty more duties waiting for him.

'Harry's home, Harry's home, Harry's home,' he could not help saying, stopping everyone he met.

Finally it seemed that only Kitty was unaware that Harry was home.

'Who's that, Kitty?' Partita nodded ahead of them the next morning. 'I'm dashed if I don't think I know that figure rather well.'

They had just finished clearing the patients' breakfast. Kitty turned from her work and stared out of the vast arched window. Partita was right. There was a familiar figure outside. Below them on the lawn, hands in pockets, standing smiling up at them was Harry.

Partita smiled. 'Out you go, Kitty Rolfe. Go and see Harry, before Harry comes to see us.'

'You might have said you were coming,' Kitty called as she hurried out to him.

'Why? Is there someone you don't want me to see?'

'No, no, of course not.' Kitty stopped, taking off her apron and patting her hair. 'No, no, it's just that we're all so busy—'

'Of course you are, that's why I didn't say I was coming. You would say you were too busy.'

'Of course I wouldn't. Oh, Harry, it is so, so good to see you, and in one piece!'

Kitty stood back from him. If she hadn't known he would hate it, she could have cried with relief.

'I'm not only in one piece, Kitty, I am better than I was. Even Father was forced to say so. "Better than you were before you left Bauders, Harry," he said last night.'

'You certainly look as fit as a general.'

Harry nodded and, taking in the sight he had dreamed of for so long amid the blood and the horror, amid the terror and the waste, he could have burst into tears, except he knew Kitty would hate it.

'Come for a walk, Kitty, please?'

'Harry . . .' Kitty protested feebly, looking back at the house where she knew Partita would be watching them. 'Of course I can't come for a walk. Besides, I have work to do. I can't just drop everything. You really are impossible sometimes.'

'Of course I'm impossible. Would I be Harry if I was possible? Besides, have I asked you to drop everything just because I'm here? Do you even know it was you I came to see? I might have come to see my father – or the Duchess. Or Partita – or even Percy, our magnificent peacock here. Don't jump to conclusions, Miss Rolfe – won't do you no good, not never.'

'Stop putting on silly voices, Harry,' Kitty chided him, finding herself becoming quite flustered. 'And tell me what you want exactly?'

'How do you know I want anything, Miss Rolfe?'

'Because I can tell by the expression on your face – and stop calling me Miss Rolfe.'

'Yes, miss.'

'Harry . . .'

But it was no good – as always the particular expression now on Harry's face made her start to laugh and once she began to laugh she knew she was undone.

'Fine,' he said, taking her by the arm and

walking her back towards the house. 'What I want is a multitude of things but I don't think we have the time to discuss them all – except the most pressing of them, and that is to find out if you will come out with me tonight? I only have a forty-eight-hour pass, and lucky beyond belief to get that.'

'Come out with you?' Kitty echoed, putting a hand automatically to her neck. 'What do you mean?'

'Oh, surely you know what going out with someone entails, Kitty? We get all dressed up to the nines and—'

'I don't understand, Harry. I don't understand why you – why do you want to take me out?'

Harry didn't bother with an answer. He simply raised his eyes to the heavens and laughed.

'Harry . . .'

'Father suggested – there is some sort of hop this evening at The Wycombe,' he said. 'The hotel on the road into town? I don't know about you, but I can't remember the last time I went dancing. I would *love* to go dancing. And most – most of all – I would *love* to go dancing *with you*.'

'Should I?' she asked Partita later that morning when they had a break from their work. 'I'm not sure whether I should go dancing. It really does not seem at all seemly, at this time. I'm really not sure I should go, Tita.'

'If you think it's unseemly then you must go. No fun in doing anything seemly, surely?'

'You're as bad as Harry.'

'Come along – if it's a lesson in protocol you want, then we'd better consult the oracle. We had better speak to Mamma.'

But the Duchess was quite adamant.

'Of course you must go. You can't be hidebound by the latest news, my dear, you know you can't. You're a young woman, you must go dancing.'

Kitty shook her head. 'It really doesn't seem right.'

Circe stood up and went to Kitty, taking her hands in her own. 'Kitty, what is right during a time of war? A war that has taken so many, that is not right. You must have some gaiety in your life. You can't become an old maid because Almeric was killed. Truly, you can't.'

'Even so . . .' Kitty dropped her eyes.

'Almeric loved Harry, Kitty, you know that.' The Duchess touched Kitty briefly on the cheek. 'He loved you. Most of all he loved fun. Off you go.'

Partita helped Kitty get dressed for the evening, just as they both always used to when Kitty first came to stay at Bauders, fussing round her as if she was a mother sending Kitty, her favourite daughter, out on a date, while Bridie stood back to sigh, cluck or admire, depending. If they made Kitty change her dress once, they must have made her change half a dozen times until finally, in a state of mock exhaustion, Partita declared Kitty ready, while Bridie sat down fanning herself with a hand mirror.

'Sure you will pass the mustard always providing you doesn't go fiddling with your hair. Oh, how me poor old feet are killing me.'

'I didn't ask you to help me, Bridie. You volunteered.'

'And sure wasn't I born with me arm stuck up in the air? Don't worry, Miss Kitty – I'll call in the favour when I gets married. You can help me get dressed.'

'Of course I will.'

'Me, too,' said Partita. 'We can get our own back for all the sighs and groans we've had to put up with from you.'

'Any news on that front, Bridie?' Kitty wondered, taking one last look in the glass. 'How is Tully?'

'Ah, he's going to be fine, thank you, Miss Kitty. 'The wonder is he got off so lightly. I mean 'twas dreadful, the Lord only knows, but when you think . . . No, he's going to be just fine and dandy, and God and everyone willing, we'll be wedded as soon as we can.'

'Wed, Bridie,' Partita corrected her. 'You will be wed as soon as possible.'

'Not me, Lady Partita.' Bridie raised her eyebrows and smiled. 'Me, I intend to be well and truly wedded.'

'You won't guess who I'm working for, Kitty,' Harry remarked as he drove them to the hotel. 'Not for all the tea in China.'

'Dr Charles,' Kitty promptly replied, taking the

wind clean out of his sails. 'Dr Richard Charles, to be precise. And if you're wondering how on earth I know – my mother mentioned it in her last letter.'

'Don't you think that's amazing?'

'Astonishing, to say the least,' Kitty agreed.

'Yet you didn't mention it?'

'I wanted to win all that tea.'

'He's a fine doctor and a brave man. No one to touch him, not in my book.'

'Really?' Kitty stared out of the window at the passing countryside. 'I don't know very much about him, other than the fact that he was in general practice and my mother ran off with him.'

'Your mother – your mother ran off with him?'

'Yes. I really could not blame her, although it was something of a shock at the time. My father – my father is completely horrid, you know. Although I believe he has been trying to make amends in the trenches. His men love him, apparently. Which is just as well, because very few other people could. And it all goes to show something good can come out of something – or in his case *someone* – so terrible.'

'You would admire Dr Charles. He's become a brilliant surgeon. Like so many thrown into the work, he has proved himself to be quite extraordinary. He could operate not just under fire, but with shells exploding round him, and not make a mistake.'

Kitty was silent. Her mother and Dr Charles

was still not a subject that she enjoyed either to think about or talk about.

'It's all in the past, Harry.'

Harry pulled on the brake.

'Good. In that case let's not talk about it any more,' he agreed. 'Let's just have what we haven't had for centuries – fun.'

The hotel ballroom was crowded but the band good, playing all the latest music including a selection from the latest hit musical in London, *Chu Chin Chow*.

Harry and Kitty danced and they talked; they talked while they danced and they danced while they talked. In the end they just danced, and the slower the music got and the more they danced, the more they both knew where the dancing and the talking was leading them.

As Harry drove them back to Bauders he started to wonder if he had forgotten how to kiss a girl, but as soon as he started to kiss Kitty, he realised that he hadn't forgotten at all but, more than that, he had never kissed a girl the way he was kissing Kitty, nor had he been kissed the way Kitty kissed him.

The parkland was lit by a full moon, there was an owl calling somewhere in the distance, and then as they began to walk back towards the house in the small woodland close a nightingale sang a heavenly song.

'You see,' Harry said *sotto voce* as they listened. 'It's so beautiful it's almost unbearable. You could almost wish him to stop, to put you out of your sublime agony.' He turned to Kitty. 'You feel the same.'

Kitty felt quite the same. More than that, for the first time in her life she felt at peace, knowing that, in some strange way, not only had Harry come home, but so had she.

Chapter Seventeen

The Last to Come Home

At last the ones who were destined to come home had come home, while those who had fallen had to be left where they had fallen, so many were they. Finally Gus came home, as his mother knew that he would.

All the young went to greet him at the station, Jossy driving ahead with Trotty pulling the trap, and the rest piling into whatever they could find. Once back at the castle gates, the pony was taken from the shafts, and everyone pulled the trap up to the castle doors where his father and mother were waiting to greet him.

James was long home, recovered from his ordeal and nursed to health by Allegra, to whom he was now married. Valentine – the dark horse of them all – had also returned, quietly and without fanfare, reunited with Livia. Dr Charles was home, his war done and the VC and bar he was awarded for showing exceptional courage in the treatment of the wounded under fire was put modestly away in his desk drawer, never to be again referred to either by himself or Violet.

Tully was home to Bauders, healthy and fit once more, and looking forward to marrying Bridie, when they had saved up enough money for some furniture, both of them determined to stay working at Bauders.

Pug was home to Elizabeth, minus an eye, lost in one of what he was in the habit of referring to as 'mes skirmishes petites, my deahs'. Pug, having been fitted with a glass eye, happily revived the use of his long-abandoned monocle, which he allowed to drop from his glass eye whenever registering shock, horror or dismay.

'And even Scrap has survived!' he wrote to a friend. 'Bit greyer, bit wiser, but still with us.'

Finally, too, Peregrine came home, released at last from his captivity, even leaner than when he had left but, in Partita's eyes, still as elegant, and a great deal more handsome, if that were possible.

'I so very nearly made it,' he told the welcoming party at Bauders. 'So nearly made it. There we were in a heavy mining area and making my way, because I speak fluent French and luckily Jerry couldn't really distinguish between a Belgian accent and a French one, I so nearly made it. Then as I was sitting in a bar actually in the port where I was to get on this cargo boat, I allowed myself to have a large brandy. And while I was drinking it, I dropped my matches just as a German officer was walking by. He very kindly handed them back to me, and I thanked him. In English – whereupon he invited me to journey with him to a really rather flea-bitten sort of prison camp, from which I was then transferred to an officer camp in a very draughty *Schloss* – which I duly survived, as you can see – thanks to your unending stream of parcels.'

'Thank heavens for Nestles milk, butter and Cadbury's chocolate.'

'Thank heavens to each of you, to all of you, for your letters. Letters are what kept us all going, right the way through – even Mamma's!' He turned to Partita. 'Come on, Mischief, time I took you for a walk.'

Just as Kitty and Harry had done, the two of them walked, at first in silence through the castle grounds, until eventually Peregrine turned to Partita.

'I meant what I said about letters, Mischief, especially your letters.' He stopped and looked at her for the first time in her life with real love. 'You are so like your letters, you know, or rather your letters are so like you. But not the child I once knew, the grown-up woman.'

Partita looked away. 'I hope I'm not *that* grown up, Perry. I hope Mischief is still around somewhere, although I do admit I have a hard time trying to find her sometimes. All the gaiety goes out of one when one sees so much suffering. You don't mean it to, but it does.'

'We are bound to have changed, but perhaps

in some strange way, we have changed for the better? Perhaps that is what heartbreak is all about? Getting better, becoming more as we should be as a result, more caring, more loving?'

Partita shook her head, all impatience once more. 'No, I don't believe that, not for a single second. That is just something that happens by accident. It's not something that *should* happen. No war should happen, especially not a war like this war. No, not ever, never should a war like this war ever happen again. What a bunch of fools we have been led by, and we can't even bring our boys home. Almeric, think of Almeric, Perry, he has to stay out there, all alone. Not a day goes by when I don't think of that.'

No one was more aware of this fact than Miss Gertrude Jekyll and her partner, Mr Ned Lutyens, so that even as Peregrine consoled Partita, and very eventually, she allowed him to take her in his arms and console her as a lover does best, the designer and architect were thinking of how best to treat the boys who had to stay out there, who would never return. It was a question that concerned them both deeply.

However many had returned, against all the odds, there was still one person who had not – Jossy's youngest boy, Ben – and nor was there any news of him.

They knew he was safe, of course – that at least was known – but they had no idea when he was due to arrive nor why he had been so delayed, and nothing anyone could do helped to unravel the mystery.

The war had ended with the Armistice signed on 11 November, yet they were still waiting, until one fine, crisp December morning they had the call.

It was midday when the telephone rang with the last of the good news to be relayed to Bauders.

'My dear, Jossy's Ben is home at last.' The Duke walked into the library unannounced to find Circe.

'Ben is home? Oh, John, that is fine, so fine.'

'We will all go to meet him, I think, we will all go. After all, he is the last to come back, and that is not nothing, is it, Circe?'

John looked across at Circe, who was hastily putting away some papers. He knew very well what they were, but he said nothing.

'Come, we will go in that confounded vehicle that Tully so enjoys us going about in. We can all pile in, huggermugger, and leave Jossy to follow in the trap.'

'The last of us home, John, imagine that. Ben, your boy, the last one home, Jossy, isn't that too marvellous?' the Duchess shouted to Jossy above the sound of Tully revving the new motor car.

'Aye, but I only 'ope he's had a hair cut and a shave, with all of us turning out to him. I only 'ope he doesn't look like summat the cat wouldn't bring in,' Jossy grumbled to the pony as he shook up the reins and set off.

The train was late, as it always seemed to be when it was not meant to be, when so many hearts were centred on its arriving on time, when so much depended on its arriving on time.

'It had to be late, on this day of all days. Couldn't be on time, could it?' the Duchess murmured to Tully as they all walked up and down the platform in an effort to keep warm.

'Never mind, Your Grace, so long as it gets here, that's all that matters.'

Jossy could see that the Duke, always the most punctilious of men, was beginning to get agitated because he had started to follow the poor station-master up and down the platform, muttering that since the war was now well *over* trains were not *expected* to be late, when all of a sudden in the distance they heard the sweet sound of wheels and engine, and the station-master at once started to blow his whistle, if only perhaps to drown out the Duke's remonstrations.

It was the usual passenger train bearing with it a large cargo van coupled between the last carriage and the guard's van.

Ben was the first to alight and, to Jossy's relief, he had had his hair cut, and he had shaved, and he went straight up to the Duke and saluted, like a good 'un.

'Glad to have you home, Ben.' The Duke saluted back.

'Glad to be 'ome, sir.'

'What kept you? A Parisian poodle, perhaps?'

'No, sir, not a poodle,' Ben laughed. 'Myself,

I'm more of a terrier man. No, something else kept me, Your Grace.'

At that moment the Duke heard the unmistakable sound of hoofs. He turned slowly, and stared. It seemed that Ben and the other two passengers had not been the only ones on the train.

'What the devil, Ben? What the devil have you brought back to Bauders?'

'An old friend, Your Grace. He's a bit battered, but he's in one piece, and if that's not a bloomin' miracle, I don't know what is.'

Of course the old horse was visibly battle worn, one of his ears holed by a bullet, a long scar down one side of his noble head, a wound that had cost him the sight of an eye, and evidence of another wound on one flank, an injury that seemed not to have affected his walk. But other than that he looked a picture.

'I can't believe it,' the Duke muttered, clearing his throat several times. 'Well, I'll be dashed. I can't believe it. I really will be well and truly dashed, I can't believe it. Look, Circe, the old boy's come home.'

But of course Circe couldn't look. As the train finally pulled out of the station she turned and walked a little way off, leaving the Duke to go forward, alone.

John put his hand up to the horse's head and pulled gently on his one undamaged ear, stroked his nose and ran his hand under his mouth to scratch the animal's chin, after which the two of them stood side by side for a while, until the horse finally lowered his head and laid it over his master's shoulder.

So it was they stood for a while surrounded by those that were left from the great house and stables, until taking the halter from Ben, the Duke led him off the platform and out of the station.

He walked Barrymore Boy all the way home. It took him well over an hour and a half, only stopping now and then to allow the old chap to take a pick of grass from the verge, and Ben walked behind them, occasionally patting the old chap on his flank.

'You're home, old boy,' John said as they passed the gate lodge and walked into the entrance of the long drive. 'There you are, old fellow, *dulce domum.*'

Because it was a fine, sunlit day, after he had been fed and they had put a good, heavy rug on him, the Duke and Ben led the weary old horse out into the home paddock, an enclosure clearly visible from the house.

The horse stood at the gate for minutes, looking around at his surroundings, as if unable quite to take in where he was. He stood there for so long that the Duke started to worry that he had been set fast and was unable to move, when all of a sudden, with a tremendous snort, he galloped forward, as if the years had fallen off him, kicking his heels in the air and ducking and twisting his head in joy. Round and round he charged, before rolling over and over in the sweet grass, all four legs in the air, finally getting to his feet for a good shake.

Naturally everyone that could, very promptly and very eagerly celebrated Ben and the old horse's return, laughing and talking and drinking champagne. Wavell circled round them with bottle after bottle, topping up everyone's glasses, over and over, frequently moving across to the Duke, who never moved from the library window, watching his old friend intently, still not quite able to believe that it was really him moving steadily through the winter grass, before being led back into his old box.

Circe's garden of remembrance for Almeric had been planted out for the spring when Miss Gertrude Jekyll and Mr Ned Lutyens both found they had arrived at the same conclusions.

'Where the fallen are buried, Ned, they are in foreign fields,' Miss Jekyll stated, adjusting her firmly rounded figure at her desk and staring at her partner through the thickest of spectacle lenses. 'We must be sure to see – to see that they will all lie among the flowers of home.'

'And we must see to it that the cemeteries are filled with light. I'll have none of those weeping dark cypresses for our young men.'

Miss Jekyll's eyesight was all but gone, but in her mind's eye she could see Ned's light, and she could see the colours of the flowers she could command to fill in the square after square, the field after field of enclosed light.

'Good, that is good, Ned. They must have light, and flowers, so when their loved ones come to visit them, as they will surely do, they will see only English flowers, Ned, Shakespeare's flowers. English roses, and cornflowers and columbines, wild thyme on the banks, and all manner of plantings that will tell them that whatever the place where their boys fell, however far from home, in distant fields, they are yet in England.'

Postscript

The Halt has long gone, and the railway that brought the few back, but Bauders is still approached by the same long road. The parkland is still beautifully kept, grazed by herds of rare-breed cattle and sheep, as well as the famous white deer. The lake is fished by permit, but rarely freezes over.

The house is unchanged, although the family live in only one wing, which allows the visitors freedom to see over the great rooms. Yet there is evidence of family life everywhere as successive dukes have maintained the tradition of trying to keep the house as a home, and not a museum. There are family portraits, naturally, but they are greatly outnumbered by silver-framed photographs. Children on ponies, friends with their dogs, wedding groups, all the usual paraphernalia that crowd table tops in reception rooms and private sitting rooms everywhere, all speaking of time passing, but also in some strange way, standing still.

The most popular room with the summer visitors is that known as the Pirate Room. In this small gallery there hangs a collection of photographs and informal pencil portraits, and the occasional oil, of all the members of something once called, it seems, the Pirate Club. In this room there are also paintings taken from old photographs of family and friends in costume, and a fine portrait of Valentine Wynyard Errol, who, after the war, became the well-known British film star, Valentine Errol.

'The family used to put on full-scale operettas in the house, for the amusement of themselves and the estate workers,' the guides will always explain. 'However, this is the first time – this production *The Pirates of Penzance*, evidence of which you see here – this is the first time they were able to put on an operetta as a family, which is obviously why everything has been kept from that production – the programmes, the costumes, the music sheets, all of it.'

'All right for all of them, having the time and money to do that kind of thing, while everyone else around them waits on them hand and foot,' someone in the crowd will always, inevitably, be heard to mutter.

'Quite so,' the guides are trained to retort. 'But you will also note that many of the young people you can see here died in the First World War; and when you go outside you will be able to see the Duchess's garden that Miss Jekyll and Mr Lutyens designed for her, and which eventually became a memorial to her son, Lord Almeric, killed at the battle of Loos as was his friend Teddy. He was succeeded by his brother, Lord Augustus, whom you see here. He is always known in the family as the *motoring* duke. He married Miss Lavinia Ponsonby and had four sons. Now if you turn to your left, you will see a portrait of Lady Partita Knowle, the youngest and most beautiful of his three sisters, all of whom are depicted here. Lady Allegra, who married a Mr Millings; Lady Cecilia, who married Lord Milborne, and lastly Lady Partita, the most beautiful, as I said, who married a Mr Peregrine Catesby of Catesby House, situated not ten miles from here. They had eight children, seven sons and a daughter, Lady Katherine, who became a famous actress, acting under the family name of Knowle. And then of course we have family friends such as Emerald Bickford who was sadly killed whilst driving an ambulance in the Great War. Last but not least, we have a portrait of the family servants. Mr Wavell, Mrs Coggle, and so on, a few of whom came back to the house after the war was over. Mr Harry Wavell, here, was the son of the butler, and he married into the aristocracy, a Miss Rolfe, and eventually became the well known author, H. R. Wavell.

'Now we move on to the kitchens, always so popular, we find, since the television series *Upstairs Downstairs*.'

The other favourite place for visitors, particularly the older ones, is Circe's secret garden, always known as 'the Duchess's Garden'. It is a place of great tranquillity, at the centre of which is a memorial to Almeric. The garden is lovingly tended by a team of gardeners, a few of whom are directly descended from those who worked on the original design.

In summer, if visitors choose to sit on one of the fine old oak benches, they can see up to the acres beyond the garden where the Duke and Duchess planted thousands of blood-red poppies. On a summer's day when the flowers sway, their frail heads catching the sunlight, they seem to be saying, '*Lest you forget*' – lest you forget!

THE END

If you enjoyed In Distant Fields, *look out
for Charlotte Bingham's next novel,*
The White Marriage.

*Charlotte Bingham would like to invite you to visit
her website at www.charlottebingham.com*

THE MAGIC HOUR
by Charlotte Bingham

When Alexandra goes to stay with her cousins at Knighton Hall she is made to feel the poor relation; the daughters of the house are both beautiful and wealthy. She is not to meet the handsome stable lad, Tom O'Brien, until much later.

When Alexandra returns home, her father remarries and she is forced to become a maid-of-all-work. Alexandra makes a success of her new life and meets the lovely Bob Atkins. Meanwhile, Tom O'Brien has become impassioned by the beautiful Lady Florazel Compton who introduces him to the sophistications of 1950s London. Sadly, Alexandra's contentment with Bob is short-lived and Tom comes back into her life.

But the past seems destined to wreck the happiness of the present, as the still-beautiful Lady Florazel is determined to re-capture her former love and destroy the magic hour of Tom and Alexandra's meeting.

'An engaging, romantic and nostalgic read'
Daily Mail

055381592X

BANTAM BOOKS

OUT OF THE BLUE
by Charlotte Bingham

Florence Fontaine has still not recovered from a
family tragedy when she discovers a strangely
dressed young man asleep in her guest cottage at the
Old Rectory. Against her better judgement she offers
him breakfast, only to rue the day as she finds
herself caught up in the resulting drama of his life.
Florence's young and beautiful daughter, Amadea, is
immediately suspicious of Edward, as he appears to
be called, fearing that he might be a fraud.

Against everyone's advice, Florence enlists friends
and neighbours to help restore Edward's now
wandering mind and discover who he might be. As
the mystery unfolds, it becomes apparent that
Edward's history is entwined with that of nearby
Harlington Hall, but that his real identity is
something quite other.

Florence and Amadea become united in their quest,
an adventure that takes them into many pasts, not
least that of the young man whom they are now
dedicated to help. In doing so they are finally able to
put tragedy behind them, repair their once
disjointed lives, and embrace a new and
happy future.

0553815946

BANTAM BOOKS

FRIDAY'S GIRL
by Charlotte Bingham

When Napier Todd, a famous portrait painter, comes
across a beautiful woman, Edith, working in a
London inn, he determines to marry her. Spirited
away to his country house, Edith soon discovers that
Napier has no use for her except as his muse.

Meanwhile, Napier's best friend, Sheridan Montague
Robertson, has eloped with Celandine Benyon to
Cornwall, drawn there by the vibrant community of
artists and dramatic light. It is here that
the two couples meet.

So shocked is Celandine by Napier's treatment of
Edith that she sets about trying to help the
troubled marriage, but her good intentions
bring nothing but tragedy.

0553815938

BANTAM BOOKS

THE CHESTNUT TREE
by Charlotte Bingham

It is the summer of 1939, and the residents of the idyllic fishing village of Bexham are preparing for war. Beautiful Judy Melton, daughter of a naval war hero, the social butterfly Meggie Gore-Stewart, seemingly demure Mathilda Eastcott, and Rusty Todd, the tomboy daughter of the owner of the local boatyard, are all determined to play an active role while their husbands and brothers, fathers and lovers are away fighting. But knitting socks and dodging bombs is not what they have in mind.

It is not just the young women who are determined to find new roles for themselves – so are their mothers. In this manner the little Sussex port, facing as it does the coastline of Nazi-invaded France, finds its closely sewn social fabric begin to unstitch, inch by inch.

The women of Bexham meet under the chestnut tree on the green to look back on a landscape that has changed irrevocably, and which they have helped to alter. None of them are the same and yet, as the men return from war, they are expected to slip back into their simple roles of mother, daughter, grandmother. Only the chestnut tree flourishes in the accepted manner, becoming the uniting symbol of all that has passed forever.

The Chestnut Tree is part of the Bexham trilogy, which continues with *The Wind off the Sea* and ends with *The Moon at Midnight*.

0553812777

BANTAM BOOKS

DAUGHTERS OF EDEN
by Charlotte Bingham

Daughters of Eden focuses on the lives and fortunes of
four very different young women at the outbreak of the
Second World War. Marjorie, left at a boarding school
by her emigrating mother; plain Poppy, pushed
into marriage with a mean-spirited aristocrat; Kate,
despised by her father, but determined to prove
herself; and man-mad Lily, who turns out to
be the bravest of them all.

That all of them are chosen to work undercover for the
espionage unit at a beautiful stately home is a surprise, not
least to them. At Eden Park they not only meet each other,
but become involved with three unusual young men –
Eugene, the seemingly feckless Irishman; Robert, Kate's
brother; and dashing Sholto, a master of disguise, and the
undisputed favourite of the unit. While there is hardly
time for romance before each is sent out into the field,
there is just enough for passionate new relationships to
form. Only Jack Ward, the mysterious spymaster, manages
to remain aloof as he guides their destinies. The fact that
they will look back on this time as having made them
feel more exquisitely alive than ever before is not
something they will know until much later.

Daughters of Eden is part of the Eden series, which
continues with *The House of Flowers*.

0553815911

BANTAM BOOKS

A LIST OF OTHER CHARLOTTE BINGHAM TITLES
AVAILABLE FROM BANTAM BOOKS

THE PRICES SHOWN BELOW WERE CORRECT AT THE TIME OF GOING TO PRESS. HOWEVER TRANSWORLD PUBLISHERS RESERVE THE RIGHT TO SHOW NEW RETAIL PRICES ON COVERS WHICH MAY DIFFER FROM THOSE PREVIOUSLY ADVERTISED IN THE TEXT OR ELSEWHERE.

All Transworld titles are available by post from:
Bookpost, PO Box 29, Douglas, Isle of Man IM99 1BQ
Credit cards accepted. Please telephone +44(0)1624 677237, fax +44(0)1624 670923,
Internet http://www.bookpost.co.uk or
e-mail: bookshop@enterprise.net for details.
Free postage and packing in the UK.
Overseas customers allow £2 per book (paperbacks) and £3 per book (hardback).